S

By Diane E Young

Copyright © 2019 by Diane E Young

All rights reserved. This book or any portion thereof may not be reproduced or used in any manner whatsoever without the express written permission of the publisher except for the use of brief quotations in a book review.

Edited by Gillian Radel

Cover Art by Devon Vander Voort

Chapter One

"What's the worst that could happen?" Ann Marie's voice was persistent on the other end of the phone.

"We could be dumped and humiliated on national TV. That's pretty bad," Katie answered, her voice equally insistent.

"I don't mean that. I mean the auditions. For God's sake, what's the worst that could happen? We try out and we don't make the cut. Come on, Katie. It can't hurt to audition. It's just another part."

"It's not the part I've always dreamed of."

"No, but it would get your face on TV. Exposure is the biggest step toward landing that 'dream part.' And you never know. You could find *love*."

"Love," Katie snorted. "We're actors, remember? Who's to say this guy isn't an aspiring actor, just like us? You'd have to be mad to believe you could actually fall in love on one of these reality TV shows."

"It could happen. But seriously, who cares if he is an actor? We could handle that. We'd have an advantage over the non-actresses. Those poor saps would be pretty upset to find out their true love was all an act. For us, it would make for a good TV show. You have to go into the experience with an open mind. I'm not counting on falling in love. It sounds like fun."

"You have a strange perception of fun."

"What do you mean? It doesn't sound fun to you? We'd get to hang out all day, sunbathing, eating and drinking whatever we want for free and going out on glamorous, all-expense paid dates with some hunk. How can you say that doesn't sound like fun?"

"So, what do you need me for?"

"I don't want to go alone. It would be more fun together. Besides, it's not like you have anything better to do."

"I have a job."

"You have a part-time job that no offense, anyone could do. You've had no prospects for any decent parts in months. This could be a great opportunity for your career. It couldn't hurt your love life either."

"My life is crap."

"It's not!" Ann Marie inserted quickly, not having meant to insult her best friend. "I'm sorry. It's not crap, but it could be a lot better."

"No, it is. My life is crap. You're right. I hate my job; I haven't had an audition in months, let alone a part. My love life is practically non-existent. But that doesn't mean I can afford to quit my pathetic job to go on some TV show – does it even pay anything? And what exposure do you expect to get? Do you really think producers scan reality TV shows looking for new faces?"

"It's television exposure whether you benefit from it or not. It's our opportunity to see ourselves on TV, at the very least. That's good enough for me at this point."

"Okay, but how desperate would I look sharing a date with twenty other girls?"

"Desperate or not, do you know how many guys will recognize you from the show and ask you out? I'm telling you, it might not end up being a huge career booster, but it will definitely be a love life booster."

"I can hear the pick-up lines already," Katie interjected. "'Aren't you that loser I saw on TV the other night?' And if we get eliminated on the first round, no one would recognize us anyway."

"You'd be surprised. I can't guarantee that we won't get eliminated in the first round, but I'll bet you this. The better your acting skills, the longer you'll stick around. It's not like you have to win the whole thing to get something out of the experience. I would like to get to the top four, because you get a lot of air time."

"Ann Marie, do you hear yourself? You are openly admitting the only reason you want to do this show is to further your acting career. You are going to be the biggest hypocrite on the show. I don't want to be perceived as a desperate bimbo. I know I'd only be acting, but the rest of the world doesn't know that. I would gladly have my first role be a desperate bimbo; I can play the part. The problem is if I act well, I become the bimbo, because I'm on a reality show being myself not a smart actress playing a bimbo on TV. How am I going to break into acting from there? And if I could convince a producer I was just acting and am capable of playing other characters, and I miraculously got a role out of this hoax, how could I ever live down the reputation of a bimbo? I don't want to start my career with a reputation like Jessica Simpson. Bimbo might work for her, but I want to be taken seriously."

Ann Marie was silent for a moment. Katie knew her best friend was taking a breath to gear up for her final rebuttal. Katie also knew that they were both going to audition for this show in the end, no matter what she said. That's how things went every time. Whatever Ann Marie wanted Ann Marie got, because she was relentless. She would argue until her opponent dropped from exhaustion. She would get her way in the end, because Katie simply couldn't say no to her.

"You are not going to be perceived as a bimbo," Ann Marie proceeded calmly. "You control your audience's perception of you. You need to think things through a little more, and I know you'll see the benefits of doing this with me. Take a chance for once in your life. We might not even make it. You can't deny the fact that you would benefit from auditioning, period. Every audition is a learning experience. We can at least audition for the sake of auditioning. If you get the call, you can make the decision then. You can always say no if you decide it's not for you. But you won't get the opportunity to say no if you don't audition."

This time Katie was silent for a moment. She had to admit Ann Marie made a compelling argument.

"All right," Katie sighed. "I'll do it."

Ann Marie squealed in delight.

"I'll audition with you, that is. I'm not making any promises."

"That's fine. We might not even make it. Let's not get too far ahead of ourselves."

"When are the auditions?"

"Monday."

"Monday? It's Thursday! I don't even know if I can get the day off. And how do we even know we can get in? It isn't an open audition, is it?"

"Katie, calm down. My agent already took care of it. It is not an open aud. They are apparently quite exclusive. You have to go through some lengthy, online application and screening process, or you have to know somebody. Gladys knows the producer personally. That doesn't guarantee anything, obviously, but it's definitely an advantage."

"And you already took care of this?"

"Yep."

"Before you even asked me?"

"I knew you'd say yes."

"Of course. I can never say no to you. So, why did you bother convincing me to audition? You could have just sent me a train ticket."

"I couldn't resist the challenge. Plus, I wanted you to feel good about your decision."

"And you call yourself my best friend," Katie feigned irritation.

"Who else would get you an audition for *Soulmates*? We are so in, Katie! I'll tell you, I was beginning to consider switching agents, but Gladys finally came through. She actually went to college with Verne Bauer. They hung out in the same circles. I think they were in a show together. She acted like they had something going on at some point. Who knows? Gladys rambled on and on, when all I wanted to know was when and where. After I found out how tight she was with Mr. Producer, I asked her to put in a good word for you, too. It was simple. I'm so excited!"

"I hate to admit it, but I am too. I haven't auditioned for anything in six months – longer than that, eight months. My God, what have I been doing? I'm literally wasting away my life as a part-time Accounts Payable Clerk. I'm quitting. I miss the city. Even if I don't get a part, I've got to get back to New York."

"You should. You're not going to get any further ahead in Glens Falls. Quit your job and get down here. Spend the weekend. We'll go have some drinks and go shopping for the perfect audition outfits."

"After I quit my job and pay for a train ticket, I'm not going to be able to afford drinks and a new outfit. Can't I just bring a bottle of vodka and raid your closet?"

"I guess," Ann Marie pouted. "So, when are you coming?"

"I don't know. I have to make some phone calls."

"Call me back, then."

"All right. I'll talk to you later."

"And Katie?"

"Yeah?"

"Thanks."

"You're welcome." Katie hung up the phone, shook her head and smiled. Her entire life was being turned upside-down, all because of one little phone call from Ann Marie.

They both knew it was more than simply another audition. It was a career move. From how Ann Marie spoke, it was a sure thing. Of course, there were no guarantees, but when your agent is a close personal friend of the producer, your chances were pretty good. This part could be the spark that Katie's dying acting career needed.

The prospect was exciting but terrifying. Her last audition had gone so well, Katie had been shocked at hearing the rejection. In devastation, she gave up her apartment in the city and moved back to her hometown in upstate New York. She had lived in the City nearly three years and hadn't landed any decent acting parts. She paid the bills by getting a few commercials and doing accounting part-time during tax season. She felt like it was never going to happen for her. She had forced herself to face the reality that maybe she wasn't meant to be an actress.

How easily Ann Marie had changed her mind! Here she was, only eight months after giving it all up, ready to jump back into the rat race. She was beginning to regret it already. There was so much to consider! Was she prepared to dive back into the acting world? There was no point quitting her job yet. She would take Monday off for the audition and postpone any career decisions until after then. If she didn't get the part, she would go back to work on Tuesday with little harm done other than a bruised ego and the loss of a day's wages. She could handle one day without pay under normal circumstances, except that she'd also have to pay for the trip to New York.

Unsure if she was doing the right thing, she resolved to take one last chance. If she wasn't fated to be an actress, she had no idea what her future held in store for her. She had no other career prospects. She had some accounting skills, but wouldn't get far without the degree; the idea of going back to college was not appealing. That would mean admitting defeat, rendering her entire life up until now meaningless. She was determined to do her best at this audition, to make this the turning point in her life. She needed this part worse than she'd ever needed anything in her life, and that fact was petrifying.

She took a good, long look at herself in the bathroom mirror. She looked like an actress. She had expressive, dark eyes and dirty-blonde hair. She leaned closer, noticing something in her hair. It was a gray one! She got them once in a while. They didn't come in subtly; they came in thick, gray and with a vengeance. She took it as a sign she wasn't getting any younger. She was twenty-five, still plenty of time to make her dream-career happen. First, she had to do something about the gray hair. She didn't want to look thirty-five! She decided to take her chances and go lighter. Hopefully the *Soulmate* liked blondes.

This audition was already putting her in debt; she might as well add a dye job to the bill. She was looking awfully pale, too. She'd better hit the tanning salon this afternoon also. One session wasn't going to do much. She would have to hit another one in the city over the weekend. Her bottom line on indebtedness was growing by the minute, as she thought of more things she needed to buy.

Two days and four-hundred dollars later, she boarded a train to New York. She might go back to work on Tuesday with her tail between her legs, but she would look fabulous with her new hairdo, manicure and suntan.

Maybe her love life would benefit from this audition after all. Even if she didn't get a part, her new look might finally attract the attention of that hot guy who worked on the third floor of her building. How many times she had been in the elevator with him to no avail … She made a pact with herself that if she didn't get this part, she was going to ask him out. While she was taking chances, she might as well take one more. Two rejections in one week would be no more difficult to withstand than one. She might as well go for broke.

Chapter Two

Katie worried the entire train ride to New York that she had made a mistake. She couldn't help feeling rather guilty for splurging so thoughtlessly on a stupid audition when she couldn't even afford a car. She had a small, one-bedroom apartment above an antique shop in downtown Glens Falls. She walked six blocks to work every day and rode the bus anywhere else she needed to go. When she'd retreated to her hometown, it was either move back in with her mother or forgo a vehicle. She chose the latter.

She loved her mother dearly, and they had a good relationship, but she couldn't bear the thought of living with her again. Her mother was a bit of a control freak, and Katie had always reveled in her independence. Moving back in with her mother would feel like a death sentence. She had been depressed enough to give up living in the city, she couldn't imagine crawling back home to her mother after being on her own all those years. She was used to taking care of herself and making her own decisions. She needed to continue doing so to maintain some semblance of sanity.

She desperately needed to land this part. It didn't matter that she didn't have her heart set on debuting her acting career on a reality TV show. If she didn't get it, the rejection would be just as disappointing a loss. She didn't want to approach this audition with a desperate attitude, but she had to be blatantly honest with herself. This audition, if unsuccessful, would probably be her last. She hated to think negatively, but she was twenty-five years old and frankly, tired of pursuing a career that continued slipping further and further out of her reach. She was confident in her acting skills; she had relentlessly pursued her dream for three years – on top of the four years spent in college earning the degree. She had no doubts of her ability to succeed in this business; she simply had not been afforded the opportunity. She hadn't gotten lucky. She had tried out for everything she heard of, with little success other than a few commercials, the last of which could just as easily be attributed to her gorgeous hair as to her acting skills.

Ann Marie met Katie at Grand Central and they walked over to Macy's for a few last-minute items. Katie refrained from any more purchases, but encouraged her best friend to indulge. Ann Marie got a new silk suit, shoes to match and a leather purse. Ann Marie looked stunning, her fiery red hair brushing the shoulders of the creamy ivory silk suit. Between her good looks and magnetic personality, Ann Marie had little chance of failure.

"We are both destined to do this show," Ann Marie assured Katie when she verbalized her opinion. "It was so easy getting the audition. It's fate. Plus, it's the perfect job. All we have to do is be ourselves."

"It would be a cake job, no doubt," Katie agreed. "I've just been disappointed too many times not to keep my guard up."

Katie peppered Ann Marie with questions all weekend long about the audition – what she thought it would be like, what answers would be the best for the questions they assumed they would be asked. Fortunately, Ann Marie loved to indulge in pre-audition strategy sessions. She didn't interpret Katie's questions as insecurity, but rather as a desire to be prepared. The weekend couldn't have gone quicker, and when Monday morning came the girls found themselves seated in a room with at least three-hundred other girls. They eyed the competition with intrigue, but felt very well prepared for whatever the day may bring.

Eventually they were separated into smaller groups of twenty-five and escorted to a room with computer terminals. They had to fill out online paperwork. Evidently some of the girls had already completed the paperwork and some hadn't. There weren't enough computers for everyone, so they rotated between computers and an interviewing room.

Katie was one of the first to enter the room and had gotten a computer. She was relieved, because that gave her some extra time to gain her composure and practice her answers for the interview questions. Ann Marie was equally relieved to be one of the first to interview. Ann Marie liked to go first and set the bar high, and when she returned from the interview room, she was certain she had done so. Ann Marie was obviously pleased with herself. She reiterated the experience to Katie, who was grateful for the advance information. Katie was feeling much more relaxed by the time it was her turn before the panel.

There were four of them. She didn't recognize any of them, nor did their names sound familiar. Three were male and one was female. She smiled brilliantly at each of the panelists in turn before taking a seat in the middle of the room. She felt a spark of attraction to two of the men instantly, and she knew it was mutual. There was no denying that feeling you get when a man is looking at you as though he can see right through your clothes.

"Please state your name and audition number," the woman instructed. The cameras were rolling.

"Katie Cohen. My number is 1415."

"Welcome, number 1415. You should listen for your number for the remainder of the audition, as opposed to your name. We will be taping the interviews and reviewing them to see how you come across on camera. We are going to end up with twenty-five girls for the show, plus two alternates. Six of the total twenty-seven chosen will be from this New York audition. We will ask you some questions, and encourage you to be yourself."

Katie nodded and continued smiling.

"Candidate number 1415, there are over three-hundred women here to audition today. What makes you different from the others?"

"The biggest difference is that I do have BA from SUNY New Paltz with a major in Theatre. My experience in acting can only help me to be successful in a role such as this. I am familiar with the show and feel very comfortable in front of a camera, whether it be for a few minutes or even all day. I feel like I can be myself on camera, whereas others might be reserved in this situation, especially being placed in intimate dating situations."

"Acting experience is very beneficial, although not entirely necessary. We sometimes select candidates with some background in acting, but we don't require it. What qualities do you have other than acting that would make you stand out?"

"I am outgoing and adventurous. I am willing to try new things." Katie focused on one of the men who was looking her up and down. "I feel I have sex appeal and would bring a certain spiciness to the show. I don't date much, so my desire to meet someone is genuine. I am also very down-to-earth and easy to get along with, so I'm sure I could interact well with the other women on the show, as well as the leading male."

"Do you look at Soulmates as a job or as an opportunity to find true love?"

"Honestly, both. I admit I would relish being on camera 24/7 but I am even more interested in meeting an eligible bachelor, even if I have to do it on television. I think you can find true love anywhere. If the chemistry is there, you will know it, whether you're on a TV show, in the grocery store, or even a random audition," Katie laughed, and the three male panelists laughed along with her.

"We appreciate your candor. If you will step back into the other room, we'll call you shortly for a reading."

Katie smiled again at each of the panelists, specifically making eye contact with each for a few seconds. "Thank you very much."

"Thank you," they said in return.

Katie couldn't help the sinking feeling that overcame her as she exited the interview. They had barely asked her anything at all. That couldn't be a good sign. They had asked Ann Marie almost a dozen questions, according to her rendition of the interview. Keeping in mind that Ann Marie tended to exaggerate, Katie pushed the self-doubt from her thoughts. She had been confident in her answers and couldn't think of anything she could have done differently. She had no control over their selections. She had been herself, and that was the most she could do at this point.

Ann Marie looked up from one of the computer terminals. "How'd it go?"

"I think it went pretty well."

"You weren't in there very long."

"I know. That scares me."

"It shouldn't. It could go either way. Maybe they knew right away they wanted you."

"Maybe…"

Ann Marie shook Katie's arm in encouragement and turned back to the computer screen. Katie noted her friend was nearing the end of the online questionnaire.

"They want your whole life story," Katie commented, nodding toward the computer screen. She turned and sat down in an empty chair not far from Ann Marie. She couldn't help but breathe a temporary sigh of relief. She was done for the moment. The panelists had indicated reading would be next. She had read for hundreds of parts. That would be a breeze.

Katie surveyed the room while Ann Marie clicked away at the computer terminal. She couldn't help but notice the girl closest to them. Her fake fingernails were so long, she was having trouble typing. She was mostly using one finger on her left hand and hovering her right index finger over the backspace key. Her hair was bleached blonde and obviously as fake as her nails. The girl must have felt Katie's stare and looked up briefly. Katie averted her gaze quickly, but had caught a glimpse of the bluest eyes she had ever seen – probably colored contacts. This girl was totally fake, and her outfit was something a hooker would wear. Her stiletto heels looked about to buckle under her pudgy, little feet. Her skirt couldn't have been any shorter without exposing a bikini-wax rash. Her blouse hung open down the middle to her navel, leaving not only her cleavage, but half of each breast exposed. Katie couldn't imagine what this girl must have been thinking when she'd gotten dressed that morning.

The girl suddenly turned around and said, "Hi, I'm Kristin."

"Hi. Katie." Katie stood and shook the girl's hand briefly.

"Did you go in there already?" Kristin asked.
"Yeah. I just came out."
"How long did it take?"
"Five minutes."
"Good, because I have another audition this afternoon. I didn't really want this one, but I figured what the hell."

Katie smiled politely and then turned away. Ann Marie was finished filling out her questionnaire and pulled her chair very close to Katie.

"That genius has been filling out the questionnaire since we got here."

"I thought so," Katie nodded, glancing over at Kristin. She was still plucking one key at a time with her left index finger and backspacing with the right. She actually seemed to be getting more proficient, typing at least three or four letters before needing to backspace.

"Her eyes creep me out," Katie added.

In the meantime, another girl exited the interviewing room and walked past them to an empty seat. A very tall, slender woman went in next. She seemed much too sophisticated for the show – the total opposite of Kristin. Katie knew variety was the key to any successful show. They needed a sophisticated lady and a slutty one. Ann Marie could fill the position of token redhead. And that left Katie as the all-around nice American girl. She had as good a chance as anyone. She had given it her all, and that was what mattered. Perhaps her life was due for a change.

"Did they tell you they're only choosing six girls from this audition?" she asked Ann Marie in a hushed tone.

"No way. What about the rest?"

Katie paused, as the door to the interview room opened, and the tall sophisticate re-entered the holding room. Her expression was unchanged. She had been in there less time than Katie. That could mean they liked her right away, or they didn't like her right away. Who knew? There was no point obsessing over something she had no control over.

A black girl passed them and entered the interviewing room. Katie couldn't help but notice the girl was stunning.

"They told me they were picking six from the New York audition. They didn't say where the others were coming from."

"No shit. They told you that?"

"Yeah."

"That sucks." Ann Marie groaned. "I thought were sitting pretty – twenty-five out of two-hundred."

"Three-hundred," Katie corrected her. "Six out of over three-hundred, according to the interview lady."

"Michaelina."

"Did you know her?"

"No, I have no idea who she is, but I took care to call her by name during the interview."

"Smart. I didn't recognize her either. I didn't recognize any of the panelists, but I did think two of them were hot."

Ann Marie laughed. "You would."

Katie didn't bother to argue with Ann Marie. Ann Marie always noticed good-looking men. She'd probably flirted with them mercilessly during her interview. It was just like her to deny she thought they were hot.

"Actually, I did some research on the show, and none of them were part of the casting crew last season. I was surprised not to recognize any of the names."

Katie nodded, not sure if a change in the casting crew was good or bad. She turned her attention back to Kristin, who was triumphantly hitting the submit button.

"Good thing she finished. She has another audition to get to," Ann Marie sneered in Katie's ear.

"I don't want to be here all day either…"

"Do you have another audition I don't know about?"

"No but I have a train to catch this afternoon."

"Don't stress over it. It'll show through on your audition."

"I can't help it," Katie defended herself. "I have to work tomorrow, whether I make it or not."

The black girl exited the interview room, looking satisfied with herself.

"Am I next?" Kristin asked to no one in particular, as she stood and looked around. No one answered. A few people shrugged. Kristin didn't wait for an answer, but teetered in her stiletto heels over to the ominous door. Katie and Ann Marie exchanged glances.

Kristin was in the interview room for what seemed like forever. They could even hear spontaneous laughter from behind the closed door. Ann Marie kept rolling her eyes at Katie. The other girls in the room didn't seem to be paying any attention. Some were reading a magazine or newspaper. One was filing her nails. One was knitting. Several were holding conversations on cell phones. One had pulled out a laptop and appeared to be checking her email.

When Kristin finally came out of the screening room, the four panelists exited as well. They all looked amused, as though they had shared some great joke. One of the men had his glasses off and was wiping his eyes on the back of his hand. Katie watched as the panelists gained their composure.

"Thank you, ladies," the woman, Michaelina was saying. "We'll be calling numbers. If you hear your number, please proceed down the hall to the second door on the left, for the next phase of the audition process. If you do not hear your number, I'm sorry, your audition is over. You can reapply online for the show after eighteen months. We will keep your application on file throughout that time frame, and have been known to call people back on occasion. With that said, thank you for participating. We do appreciate your time, and wish you the best on your own personal quest to find your *Soulmate*."

Katie couldn't help sneaking a smile at Ann Marie. The prepared rejection speech had been amusing, the last line being taken directly from the show. Each week as girls were eliminated, the host wished them well on their *Soulmate* search. Katie hoped it wouldn't be the last time she heard those words – not that she was looking forward to hearing them again, if they were directed at her. That would mean she'd been eliminated from the show. But it would also mean that she had made it onto the show, which was the important thing right now. One step at a time.

"When your number is called, please proceed down the hall to the second door on the left. Thank you, ladies."

Michaelina exited the room, accompanied by one of the male panelists. The other two stayed behind, the guy with the glasses adjusting them on his nose to read the numbers.

Ann Marie's number was the first to be called. She stood and smiled, squeezed Katie's arm again and headed for the door. Katie held her breath as the numbers kept coming.

At least ten numbers were called before Katie heard her own, and several other numbers were called as she made her way to the exit. Approximately half the girls in the room were moving on, including Kristin, the tall sophisticate and the black girl. They headed down the hall as instructed and joined the others in a large auditorium-like room. Katie was expecting to see hundreds of girls waiting in there, but there were only four seated in the front row. As they filled in the seats in the front two rows, Katie counted eighteen girls in all. She looked around and wondered if more were coming yet.

Katie wracked her brain trying to figure out how things worked. She always overthought auditions, and in reality, never truly figured out how they worked. They were all different. Seldom did she have a clue if she was doing well or how her chances were. Once in a while if she was lucky, she would get a smile from one of the judges. Otherwise, she had to rely on her gut feelings, which meant nothing in this line of work. In college, things had been so much simpler. Unless they had a guest director, she knew basically how the auditions worked depending on who was directing. They read for various parts and usually had some sort of impromptu exercise. Until Katie had graduated into the real world of auditions, she knew exactly what to expect and how she had done.

The set looked simple enough. Two chairs faced each other. Off to one side was a large gray screen, much like a backdrop at a photography studio. The cameras surrounded both chairs. Michaelina was bustling around the filming area making last-minute adjustments.

A younger guy, perhaps an intern, was handing out scripts. Katie quickly skimmed through it. The lines were easy; the reading would be no sweat.

The man with the glasses entered the room and immediately went to confer with Michaelina. He made one adjustment to a camera that Michaelina had just finished adjusting, then directed the girls, two at a time, to take the seats on the set. They had to read through the lines twice, once as Character A and once as Character B. The candidates were advised no acting experience was required for the parts; they could read the lines however they liked; they were merely screening the girls to see how they looked on camera.

After all eighteen girls had read both parts, they took a break. The girls were instructed to return in one hour for a final exercise.

Katie didn't feel like eating, but Ann Marie insisted. There was a sandwich shop down the street, where they could grab a quick bite and gab for a few minutes. Katie picked at her ham and cheese sandwich per Ann Marie's encouragement. Ann Marie, who had been through "hundreds" of these auditions, informed Katie matter-of-factly that one final exercise was probably going to take the rest of the afternoon.

"Seen it a hundred times," Ann Marie was saying. "They wouldn't have bothered to break if it was a quick exercise. Besides, you won't have to worry about getting something on the way to the station."

Katie nodded and took a bite of the sandwich, which she chewed and over-chewed before choking it down. She drank some of her bottled water – soda made her burp – to wash it down. Eating was the last thing she felt like doing.

"You don't know where your next meal is going to come from," Ann Marie continued.

"MacDonald's in Glens Falls," Katie retorted.

The girls ate what they could and walked back to the studio. Ann Marie was still confident that both of them would get cast. Katie had her money on Kristin and the tall sophisticate. Kristin already appeared to be in, judging from the grand old time they all seemed to have during her interview. The tall sophisticate had a French accent, Katie had noticed during the reading. She seemed leagues above the other candidates, and seemed to know it. Her confidence was appalling, but even more annoying was her carefree attitude. She didn't appear to want a part, and acted as though it was below her to be here with the rest of them.

"This audition is basically a formality," Ann Marie was saying as they reached the studio. "I'm sure your right about Kristin and the tall one. They seem like *Soulmates* material."

"Why would someone like Frenchie be auditioning in the first place? She doesn't seem to care if she gets a part or not."

"It's all part of her strategy. Trust me, I've seen her type. She wants the part. She's dying to be on TV."

Katie smirked, as they reconvened in the auditorium, and the tall, French sophisticate was already seated, front and center, waiting for the next phase of the audition.

"Perhaps she never left," Ann Marie surmised, leading Katie to the second row and sitting as far away from Frenchie as possible. That meant being in close proximity to Kristin, but at least Kristin was friendly.

The hour-long break slowly dragged into an hour-and-forty-five minutes. Katie kept tapping her foot anxiously, and Ann Marie kept slapping Katie's knee to stop it. Kristin chewed gum and snapped it loudly every fifteen seconds.

"Thank you for your patience, ladies. We're ready to run the final screen test," Michaelina announced without really looking at any of them. "What we would like you do is step in front of the gray screen when it's your turn. It doesn't matter what order you're in; just come up in the order you're sitting. We'd like you to record a message to our *Soulmate* – we'll call him John. Introduce yourself with your number, as though you are taping a video greeting to the *Soulmate*. You can tell him anything you'd like, anything that you think might persuade him to want to meet you in person. The time limit will be seventy seconds. You'll hear a warning beep at sixty seconds. We want to keep these brief, so you will be cut off when time is up, whether you're finished or not. We're not looking for profound messages. Have fun with it. Let your personality shine through. We're looking for spontaneity. We'll take about two minutes, and then call the first person to begin."

A few of the girls groaned, and more than a few looked around nervously, as Michaelina made her way back to the adjudicator's table several rows back. Katie was finally feeling some confidence. She could improvise with no problem. She knew Ann Marie could too. Acting experience was definitely going to give them an edge.

Katie had to hold back giggles, as the first girl took her turn. She was a small brunette, very young. She was trying to make her voice haute and kept batting her eyes. It looked more like she had a nervous twitch.

"Hi, John," she said in an abnormally gruff tone. "I'm number 1440. I can't wait to meet you. I like moonlit walks on the beach, champagne and strawberries, and long, hot bubble baths..."

Katie thought she'd explode with laughter. She didn't dare sneak a glance at Ann Marie.

"If you pick me, I know you won't be disappointed."

"Thank you," the guy with the glasses called.

"Was that long enough?" the girl asked, in her normal voice.

"It was fine. Next please!"

Katie couldn't suppress the urge to giggle as girl after girl delivered trite video messages to some guy they'd never met. She vowed not to appear so pathetically desperate. She purposely ignored the next two girls' tapings in order to regain her composure. She had to get into character. She hadn't really decided on a character, so more specifically she had to prepare to be herself. This had to be the most bizarre audition she'd been through.

Ann Marie went before Katie. Katie honestly had no idea what Ann Marie had said up there, but it was inconsequential. Ann Marie looked great. She was the only redhead in the room, and her personality was even more radiant than her hair. The adjudicators were mesmerized. Katie knew it would be difficult to impress the panel as much as her friend had just done. She knew in her heart Ann Marie would be selected. She hoped now more than ever that she would be joining her best friend in celebrating their success while they embarked on this incredible adventure.

Katie held her head high as she approached the gray screen. She felt dazed, but remembered to make eye contact with each of the four panelists on her way across the stage. She felt like she was in slow motion; it took what seemed like an eternity to walk across the room to the prominent, gray screen. She took a deep breath as she turned her back to the screen and faced the camera. The cameraman signaled for her to begin.

Katie nodded with a smile, tossed her newly blonde locks over her shoulder and began.

"Hi there, John. My number is 1415, and my name is Katie. Numbers are so impersonal," she paused and smiled. "I'm very curious to meet you, and to see if we would be compatible. I'm an adventurous person. I enjoy meeting new people, making friends and tackling challenges. I know if we got together, we'd have a lot of fun, no matter how things turn out. I'm willing to give this a try to see if we could possibly be *Soulmates*. You never know…"

Katie smiled again and could feel her eyes sparkling. She had been thinking about being in love, pretending she was speaking to the man in the elevator in her building that she had a crush on. She hoped she came across as flirty and playful, but not desperate. She had been the only one to use the word *Soulmates*. She hoped it wasn't cliché, but every one of the ladies who went after her worked it in to their introductions as well, so it must have been a good idea. Overall, Katie felt good about her performance. Her chances were as good as any of the others. Most of all, she was glad it was over!

Chapter Three

Katie grew impatient as the afternoon passed. She was grateful they were getting results today, but she also didn't want to miss her train. It was after 4 o'clock by the time the panel reached their decision.

"Thank you, ladies," Michaelina was saying. "We appreciate your patience while we reviewed the tapes. We want to emphasize that you were all great, and our decisions are based on the best potential matches for our current *Soulmate*. We will keep applications on file, again, for eighteen months. That means you are automatically considered for future seasons within that time frame without having to audition again. Just because you were not a fit this season, doesn't mean you won't fit it perfectly in a future season. With that said, I will be calling the numbers of the six ladies we've selected, and we ask that those selected remain in the studio for a brief informative meeting. If your number is not called, you are free to leave. Ron will be in the media room where most of you began, so you can see where you stand on the alternate list. I do want to mention that our first two alternates have been selected from the LA audition, so the first on this list is actually the third alternate. I also want to stress that all the candidates are subject to a background check, and we have filled spots with alternates every season. If we do need alternates, we will notify you within three weeks."

She paused and looked around.

Katie's mouth was dry, as Michaelina began calling numbers. Ann Marie was the first one called. She beamed at Katie and squeezed her arm. Katie smiled back. No surprises there. Katie held her breath as two more numbers were called. Ann Marie grabbed her had supportively.

"1415."

"Katie!" Ann Marie squealed. She jumped up and threw her arms around her.

"I can't believe it!" Katie cried.

Michaelina continued calling numbers, but Katie and Ann Marie were too busy celebrating to notice who was reacting. After the candidates who had not been chosen filed out of the room, Katie regained her composure and scanned the results. One was a short woman with dirty-blonde hair and a New Jersey accent. The tall sophisticate, seated front and center, looked smug as she accepted a handout from one of the interns. Kristin had made it, as well as a brunette girl.

"We've got some important items to go over," Michaelina was saying. "On the handout you are receiving, is a URL. Everything you need to join the *Soulmates* team is on that website. Your user ID is your last name followed by your audition number. Your password is your audition number. You may change your password after you log in the first time. On the website, you will find several items that require your attention. First is your contract. Print it, read it thoroughly, have your agent or your attorney peruse it if you'd like. There is nothing out of the ordinary, but I will point out clause 11.B which basically states you do not speak to the press before, during or after taping. Nothing can be posted on social media regarding the show and your part in it. This clause is in effect until the season finale airs. We insist on your commitment to protect the integrity of the show. You will sign and date on the back two pages electronically by the deadline, which is one week from today. There is also a phone number to our legal liaison should you have any questions."

Michaelina paused and looked around to ensure she had everyone's attention.

"Item #2 is the taping schedule. Please note we will meet here on Monday, May 4 to begin taping interviews. You are responsible for your travel arrangements to the studio. All subsequent travel is arranged by *Soulmates* and will be provided to you on May 4. We will put you up in a hotel here in New York Monday night and proceed to fly out Tuesday morning to LA for the taping of the premiere."

She paused again and glanced around the room. Satisfied that everyone was on track, she continued.

"You will find a list of what you will need to pack. Keep in mind *Soulmates* has wonderful sponsors, and much of your wardrobe, etc. will be provided to you. Try not to over-pack as space is limited. If it isn't on the list, you don't need it. You may want room in your suitcase anyway, because you will leave with more than you came with, even if you leave early on. There is a medical form you will need to fill out, as well as an emergency contact form. Very importantly, there is a guide that outlines the interviews we will be taping here on May 4. You do not need to memorize any responses, but you should be familiar with the topics. Be prepared to speak about yourself."

"Everything I've highlighted is on the website. I would like to say, on behalf of the *Soulmates* production staff, congratulations and welcome to the show. We will see you here on May 4."

The people remaining in the room applauded politely, staff and newly-cast members alike.

Katie felt like she was dreaming. She wanted to stay and celebrate with Ann Marie, but she had to hurry to get the train on time.

"Call me when you get home," Ann Marie ordered and embraced her friend.

"I will! I can't believe it!" Katie exclaimed.

"I can! This is awesome! Hurry – go. Call me. Love ya."

Katie waved as she scooted from the room to catch a cab outside. She did make the train, with little time to spare. She could hardly believe her good fortune. She had finally gotten a break. It might not be the "big break" she dreamed of, but it was definitely a start.

She wasted no time caring for all the details to facilitate her arrival back at the studio on May 4. She had put in her two-week notice at work, banking on making it past the first round and securing the $5000 bonus. If she didn't launch an acting career after making her TV debut on *Soulmates*, she would have enough money to hold her over until she found another crappy part-time job. Smithton-Curry was not a career, and they were just as well to see her go. Tax time was over, and they were going to be letting people go anyway. Katie's only regret was that she didn't run into the cute guy in the elevator and would probably never see him again.

The biggest obstacle she had encountered was her mother. Sharon Cohen had humored Katie in her will to pursue an acting career, but had never fully approved. In fact, she had more-or-less been waiting in the background to gloat an "I told you so" when Katie failed. Katie knew very well her mother was not going to approve of her quitting her "real" job to accept a part on a reality TV show. Katie didn't allow her mother's disapproval to sway her decision. Her mother disapproved of most things Katie did in her life, but was still Katie's life. It was her career and her decision. Deep down, Katie knew her mother wanted the best for her.

Katie's upbringing by her single mother had been rather strict. Katie's father left when she was very young, and she had little recollection of him. Her mother's poor marital experience made Katie cynical of love and relationships with men. Even though it had been her mother burned by love, she felt as though her father had dumped her, too. Her own personal romantic relationships thus far had been very guarded. She had spent her entire life building a wall around her heart. She didn't want to go through what her mother went through. Still, there was a small part of her that didn't want to miss out on experiencing true love.

The idea of meeting her husband on a reality TV show was not exactly the true love Katie had imagined in her life. Katie almost had to laugh at the prospect, but that was what *Soulmates* was all about. Katie spent the next three weeks becoming a girl who believed you could find true love on TV. She got herself into character. By the time she reported to New York to start taping interviews, she had herself nearly believing she could meet her *Soulmate* soon. The hopeless romantic in Katie's heart wanted nothing more than to be swept off her feet and carried into the sunset, while the practical, level-headed daughter of Sharon Cohen pushed away any frivolous fantasies of true love. Thus, her strategy for success on *Soulmates* without getting hurt was established.

Katie took the train to New York on Sunday and spent the night at Ann Marie's apartment. They gossiped all night about what they thought the show would be like, and what the other girls were going to be like, and most importantly what the guy was going to look like! Katie had no idea what to expect, but she was prepared for anything. Whatever happened was better than living in her hometown and working for an accounting firm.

Katie and Ann Marie caught a cab to the studio Monday morning. All the other girls were there already except Kristin, who showed up about two minutes late. A woman named Barbara was in charge, and looked very perturbed. In fact, she looked perturbed with Kristin all day long. Otherwise, she was stone-faced and efficiently moved the girls through the process of completing all the last-minute details and taping interviews.

One girl taped at a time, so the others sat around and talked while they observed. They were all anxious to get to LA and start the interactive part of the show. The interviews would be edited and diced up before they aired – they felt more like another audition than part of the actual show.

The brunette from auditions interviewed first. Her name was Valerie Beck and she was from Boston. She was quick with her answers and came across as somewhat conceited and brash. The questions varied in nature from "what do you do for a living" to "how does your age compare to your level of maturity." The questions were fairly broad, more of a get-to-know-you and your aspirations for the future. Katie knew from seeing the show, the interviews continued throughout the season, and the questions grew more intimate.

Valerie's interview took almost an hour, mostly due to technical difficulties. Katie went second, and her interview only took half an hour. She was asked many of the same questions as Valerie. She was also asked if she wanted children, how she felt about love-at-first-sight and if she would consider relocating her residence. Her responses were concise and mostly honest. She left out her acting aspirations and described her line of work as an accounting assistant. She admitted she wanted children someday, but was not ready yet. She said love-at-first sight was definitely possible, but she obviously had never experienced it personally; she also stated she felt it was better to get to know someone you planned on entering into a relationship with. As far as relocating, she was absolutely willing to do so. She was open to exploring any location and looked forward to seeing other parts of the country.

Katie felt confident the interview went well. Barbara gave her an approving nod, which Katie interpreted as gratitude for not having to re-tape any of her responses. She joined the other girls once again, and a dirty-blonde named Lois Denato was next. Katie listened to the interview long enough to gather Lois was from New Jersey, was outspoken, blunt and at times tacky. Katie passed Lois off as white trash, and turned to gossip with Ann Marie.

Ann Marie was now on a first-name basis with the other girls and introduced Katie to Brittany, Valerie and Kristin. Katie nodded that she had met Kristin at the audition, and shook hands with each of them. Brittany Latrelle was the one they had referred to as the tall sophisticate, or Frenchie. The woman was quite striking. She stood at least five-feet-ten inches tall and had long, straight brown hair with perfectly golden highlights. Her make-up looked professionally applied, and her French manicure was impeccable. She had a French accent and said she was from Montreal. She was friendlier today than at the auditions, but rather condescending. Katie gathered Brittany was not overly fond of Americans and held herself in high esteem as a Canadian. Katie couldn't help but wonder what interest Brittany might have in meeting an American man on *Soulmates*, but then whoever said the *Soulmate* was going to be an American?

Still, talking to Brittany was far more interesting than eavesdropping on Lois's interview. Even though

Brittany was a snob, she was an able conversationalist, and her French accent was pleasant to listen to.

Lois turned out to be incredibly long-winded, and her interview took them through to an early lunch break. The intern, Neil, had ordered lunch already and was busy getting it set up. There were salads, deli meats and fresh fruit and vegetables. It was nothing outstanding, but it was adequate – and it was free.

After lunch, Barbara instructed Valerie back to the interview chair to re-tape some of her responses. Apparently, the technical difficulties had not been sufficiently overcome. Brittany was up next, and Katie was glad to have a break from her by then. Brittany was smart, successful and interesting, and she knew it. Her "I'm wonderful" attitude was beginning to wear on Katie's nerves. Brittany's spent about forty-five minutes in front of the cameras talking about herself, and then returned to the group of girls to talk about herself some more. Katie forced herself to listen for a few minutes, then excused herself to the ladies' room. When she returned, she sat closer to the interview area so that she could watch Ann Marie.

Ann Marie's interview went well, which was no surprise to Katie. Ann Marie showcased her outgoing personality and had obviously won over Barbara's approval; Barbara was actually smiling for the first time today. No doubt Ann Marie would win the heart of the *Soulmate* as well as the viewing public. She had a universal girl-next-door appeal. She was the kind of person you wanted as a best friend, and Katie was proud and grateful to have that claim.

After Ann Marie's interview, Katie waved her over to where she had relocated her seat. Kristin took her spot in the hot seat. The girls tried to converse, but kept being interrupted by outbursts of laughter on the set. Kristin was no comedienne, but she seemed to be the one that things happened to. A light fell over and she let out a blood-curdling scream. She recovered from the scare with laughter. Then she got the hiccups. They had to re-tape nearly every response and stop for Kristin to perform various methods of curtailing hiccups. She gargled water, drank from the wrong side of the glass. Neither worked. There was a major production to find a pencil for her to hold in her teeth while she drank water. She held her breath. She begged no one to scare her, as that was what had given her the damn hiccups in the first place. Eventually they got enough taped, with Kristin answering questions as quickly as possible and invariably letting out a loud hiccup at the end of her sentence.

Everyone was relieved when Barbara called it quits. She instructed them to take a fifteen-minute break, and then reassemble for a brief meeting. It was already after five, and the girls were tired from sitting around all day. They commented on how amazing it was that doing nothing could be so exhausting. When they reassembled, Barbara was busy reviewing footage, so her assistant, Zeb, facilitated the meeting. He explained which hotel they'd be staying at tonight, and what time to meet in the lobby for their transfer to the airport in the morning. He told them they'd be two-to-a-room tonight, and they could choose who they wanted to bunk with. He explained their luggage had already been transported to the hotel and provided them each a claim ticket to pick up their luggage at the baggage check. He handed out vouchers to the hotel restaurant for dinner. He gave them itinerary sheets for tomorrow. Finally, he answered questions, while Barbara finished reviewing the coverage.

Barbara dismissed them all but Kristin to go back to the hotel. She was dissatisfied with Kristin's interview and wanted to re-do everything now that Kristin's untimely case of the hiccups had been cured. The other girls were just as glad to be without Kristin, and made plans to meet in the hotel restaurant after checking in. Katie and Ann Marie had naturally paired up and Valerie had latched onto Brittany. Valerie made it clear she had no intention of rooming with Kristin. Lois didn't care who she roomed with and shrugged indifferently. They set off to the hotel having cordially settled the first decision.

Katie was glad to have Ann Marie there with her. Rooming with a stranger was not very appealing, even if for one night. Spending the night with Ann Marie was going to be fun. No wonder Ann Marie had insisted Katie audition with her. This trip was more than meeting a guy and getting television exposure. It was an all-expense paid dream vacation. Katie hoped it didn't end too soon!

The vacation kept getting better and better. As their plane landed in LAX the next day, the pilot announced the current temperature of 73° and a high expected today of 85°. Ann Marie let out a whoop from three rows up. Katie giggled to herself.

The girls were tired from the flight, and the three-hour time difference made for an even longer day. They had little spare time that afternoon, between getting checked into the hotel and preparing for the premiere shoot. They had been advised to sleep on the plane, but of course Katie couldn't. She was too excited!

The afternoon was a bustle doing hair and makeup, steaming dresses, making last-minute alterations and repairs for the inevitable wardrobe mishaps. Katie was pleased with the result. Her hair was down, which she thought looked sexier than an up-do. She had chosen a black strapless dress, so that her hair gently brushed her shoulders. The dress was long and fitted, which accentuated her slim, attractive figure and pronounced a full, but not overflowing bosom. Her manicure and pedicure was a dark cabernet color that popped against the black dress. Her makeup was perfect, including cabernet lipstick to match her polish. She made a mental note not to drink too much, so as not to lose too much of the perfectly-coordinated lipstick around the rim of her glass. She wasn't about to waste valuable air time in the powder room having her makeup reapplied.

Katie and Ann Marie took the elevator together to the Grand Ballroom. However good Katie thought she looked, she knew Ann Marie blew her away. Her best friend was brilliant in a turquoise, sequined gown. It had a daringly plunging back. The long sleeves came to a tip on the back of her hand and were trimmed with tiny crystals. Her wavy, red hair cascaded over her shoulders and sparkled with glitter.

"Is it too much?" Ann Marie asked. "Be honest, do I look like the Little Mermaid?"

"You look fabulous. I wouldn't change a thing. Don't stand near me when we get downstairs."

"I think I'll stand between Kristin and Lois," Ann Marie shot back. "We'll show this guy what class looks like."

"I wonder what he looks like," Katie pondered aloud.

"I'm sure he'll be *fine*."

"No doubt. All the girls will be mauling each other to get next to him. I'd put more stock in our wrestling skills than our acting skills at this point. Easy for you – you grew up with brothers."

"Just make sure to connect with him," Ann Marie instructed. "Pour on the charm. We do not want to go home tomorrow!"

"I'm in this for the duration. What more could you ask for? Free food, free drinks, parties, dresses, dates, 80° weather… I have no desire to go home tomorrow, even if the guy turns out to be a huge nerd."

"This is pretty awesome," Ann Marie agreed with a smug grin. "And I'm sure he won't be a nerd."

The elevator came to a stop at the Mezzanine level, and the girls exchanged ready glances and took a deep breath before stepping into a huge reception hall outside the Grand Ballroom.

"Here goes nothing," Katie whispered. She tossed her hair over one shoulder and stepped across the threshold onto lavish carpet. Ann Marie followed suit, strutting confidently to a reception table set up outside the entrance to the ballroom, which was presently closed. Neil was manning the table and handing out name tags with first names only. He instructed the girls to line up alphabetically by first name.

Katie accepted the name tag, but struggled where to put it, considering she was wearing a strapless dress. She wasn't about to obscure her cleavage with a name tag. She fastened it over one hip and wandered over to where she assumed the middle of the line would be.

A short girl with strawberry-blonde hair and an obnoxious, red, satin dress took a spot directly in front of the closed doors.

"A," she called. "Any other A's? I'm first. Can anyone beat Amanda?"

"I'd like to beat Amanda," Katie murmured to Ann Marie, who had moseyed up beside her.

"I'm going to have to stand next to her," Ann Marie responded with a slap to Katie's arm.

"Have fun," Katie said and gave her a friendly push toward the double doors. Katie wondered if they were being filmed already. She didn't see any cameras yet, but that meant nothing. She wasn't about to make a spectacle of herself like Amanda. She stood back and let the others fill in around her. She watched to see if there were any Adriana's or Allison's that could "beat Amanda" but none showed. There was one dark-haired girl between Amanda and Ann Marie. Katie wondered what name she could possibly have. She was sure Ann Marie didn't care, as long as she provided an adequate buffer between herself and Amanda.

Katie was settled in line in front of Kristin and behind a girl named Karen. She felt comfortable with her position. No one in front of her looked exceptional, other than Ann Marie and Brittany. Those two were far enough away from Katie that they wouldn't be directly compared. The girls immediately in front of Katie were not spectacular, in her opinion. Thankfully, half-dressed Kristin was behind her, so she would not pose any unwelcomed distraction.

Barbara stepped out from behind the closed doors, carefully securing them shut behind her and held up a hand for attention.

"Thank you, ladies. I'm losing my voice, so if you could keep it down for a minute, I want to go through a few logistics. We will not be re-shooting anything tonight, unless there is some major catastrophe. There are various cameras and they will run constantly. What you do, what you say, what you act like may be captured on camera, and may be aired on national television. If you trip … if you throw up … if you get the hiccups, that is how you will be seen my millions of American viewers. We want tonight to be spontaneous, and we want to capture you as you truly are. Be yourselves, but be aware that you are being filmed at every moment."

There were a few outbursts from the crowd, mostly groans and giggles. Katie snuck a glance at Kristin, who looked appalled that Barbara had brought up the hiccups.

"We'd like to get filming, and I know you are all eager to meet this season's Soulmate. Let me give you an overview of how this evening works, and we will jump into filming. You will each meet our Soulmate one at a time, but we will pause after each group of five. After you introduce yourself to our handsome gentleman, please move to the left, away from the main camera area. You will see five X's taped on the floor, and we will line up on the X's in groups of five. The camera will sweep each of you again, and then Zeb will direct you to your table.

"The tables are set for six. Please sit together with your group of five, and our Soulmate will be sitting with each table throughout the night. You will all get to spend a few minutes with him. I will go ahead and tell you now, his name is Eric."

Oohs and aahs rang throughout the corridor. Barbara held her hand up for silence again.

"This is not a free-for all. We will ensure that each lady gets time with Eric, so don't worry about getting left out. You will all meet him, five-at-a-time, and take your seats. We will break for more instructions at various points throughout the evening, but again, cameras will be rolling at all times. A brief overview of what to expect: we will have an unstructured cocktail hour, followed by a sit-down dinner. Your host for the evening, of course, our *Soulmates* host Shane Theron. Shane will direct you somewhat, but you are not to approach him at any time. Any questions should come directly to me and my team, not Shane. Anything you say to Shane can be aired. I am not on the show, period, so you may feel free to speak openly to me about any concerns."

"I don't trust her," Kristin murmured behind Katie. Katie raised her eyebrows and turned back to Barbara. Kristin was probably right. Just because Barbara was never shown on TV didn't mean someone having a conversation with her wouldn't be. Katie doubted she would have any questions or concerns important enough to approach Barbara, but the hall was filled with drama queens vying for attention.

"After dinner, we will have dancing and some more time for mingling. After the party, Eric will make his decision on which fifteen girls he would officially like to date. More instructions will come throughout the evening, but that is an overview of what to expect. Let's try to get through the introductions. If I yell 'cut' it means there is a technical hold-up. Please stop whatever you are doing at that time and listen for instructions. We generally tape through with minimal interruptions, but you never know. We want to maintain the integrity and spontaneity of the show. Have a fun time, and most importantly be yourselves!"

Barbara conferred momentarily with a tall, bald man and then disappeared behind the closed doors, leaving the bald man guard. He had a headset on, but looked more like a bouncer than a production assistant. The girls chatted anxiously as they waited to gain entrance to the Grand Ballroom. Katie kept her back to Kristin to avoid small talk and sized up the competition.

The first in line, Amanda, was no problem. The second girl in line was pretty, dark, Latino. She was short in spite of six-inch heels. She was one of several in a black dress, but this dress was very different from Katie's. It was just below the knee, and had several layers of ruffles. It looked ethnic, and accentuated the girl's voluptuous figure, but not the kind of dress that would flatter just anyone. The girl looked fantastic. Katie hoped Eric would prefer blondes.

Ann Marie stood behind her in stark contrast, with Brittany behind her. Brittany was stunning, of course, in a long, straight, cream-colored gown with a huge slit up the back. The dress was dappled with rhinestones that sparkled as she moved. Her hair and make-up were predictably perfect. Brittany was a sure bet to make it to the next round. The final girl in the first group of five was not so certainly advancing. She had curly, dark-blonde hair and was not striking in any way. She wore a nondescript dress in black-and-white and had an easily forgettable face. Katie felt sorry for her, having to follow Brittany. Anyone directly behind Brittany was destined to be overlooked.

A good fifteen minutes passed before the bald bouncer got the signal to send the first girl in. He pulled the door open just enough for Amanda to slip through, then resumed his position with arms crossed over his chest.

Ann Marie turned and gave Katie a thumbs-up. Katie smiled and returned the gesture. The adventure was about to begin!

Chapter Four

The first set of five had been in the room for what seemed like forever, with no indication that the others would be joining them soon. Katie grew antsy, wondering what was going on in there. She was sick of standing in her high heels and shifted her weight from one foot to the other intermittently. They could have lined up chairs easily enough.

Katie studied the next set of girls. She was close enough to read their name tags. Danine was first outside the double doors. She looked Italian, with thick, brunette hair and brown eyes. She had on a short, plain white dress, and funky strap-up sandals. Her shapely, tanned legs were enough to get her through to the next round.

After Danine was Desirae. Desirae was mousy, with short-brown hair and a plain face. Her dress looked like a prom dress from the eighties – light blue, puffy and tacky. Unless this girl had killer personality, she was toast.

The next girl, Faith, was kind of pretty. She had unusually pale skin for such dark hair. Her hair was perfectly black, with no highlights, and perfectly straight. She also wore a black dress. Her dress had a gothic look, like something from the Renaissance. It was a unique look, but risky. Eric would either love it or hate it. Katie thought Faith had a cool look, and probably had a pretty good chance if Eric was into that kind of thing. Faith was slightly different from the other girls, and one definitely needed to stand out in this game.

The next girl's dress was absolutely hideous. Heather had a very pretty face, curly brown hair and bright blue eyes. The dress was dark blue with a psychedelic pattern that could make you dizzy if you stared too long. Katie was mesmerized for some time by the dress, but was pulled back to reality by the bald guy, who began talking into his Bluetooth. After a moment, he stepped aside and swept one door open, allowing Danine entrance to the Grand Ballroom.

Katie blinked heavily to moisten her dry eyes and moved on to the next girl in line, Iris. Iris was a tall, pale blonde who had such an athletic build she looked almost masculine from behind – which was probably why she was wearing a very feminine, pink floral. Katie would have bet money Iris would be on the next flight home.

As the girls continued to enter the Grand Ballroom one-at-a-time, Katie surveyed the five ladies in her own group. Jennifer would be first, followed by Julia, Karen, herself and then Kristin. Katie could see her biggest competition of the five was definitely Jennifer. Jennifer was extremely attractive. She was a petite blonde with a charming southern accent. She seemed very sweet and friendly. Her dress was deep green, which accentuated her green eyes splendidly.

"Call me Jenny, please," she giggled to the girl behind her, Julia.

"If you insist," Julia answered with an undisguised touch of disdain. Julia also had a southern drawl, but where Jenny was sweet and bubbly, Julia seemed to be a snooty southern belle. Obviously, Julia felt superior to Jenny; she undoubtedly felt superior to all the others. Katie had to admit she was beautiful, although stiff and almost mannequin-like. Her dress was burgundy, long and classically elegant. It set off her wavy black hair and green eyes superbly. She clearly meant business and could be trouble if she had any personality beneath her prude exterior. Katie was banking on first impressions being the key to success tonight. Eric wasn't going to have time to break through Julia's shell. Hopefully he would presume her a waste of his time.

Karen was another waste of time, in Katie's opinion. Karen was nervous and self-conscious. She kept checking her bra straps to make sure they weren't showing. She should have worn a strapless bra. The straps on the dress were wide enough to accommodate a bra, but Karen's paranoia was unattractively drawing attention to them. She was so nervous her skin was becoming blotchy, which was especially pronounced against the white dress. She wasn't an unattractive person, but her uneasiness was evident. She hadn't spoken a word to the girls around her and would be lucky to find her voice to speak to Eric.

The second set of five had all gained entrance to the Grand Ballroom, and Baldy was getting the call to let the next one in. Jenny made an excited, squeaky noise and ducked under the bald man's arm. Katie took a deep breath and tried to prepare mentally. She had no idea how she was going to feel about Eric when she saw him, but she knew how she had to make him feel about her. No matter how she felt about him, she had to pour on the charm and make a big impression. It was all a game tonight. She needed to get through this round, because she desperately needed that $5,000 bonus. Otherwise, she was totally screwed. She would be going home with no money, no love interest, and no job to face her "I told you so" mother. She intended to play this game strategically. She was not going home so soon!

Julie was allowed to enter. Katie was growing impatient, but she planted an encouraging smile on her face for Karen, who was going next. Katie knew she would be wearing that smile for the next few hours, no matter how she felt about some of the other girls. She would don her poker face and play the role of Miss Congeniality for the night. Besides, she and Ann Marie could rehash all the details later. She was so lucky to have her best friend here with her. The other girls didn't have that luxury; they didn't know who they could trust. Betrayal was a prevalent outcome in this situation.

Karen was being sent in. That put Katie at the front of the line. Her heart started beating faster. She reminded herself it was just another role. She needed to give the performance of a lifetime. She shifted her weight from one foot to the other to keep the blood flowing through her legs. The last thing she needed was for her foot to fall asleep. It seemed like an eternity that she stood at the closed double doors, watching the bald guy for a signal. At last the Bluetooth showed some activity, and he swung the door open.

"See you in there," Kristin said, and patted her back.

Katie managed to flash a smile, then inhaled deeply and stepped over the threshold into the Grand

Ballroom. She felt like Cinderella walking into the ball. All eyes were on her. Katie pretended she was a princess, and the cameras were paparazzi. She imagined herself walking down the red carpet and smiled brilliantly. The room was breathtaking, exactly how she would have imagined a grand ballroom would be in a fairy tale. She was taken in by the grandeur, but even more taken in when she saw Eric.

He was very attractive, and his gaze was glued to her, his smile encouraging her and beckoning her to him. Katie was pleasantly surprised by Eric's good looks. She was not naïve enough to be struck by love-at-first-sight, but he was certainly worth getting to know. He stood about five-feet-ten, somewhat shorter than she usually dated, but still tall enough to see the top of her head when she wore heels. His hair was thick and brown, with golden highlights, probably from the sun. He seemed to fill out the black tuxedo nicely. He was not too thin and not too muscular. She would have to see him in a bathing suit to make final judgment on his physique, but was fairly sure if Eric looked that good in a tux, he would definitely look good in a bathing suit.

He smiled at Katie, as she approached. He had a great smile. "Hi."

"Hi, Eric! I'm Katie," she beamed back, gesturing to the name tag attached at her hip. Eric's eyes followed Katie's gesture.

"I see that," Eric replied as he unabashedly scanned Katie's body.

"I didn't have anywhere else to put it on this dress."

"I see that as well," Eric laughed.

"I'm sure you won't forget my name anyway."

"Of course not, Katie." His green eyes danced. He was a merciless flirt.

"Thank you," Katie smiled and gave him a quick hug. "I'm glad to finally meet you!"

"Likewise," he said, as Katie turned to take her place on one of the five X's nearby. She could feel his gaze on her, and when she turned around he was still looking at her. She gave him another brilliant smile. She absolutely felt a connection. He wouldn't be forgetting her any too soon. He might not be the man of her dreams, but then again, maybe he was … He was worthy of her attention. She wanted to stick around now more than ever. The bonus was imperative, but Eric was hot! She was looking forward to the challenge of enticing him.

    Her moment in the spotlight was over. The ballroom doors opened, and in came Kristin. Even though her look was revealing, on the verge of slutty, she was still captivating. Her silver sequined dress glittered blindingly as she strode across the room. Even her silver shoes glittered. Her blonde hair cascaded over her partially-exposed breasts. Eric couldn't take his eyes off them.

    Kristin was either nervous or exceedingly calculating, because she got the hiccups again. She giggled and pulled at Eric's arm.

    "I knew that was going to happen!"

    Eric grabbed a glass of water off a nearby table and chivalrously came to her rescue.

    "Aren't you sweet?"

    Eric wouldn't be forgetting Kristin any time soon either. She carried her water with her to the designated X on the floor. The camera scanned over the five ladies again. Katie suddenly realized how competing in a Miss America pageant must feel.

    Zeb motioned the girls over to table number three. They sat down quietly and positioned themselves to watch the remaining procession.

    Lois was making her way toward Eric. At first glance, she looked nice, and Katie was feeling guilty for assuming she was white trash based on her New Jersey accent. She cleaned up nicely. But as she started talking, that white trash air about her returned. Katie couldn't help but notice her black and gold dress was more loud than classy. It was too short in the back and too low in the front. She didn't have the curves to carry it off. Her legs were too skinny, and her chest too flat. Her dirty-blonde hair, pulled up off her neck, was her only redeeming factor. It framed her face nicely, but her face was a little too rough to be framed so delicately.

Eric smiled at Lois, just as he had at Katie and Kristin. Katie wondered if she had truly made an impression, or if Eric was playing her. Maybe the connection she felt was manufactured. He was playing them all, wasn't he? That was the point of the show.

Lois turned and stood on the first X, as the doors opened again. Maeve was the next to enter. She was one of the girls in black, but Katie did not feel threatened by her. Maeve's dress was sequined, but the sequins were black and didn't catch the light. The length seemed to be wrong as well. The hemline fell just to the knee and gave Maeve's legs a chunky look. She wasn't particularly chunky, but the cut of the dress was not flattering. Her red hair was short and fine, not full and radiant like Ann Marie's. In fact, Maeve's hair was more orange than red, and rather dull. It reminded Katie of overcooked carrots that had lost their color and flavor.

Eric greeted her fondly, but Katie detected a change in him. There was no chemistry between them, and it seemed Eric couldn't fabricate any. His mannerisms were polite and friendly, but not flirtatious as they had been with the other girls. It gave Katie confidence that she had indeed caught Eric's eye.

Madison came next. She was a lovely girl with an extremely pretty face, brown hair and bright blue eyes. Her dress was midnight blue, and fit her perfectly. It was silk and clingy, classy yet sexy. Eric was clearly impressed.

Olivia followed Madison. Olivia was also very pretty, but had more of a natural look. Olivia was the type of girl that looked as though she had no make-up on, and didn't appear to need any. Her skin was fresh and blemish-free. Her green-hazel eyes needed no accentuation. She wore a light green dress, so pale you could barely tell it was green, almost like mother-of-pearl. It was a short, plain dress, but very flattering. Olivia introduced herself to Eric and found her X. Eric seemed to like her, too.

The last in that group was Patty. She was a brunette with a bright red dress. The dress was obnoxiously red, on the verge of hot pink. Maybe it was the lighting, but Katie felt the urge to shield her eyes. It looked like a leftover bridesmaid dress that had the wrong dye lot. Katie continued smiling and took care not to let the contempt show on her face. The main camera was busy scanning the fourth set of girls occupying the X's, but the other cameras around the room scanned continuously. She reminded herself she could be captured at any time, and didn't want to be wearing a salty expression when she was.

Group four made their transition from the X's to their designated table, and the ballroom doors opened again. Another attractive girl entered the room. Katie wasn't positive, but the name tag looked like Riann. She had dark hair and eyes and wore a black dress. Eric seemed to like her, although there was nothing notable or unique about her. They chatted longer than most of the others before Riann found her way to the X's.

Samantha was next. She had silky, white-blonde hair and a pale, peach-colored dress. She looked very feminine and soft. She had a nice smile, warm and caring. She was quite pretty, but her genuine personality made her even prettier. She exuded sincerity.

Samantha was followed by Simone. Simone had a cute face and bounced when she walked. She was petite, peppy and outgoing. Her laugh resonated throughout the room. Most of the other girls couldn't hear what she was saying, but laughed right along with her, because her personality was infectious. She had light brown hair with soft, red highlights. Her green eyes were offset by her olive-colored dress. The dress itself was nondescript, but it honestly didn't matter what she was wearing. Simone's magnetic personality lit up the room.

Katie breathed a sigh of relief when Simone took her place on one of the X's. She didn't know how much competition she could take! Katie had seen some very pretty girls enter the room, and Eric looked equally impressed by most of them. They were almost done!

Tina came out next. She was the only black girl, and she was stunning. She was very tall and had very dark skin. Her hot coral dress was bright against her skin, but still tasteful. She stood out from the other girls, which was to her benefit, and Eric seemed to like her. What man wouldn't? Tina was gorgeous. Katie figured she had a free ticket to round two, based on the fact that she was the only black girl. Historically on the show, whether purposefully or coincidentally, the person of opposite color always made it to round two but had never been chosen as the final winner. So, while Tina was an immediate threat, Katie thought she had her beat in the long run.

The grand ballroom doors opened a final time, and Valerie made her entrance. She stepped over the threshold, raised her arms and struck a pose.

"Last but not least!" she called, which brought a chuckle from the crowd. She looked spectacular, which was no surprise. She strode confidently across the ballroom floor and gave Eric a strong handshake and a kiss on the cheek.

"Hi, Eric. I'm Valerie."

"Hi, Valerie." Eric looked awed.

"I'm so glad to meet you. How are you?"

"I'm great."

"I bet you are," she laughed, motioning to the twenty-four girls behind them.

"I'm a little overwhelmed right now," Eric admitted.

"I would imagine you are," Valerie concurred. "I will let you take a breather. It was great to finally meet you, and I'll talk to you later tonight."

"Absolutely."

Valerie kissed his cheek again, and turned toward her table. Zeb caught her attention and reminded her she was supposed to be standing on the last X. She covered her mistake gracefully and did an about-face. The camera scanned the final group of five, then focused on Shane Theron, who had magically appeared where a sixth X would have been next to Valerie.

"There you have them," he announced. "Twenty-five eligible women! Ladies, welcome to *Soulmates* Season Seven."

The ladies cheered and applauded. Zeb gestured for the last group to move to their table, and another camera closed in from the side to get Shane and Eric in the shot together.

"Could one of these lovely ladies be your *Soulmate*, Eric?"

"I'm optimistic, Shane. I'm looking forward to getting to know everyone a little better."

"Let's get to it! Tonight is all about getting to know each other, beginning with our *Soulmate*, Eric Werner. Take a look …"

Curtains behind Shane and Eric opened to reveal a huge screen. A video began. The *Soulmates* logo filled the screen and faded into a huge picture of Eric. The short film was an overview of his life, narrated by none other than Shane Theron. It consisted of pictures of Eric in a slideshow format, highlighting critical moments throughout his life: a baby picture, receiving an athletic award in elementary school, playing high-school football, the senior prom. The narration described him as being from Pittsburgh, PA. He came from a large family with four siblings – two sisters and two brothers. He was a high school athlete, and still a huge fan of the Pittsburgh Steelers, Pirates and Penguins. He was thirty years old, owned his own home, and had a successful career as a computer programmer. All he lacked was a mate. He was sick of the dating scene, and had agreed to go on the show. He was ready to settle down, and knew the perfect someone had to be out there.

The room applauded, and the screen faded to black, then to the *Soulmates* logo.

"Could Eric's *Soulmate* be in this room? We'll find out as Season Seven unfolds…"

Shane paused, and Barbara started calling out instructions. Apparently, Shane had pre-taped much of his banter, but Barbara wanted him to tape everything again in front of the ladies. She insisted on capturing their honest reactions to Shane to maintain the illusion of the show. She wanted footage of Shane and the ladies in the same room, and Shane was giving pushback. Barbara won the battle, as she was the director, and Shane reclaimed his position on the imaginary sixth X.

"We've got a great evening planned to kick off the season," Shane began, and his welcoming personality and winning smile were back, as though there were no place he'd rather be. "Ladies, you will have one hour of cocktails with Eric before dinner. This is your opportunity to get to know one another a little. It is also the time to make an impression. In fact, Eric will be dining at the table of his choice. That gives five special ladies some bonus time with Eric."

The ladies responded with ooh's and aah's.

"After dinner, we'll have dancing. Eric will ask the lady of his choice to start things out on the dance floor. Don't worry, you'll each get a chance. Enjoy yourselves, but remember all good things must come to an end. At the end of the night, Eric must make his decision of who will stay and who will go. Ten ladies will be going back home. Fifteen lucky ladies will be moving on – and moving in to the *Soulmates* mansion."

The ladies cheered again. Lois whistled through her fingers.

"You've got a rowdy bunch here, Eric!"

Eric grinned in anticipation.

"I'll leave you to it," Shane concluded and stepped back. He took a seat next to Barbara, who instantly vacated hers to bark out more instructions.

"Cocktail hour is very upbeat and casual. Spontaneity is the goal here. I want everyone to socialize and let Eric do the mingling, so no one monopolizes his time. The adjacent bar and lounge area will be used. The dinner area should be vacated completely. We will probably run longer than an hour, depending on Eric's feedback. For the most part, we will leave you alone to socialize. Remember, cameras are always running. Anything you say or do can be aired on national television.

We are going to take a fifteen-minute break and reconvene in the bar and lounge area."

Ann Marie and Katie stayed away from each other during the break and started making connections with the girls at their respective tables. They had agreed that they would both benefit by dividing and conquering. Their strategy was to size up the competition and pair up with some of the obvious threats to ensure none of them got too much time with Eric. They would tag-team their time with Eric and covertly draw other girls to and from Eric in the meantime.

Ann Marie buddied up with Andrea and Chelsea, and Katie took Jenny and Julia. Ann Marie got to Eric first. Katie chatted with her tablemates for a few minutes, then rotated the three of them in to take their turn talking to Eric. Ann Marie stepped back, and Andrea and Chelsea politely followed suit. Ann Marie struck up a conversation with Heather next; she and Heather talked for a few moments and then made a play for Eric's attention.

The two worked the room efficiently and both spent a considerable amount of time talking to the man of the hour. Their tactic didn't work with some of the more aggressive girls, and they both stayed away from a few specific girls they didn't feel comfortable around. For Ann Marie, that was Maeve, the other redhead. Katie could have told Ann Marie that Maeve was no competition for her, or anyone else, but Ann Marie had a thing about being the only redhead in the room. Katie herself avoided Kristin and Valerie for the simple fact that they made her feel self-conscious. Kristin's huge boobs were no competition for Katie, and Valerie's quick-witted tongue was too unpredictable. Katie also didn't waste any time on those she felt were definitely in or surely out. For example, she had no doubt Eric would keep Brittany the French Princess and Tina the Black Beauty. She had equally strong feelings that he *wouldn't* be keeping anxiety-ridden Karen or Amanda the Amazing Ditz – who, by the way, was drunk. She was also fairly sure she didn't need to worry about Trailer-Trash Lois, Iris the Green Giant or Dowdy Desirae.

Together, Ann Marie and Katie maximized their individual time spent with Eric. Katie made sure to cover her name tag and quiz Eric to see if he remembered it. He hadn't forgotten. Katie felt the night was going well. After an hour, Shane entered the scene again. He held up his arms to gain their attention.

"Ladies! Cocktail hour has come to a close. Please take your seats, and Eric will decide which table to join for dinner."

The ladies moaned at having to give up their social time with Eric. They reluctantly trooped back to their respective tables.

"Eric, can I have your decision?"

"Yes, Shane. I've given it some thought, and I want to be fair to everyone. I've decided to split my time between all the tables."

"Sounds good. Choose your starting table, and I'll have the first course served."

Eric sat at table number five, after reasoning since they had waited the longest to meet him, they should get him first.

"Salad is a quick course," Jenny told her table enthusiastically. "Maybe we'll get him for the main course."

"Or dessert," Kristin added, as she picked at her salad. Katie couldn't help but notice Kristin was about as good with a fork as she was with a computer keyboard. Why she wanted those humungous, fake nails was a mystery.

As it turned out, Eric joined table number three for the third course, which was minestrone soup. He had survived salads with table number five and shrimp cocktails with table number four. Katie was just as glad to have Eric with them during the soup, because it was not messy and only took a few minutes to eat. They got more quality time with him. It was much easier to have a conversation between sips of soup than trying to talk with a huge chunk of meat in your mouth.

Eric sat between Karen and Jenny. Karen turned redder by the minute, but Jenny had no problem carrying the conversation for both of them. Kristin, who was next to Karen, kept leaning forward to talk around her. Every time she did the whole table got flashed by her chest. Katie couldn't help exchanging glances with Julia every time it happened. It would all be caught on camera, but Katie didn't care if she and Julie looked catty.

Katie was seated directly across from Eric at the round table. If she couldn't sit next to him, across from him suited her just as well. He had no choice but to look at her, even if their conversation was a little strained. Katie kept a gracious smile on her face and nodded along with the other girls.

Julia was in the most difficult position, between Katie and Jenny. She was half hidden from Eric's view, and was too polite to interrupt any part of the conversation. Julie was probably not going to be sent home regardless; she was charming.

The course didn't last nearly long enough. Eric was quickly moving on to table number two with Danine, Desirae, Faith, Heather and Iris. Katie and her cohorts lusted after him as he sauntered away and sat between Danine and Heather. Kristin broke the silence.

"Karen, are you having an allergic reaction?" she asked loudly, as she was just noticing Karen's bright red blotches. "Did you eat the shrimp?"

"No, I'm not allergic to shrimp," Karen answered with a weak smile.

"Is it sun burn?" Kristin offered, a semi-disgusted look on her face.

"No, I think it's just nerves. It started earlier," Karen replied meekly.

"You should put something on that," Kristin insisted.

"Like a sweatshirt..." Katie thought.

"This filet looks delicious," Julia changed the subject tactfully.

"I don't eat red meat." Kristin pushed the meat to the side of her plate and dug into the garlic mashed potatoes. The others didn't respond, but began picking at their own plates. Dinner was a little uncomfortable, but it went quickly. Dessert was chocolate cheesecake, and Eric shared that with table number one. Katie wondered if Kristin was going to have some aversion to cheesecake as well, but she ate every bit on her plate. Besides the potatoes, it was all Kristin had eaten all evening.

Katie ate a few bites of the cheesecake, but didn't want to stuff herself. She was already beginning to feel like she was in the Twilight Zone. This was the most bizarre dinner she'd ever had. It was like going to the prom stag and fighting over one guy with twenty-four other girls. How had she ever allowed Ann Marie to talk her into this?

As the tables were being cleared, Shane came back on the scene. He had cowered next to Barbara most of the evening and sucked down scotch after scotch. He had eaten even less than Kristin, but was not noticeably fazed by the alcohol.

"I hope you all enjoyed dinner," he began. "I'm going to invite Eric to the dance floor at this time. He will make his choice who gets the first dance."

Eric stood and joined Shane in front of the tables.

"Who have you selected, Eric?"

"I'm hoping to dance with everyone, but I'll start with Brittany."

Brittany smiled and stepped forward. The lights dimmed and the music began. Eric and Brittany slow danced, as the others looked on wistfully, waiting their turns to be in Eric's arms. Brittany and Eric made an odd couple. Brittany was several inches taller than him in spite of her moderate-sized heels. She was a graceful dancer, even though she appeared to be leading most of the time. She seemed out of Eric's league.

Katie wondered if they would all actually get a chance to dance with Eric. No instructions had been forthcoming, in spite of Barbara's promises. It would be nice to see if there was any chemistry between them. It wasn't clear if Eric was going to choose all his dance partners, or merely the first one. Hopefully it was organized and not a free-for-all cutting in. Katie wished she knew what was going on so she could prepare herself. Spontaneity was not in her nature.

Katie's curiosity was satiated soon enough. Brittany got to dance the entire song with Eric. As the song ended, Zeb was busy lining up the girls to dance. The next song started, and Andrea stepped forward to dance with Eric. They only danced about a minute before Zeb sent Ann Marie to cut in. It reminded Katie of a dollar dance at a wedding reception, minus the cash.

Katie felt like an idiot waiting in line to dance with a guy. She stood patiently and smiled politely as the other girls took their thirty-to-forty seconds in the spotlight. The line moved along quickly, and before she knew it, Zeb gave her the nod. She had somehow ended up after Iris, and she gently tapped Iris's shoulder to cut in. Iris stepped aside quickly, as though she was glad to be relieved. Eric looked relieved as well.

"Hi, Katie," he said, remembering her name.

"How are you doing? Are you hanging in there?" she asked.

"I'm OK. It's a little overwhelming, but I can't say I'm not enjoying it!"

"I'm sure!" Katie smiled, and their eyes met. Eric had green, vibrant eyes. They were playful and a little mischievous. Katie's instinct was to look away, but she held her gaze flirtatiously. She had another unexpected urge to kiss him. She smiled instead and tried to cover her nervousness. She couldn't understand why she kept having these weird feelings.

"Are you enjoying yourself?" Eric asked.

"Definitely. I would absolutely like to stick around and see what happens."

"Good," he said and smiled.

The room was crowded full of people, but to Katie it felt like just the two of them.

"Pittsburgh, huh?" Katie asked, lightening the conversation.

"Pittsburgh. How about you? Where are you from?"

"I'm from Glens Falls, New York."

Eric nodded and smiled, but obviously had never heard of it.

"It's upstate New York. I used to live in the City, but I moved back to my hometown last year."

"Any plans to relocate in the future?"

"Oh, I'll definitely move again. I just needed a change from the City. It's so expensive."

"Yeah," Eric agreed.

Julia was patiently waiting to cut in. Katie smiled and politely stepped aside.

"Thank you, Eric," she said and squeezed his hand.

"Thank you, Katie."

Katie walked dazedly back to her table. She was pleased with how it had gone. She felt a connection with Eric. It was natural, not forced. She looked on, as the other women danced with Eric. How strange it was to share a man with a room full of gorgeous women! If she made it to the next round, she knew it would get stranger yet. She hoped she made it to the next round, but she couldn't be totally sure how Eric felt. He seemed to like her, but he obviously liked a lot of the others, too. She had no choice but to wait and see.

Chapter Five

Once all the girls had danced with Eric, Zeb instructed them to socialize freely. There was a mad dash toward Eric. He seemed to be loving it. Katie hung back with Julia and a few others.

"I definitely need more time with Eric," Julia was saying. "I barely got to talk to him at dinner."

"I know," Katie answered and noticed a camera was on them. "It was hard to talk across the table."

Both girls took care not to say anything derogatory. Julie was too polite to do so, and Katie was too calculating. She didn't want to look bad on camera – unless the season needed a "bad girl." She hadn't yet decided what role she was going to play.

They grabbed a glass of wine and made their way to Eric. They were quickly pushed aside by Jenny and Kristin, who wanted their turn. Katie took the opportunity to talk to Ann Marie for a minute.

"How's it going?" she asked.

"Great! How about you?"

"It's been a weird night, but it's fun."

"Yeah, baby!" Ann Marie hooted and moved on. A couple of the other girls rallied around her. That was Ann Marie, always the life of the party. If Eric didn't like her, the other women certainly did.

Shane stepped into the crowd with an empty glass in his hand. He was tapping it with a spoon to gain their attention.

"The bride and groom are supposed to kiss!" Amanda called and threw her arms around Eric's neck. She planted a big one right on his lips. She almost fell over in the process, in her inebriated state. Eric caught her before she fell. He looked embarrassed. The other girls giggled with their hands cupped over their mouths.

"Good lord!" cried Lois. "How much did that girl drink?"

"I didn't think she had very much," Andrea offered, "but she didn't eat all day."

"None of us did," Lois cackled.

"Ladies!" Shane called over the laughter. "As I said earlier, all good things must come to an end."

The laughter turned into groans of disappointment.

"Yes, ladies. The time has come for Eric to make his decisions. We'll give him some time alone. When we come back, be ready to hear his choices."

The ladies looked at each other nervously and watched Shane escort Eric from the room. Zeb directed them to the dance floor area, while the crew rearranged the filming area for the elimination shoot. They moved out the tables and slightly shifted the camera angles to face the curtained back wall, where the video screen had been. They taped off more X's on the floor. A cart draped in velvet was wheeled out to the approximate location where table number three had been. A large gold box rested on top of the cart.

Katie recognized it as the infamous, gold box that held the gifts for those women asked to advance. At every elimination gifts were presented to those that were moving forward, usually jewelry, and incrementally higher in value as the field of women narrowed. The last girl remaining theoretically received an engagement ring. The relationships that evolved from the show did not have good track records, but the statistics didn't deter women from wanting to participate. That was evident from the auditions and the extensive applicant screening. Thousands had applied to be on the show, and only a handful were chosen. For the ten who would be eliminated tonight, it had been a futile effort.

Once the room was set up for the elimination shot, the girls were lined up on the X's in a U shape with thirteen in the back row and twelve in the front. They were staggered appropriately so that each person was visible. They were alphabetical from front left to back right, so Ann Marie was third from the left in the front row, and Katie was nearly behind her.

They stood in position more than twenty minutes before Shane escorted Eric back into the room. They chatted nervously as they waited, and shifted as directed by

Barbara to ensure they were perfectly aligned for the shot. Eric and Shane stopped next to the velvet-covered cart.

"Ladies, it's the moment you've all been waiting for. Eric has made his choices. I'm sorry to say ten of you will be leaving us tonight. Fifteen of you, however, will be receiving a necklace as a gift from Eric and an invitation to move into the *Soulmates* mansion."

Shane opened the ceremonial gold box and held up a necklace for all to see. It was a gold chain with a Soulmates logo as a charm, an S intertwined with hearts. Katie thought it was tacky, nothing she would ever wear. The necklace didn't matter though; it was merely a symbol. There was a $5000 bonus at stake – and better jewelry to come if she were to advance.

"Eric would like to say a few words before we begin," Shane explained and stepped aside. Eric flashed his winning smile and addressed the ladies.

"I just wanted to say thank you to all of you for taking a chance on me. I had a really great time tonight, and I hope you did, too. We all came into this night with high expectations. This has been a tough decision for me – harder than I thought possible. I think you are all great. I know we didn't get to spend much time together, so I had to base my decisions on first impressions and who I felt I had a connection with. I hope I made the right choices. All I can say is, it's really hard letting ten of you go when we hardly had enough time to get to know each other, but I did feel a stronger connection with some, and I'm going with my gut. I do wish you all well."

Eric looked at Shane, who nodded and gestured at the fifteen necklaces awaiting placement around fifteen lucky necks. Eric picked up the first one and took a breath.

"Madison," he said.

Madison's face lit up as she squeezed between Chelsea and Danine to receive her necklace. Eric fastened it around her neck. It hung perfectly over the neckline of her midnight blue gown. She conveniently had not worn a necklace that evening. Katie thought she was a presumptuous bitch, but she smiled politely, as though Madison was her new best friend.

"Thank you!" she beamed at Eric.

"You're welcome," Eric responded, and gave Madison a quick hug.

She turned on her heel. Her expression was undeniably gloating, as she faced the women to resume her place in line. The women looked on and smiled, trying to conceal their jealousy. Chelsea turned around to check out the bling.

Eric in the meantime, was picking up the second necklace. The girls took notice and straightened up to listen to the next name.

"Brittany," he said.

Brittany was right in front, next to Ann Marie, and stepped forward to receive her gift. Eric clasped the necklace and embraced her briefly.

"Thank you, Eric," she said stiffly, in her lofty French accent, and turned away from him. Her expression, too, was unmistakably boastful, in spite of the fact that in real life Brittany wouldn't be caught dead in that necklace. Katie loathed her, but was careful not to let contempt show on her face. Ann Marie congratulated Brittany congenially. Either Ann Marie had double the acting ability of Katie, or she didn't find Brittany as annoying, because she truly looked happy for Brittany.

Katie drew a slow breath in and prayed she was chosen. She wasn't a religious person so it was a simple prayer, "Oh, God, please let me make it to the next round."

"Danine," Eric said.

The attractive Italian took minimal steps to reach Eric. He put the third necklace around her neck and gave her a hug. Danine pecked his cheek and thanked him, then returned to her position.

Eric called Tina next, followed by Kristin, Samantha, Jenny and Ann Marie, none of which came as a surprise to Katie. She was busy congratulating her best friend, when Eric called Valerie. Katie felt like puking. She shouldn't have eaten.

Valerie made a gesture of relief, whipping her forehead with the back of her hand, and the other girls laughed. It broke the tension slightly, but the relief was short-lived. After Valerie stepped back into line the silence loomed again heavily.

"Olivia," said Eric.

The exhalations were audible after each name. Katie had been keeping track, and the count was up to ten. Her confidence was waning. Her palms were sweating. Her knees felt like they would buckle. Ann Marie was staying, and she would have to skulk back to New York with her tail between her legs. It would be difficult to be happy for Ann Marie. Best friend or not, she was jealous as hell.

"Katie," Eric said.

Katie put her hand over her heart. She couldn't contain her surprise and excitement. She smiled from ear to ear as she slipped between Amanda and Andrea, being careful not to bump drunken Amanda onto the floor.

"Hi," she said nervously, and the girls behind her giggled.

"Hi, Katie," Eric said and lifted the necklace to Katie's throat. It felt cold on her chest, but Eric's hot hands brushed against her neck. Her heart pounded in excitement. She smiled up at him and tried to keep her cool. His green eyes were incredibly tantalizing.

"Thank you." She leaned forward to hug him. She didn't have the nerve to kiss him, even on the cheek. She didn't know why she was having such difficulty remaining in control. He wasn't even her type. It was the eyes, drawing her in, and the softly inviting lips …

Katie grinned and turned away from him. It was hard not to gloat, as she faced the other women. Those who had already received necklaces looked sincerely happy for her, while those that hadn't looked like they wanted to tear her head off. She dazedly took her place and breathed a sigh of relief. Her hand fingered the necklace, resting on top of the one she had already been wearing. She didn't care if it was tacky, it was around her neck. She had done it. No matter what happened from here, she was getting the $5000 bonus and could go home proudly.

She was barely aware of Eric calling Julia next. She was drawn back to reality when he called Lois. That was a surprise. Lois was so different from the other girls. She was loud, gruff and obnoxious. She lacked the class and finesse of most the other women Eric had chosen – save Kristin, whom he obviously chose for her huge breasts. Lois seemed more like a tomboy. She was petite, but her figure was not feminine. She looked almost awkward in a dress.

Lois was only two people down in line, separated from Katie by only Kristin, so Katie put on a supportive expression.

"Congratulations, Lois!" she said in turn.

"Heather," Eric was saying.

Katie's faith in Eric was restored. She didn't appreciate being classified with someone like Lois. How could Eric have felt a connection with her? At least Heather was pretty, a justifiable choice. Evidently Eric had been able to draw his focus from her hypnotizing dress to her angelic face.

Eric fastened the necklace on Heather. And they were down to one. Katie felt Karen tense up beside her. Katie almost felt sorry for her. The poor lobster actually thought she still had a chance. Katie would have put money on Simone, but Eric preferred Riann.

Riann let out a delighted squeal and practically danced forward to receive her necklace. The disappointment on the other girls' faces was pronounced. Ten girls' dreams had just been crushed. Katie felt the extreme mixed emotions in the room, ranging from overjoyed to terribly rejected. She almost felt guilty to display her pleasure.

Riann returned to her spot in the lineup. The tension in the room had magically vanished. The first elimination was over. The adventure was about to begin.

Shane stepped forward and spoke, "Thank you ladies. If you did not receive a necklace tonight, I'm sorry. Your journey has ended. You must say goodbye to Eric.

We want to wish you the best on your own personal quest to find your *Soulmate*."

The ladies who were not chosen came forward one at a time to say goodbye to Eric. Amanda was supposed to go first, but stuck her nose up in the air and walked straight past Eric – well, not exactly straight. She swaggered directly past Eric and made her way to the double doors at the end of the room. She had trouble getting them open. The whole room was staring at her, including the cameramen. There was no way that footage was getting left on the editing room floor.

Andrea stepped forward. She was a good sport and hugged Eric congenially before exiting. The rest of the rejected women followed suit, including Chelsea, Desirae, Faith, Iris, Karen, Maeve, Patty and Simone. Ten were gone. The remaining fifteen were handed champagne flutes and rearranged to a more concise grouping.

Eric rose his glass as he spoke.

"I want to make a toast to you beautiful fifteen ladies. I am looking forward to getting to know each of you better. I feel confident that we have a really good group here, and no matter what happens, we're going to have a great time. Here's to beginning our journey on *Soulmates* together."

The girls raised their glasses as well.

"Hold right there!" Barbara called.

Two cameras panned the rows of women with their champagne flutes raised.

"And ... drink."

Katie raised her glass to her lips. She was used to taking direction, but this situation was different, almost surreal. She was acting, but she was experiencing real emotions. She sensed this project was only going to get weirder.

"Cut!" Barbara called. Eric was being whisked away, and Shane had already disappeared. "Thank you, ladies. We need to go over a few details with you before you go."

She turned to Zeb, who took over with the instructions.

"We will meet back in the Grand Ballroom at 8:00AM tomorrow. You have the option of coming at 7:00AM for the breakfast buffet. We are going to move you into the *Soulmates* mansion immediately following, so please have your bags completely packed and placed just inside your hotel room door for our staff to pick up. We have green luggage tags for you on the table by the door. Please pick them up as you leave tonight and attach them to your luggage, as they identify it as part of the *Soulmates* group. In other words, if you expect your luggage to be at the mansion when you arrive, you need to use the green tags. You will receive further instructions tomorrow morning, but to give you an overview, tomorrow will be spent traveling and getting settled into the mansion. Cameras will be rolling as usual. We will go over everything in detail tomorrow, but if you have any questions that can't wait, please see me. Enjoy the rest of your evening. Thank you."

The crew was bustling around, Barbara shouting directions, as Zeb finished his speech. He tried to take his leave, but Madison cornered him and started peppering him with questions. The remaining fourteen women were left alone, finally able to relax. They congratulated each other sincerely, as the immediate pressure was off. The atmosphere was much more festive now that they didn't have to worry about trying to impress Eric. They made a point of collecting their luggage tags and headed back to their rooms. One cameraman happened to be in the same elevator with Ann Marie and Katie, so they rode silently to their prospective floors. Katie wasn't in her room five minutes when her phone rang.

"We did it, girlfriend!" Ann Marie shouted.

"I know! It's like a dream."

"It really is. Nothing like I expected."

"I didn't know what to expect," Katie admitted.

"I thought it would be more organized. Barbara keeps saying instructions will be forthcoming, and they never are. But whatever, how about Eric? What do you think of him?"

"I was pleasantly surprised. He's not bad looking."

"He's a hottie."

"He's cute. He's not really my type, but he seems nice."

"So, he's not your *Soulmate*?" Ann Marie teased.

"There was no love-at-first sight, but I didn't think there would be. Do you like him?"

"Sure, based on looks. Our conversations were difficult with so many people around."

"I know what you mean. Plus, at dinner I was on the opposite side of the table. I couldn't even hear the conversation."

"I was opposite, too. At least we got a lot of eye contact. Hey, there's a mini bar in here. I'm breaking into it."

"Why not? We aren't paying for it," Katie agreed, but she was too tired to move from her position on the bed to check out the room's mini bar stash.

"What'd you think of our competition?" Ann Marie asked, cracking open a shot-size bottle of whiskey.

"There's a lot of pretty girls. I can't really predict how long we'll stay. It depends on who Eric likes."

"What the hell am I going to mix this with?" Ann Marie interrupted.

"It doesn't matter," Katie continued, ignoring her friend's outburst. "We got our $5000 bonus. We can go home any time."

"Don't speak too soon. The mansion is going to be a riot."

"I'm sure it is! Don't get me wrong, I don't want to go home, but if I do go home after the next round at least I'll have something to show for it."

Ann Marie laughed. "All right, chicky. I've got to go find the ice machine. Are you going to breakfast in the morning?"

"I doubt it. I don't care about eating. I'll probably go down around 7:45 to grab some coffee."

"There's a coffee maker in the room," Ann Marie pointed out.

"Yeah, but that coffee always sucks. I'll grab some downstairs."

"I'll probably need some decent coffee too, if I hit this mini bar hard. I'll meet you in the Grand Ballroom in the morning then."

"Good night."

Chapter Six

Katie got her luggage ready the next morning and left it inside the door as instructed. She hit the elevator button at 7:40AM to head down to the Grand Ballroom for coffee. Brittany was in the elevator when she got in.

"Good morning," she said.

"Good morning, Katie."

"How are you today?"

"Well, and yourself?"

"Great," Katie answered, as the elevator stopped on another floor. The doors slid open, but no one was waiting to get on. Brittany hit the button to close the doors, and the elevator slowly started down again.

"So, we're moving into the mansion today," Brittany broke the deafening silence. "I hope it's worth it."

"It looks nice on TV."

"Really?"

"Yeah, haven't you ever seen the show?" Katie was astonished.

"No."

Katie wanted to ask Brittany how she'd happened on an audition for a show she'd never even seen, but the elevator bell sounded their floor, and the doors slid open once again. Brittany motioned for Katie to exit first.

"This meeting better not last too long. I've got phone calls to make. This time zone is killing me."

Katie made no comment. They strolled down the corridor to the double doors that led into the Grand Ballroom. The very doors that had stood closed so tauntingly last night were propped open invitingly this morning.

The breakfast buffet smelled wonderful. Katie wasn't a big breakfast eater, but she grabbed a cheese Danish and some fresh fruit. She didn't know where her next meal was coming from, after all. Brittany grabbed a croissant and joined Katie at the coffee station.

"Much different in here from last night," Katie commented, noting there were only three tables set for five each. The backdrops had been removed, the bar area was empty, and the array of lights, people and decorations were painstakingly absent. One of the three tables was filled by Danine, Riann, Samantha, Tina and Lois. One was semi-occupied by Jenny and Julia, and the third was empty.

Brittany snorted in reply, and led the way to join Jenny and Julia. A few minutes later, Madison entered the room to complete the second table.

"Good morning."

"Do I have time to eat?" Madison asked.

"Eat if you want to eat," Brittany ordered flippantly.

Madison stood and approached the buffet, much like a young child being told by her mother to eat.

The remaining five ladies strolled in one minute before eight. Barbara was already there, bustling around and organizing her camera crew. Zeb was busy picking over the breakfast buffet.

Kristin bobbled through the door in stiletto heels, a short skirt and spaghetti strap shirt that left nothing to the imagination. If there was any walking involved in reaching their final destination, Kristin was not going to make it; she'd better hope for door-to-door limousine service.

Heather followed closely behind and was dressed similarly. So, Katie thought, last night's psychedelic dress wasn't merely a clever ploy to let Eric think she was a bad dresser. Good taste in clothes clearly eluded Heather. Her skirt was as short as Kristin's. Her shirt didn't have spaghetti straps, but was more of a T-shirt. It was a very tight, V-neck cut-off that showed a lot of cleavage, a lot of stomach and not a lot of class. It was hot pink and read "Diva" across the front in sparkly gold writing. Her curly brown hair was pulled up on top of her head, giving an afro-like appearance. She looked tacky, but had a pretty face in spite of it all.

Ann Marie and Olivia walked side-by-side between the two sleazes. Ann Marie was walking on her tippy-toes and shaking her butt from side to side in her best Kristin imitation. Then she pulled her hair atop her head and strutted like Heather. Olivia walked next to her and giggled uncontrollably. Some of the other girls were watching and giggling as well.

Ann Marie was fully aware of the cameras rolling in the room, but continued her act regardless. She pursed her lips and threw her chest out. Then she looked down and took on a shocked expression, as though someone had stolen her large breasts. She grabbed her chest, looked down her shirt. Katie couldn't help wondering if Ann Marie had gotten into the mini bar a little too much last night. Maybe she was still drunk.

The entire room was laughing now, except Brittany, who kept her naturally-disdained expression. Valerie had just come in behind Ann Marie and Olivia, and got a bird's eye view of the show. Valerie giggled, although she looked slightly embarrassed. Kristin and Heather had reached the empty table, and looked around to see what was so funny. Ann Marie quickly dropped her purse and bent to pick it up, in a quick attempt to appear innocent.

Barbara had pulled her glasses to the end of her nose to peer over them at Ann Marie. She snapped them back into place on her face now, with a look that could have been either amusement or irritation. Barbara was hard to read.

"Thank you for joining us, ladies," Barbara began sarcastically with a smirk. Apparently, she was both amused and irritated. "We're going to be moving into the mansion shortly. We've got two vans to take you, and one videographer for each van. Your luggage is being transported separately, and will be waiting for you in your room assignments, which will be announced upon arrival at the mansion. Shane will be there to greet you and explain the boarding situation, as well as some ground rules. A few things he won't mention on tape, but are imperative: no one leaves the premises unless escorted by *Soulmates* staff. Zeb, as well as Sherry here," she motioned toward a tall, mousy-haired woman, "will be on site should you need anything. They can send for anything you need from the drug store, care for special dietary needs, dry cleaning, whatever.

"Cameras. Let's talk about expectations for a moment. Obviously during official *Soulmates* events such as dates and elimination ceremonies, footage is comprehensive. In addition, the two videographers who have been following you around will continue to do so. They will cover you all candidly 24/7 excluding the bathrooms. Just to ease your minds, there are no hidden cameras. If you are in your bedroom, for example, and no videographer is in there with you" – a few giggles – "then you are not being recorded. No one is going to barge in on you while you're in the shower, or getting dressed, in other words. No one will intentionally invade your privacy. Hopefully I needn't say it, but there is to be no nudity in the public areas of the mansion. Keep in mind this is not an R-rated show. If you say or do anything inappropriate, it will be edited accordingly. That is not to say it will be cut from the show; it may be edited for suitable viewing. Keep that in mind."

Barbara paused and looked over her glasses directly at Ann Marie. Some of the girls giggled and whispered comments to each other. Ann Marie met Barbara's stare with a wide-eyed, innocent expression as though she had no idea Barbara was referring to her.

"Cell phones. While cell phone usage is permitted, we ask that you make your personal phone calls in private, away from the cameras, etc. Please do not carry your cell phone around with you. If you are awaiting an important call, you may give your phone to Zeb or Sherry, who will monitor it for you. The ringer should be off at all times. I am not spending my time editing out phone calls. There are also phones at the mansion available for personal use. As you recall from the contract you all signed, you will not post anything on social media, nor will you discuss the show. This is a job, for which you have been paid."

Madison raised her hand during the cell phone speech. Zeb pointed at her, nodded his head and jotted something down. He was obviously accustomed to working quickly and efficiently with Barbara without interfering with her.

"There is no smoking inside the mansion," Barbara was saying, "even in the bathrooms and bedrooms. This includes e-cigarettes. If you must smoke, you must smoke outside. And please dispose of your trash appropriately – cigarettes and otherwise. When you get to your room, a welcome package will be on your bed. Inside you will find these guidelines in writing. You will also find a journal for your personal use, as well as a few gifts from sponsors.

"You are expected to participate in all *Soulmates* functions," she continued. "Most of your meals will be organized and many meals will be taken while on a date. We will also have catered functions at the mansion, which may have bar staff, cocktail waitresses, etc. There is no tipping necessary, I might add. Some of these events will not be pre-announced, because we like the element of surprise. Our caterer will be providing three meals daily plus snacks, for those that may not be on the date at meal time. The kitchen is also open 24/7 and is fully stocked. If you are hungry after hours, or you don't like what is on the menu, you may responsibly use the kitchen, and care for clean up when you are done. I believe anyone with food allergies has already made me aware, but if you have not, please see Zeb or Sherry know during the Q&A period. There is also a full bar on site. You may eat and drink at your leisure, but remember you are being filmed. I wouldn't advise getting drunk and doing something stupid on tape, and I might add I wouldn't think Eric is interested in an alcoholic *Soulmate*, as you may have already gathered last night.

"These are the general rules of the house. When we arrive at the mansion, Shane will brief you on the general rules of the game. I'm going to leave you with Zeb now, who will answer any questions. If you need anything, please let Zeb or Sherry know and they will arrange to get it for you."

Barbara turned and exited before anyone could say anything. Barbara's speeches always seemed to end abruptly. She would drop a few bombs and then turn things over to poor Zeb. He must have been accustomed to doing all the dirty work, because he never flinched. He consistently stepped up to the occasion like a relief pitcher stepping up to the mound.

The question and answer forum turned out more annoying than informative. Heather asked more questions than she had brain cells. Most of her questions were either irrelevant or had already been answered. Madison, after dictating not only her extensive list of food allergies, but also her medical history at large, started asking questions about the next round of dates, none of which Zeb could answer. She even resorted to beginning her questions with "maybe you can't answer this, but…" to which Zeb would reply, "As Barbara said, Shane will be going over those details with you."

Brittany kept rolling her eyes and tapping her fingers. Kristin was text messaging on her cell phone at the next table. She could type on her cell phone a lot faster than she could type on a keyboard.

Lois finally spoke up in frustration.

"Does anyone have a question that Zeb can answer? If not, let's get out of here!"

"Yeah," added Ann Marie. "Our mansion awaits."

"And our open bar," Brittany said under her breath. Katie hated to admit it, but she felt the same way as Brittany. Although Katie didn't want to look uncompassionate, Brittany clearly cared little of what others thought.

Zeb seemed relieved that no one voiced any more questions. Katie had already learned that asking questions was pointless. Barbara wanted spontaneity and gave up information only as necessary.

Zeb called for the first eight girls in alphabetical order, which included Ann Marie through Kristin for the first van. The other seven women got van number two. The ride took more than an hour, and traffic was horrendous. By the time the van pulled onto a private road, Katie was beginning to feel car sick. She was glad she had opted to sit in the back when the videographer turned around and started taping.

Black, iron security gates opened, and the van rolled forward. The girls leaned from side to side trying to see around each other and be the first to catch a glimpse of the mansion. They rounded a curve, and there it stood in from of them, magnificent and impressive. It was a huge, gray stone building with a circular drive that wound around a stone fountain. The front porch was open like a patio, with three cement steps extending the entire length across the front. The double doors were flanked with urns bearing manicured cedars and ivy trailing playfully over the edges.

The porch was large enough to hold all fifteen women comfortably. They were instructed to assemble there, while last-minute preparations were being made inside. Momentarily, Shane opened the double doors ceremoniously and held his arms open as a gesture for them to enter. The girls did so, their faces filled with awe from the sheer magnitude of the foyer. Normally a foyer filled with fifteen women, one host and various cameras and crew would have been crowded. The ladies filed through three- and four-abreast with ease. Shane led them past a majestic, meandering staircase to a set of French doors on the left that led to a large sitting room.

The room was splendid, entirely in white with a few colorful accents. Three couches were set up in a U shape around the fireplace. In spite of the white-on-white decorating scheme, it did not look bland or uninviting, but rather crisp and luxurious, full of textures including an area rug over the white marble floor and layers of throw pillows on the couches. The enormous floor-to-ceiling windows were treated with white sheers under heavy white draperies, tied back with rich gold cording. The mantle over the white, brick fireplace was covered from one end to the other with white candles of all shapes and sizes and flanked by two huge vases filled with white flowers. The colorful artwork on the walls was exquisite. Most of the paintings were garden scenes dappled with soft purples, greens and buttery yellows, framed in gold. A large ficus tree softened one corner, and a Boston fern sat atop a white ceramic pillar between two armchairs in another corner to form a quaint reading nook.

Katie had never been in a mansion, unless she counted fraternity parties in college. Pure size does not a mansion make. The fraternities she had seen in college looked gorgeous from the outside and had the remains of what was once luxury, but had been heavily beaten down. Fireplaces had been boarded shut, hardwood floors permanently stained with beer, and velvet window coverings tattered with cigarette burns and infested with the smell of stale smoke. Furniture had been obsolete, other than the occasional pool table in the center of the living room. Although Katie had never been in a sorority herself, she knew their houses were slightly less dilapidated than the fraternities. Neither compared to the *Soulmates* mansion. The *Soulmates* mansion was a sophisticated edifice intended for elite tenancy. Katie couldn't wait to see the rest of the place.

For now, the girls settled in the sitting room. The couches were large enough to seat four comfortably, and the other three perched on the arms. Shane stood in from of the fireplace. The camera crew filled in around them. Katie sat on the couch closes to Shane, with Brittany next to her. She looked around the room and noticed the couches did not form a perfect U with the fireplace as the focal point, but were angled slightly so that no backs would be toward the cameras. Katie was blown away at how large the room was. The entire first floor of her mother's house could have fit in just the sitting room and foyer.

"Welcome, Ladies!," Shane was saying. "And congratulations! The *Soulmates* mansion will be your home temporarily, so enjoy! Make yourselves comfortable. Your luggage has arrived and has been brought up to your rooms. As you may know, the *Soulmates* mansion has seven bedrooms on the second floor and one private suite on the third floor. Considering there are fifteen of you, fourteen will be bunking up. One lucky lady will be occupying the private suite. To be fair, we drew names earlier to determine who will get the suite. Incidentally, the lucky lady who retains the suite will also be getting a single date with Eric this round, which leads me to our second subject: round two. Let me explain how things will work, and then we'll get you settled into your rooms."

Shane spoke dramatically, looking around the room to captivate the ladies' attention. Anyone who had seen the show before knew exactly what was coming. They mixed things up a little bit, but for the most part used the same format each season. It was one of the highest-rated shows on primetime. As they say, why fix it if it ain't broke?

"Round two," Shane continued, "will consist of two singe dates and two group dates. As I mentioned, the recipient of one of the single dates has been selected at random. Eric has chosen one lady for the other single date, which will take place tonight. That leaves thirteen women, who will be divided into two groups at Eric's discretion."

Shane paused, as the cameras panned his audience for reactions.

"I know you're anxious to get settled in, so let's start with your room assignments. Earlier we drew names from a hat to determine who will be roommates, and who will begin in the third-floor suite. If the person who occupies the suite is eliminated in a future round, the suite will be reassigned. We will draw names again to move a different lady into the suite. It is well worth the move, I might add."

The girls nodded in agreement, excluding Brittany, who claimed she'd never seen the show. Katie and the majority of the others knew the suite occupied the entire third story of the mansion, had a private entrance and was furnished lavishly with a king-sized canopy bed, separate living room and master bathroom with a Jacuzzi.

"Without further ado, here are the results of the drawing." Shane hit a remote. The picture above the fireplace mantle rose slowly to reveal a flat screen. A video began.

"Welcome to the *Soulmates* mansion," said the Shane on the video screen.

"I look good, don't I?" said the live Shane, drawing polite giggles of agreement from the crowd.

"We are about to draw names for your room assignments. The last name drawn will be entitled to the private suite on the third floor, as well as a single date with Eric. Let's begin."

Shane thrust his arm into a black container and pulled out a name. "Jenny ... and," pulling out another name, "...Riann."

"Heather ... and ... Brittany. Ann Marie ... and Samantha." Ann Marie gave Samantha a thumbs-up as though they were best friends. Katie had been secretly hoping she and Ann Marie would miraculously get paired up, but there was still hope for the private suite on the third floor.

"Valerie ... and ... Danine. Kristin ... and ... Madison. Tina ... and Katie."

Katie smiled at Tina. Things could be worse.

"That leaves three names. The first two will share the final double room. The last name remaining shall inhabit the private suite at the very least for round two, and will also secure a single date with Eric."

Shane put his hand in the black container.

"Olivia..." he read dramatically. "And ... Julia!"

He pulled out the final name, but Lois was already cheering as though she were in a sports bar.

"Congratulations, Lois!"

The video went black. Live Shane hit the remote, and the painting returned to its original position over the mantle.

"Congratulations, Lois," he repeated. "You can relax in your private suite for two full days. Your single date will take place Friday night."

Shane gave the ladies a moment to gather their composure.

"There will be two group dates, ladies. One will be tomorrow, and the other will be Friday afternoon. You'll be receiving invitations from Eric to that effect. I do have one final announcement to make before I leave you. One lucky lady, of Eric's choice, will be joining him for dinner tonight. The rest of you will have the evening to spend at your leisure, with a catered dinner at seven-thirty in the dining room."

The ladies seemed pleased with the announcement. Catered dinner and a night of leisure in the mansion sounded almost as good as a dinner-date with Eric.

"This lady was selected by Eric, as the one who made the best first impression. Eric will be picking you up at seven and taking you out for a private, romantic dinner for two …"

Shane had to drag out every announcement. His attempts to be suspenseful were in reality, quite annoying.

"The lucky lady is … Madison!"

Chapter Seven

Katie and the others tried not to be too disappointed about Madison securing the single date. It was early in the game, and although single dates were key, they increased in importance as the game went on. A single date in round two was almost always a free ticket to round three, but a single date in a later round could mean being the last girl standing.

Shane left the girls on their own to examine their quarters and explore the rest of the mansion. The main cameras packed up to relocate to the site of Eric and Madison's date. The two videographers stayed behind, one of them glued to Madison as she swooned over her good fortune, and the other followed Lois up to the private suite to capture her reaction.

"What a relief to have a minute alone." Tina told Katie, and gestured toward the videographer a few steps ahead of them. He was zooming in on Madison, as she headed upstairs to her room. The girls' names were attached to their bedroom doors like stars' dressing rooms. The room Madison would share with Kristin happened to be just across the corridor from the landing at the top of the stairs. The room assigned to Katie and Tina was the next door down and occupied the back right-hand corner of the second floor. This story of the mansion had seven bedrooms, three in the front, four across the back of the building, and two huge bathrooms. The immediate area at the top of the stairs was open to the foyer below. If you stood on the landing at the top of the staircase, you could monitor the front door perfectly.

Some of the girls flitted from room to room, checking everything out and making comparisons of which room was bigger and which had a better view. Katie and Tina preferred to unpack and relax. Neither girl particularly cared whose room was the biggest.

"Do you have a preference?" Katie motioned toward the beds.

"It makes no difference to me," Tina replied.

Since Katie had entered the room first, she made her way to the bed further from the door.

"This room is fabulous," Tina was saying.

"It is. I couldn't believe the sitting room downstairs. It was gorgeous! I've seen it on TV, but it is so huge …"

"I know, I was thinking the same thing. It is breathtaking in person. What do you say we get settled in, hit the lunch buffet and check out the rest of the place?"

"I'd love to," Katie agreed. She had wandered past her bed to her window, which had a splendid view of the back yard. "I wouldn't mind testing out the pool, either."

"Absolutely. Can you see it?" Tina hurried over to the other window.

"You can just see the end of it. It looks like that terrace runs alongside it. It looks beautiful, from what I can see."

"Yes, it does," Tina agreed.

"You know what, I'd better call my mother before I forget. She'll want to know I made it here."

"Good idea. I think I'll just hit the restroom first." Tina headed for the door, while Katie dialed her mother's cell phone number. Katie knew her mother never answered her cell phone at work, so she left a voice mail. It was much easier than having to speak with her directly.

Tina was only gone a few minutes and was obviously amused when she returned. Katie raised her eyebrows.

"I can't help but laugh," Tina began.

"Is the bathroom that odd?" Katie wondered aloud.

"Let me just tell you. Now, I don't want you to think I'm not a nice person, because I really am not catty or anything. It's just, when I came out of the restroom – which is right outside our door I might add – Kristin and Madison were coming out of their rooms with their bikinis on. And you know the videographer was all over that. So, Kristin comes out first, all hanging out of her suit," Tina held her hands out in front of her chest to demonstrate the enormousness of Kristin's breasts. "And here comes little Madison behind her, with this look of total inadequacy. I'm sorry, but it struck me funny."

Katie couldn't help but laugh. "Trust me, I was glad Kristin was behind me and not ahead of me in line last night."

Tina laughed even louder. "She had to have had a boob job. Those just aren't natural."

"I wouldn't be surprised."

"Did you get ahold of your mother?" Tina asked.

"No, I left her a message. I'm sure she's still at work. It's just as well, I don't feel like dealing with all her questions."

"I hear you, girl," Tina said, while methodically pulling articles of clothing out of her suitcase, shaking them out and hanging them in the closet. "My mother, Estelle, is the same way. She was not thrilled when I told her about the show."

"My mother wasn't either!" Katie admitted. "And this is probably going to sound shallow, but thank God, I made it to this round. I couldn't have faced my mother otherwise. I really need that $5000 bonus."

"What bonus?"

Katie looked up, startled. Had Tina not read the contract, or had she, in fact read it wrong? A wave of panic rushed over her, then Tina started to laugh.

"I'm kidding!"

Katie breathed a sigh of relief.

"You should have seen your face!" Tina laughed. "But seriously, girl, I felt the same way. That money justifies taking off work to come here. I'm a realtor, and every hour I take off could kill a sale. It was a risk."

"It's a good thing that you have a career to go back to, though. Plus, if things worked out with Eric, you could literally work anywhere."

"That's true," Tina agreed.

"I actually quit my job to come here. It was a part-time thing, so it's not like I gave up my career."

"So, you took a big risk, too. And since you're between jobs, you could literally work anywhere ... if things worked out with Eric."

"Good point." Katie nodded. "What did you think of Eric?"

"He's cute," Tina smiled sheepishly.

"He is," Katie gushed, relieved to be able to admit freely what she thought of their leading man. "And honestly, I'm glad money isn't an issue any more. I think if they gave bonuses after every round, a lot of girls would only be here for the money."

"I agree."

"How do you feel about interracial relationships? Did they grill you about it when you auditioned?"

"I'm fine with it," Tina told her. "They asked me, sure, but I date all kinds of men – black, white, it makes no difference to me."

"That's cool. You and Eric would make a very nice couple."

"Stop," Tina protested with a laugh. "I've barely talked to him."

"But you look good together. Some of the other girls here don't even look good with him. Like, they don't match."

Tina laughed harder.

"I'm serious."

"I know you are. I agree with you, it's just funny."

Katie and Tina chatted more as they unpacked their suitcases. They inspected their room from top to bottom and went through their welcome packages. The rules of the house were in there as Barbara had promised, but neither bothered to review them. The journals Barbara had promised were in there as well, along with several pens, stationery and envelops with the *Soulmates* logo. There was also a variety of items with other company logos, presumably sponsors, such as T-shirts, visors, golf shirts, flip-flops, beach towels and a slew of health and beauty care items – hair products, make up, etc.

"This is better than Christmas," Tina commented.

Katie nodded, but didn't foresee wearing any of the clothes while on the show. Maybe they were supposed to, but she didn't want to walk around the house wearing the same T-shirt as five other girls. She also wasn't thrilled about handing out any free endorsements. If these big companies wanted their products endorsed, they should pay her for it. She felt like she would be taking ad work away from starving actors such as herself if she stooped to wearing sponsors' products on the show. She wasn't adverse to testing the hair products and make up, but she didn't recall reading anything in the contract about providing free endorsements. She couldn't wait to hear what Ann Marie had to say on the subject.

Katie and Tina decided to get their swimsuits on and get a closer look at the pool. They explored the ground floor of the mansion on their search for the back terrace. They discovered the lunch buffet while on their tour, and filled plates before heading outside. Neither was very hungry, but the buffet had a nice array of fruits, salads and vegetables that looked appetizing but not too filling. This place was spectacular, and the grounds were equally impressive. They found two unoccupied lounge chairs by the pool and turned them to get a better angle of the sun.

"This weather is amazing," Katie commented.

"Where are you from?"

"I'm from upstate New York, Glens Falls."

"Pretty cold up there?"

"Yeah, it is. It's nice in July and August. That's about it."

"I'm from Richmond, Virginia. It's pretty fair, climate-wise, but I don't usually get to enjoy it. I'm always working."

"You're probably busy year-round with your job, aren't you?"

"Yes, I am. We have our busier times, but the market is pretty good right now."

"If I ever move to Virginia, I'll call you."

"I'll hook you up," Tina smiled and fell silent to take a few bites of food. Katie picked at her own plate and took the opportunity to look around. She wore sunglasses, so no one would catch her staring at them. Kristin and Madison were lying on their backs on lounge chairs on the opposite side of the pool. Kristin was text messaging on her phone again. Madison appeared to be asleep. Heather was lying on her stomach, more near the deep end, so Katie couldn't tell if she was awake or asleep. Olivia, Riann and Jenny were swimming.

Ann Marie, Lois and Samantha were approaching from the house. They had found the open bar. Ann Marie had thoughtfully made a pitcher of strawberry daiquiris, and Samantha carried a stack of plastic cups. They bypassed the near side of the pool and brought the drinks over by where Tina and Katie were sitting. The three girls in the pool jumped out and joined them.

Ann Marie poured the drinks, and Samantha handed them out. Lois was busy bragging about her private suite.

"Did you make these?" Tina asked.

"I did," Ann Marie answered proudly.

"Thank you! They are delicious."

"Yes, ma'am," Samantha agreed and raised her glass to Ann Marie. "Thank you, Ann Marie!"

The other girls chimed in their compliments, and Ann Marie curtsied and winked at Katie. That was typical Ann Marie, always the life of the party. She emptied the pitcher and ran inside to make more.

Kristin and Heather relocated to the party-side of the pool. Danine and Valerie must have met up with Ann Marie inside, because Ann Marie enlisted their help in carrying out round two of drinks. Madison hadn't moved from her spot. Katie wondered how anyone could sleep at a time like this. The weather was perfect, the drinks were free and the company was entertaining.

Unfortunately for Madison, no one woke her up to join the party. By the time she went in to get ready for her date, she was severely sunburned.

The other girls had gathered in the front room for cocktails before their seven-thirty dinner – and for a glimpse of Eric when he arrived to pick up Madison. Madison still had not come downstairs, and Eric was due any minute. The girls were beginning to think she wasn't coming down.

"She's probably waiting to make a dramatic entrance for Eric," Kristin surmised. "You know that girl loves the attention."

"Still, I think someone better check on her," Danine said, and Tina offered to tag along. Fifteen minutes passed, and still Madison hadn't come down, and neither did the girls who had gone to retrieve her. In the meantime, the doorbell rang. Jenny, who was conveniently standing in the doorway of the sitting room, raced to answer it.

"Hi, there, sweetie," they heard Jenny greet Eric in her sing-song voice with her adorable southern accent.

"How are you…"

"Jenny," she said. Katie smirked. Eric hadn't forgotten *her* name.

"Jenny," Eric repeated. "I'm sorry."

"That's OK. How are you doing?"

"Not bad, not bad."

"Did you get some rest today?" Her voice grew louder as the two of them neared the sitting room.

"A little bit. I moved into the guest house this morning."

"The guest house," Heather repeated loudly.

"Where is the guest house?" Brittany asked.

"It's just down the walkway past the end of the pool."

"So, you don't stay in this house?" Brittany asked.

"No way!" Lois shouted. "That would be dangerous!"

"Too bad," Brittany said with a little pout.

"You might as well join us for a drink," Ann Marie ordered. "Madison is MIA."

"She is?" Eric couldn't tell if Ann Marie was joking or serious, but he joined the girls for a drink in the front room.

It was another twenty minutes before Madison finally came down. Everyone was having such a good time that they'd forgotten all about her. They were somewhat disappointed to see her, and she was obviously disappointed to have missed making a grand entrance. Even Eric seemed reluctant to leave the party, but he rose and politely greeted Madison.

She looked as though she had been crying and had tried to cover it up by applying heavy makeup. The makeup was ineffective in hiding her red eyes, as well as her beet-red skin. Sunburn had a way of darkening after the sun went down.

A few of the sincerely compassionate girls stepped up to inquire if Madison was OK. In Kristin's case, it was clearly an attempt to draw attention to Madison's condition, rather than an act of empathy. Kristin was Madison's roommate, after all. If she had truly been concerned, she would have been upstairs with her all this time. Instead, it had been Julia upstairs tending to Madison's sunburn, later joined by Danine and Tina.

Eric acted the gentleman. He must have sensed how uncomfortable Madison was, and he hastened their departure. The other girls called goodbye wistfully, and moved on to the dining room for their own dinner.

The main topic of conversation during dinner was Madison. Danine was quite the gossip, and relayed to the other girls almost word-for-word what had happened upstairs. Julia interrupted the story twice, and insisted it wasn't as dramatic as Danine was making it out to be. Tina contributed nothing to the conversation, but met Katie's gaze every few minutes and rolled her eyes. Later that evening, in the privacy of their own room, Tina gave Katie the real story.

Although Danine did exaggerate a bit, Tina confirmed that Madison was the drama queen of the house. She had been sobbing uncontrollably at how awful she looked, and how Eric was going to laugh at her, and how she hurt so bad…

According to Tina, it was quite a show. She gave Katie all the details, and went on to give her opinion on some of the other girls, while she was at it. Danine was a two-faced, gossipy bitch, who had only been upstairs under the pretense of taking care of Madison; in reality, she was getting ammunition to use against Madison, which she'd proven at dinner. Julia, on the other hand, was too sweet for her own good and was going to have to be more assertive and quit worrying about the others if she was going to get Eric to notice her. Julia had fixed Madison's makeup three times, rubbed aloe vera lotion all over her, brushed her hair and helped her change her clothes, all the while making assuring comments and soothing little noises.

"I would have had to leave," Katie commented, wrinkling up her nose.

"I wasn't missing the show!" Tina insisted.

The next day an invitation to dinner arrived for eight of the girls. Katie was pleased to hear that she was one of the girls chosen to go, but couldn't help but feel a little jealous towards the others. Madison and Lois got single dates with Eric, and didn't have any competition. The group that was going somewhere tomorrow had only five girls. Her group was large. She had to keep reminding herself that eight girls was better than twenty-five, as it had been the other night.

The group of eight consisted of Katie, Ann Marie, Heather, Julia, Olivia, Riann, Tina and Valerie. Katie felt satisfied with the group. If she had made the list herself, she would perhaps have exchanged Valerie for Jenny. Valerie was a bit overbearing, while Jenny was pleasant. Katie was relieved not to have to spend an evening with Brittany, Kristin or Danine. Katie hadn't made an opinion of Samantha yet, but Ann Marie confided that her roommate was very sweet. Sweet meant competition as far as Katie was concerned. She found herself more poised to compete with the catty and gaudy girls than the sweet ones.

Tina was equally pleased with the group. She and Katie were getting along fabulously, and shared many similar opinions of the other girls. Katie had thought she would miss her gossip sessions with Ann Marie, but Tina filled the void perfectly. Katie didn't feel as though she were in competition with Tina. She simply felt they were friends. Thus far it made the experience much less stressful than had she drawn Kristin or Madison, or even Samantha for a roommate.

The girls got ready and met the other six participants downstairs. The ones who were not joining in today's date conveniently showed up in the bikinis to see the others off. Madison was the only one with clothes on, because she had wisely stayed out of the sun today. Her sunburn looked even more painful than yesterday, but she was done crying about it. She hadn't yet given up many details of her date with Eric, but she was visibly smitten.

Eric picked up the girls before six. The nine of them climbed into the *Soulmates* limo, along with a videographer. They immediately broke open the champagne. They had only just gotten the glasses filled when the car rolled to a halt. They hadn't gone half a mile, and were still on the access road. They wondered if something was wrong with the car, but the chauffer opened the door to let them out.

Eric held up his glass and said, "To a great night with eight beautiful ladies."

The girls raised their glasses to toast.

"To a great night," Ann Marie added, "with one hot guy."

The other girls laughed and chinked their glasses together. They looked on questioningly as Eric climbed out of the limo. Ann Marie shrugged and followed him. The other girls did likewise. Eric let them into the woods a short way. They came to a clearing, and there, behind the guest house, was a patio set for dinner. The cameras were already set up and rolling.

The arrangement was incredible. One long table stood in the middle of the patio. The entire center of the table was covered in candles. Torches set up around the perimeter of the patio provided additional lighting. Off the end of the patio, a fire was lit in the fire pit, which was surrounded by inviting, cushioned seating. It was so secluded, it was very romantic in spite of the ratio of eight women to one man.

Eric opened more champagne and refilled the glasses. Julia hadn't finished hers and protested when Eric tried to top her off.

"I'm not much of a champagne drinker," she explained.

"I can get you some wine," Eric offered.

"That's not necessary. I'm fine."

"It's no problem. Do you like red or white?"

"No, really. I don't want any."

"Mixed drink? Beer?" Eric kept trying.

"I really don't drink," Julia explained.

The other girls looked at her as though she were a leper.

"Why not?" Heather asked tactlessly, snapping her gum as she awaited the answer. Her manners were even worse than her wardrobe – although she fortunately wasn't wearing her Diva shirt tonight.

"I live in a dry county, so it's not something I go out of my way to do," Julia explained politely.

Heather didn't respond, but continued snapping her gum with a disgusted look on her face. She wasn't very attractive when she let her personality shine through.

Eric offered Julia a soda. She insisted water would be fine. They walked over to the table, which was exquisitely set. Eric pulled out a chair for Julia at the end of the table closest to where they'd been standing. As they took their seats, a server came with pitchers of water. Eric sat at the head of the table, which happened to be as far away from Julia as physically possible. It probably wasn't intentional, but it was notable.

Valerie had raced to the opposite end of the table and secured one of the spots next to Eric. Ann Marie got the other. Katie grabbed the chair next to Ann Marie; she wasn't missing out on dinner conversation again. Tina sat on the other side of Katie, and Olivia was at the end, across the table from Julia. Heather was pouting because she didn't like her seat. Katie had a momentary flashback to third grade, playing a round of musical chairs. This entire situation was juvenile.

"We didn't get much time together the other night," Eric was saying. "I'd like to do a little ice breaking – no stupid games or anything like that. I've been studying your profiles, and I thought I'd test my memory."

The girls nodded and agreed.

"Valerie, I'll start with you."

Valerie sat up straighter in her chair.

"You're from Boston – easy to remember with your accent. You are thirty-one – does anyone mind my saying their age? And you are a legal assistant, right?"

"Perfect! Bravo!"

"Great. Now let's see, Riann."

"You don't have to say my age."

"Thirty-two," Eric guessed and pointed at her.

"Yes," Riann admitted.

"It's all right, I'm thirty, right behind you. You're from Cleveland, I remember, not too far from Pittsburgh. And … I don't have any idea what you do for a living."

"I work at a day care center."

"Day care," Eric repeated, as though it had been on the tip of his tongue. "OK, Heather. You are from Louisville, also not too far from Pittsburgh. Now, your profile said you were a dancer. What kind of dancing do you do?"

"Exotic," Heather said bluntly. Ann Marie almost spit her champagne out. She started a coughing fit to cover it up. Katie smacked her on the back a few times.

"Thank you," Ann Marie croaked. "It went down the wrong pipe."

Eric moved on quickly. "Julia. You are from North Carolina. And, I'm sorry, I can't remember what you do."

"I do secretarial work," Julia smiled.

"That's right. I'm glad this isn't a test! Olivia," Eric went on, correctly guessing the name. "I know this one. You are twenty-four, you are from Buffalo and you're a student."

"Grad student," Olivia corrected.

"And Tina … you're from Virginia, and you sell real estate."

"Yes, but aren't you going to say my age?"

"Thirty, same as me."

"Very good. I'm impressed."

"Katie … is from New York somewhere…"

"Glens Falls."

"Yeah, some little hick town in upstate New York – nowhere near Pittsburgh."

"It's not that far, and it's got to be better than Pittsburgh," Katie shot back with a grin.

"Low blow, Katie," Eric feigned offense.

"I'm just kidding. I've never even been to Pittsburgh."

"You're missing out," Eric assured her. "It's a great place."

Katie shrugged playfully.

"You do some kind of accounting work, or something …"

"Accounts payable."

Both Ann Marie and Tina kicked Katie under the table. Ann Marie coughed again.

"Unemployed," she said during the cough. Eric didn't notice.

"And that brings us to Ann Marie," he was saying. "You are from New York City and you're an actress. What kind of acting do you do?"

"Porn star."

Eric's jaw dropped.

"I'm joking! Do I look like a porn star?" Ann Marie shouted, as the other girls had looks of horror on their faces. "I mostly do commercials, but I aspire to have my own sitcom someday."

Eric laughed, but looked as though he couldn't tell if Ann Marie was joking or serious.

"So, how did I do, ladies?" He asked the group at large.

"Great!" They all agreed. He had obviously studied some profiles more than others, but he had done quite well for only having met them once.

Servers were bringing out bread and salads. One brought several bottles of wine. Eric tasted a red and a white, then motioned to the red. The server filled his goblet, then proceeded around the table. He didn't offer the ladies to taste, but gave them the choice, red or white.

Katie took the red, in hopes that dinner was red meat. Her wish was fulfilled. It was roast beef served with garlic mashed potatoes and baby carrots. The red wine had been a good choice and complimented the meal perfectly. Katie ate too much in spite of herself; it tasted so delicious. Dessert was rich chocolate cake with thick chocolate frosting and strawberries on top. There was no point trying to resist. Hopefully, no one suggested a dip in the hot tub after dinner.

Leave it to Ann Marie to spice things up.

"Do you have a separate hot tub over here, because if we go back to the mansion the other girls will invade our date."

"No, I have to share the pool and the hot tub. But we don't have to invite the others."

"Oh, those ladies don't need an invitation!" Valerie laughed matter-of-factly.

"I'll tell you what," Eric said. "I'll get changed and meet you all in the hot tub in, say, twenty minutes?"

"Don't have to ask me twice," Ann Marie said and stood up. She started to lead the girls back through the woods to the limo.

"You want to go that way," Eric stopped her and pointed in the opposite direction.

"I can't believe we have to walk home from our date – and without an escort," Ann Marie joked.

"The date's not over yet," Eric reminded her.

Chapter Eight

The octet giggled all the way back to the mansion and plotted their strategy to evade the other girls. They went over every scenario, and no matter how things played out, they had no choice but to be rude. They had to tell them they weren't invited, because it wasn't their turn with Eric. And if the others were already in the hot tub, they were getting kicked out! Ann Marie had no problem bearing the bad news.

As it turned out, no confrontation was necessary. The others were hanging out upstairs in Lois's suite. They didn't hear the eight return from their date. If they were watching out the window for them to return, they were undoubtedly watching for the limo to pull up out front.

Ann Marie and Olivia decided to sneak up to the top of the stairs to listen for a minute. The videographer couldn't miss out on a chance to hear some dirt, so he followed them up the stairs. The remaining six got changed into their bathing suits as quickly as possible and scooted back downstairs. Ann Marie and Olivia joined them moments later, and they all went outside to the hot tub. Ann Marie swore they hadn't heard anything worth repeating, but Olivia kept giggling.

Eric wasn't there yet, but the cameras were. Eric showed up only minutes later, in his swim trunks as promised. He also had on a T-shirt, which he promptly removed. Katie made a quick assessment of his body without appearing to stare too long. He had nice legs, not too thin or too fat. His chest was muscular, and abs surprisingly sexy. All things considered, his body exceeded Katie's expectations. This experience was getting more intriguing every day.

Nine people in the hot tub was intimate – a little too intimate for Julia. She excused herself and went indoors.

"Is she coming back?" Eric asked.

"Who cares?" Heather laughed and poured herself another glass of wine. Ann Marie and Olivia held their glasses out for refills, but Heather ignored them. Ann

Marie made a face and picked up the bottle of wine. She poured Olivia and herself a glass. Olivia was having a giggling fit over the face Ann Marie had made. Eric hadn't seen any of the interaction and gave Olivia a quizzical look. Olivia was laughing too hard to explain and held her hand up to tell him never mind.

Heather, in the meantime, was glaring at Olivia. For having such a beautiful face, Heather had an equally ugly personality. Eric's interest in Heather appeared to be waning. She was trying very hard to use her body to attract his attention. Her swimsuit left nothing to the imagination, and she kept standing up to adjust her straps. She did have impressive physical attributes, but Eric seemed turned off by the fact that she was an exotic dancer. He hardly spoke to her all night and even averted his eyes. It was almost like he was embarrassed to look at a stripper in front of the other girls.

He didn't seem to have any problems checking out the others' bodies. Katie caught him looking at her several times. She also noticed him looking at Tina and Valerie. Ann Marie demanded most of his attention – so much so that Heather began to pout again and Riann looked close to tears. Ann Marie was flirting mercilessly, and Eric was obviously enjoying it. Valerie looked uncomfortable at times, but Katie, Tina and Olivia laughed right along with Ann Marie, encouraging her even more. At one point, she actually grabbed his crotch under the water.

Valerie tried to put an end to the date at that point. She announced how late it was and got out of the hot tub.

"It's been a great evening," she said with a smile as she dried herself off.

Heather and Riann took her cue and exited the hot tub as well.

"I'll walk you back to the mansion," Eric offered, and climbed out of the hot tub.

"We'll be here waiting for you," Ann Marie called. Valerie's jaw dropped. Her attempt to manipulate the others out of the hot tub had failed.

Heather gave Ann Marie a dirty look and then shot daggers through Valerie. She was plainly jealous that Ann Marie was extending her time with Eric, while she was now stuck going inside. She hesitated, as though contemplating getting back into the hot tub. It was too late. Valerie had tricked her and Riann but not the others. Heather grabbed her towel with a huff.

Riann looked almost relieved to be leaving. Maybe she didn't like Eric; it was hard to tell. She let him accompany her, Valerie and Heather back to the mansion. He wasn't gone fifteen minutes before rejoining the hot tub party.

Ann Marie promised to behave the rest of the evening. She kept pouring them all drinks, though. They ended up getting out of the hot tub and hanging out in the shallow end of the pool instead, on Tina's suggestion. She had grown warm, and advised the others it wasn't a good idea to stay in the hot tub too long, especially while drinking.

It was a warm evening, probably upper seventies. The pool water was some ten degrees warmer than the air, so it felt as relaxing as the hot tub had been. The five of them had a great time in the pool. They lounged around and talked, and the atmosphere was more fun than competitive. They got to know Eric quite a bit under such intimate circumstances. They were all attracted to Eric and flirted accordingly, but they weren't cut throat about it. The alcohol probably helped them relax and lose some of their inhibitions and jealous tendencies.

None of them got a kiss goodnight, but they each gave Eric a hug.

Olivia noticed movement at a third-story window and cut her hug short. "Someone is spying on us," she said.

"Does that surprise you?" Tina laughed.

"It shouldn't," piped in Ann Marie, "after what we heard earlier."

"What?" Eric asked. "Or don't I want to know?"

Ann Marie went into a narrative on how she, Olivia and "Ken the camera dude" had tiptoed to the top of the stairs earlier to eavesdrop on the conversation going on in Lois's suite.

"I can't name names, because I don't know the voices well enough to be one-hundred percent sure, but someone was saying pretty nasty things about Valerie."

"Really? Like what?" Tina asked. The question sounded innocent enough, but Tina was somewhat of an instigator. Katie loved that about her. Tina could come off as nonchalant, but she got the dirt to surface.

"Just mean comments about how conceited she is, and how long it takes her to get ready, and how all her stuff has to be just perfect," Olivia told them.

"Things a roommate might know," Ann Marie said as though she'd made a discovery.

"Who is Valerie's roommate?" Tina asked.

"Danine is," Olivia answered.

"The cat fights are beginning already?" Eric asked.

"Why do men have an infatuation with cat fights?" Katie demanded.

"They're a turn on," Ann Marie answered for Eric. "So, you must have been feeling pretty warm earlier, big guy. There were some dirty looks going on in the hot tub."

Eric didn't answer, but grinned.

"There's going to be even more disgruntled feelings if we stay out here much longer," Tina added. "Not that I care, but I'm getting cold, girls!"

Eric escorted the four ladies back to the mansion as promised and thanked them for an awesome evening.

"You keep us around, big guy. There's a lot more where that came from," Ann Marie assured him.

Katie was fairly confident Eric would be keeping the four of them. They all seemed to have chemistry with him. However, he could theoretically have chemistry with all five of the girls on tomorrow's date, as well. And he still had a single date with Lois. Things could go either way.

The following afternoon Brittany, Danine, Jenny, Kristin and Samantha went on their date with Eric. The invitation had mentioned fun in the sun, which could have meant anything from boating to beach volleyball. The girls had dressed for the occasion with shorts and tank tops or bikini tops.

They explained when they returned that their date had been a picnic in a park. They had a late lunch, played Frisbee, and each had a few minutes alone with Eric. The eight girls who had gone out on the date last night agreed to confess all the details of their group date, in exchange for a full recap of today's date. Once they realized Madison had been left out, they made her part of the deal. She had to spill all the details of her single date, or leave the room. Madison had no qualms about divulging the details of her special night with Eric; she was more than happy to brag about it.

Lois was the only one not included, because she was currently off on her single date with Eric.

"I'll tell you right now," said Danine. "You guys had a lot more fun than we did."

"Speak for yourself," Brittany retorted.

"I'm not saying I didn't have a good time," Danine retracted her statement. "I just feel like we got short changed. You guys got to go out all night. We only had a few hours."

"But you had more time per person," Tina reasoned. "We had eight women on our date, and none of us were alone with Eric even for a minute."

"Some of you had a lot more time with him than others," Heather said in an accusatory tone.

"You could have stayed," Ann Marie pointed out. Heather didn't reply. What could she say? Ann Marie was right. She had left of her own volition. She took silent and pouted instead.

"Let's move on to the important stuff," Valerie said impatiently. "Has anyone kissed him yet? Madison?"

"Yes," she admitted, her cheeks blushing slightly in spite of the remaining sunburn. "He kissed me goodnight after our date. It was very sweet. We didn't make out or anything."

Brittany snickered.

"We didn't," Madison insisted. "Eric was a gentleman."

"That's your loss," Brittany shrugged. "You should have taken advantage of your time with him."

"I did get the first kiss. I wasn't going to jump all over him."

"I bet Lois does," Danine interjected.

"Why, Brittany?" Madison ignored Danine. "What would you have done?"

"I will do whatever feels right at that moment. Obviously, Eric didn't want to do anything more with you, or he would have." Brittany's tone was playful, but her blue eyes were stone cold.

"It was a first date," Madison argued.

"How many dates do you think you're going to get?" Brittany refuted. "The elimination is tomorrow."

"Well, at least I kissed him. I don't think he wanted to hurt me by touching my sunburn. I appreciated him not mauling me."

"He can maul me any time," laughed Jenny, trying to lighten the mood.

"Hear, hear," added Ann Marie, and raised her wine glass.

"Did you kiss him?" Madison demanded, still glaring at Brittany.

"Absolutely. I wouldn't want to go on unless he can kiss. What would be the point?"

"And …" Katie prompted. "Can he kiss?"

"Absolutely!" Brittany raved, smiling at the recollection.

"That's a little forward, don't you think?" Riann asked. "Kissing when there's four other women on the date?"

"Not at all," Brittany waved her perfectly manicured hand as though dismissing Riann from the conversation. "We were alone. We didn't do anything in front of the others. Besides, I wasn't the only one. From what I've heard, Eric has kissed quite a few of us."

"Who else did he kiss?" Valerie wanted to know.

Jenny, Kristin and Samantha confessed. Danine tried to make a late entry, but Katie cut her off. She was probably lying, because she didn't want to be the only one on the date that hadn't gotten a kiss.

"What did you think, Jenny?" Katie asked. "We want details."

Katie couldn't help thinking about Eric's lips and how badly she had wanted to kiss them. She would jump on the first chance she got to kiss Eric. She had to give him something to make him want more.

"We went for a short walk," Jenny was saying, "and he was holding my hand the whole time. He doesn't seem like a stranger when you're with him. It felt very natural, as though we'd been friends forever. We talked a little, and he leaned in for the kiss. It was completely in the moment. It felt right. It didn't even seem like the cameras were on us."

"That sounds very sweet," Riann said with a bite of sarcasm, "but don't you find it a little disconcerting that he's kissing you, and Brittany, and Samantha, and Kristin?"

"And Madison," Ann Marie added.

"I don't really like the idea of kissing someone who just kissed someone else," Riann continued. Julia agreed, but Brittany spoke up sharply.

"Then you shouldn't be here," she said. "That's part of the game."

Riann looked as though Brittany had slapped her face.

"Maybe that's part of the problem," Madison broke in passionately. "I don't think of this as a game."

"Of course, it's a game," Brittany replied condescendingly. "It's a competition. That's a game."

"But I'm not competing with any of you," Madison insisted. "I'm here to find out if Eric is right for me. I don't feel like it has anything to do with any of the rest of you."

Some of the girls nodded in agreement.

"You're naïve," Brittany remarked.

"It is a competition," Kristin chimed in, "whether you think of it that way or not. You've got to compete for

Eric's attention and try to show him who you are, while everyone else is doing the same thing."

"All right, it's a competitive atmosphere," Madison conceded, "but I still think true love will prevail. If one of us is destined to be Eric's wife, that person will prevail."

Brittany rolled her eyes and shrugged.

"You don't even care about Eric," Madison continued. "If you're here just to play a game, you should quit now!"

"You are so naïve," Brittany repeated.

"I'm naïve because I'm here for the right reasons?" Madison demanded. She stood and glared down at Brittany.

"You're naïve if you think you are going to become Eric's wife."

"I never said that. I don't know who Eric is going to end up with. We've just met. All I'm saying is that it isn't a game to me." Madison sat back down. She thought twice about it and stood back up. "Forget it. I'm not going to sit here and argue with you."

Madison stormed from the room. They heard her footsteps go upstairs. Olivia and Heather stifled their giggles.

"If Madison doesn't know who Eric is going to end up with, then it clearly isn't her," Brittany said matter-of-factly.

"Why, who do you think is going to end up with Eric?" Valerie asked out of curiosity.

"I have to believe I am, or I wouldn't be here," Brittany said casually. "We should all believe we are the one for Eric. If you don't believe it, there is the door."

"No one should be counting themselves out," Tina translated.

"Eric is going to be counting five of us out tomorrow," Danine reminded them. "Any thoughts on who might be going?"

"I have no idea who's going," Tina answered diplomatically, "but I would bet Ann Marie, Katie and Olivia are staying."

"He seemed to like you, too, Jenny," Samantha piped in.

"He seemed to like you, too, Samantha," Jenny retorted.

"That's the problem," Katie interrupted realistically. "He seems to like a lot of us."

"Only Eric knows…" Valerie said mysteriously with a secretive wink.

"We'll all know tomorrow," Ann Marie said. "Let's make the most of tonight. Who needs a drink? I'm buying."

Chapter Nine

The fifteen girls gathered on the terrace the following evening. They had a cocktail hour and a final opportunity to speak with Eric alone, before the elimination shoot. The tension in the air was more suffocating than the humidity.

Madison avoided Brittany like the plague, but shot dirty looks at her every chance she got. Brittany didn't care, if she even noticed. She strolled around the terrace in her lofty manner, with her head held high and looked down her nose at the others.

Kristin's breasts were hanging out as usual. The others were becoming accustomed to them by now. If Kristin had any personality, she may have been a serious threat, but large breasts will only get you so far.

Lois on the other hand, while lacking in the breast department, more than made up for it with her big mouth. She bobbled about the room taking bets on who would be eliminated. She had no idea most of the women had their money on her.

Ann Marie had joined Katie and Tina in their room last night after everyone had gone upstairs to bed. They had sat up another hour discussing the events of the evening and making their own predictions on Eric's choices. They had all agreed that Lois would be gone if any of them were Eric. There was simply nothing attractive about that woman. They also agreed things didn't look good for Julia, Riann and Heather. While Julia and Riann were too reserved, Heather was too forward. From the looks on their faces tonight, those three were well aware of their impending doom, while Lois was oblivious. There was some controversy over who they thought the final victim of the elimination would be, but each felt confident in their own chances to stay.

Eric mingled freely with the women for an hour. Shane called for Eric promptly when the hour was over, and banished him to a private sitting area set up beyond the hot tub. Each woman would get a chance to speak with Eric personally before he made his final decisions.

Shane escorted the women, one at a time, to the secluded meeting area. It was totally private from the rest of the group, but the cameras prevented them from being completely alone. They were taken in alphabetical order, which put Ann Marie first, and Katie somewhere in the middle.

Katie felt nervous for the first time since she'd been there, although she didn't know exactly why. Was she nervous about what she was going to say to him? Was she suddenly scared of the cameras or was she starting to have feelings toward him? She decided it was nothing more than a little stage fright. As she stepped into the clearing and set eyes on Eric, she immediately felt calmer. His smile was reassuring.

He stood and hugged her. She didn't want to let go. She held onto him a little longer than probably intended, but he didn't pull away.

"I couldn't help but notice," he said, when he stepped back, "how well we fit together."

"Yes, we do," she agreed. "Or do you say that to all the girls?"

"No, I don't." Eric's expression was serious.

"It's great to see you," Katie was saying, trying not to feel the intensity of Eric's gaze. "It seems like weeks."

"It does. It's probably from trying to squeeze so many dates into such a small time-span." Eric sat Katie down with him on the bench.

"You must be overwhelmed."

"I am. And I don't want to hurt anyone."

"Of course not, but I think people understand it's all part of the process. Feelings are going to be hurt no matter what. That's a risk we're willing to take, or we wouldn't be here." Katie smiled kindly at Eric. His green eyes met hers, and they looked more sad than playful tonight. This elimination business what really tearing him up inside. "Do you have anything you want to know about me, or is there any way I can help you come to a decision?"

"I have a lot of questions, but let's stick with an easy one. How do you feel about me – so far?"

"I feel pretty good, Eric. I have to admit, I was skeptical about this whole thing, but so far, I think you're great. I definitely want to get to know you better. I can feel there's chemistry between us, and I'd like to stay and see what can become of it."

"Good, "Eric said, and smiled. He patted her hand, which was resting on her leg, and then stood to indicate the interview was over.

"Hang in there," she said and hugged him. "It'll be over soon."

"Thank you," he said and gave her a squeeze.

Katie gave him a reassuring smile, and turned to leave. She was surprised by Eric's sensitivity. He was truly anguished over this elimination. She wanted to believe he liked her, but couldn't help wondering if perhaps his guilt was actually directed at her. She may have misinterpreted their entire conversation. He could just as easily have felt badly about hurting her feelings as much as anyone else's. Maybe he confided in her because he was eliminating her and wanted to soften the blow.

Katie was deep in thought as she walked slowly back to the party. Shane was by her side, and she tried to keep up with his small talk. She was vaguely aware the cameras were on them, since Shane wouldn't be speaking to her otherwise. She just wanted to be alone to think! She wished Shane would shut up. She quickened her pace slightly.

"Thank you," she smiled at Shane as they neared the terrace. He nodded and went to retrieve Kristin, who was next to see Eric.

Katie sought out Ann Marie. She wanted to talk to someone she trusted. Since Tina hadn't seen Eric yet, she wouldn't have any pertinent advice. Quite frankly, Ann Marie was the only other person in the house she could trust.

Ann Marie was busy talking to Samantha. Katie caught her attention and winked. Ann Marie wrapped up her conversation with Samantha and joined her best friend.

"Let's walk," Katie said, so they wouldn't be too conspicuous. If the videographers thought they were having a juicy conversation, they would be all over them. The last thing Katie wanted was a camera zooming in on their discussion. Katie casually led the way inside to the ladies' room. Luck was with them, and none of the other girls intruded on their privacy.

"How did it go with Eric?" Katie asked as soon as they were safely in the bathroom. No cameras were allowed in there, so they could speak freely.

"I think it went well. I'm sticking to my guns on my picks."

"He didn't seem depressed at all?" Katie asked as she combed her fingers through her hair.

"Depressed? No," Ann Marie answered from the stall.

"Not really depressed. Somber is more the word I'm looking for."

"I guess he was somber, yeah, compared to the other night. You have to consider I was the first one to see him tonight. He could very well have been depressed by the time he got to you. That doesn't mean anything. What did he say?"

"He asked me how I felt about him so far. But before that, before we talked about our feelings, he said he felt bad hurting people. It didn't feel like he was referring to me, at the time. Then I started analyzing everything, and I'm not so sure. I guess I'm a little paranoid."

"I'm sure he wasn't referring to you. Who was right before you?"

Katie thought a second. "Julia."

"There you have it. Julia's a nice person he wouldn't want to hurt, but he's obviously not interested in her."

"You're probably right," Katie started piecing things together. "He did seem relieved to see me. He gave me a big hug."

"You'll be OK, kiddo," Ann Marie told her friend as she exited the stall. "He likes you."

Katie nodded. She knew Ann Marie would put things in perspective for her.

"We'd better get back out there," Katie said.

"Put on a happy face!" Ann Marie reminded her. She smiled at Katie in the mirror as she washed her hands.

They exited the restroom and rejoined the party. It certainly didn't feel like a party. It felt like waiting to find out how you did on a test. There was a fine line between a C minus and a D plus.

When Shane returned from escorting Valerie back from her visit with Eric, he addressed all the women.

"If I could have your attention ladies," he said. "Eric is finalizing his decisions. We'll take a short break. When I return with Eric, be prepared to hear his choices."

"Cut!" Barbara yelled. "Thank you, Shane. Let's take a fifteen-minute break, then get the ladies set up to shoot the elimination."

Barbara walked away to confer with Zeb and one of the cameramen. She was motioning and explaining how she wanted everyone set up.

"Even when she gives them a break, she doesn't give them a break," Kristin commented.

Katie nodded. Kristin was right. The cameramen were packing up to move. The women were left completely alone for those fifteen minutes, with no cameras whatsoever. Katie felt free. She was tempted to start screaming vulgarities just to get it out of her system. She restrained herself and caught up with Ann Marie instead.

"I wonder where we're shooting."

"I heard someone say out front."

"Really?" Katie said. She hadn't heard anything. Ann Marie had a way of finding things out. She was quite a little sleuth.

"How are you two holding up?" Tina asked as she approached.

"Not bad," Ann Marie answered for both of them.

"You know what's weird?" Tina continued. "I don't know Eric well enough to be disappointed over losing him, if I get sent home tonight, but I don't want to leave yet. I would miss you guys!"

"That's sweet!" Ann Marie exclaimed.

"We'll miss you too, Tina, when we do go. We should exchange addresses and phone numbers."

"Let's make an agreement. If one of us does get kicked off, we'll leave our address and phone number in the room when we go up to pack."

"That sounds good," Katie agreed. "And if we don't get kicked off, we should exchange information when we get back to the room, while we're thinking about it."

"Definitely," Tina said.

"What if Lois gets the boot?" Ann Marie was saying. "That would be a thirty percent chance one of us ends up in the private suite."

"That would be awesome," Katie agreed. "Not that I don't want to room with you, Tina."

"I understand. You don't need to explain."

Zeb began gathering the girls together and directing them to the front porch. The camera crew was still bustling around, but obviously previous arrangements had been made for the shoot. The porch was decorated beautifully. The urns had been moved to either end, and twinkle lights had been strung throughout the greenery.

The girls were arranged alphabetically from back to front, but were staggered on the steps like chorus risers. They were staggered in position on the steps, filling in the gaps for a perfect arrangement for a photo shoot. Barbara, of course, made last minute adjustments, moving this one an inch to the right and that one a quarter-inch to the left. It was actually becoming annoying.

Katie wasn't thrilled with the placement of the women at any rate. She had worn another black dress, as had Kristin, Samantha, Tina and Julie. The black dresses were weighing down that end of the porch. They should have been mixed up with the other colors, rather than lined up alphabetically. It made no sense for Barbara to act so picky over a quarter of an inch left or right, when she'd paid absolutely no attention to colors, heights, or any other potentially relevant attributes.

Katie found herself mentally criticizing Barbara all too often. The show's success apparently had little to do with her directing capabilities. Katie was beginning to question her own career choice. Perhaps she would have more success as a director than an actor.

Katie looked on as the velvet-colored cart bearing the gold gift box was wheeled into place. She wondered what was inside this time. She would find out soon enough. Shane and Eric were approaching from the side of the mansion. Eric waited at the edge of the set while Shane addressed the ladies. They ended up hearing his speech three times, as he kept demanding a retake. Barbara said nothing, but indulged him.

"Good evening, Ladies. As you know, Eric will be eliminating five of you tonight. The ten ladies chosen to stay will continue on this journey with Eric to find his *Soulmate*."

He opened the gold box and withdrew a gold bracelet.

"The ten ladies selected will receive a gold bracelet from Eric, as a token of friendship, anticipation, and an invitation to continue building a relationship."

He replaced the bracelet in the box.

"Eric would like to say a few words before we begin."

He lifted his arm and motioned to his left. Eric stepped forward, as Shane bowed out of the shot.

"Thank you, Shane. Good evening, ladies."

"Good evening, Eric."

"I just wanted to say thank you to all of you for sticking it out with me. I had a great time on all of our dates together and I think you are all special. It's been really difficult for me to face up to eliminations. I don't want to hurt anyone's feelings. I'm just going with my instincts on this one. If I didn't pick you, it wasn't because I didn't like you. I just felt like someone else made a better match for me."

He looked down at his shoes and took a deep breath. They could hear him exhale. He raised his head, although still averting his eyes from the ladies. He picked up the first bracelet carefully. Finally, he looked at the women.

"Jenny," he said and smiled.

Jenny's face was beaming as she cautiously stepped down from her perch to accept her gift. Eric fumbled with the clasp on the bracelet. Jenny smiled up at him reassuringly. He laughed nervously and eventually figured out how it fastened. He raised his arms triumphantly.

"Thank you," Jenny said.

"Thank you," Eric repeated and gave her a hug. Jenny returned to her assigned spot, huge smile plastered on her face.

Eric took another breath and picked up another bracelet.

"Madison."

Madison was absolutely glowing, and it wasn't entirely on account of the sunburn. In fact, her face didn't look bad at all once she'd caked on some makeup. The rest of her body was peeling disgustingly, but her face looked almost normal. She stepped forward to receive the bracelet from Eric. He was still having a little trouble with the clasp, but got it latched nonetheless. Madison gave him a hug and a kiss on the cheek. The kiss was undoubtedly for Brittany's benefit, confirmed by the gloating and hateful look on Madison's face as she returned to her spot in front of Brittany.

Brittany took it all in stride. She was a hard person to fluster. She wore a small smirk of her own, which Katie interpreted as, "Wait and see, Madison. You're not rid of me yet."

In the meantime, Eric called Ann Marie, who was in the midst of the controversy, because she stood next to Brittany. Ann Marie's heel caught on the step, and she stumbled slightly on the way down.

"I'm fine!" she called to concerned faces.

Eric had stepped forward to grab her arm.

"There's an ice breaker," she said, and the others laughed. The tension had been so thick, the laughter was a welcomed relief. Katie felt as though the laughter had been a personal reminder to breathe. Thank God for Ann Marie, or she may have passed out.

Eric was becoming more adept at fastening the bracelets, and he slipped Ann Marie's on with little problem. She gave him a huge hug.

"Are you OK?" he asked.

"Yes, I'm fine. Thank you."

"You're welcome."

Ann Marie turned around and curtsied. "My next show's at eleven!"

The ladies laughed again, letting off some steam. Ann Marie carefully and deliberately climbed the steps to resume her position.

Eric picked up the next bracelet.

"Samantha," he said.

Samantha stepped forward and held out her wrist. Eric fastened it like a pro.

"Thank you, Eric."

"You're welcome, Samantha," he replied and gave her a quick hug.

He called Tina next. Katie watched with genuine appreciation as her friend received her gift. Katie was honestly happy for Tina – and for Ann Marie –but she was growing more anxious by the minute. They were half way done already! She thought about what Tina had said earlier, and it rang true. She wanted to stay with her friends. They didn't know Eric well enough to care about getting dropped, but they would miss each other terribly.

Katie could hardly believe her ears when Eric called Lois. She had no idea what Eric could see in that tomboy. Maybe he felt guilty letting her go after their single date. It would eat Katie up if she got sent home and Lois got to stay. Lois had no attractive qualities whatsoever. She was skinny and flat chested. Her face was nothing to write home about. She was loud and pushy and tacky. Katie could not think of even one redeeming quality. Lois was out of her league. It was utterly impossible for Eric to be attracted to that woman.

Lois received her bracelet and gave Eric a kiss on the cheek. Maybe there was some strange chemistry there. Otherwise he wouldn't have chosen her. He couldn't have kept Lois on the basis of guilt alone, when there were other, lovely girls to choose from.

Lois turned and took her place in the front row, centered between Ann Marie and Brittany.

"Brittany," Eric called.

Brittany squeezed between Lois and Madison and approached Eric. Brittany and Lois were like night and day. How Eric could like both was a mystery. Brittany was so classy and elegant, her long straight hair shining as she glided by the other ladies, while Lois was so white-trashy. Of course, neither had very appealing personalities, as far as friendships went, but they were definitely at opposite ends of the spectrum.

Brittany held her arm out and watched as Eric fastened the bracelet. She spun it on her arm approvingly, and gave Eric a hug.

"Thank you, Eric."

"Thank you," he said, and watched entranced, as she made her way back to her position.

Brittany back in place and smiling triumphantly, Katie held her breath once again. Eric lifted the next bracelet from the gold box. He paused as he settled it in his hands.

"Katie," he said looking up at her.

She exhaled and hoped it wasn't audible. She slid carefully down the steps between Tina and Valerie. Tina gave her a thumbs-up as she passed. Katie couldn't stop grinning as she stood in front of Eric. He clipped the bracelet around her wrist and returned her smile.

"Thank you," she said and wrapped her arms around his neck. They embraced but a second, and Katie turned to climb up the steps once again. Tina patted her back.

Valerie in front of her, Kristin on her left, and Julia on her right each gave her the same look. They were trying to be good sports and show happiness for her, but were obviously concerned about their own fate. Only two bracelets remained, which meant at least one of them was not getting one. In addition to the three of them, four other girls waited anxiously down the porch.

Theoretically, neither Valerie, Kristin nor Julia might get chosen.

"Valerie," said Eric.

Valerie wiped her brow dramatically as a release of emotions. She chuckled as she took a few steps forward to meet Eric.

"You had me worried there," she said nervously.

Eric smiled and clasped a bracelet around her wrist. Valerie raised her arm and shook it victoriously, then laughed again.

"Thank you, Eric."

"You're welcome," he said and laughed a little. He was noticeably feeling the pressure. He glanced anxiously at the final bracelet waiting in the gold box.

Valerie drew his attention back by giving him a hug. He seemed eager to get the eliminations over with. He gave Valerie a quick, almost mechanical hug, and fidgeted, as she walked proudly back to her place.

Six girls remained unchosen.

Eric took a deep breath and raised the last bracelet from the box. He dared not look at the ladies, but played with the bracelet in his hands.

"Kristin," he said finally.

It was over. Kristin smiled with relief and teetered down the steps in her stilettos. She and her breasts waited zealously in front of Eric for the jewelry. He clasped the bracelet on her wrist and hugged her in turn. She purposely squeezed her breasts into his chest. It was unavoidable, what with the size of those things, but it was tacky nonetheless. Eric didn't appear to mind. Most men wouldn't.

"Thank you," she said delightedly and tiptoed on her stilettos to her position on the far end of the porch.

The girls were relieved it was over, but the tension had not vanished from the atmosphere as it had after the first elimination ceremony. Heather and Danine looked livid. Olivia looked totally shocked, and Riann looked as though she were ready to burst into tears. Julia smiled pleasantly. She wasn't fazed by the news and took it in stride. She was the only one to check out gracefully.

Shane stepped up next to Eric.

"Thank you, Eric," he said. "I know that was difficult for you. Ladies, I'm sorry, but if you did not receive a bracelet, your journey ends here. You must say your goodbyes. We do want to wish you well on your own personal quest to find your *Soulmate*. Danine ..."

Danine stepped up first to say goodbye to Eric.

"I don't feel like you even gave me a chance," Danine accused him.

"Everyone is getting the same chance," Eric said. "It's hard to juggle fifteen women in three days and make a decision like this. I just had to go with my gut feeling."

"I think you'll regret some of your choices," she said bitterly and stalked away.

Heather came second.

"I guess I'm just too much woman for you to handle," she said.

"I guess so," Eric replied noncommittally and shook Heather's hand. "It was nice meeting you."

Heather's mouth dropped open, but she didn't respond. She exited the set with her head held high. Eric didn't look affected by either's girl's outburst.

Julia approached him next. She shook his hand congenially and smiled.

"I had a nice time. Thank you for having me."

"Thank you. I'm sorry it didn't work out."

"It wasn't meant to be," Julia said kindly.

"Thank you," Eric said softly. Julia smiled again and exited.

Olivia stepped up to the plate. She hugged him first, then stood back and looked him in the eye.

"Can I ask why?" Her expression was hurt and confused as to how he could possibly have let her go.

"Honestly, Olivia, I feel you are a little too young for me. We are at two completely different places in our lives."

Olivia nodded, but still looked as though she didn't understand. Olivia, at twenty-four was in fact, the youngest of the group. Katie and Ann Marie were barely older at twenty-five, but there was a difference in maturity level. Eric had kindly substituted the word "young" for the word "immature."

Olivia walked away, and Riann took her place. Eric looked like he expected a hard time from her as well, since she appeared to be on the verge of tears. Maybe she was simply a sensitive person, because she certainly hadn't seemed that attached to Eric. Some people didn't deal well with rejection.

"I enjoyed meeting you," Eric said.

"It was nice meeting you, too," she said and forced a smile. "Good luck to you."

"Thank you, you too."

Riann hurried quickly from the set. Barbara sent Zeb to interview the five women who had been released from the show. She arranged the other ten women on the porch steps for the celebratory toast.

Eric had already recovered from his encounters with his newly-defined exes. He raised his glass cheerfully and addressed the remaining ten ladies.

"I just want to say thank you for bearing with me. I am very satisfied with the choices I made. I have enjoyed the time spent with each of you, and I'm looking forward to spending more time together."

They all raised their glasses.

Chapter Ten

Sunday was Mother's Day. Barbara gave the entire cast and crew the day off. Rumor had it Eric had flown home to visit his mother. The girls weren't sure if he was really gone or if it was a ploy to keep them away from the guest house while the cameras were off duty.

They didn't mind having the day to themselves. They were also thrilled to learn Madison had arranged to leave the premises for the day. She was from Los Angeles, and her mother lived close enough to meet for lunch. A taxi picked up Madison out front around eleven. Kristin took the opportunity to move her bedroom.

Shane hadn't said anything about the empty bedroom Julia and Olivia had shared. Kristin claimed it and started moving her belongings as soon as Madison was gone. Since Ann Marie and Samantha got along well, and Katie and Tina actually liked rooming together, none of them made a fuss over Kristin getting a single room. The other remaining girls already had their own rooms, since their roommates had moved out last night.

Madison was ecstatic to come home and find Kristin gone from her room. She was irritated that she hadn't gotten the choice of which room she wanted and of course, made a big deal over it. They argued all evening.

"I thought I was doing her a favor," Kristin said to the others after Madison stormed out of the sitting room and stomped up the stairs. "She would have been livid if she'd come home and I'd moved her into the spare bedroom. Plus, I gave her the good room. She has a view of the back; I have a lovely view of the driveway."

"She would have complained no matter what," Valerie said.

When Barbara learned of the room switch the next day, she ordered interviews of both Kristin and Madison to get the controversy on film. As soon as they were finished, all ten women were gathered in the sitting room for instructions from Shane.

Shane greeted them and explained there would be two single dates with Eric this round. There would also be two group dates, one of which would take place immediately following the meeting. Eric had already selected the two lucky women to receive single dates. The other eight would be competing to go on today's date – and only three of them would be attending.

"What we need to do is find out which eight ladies will be taking part in today's challenge. That means the two not competing will be going on single dates with Eric. These two women were selected by Eric as the two people he felt he needed more time with."

He paused and removed two envelopes from his jacket pocket.

"I have here two invitations from Eric. I would like to invite Jenny up here to read the first one."

Jenny hesitated and came forward, as though she was unsure if the invitation belonged to her, or if she was merely getting to read it. She carefully slit the envelope open and pulled out the invitation.

"Dear Jenny," she read. "Oh, it is mine! Dear Jenny, please join me tomorrow evening for a romantic dinner for two. I will pick you up at 7:00PM. Eric."

Jenny hugged the invitation and slipped back to her seat.

"The other invitation," Shane announced, "is for Wednesday afternoon. The next elimination will take place Wednesday night. For those of you who did not get a single date and do not win today's challenge, Eric has a group date planned for tomorrow afternoon."

The girls exchanged glances at the mention of elimination.

"Since you are all anxious to learn about today's challenge, we'll head outside very soon. I will forewarn you, since Eric is such a sports fanatic, it is a physical challenge. Eight of you will participate. Jenny, and the person whose name is on this invitation, will not need to compete."

Shane paused to add to the suspense. Katie was grateful it wasn't a live show. They would have to sit through a commercial break every time Shane was about to make an announcement.

"The second invitation belongs to … Samantha."

Samantha's face lit up. She stood and accepted her invitation from Shane. She stared at the invitation in her hands, looking as though she didn't want to open it in front of the others. Realizing privacy was not an option, she tore it open and read aloud.

"Dear Samantha … the pleasure of your company is requested on Wednesday, May 13 at 12:00PM for a romantic carriage ride through wine country with me. Eric. Sounds lovely!"

"Ladies," Shane said. "There you have it. Jenny and Samantha will be going on the two single dates. The remaining eight of you will compete for the three spots on today's group date. The other five will share some time with Eric tomorrow afternoon. I invite you know to join me outside to take part in the challenge."

The ladies exchanged glances and followed Shane outside. The shoot was set up in the grassy area behind the pool. There was a basketball hoop and some targets.

"I might as well forget it," Kristin commented after surveying the scene.

Katie had to laugh at the thought of Kristin shooting baskets with those vampire nails. Her own prospects weren't quite as bleak, but she had to admit Lois the tomboy had the advantage on this one. Madison looked ready to cry, to the extent that her lip was beginning to quiver.

Shane explained there were three events: basketball, softball and archery. All eight women would participate in the first event. They had three chances to make a basket from the foul line previously marked off. It didn't look nearly as long as a regulation foul shot. All ladies advancing would have two chances to throw a softball through a target. Those successful would then shoot an arrow at the archery target. The three with the best shot would win the date.

"What if none of us make a basket?" Valerie asked jokingly.

"We've got a tie-breaker event planned if necessary." Shane was quick with an answer as usual.

"We'll make it," Lois said confidently for all of them, clapping her hands together in encouragement. Lois's confidence was premature. Neither Brittany nor Kristin made a basket, which left only six girls to advance to softball. Valerie was the only one to miss the hole in the softball target. It was a large hole, and her second attempt was close, but she couldn't persuade Shane to give her another try.

Five girls advanced to archery. Katie had felt comfortable with basketball and softball, being relatively athletic growing up. She hadn't played any sports in college, but had completed the required four credits of physical education, two of those credits having been fulfilled by softball. Granted, that was five years ago, but she could throw a ball well enough. Archery, on the other hand, was not a common skill. Katie had tried archery once when she was eighteen. She had gone to the Renaissance Festival in Sterling, New York with Ann Marie and a group of friends. All the games and activities were themed for the period. Katie had tried archery. She had not done very well, but at least she had done it before. Most of the others had never touched a bow, Ann Marie included. Ann Marie had skipped archery in lieu of drinking ale and eating a huge turkey leg with no utensils. Little did she know that choice would have future repercussions.

Lois went first and set the bar. She struck just outside the bullseye. She claimed she had never played before, which was probably true. After all, she openly admitted to playing on a softball league for years. Katie tended to believe Lois, because she didn't seem to have anything to hide. Besides, most white trash hasn't had the opportunity to try archery.

Tina and Ann Marie were not so lucky. Neither hit the target at all. That left the door wide open for Katie and Madison. They had only to hit the target to win. The pressure of beating Lois was off. She felt much better about her prospects of hitting the target versus making a miracle shot.

Katie and Madison both hit the target. Neither came close to Lois's phenomenal shot, but that didn't matter. They had secured a position on today's date with Eric. It wasn't a single date, but three girls on a date with one guy was better than five.

Shane congratulated them and whisked them away for their date. They were allowed a few minutes to freshen up before climbing aboard the *Soulmates* limo, which was waiting out front.

Eric was in the limo already and was delighted to see them.

"I couldn't wait to find out who won," he greeted them. "How was the competition?"

"It was fun!" cried Madison. Her mood had changed completely.

"There wasn't much competition," Lois laughed, and told Eric the whole story.

"You guys are awesome," Eric said and grabbed a bottle of champagne. "I'd say this calls for a celebration."

"Yes, it does," Katie agreed and handed out the glasses. She suddenly wondered if it was even noon yet, and checked her watch. It was ten-after-twelve. They hadn't eaten lunch yet. Too much champagne on an empty stomach wouldn't be pretty.

"Don't worry," Eric said, reading her mind. "Lunch is first on the agenda."

They ate lunch at an outdoor café. A private terrace had been set up for the four of them – and the cameramen of course. It was a very romantic setting, but difficult to feel anything but plutonic. There was definitely flirting going on, but not the same interaction as having a one-on-one date.

Madison dominated most of the conversation. She was flirting and showing off for the camera, as much as for Eric. Lois and Katie exchanged glances several times, as Madison twirled her hair around her finger and laughed too loudly. Eric didn't seem to notice.

Katie tried not to feel intimidated by the situation. She remained cool, smiled and nodded continuously, and enjoyed the delightful cuisine. After lunch, they clamored back into the limo and were chauffeured to a day spa. The ladies were excited to spend the afternoon with Eric while being pampered.

They had massages first. They were all in the same room, lined up on the tables. Lois was on the end, then Eric, Katie and Madison. Madison seemed put out that she didn't get to be next to Eric. She made herself the center of attention anyway.

"Excuse me," she told the massage therapist. "I have very sensitive skin, and I'm still recovering from a horrendous sunburn. Can you take extra care with me?"

"We'll take care of you," she answered soothingly, with a slight hint of condescension. Katie smiled and turned her face toward Eric.

"This is incredible," she said. "I've never had a massage before."

"Never?" Eric repeated.

"No, I've been missing out."

"I've been missing out, too," Lois added. "I've always wanted to get one, it's just finding the time …"

"Oh, I go at least once a month," Madison bragged. "It really takes the stress off."

Katie held her breath. She happened to know that Madison was a cashier in the ladies' section of a department store. It was a big joke around the house, because her profile listed her as a "fashion consultant." Katie wanted to comment how stressful retail could be, especially around the holidays, but she bit her tongue. Madison probably believed she was a fashion consultant in the charade she called her life. Katie turned the conversation back to Eric instead.

"Do you have a stressful job, Eric?"

"It can be. I'm a computer programmer, and I mostly subcontract. The job itself is more challenging than stressful, but sometimes it can be stressful trying to meet a deadline, especially when you can't figure out why something isn't working right."

"Are you self-employed?" Katie asked.

"For tax purposes, I am. I have a couple of big clients I do a lot of work for, and I do some work for one particular company, but I'm not on anyone's payroll presently."

"Need an accountant?" Katie joked.

"Actually, I do. I got killed on my taxes last year."

"Taxes are so boring. Let's talk about something else," Madison insisted.

"This is so relaxing, I could fall asleep," Lois said, ignoring Madison. "Do you have any input as far as where the dates are held, Eric? Or is that up to the producer?"

"I have no input," Eric answered. "They come to me and tell me where we're going and when to be ready."

"But you sometimes get to choose who goes on what dates, right?" Madison chimed in. "For example, you chose me, while Lois's name was pulled out of a hat."

"I get to choose sometimes. And I try to be fair. Since I already had a date with you Madison, and with Lois, I tried to pick some other girls I hadn't spent much time with. And I was thinking, Katie, since I did get to spend some time alone with Madison and Lois previously, I'd like to spend some time alone with you today. What do you say we hit the Jacuzzi?"

"Sounds great," Katie said, sitting up carefully so as not to lose her towel. She suddenly remembered she had no bathing suit with her.

That was no problem. Barbara had full wardrobe staff on hand. Katie chose a sexy turquoise bikini and quickly changed. It wasn't a perfect fit, but she didn't mind hanging out of it a bit. She joined Eric, and the cameraman, in the Jacuzzi room. It was just big enough for a single camera setup in the corner. She didn't even care that the cameras were invading their privacy. She finally had Eric to herself, and she was taking full advantage of the situation.

"Wow. You look great," Eric said.

"You do, too," Katie smiled. "Thank you for spending some time alone with me."

"You're welcome. I've been looking forward to it."

"I have been, too. It seems like time is flying by, there's only ten girls left, and we haven't been alone together yet."

"Tell me about it," Eric laughed. "I feel like I've been forced to make some blind decisions."

"You have been. You just have to go with your instincts," Katie advised.

"I think the first cut was harder, because I had to base my decisions on first impressions. Sometimes first impressions aren't accurate. But on the other hand, there are some girls I knew I had absolutely zero chemistry with, so they had to go – especially on the second round."

"I could tell."

"Was it that obvious?"

Katie couldn't lie to Eric any easier than she could lie to her mother.

"It was obvious in two cases," Katie admitted.

"Heather?" he guessed the most obvious.

"And Julia," Katie added.

"I know. Julia was sweet, but she and I were not compatible in the least. Heather just made me uncomfortable. I mean, going to a strip club with the guys is one thing, but I felt like I was at a strip club with the girls, which is plain wrong."

Katie laughed at Eric's expression.

"I'm sure she's not the only one who slightly altered her occupation on her profile," Katie said, referring to Madison, but well aware how close she was to that category as well. She hadn't lied about anything. She was employed as an Accounts Payable Clerk at the time of her application. She was not employed as an actress at that time, nor had she been for months. It wasn't the same thing as omitting the word "exotic" before dancer, or substituting "fashion consultant" for department store clerk.

"So, Lois might not be a nurse?" Eric joked, as though he already knew Madison had pumped up her resume.

"I was generalizing," Katie met Eric's sarcasm with practicality.

"I'm sorry, I'm being totally unprofessional discussing the other girls with you. I just feel so comfortable talking to you. I don't feel like we just met."

"I know what you mean."

"You do? Good. It's like an instant friendship."

"Uh-oh. Are you saying I'll never be more than I friend to you…"

"No, not at all," Eric back-pedaled. "I'm saying I feel comfortable with you. Friendship at this point is good. I would love to see where it leads."

"I completely agree," Katie said, staring directly into his flirtatious green eyes.

It was the perfect moment to kiss, and they leaned in to meet halfway. Katie felt a surge of excitement through her whole body, as his soft lips met hers. She had been anticipating this moment since they had met. His kiss was all she'd expected and more. It was a soft, romantic kiss, lasting merely seconds. It satiated her curiosity, but left her painfully yearning for more.

"I hope you agree that that was not a kiss between old friends," he said.

"I agree," she said, though she was short of breath. She wanted nothing more than to move in for the kill, press her body firmly against his and kiss him fully until they both gave in to carnal pleasure. She knew she had to hold back. If she wanted more, she had to leave him wanting more.

"Can I tell you something?" she asked.

"Of course."

"I've wanted to kiss you since the moment we met."

"Really?" His response was more of a statement that a question. "Why didn't you?"

"It wasn't the right time."

"Is it the right time now?" he asked, his eyes greener than before, burning with desire as he impatiently awaited her reply.

Katie moved in closer and kissed him again. The bubbles enveloped them, sporadically splashing and gently caressing their bodies. Their legs were touching in the hot water, and she put her hand on his bicep and stroked slowly upwards towards his shoulder. He had his other arm around her back and pulled her closer. Katie let her breasts brush against Eric's chest. She knew the cameras couldn't capture the contact from that angle, with the bubbles spiraling around them, but Eric could feel them. She had to taunt him, to make him want more from her.

His hand was on her leg now, grabbing her thigh under the water. He went so far as to finger the string on the side of her bikini. He was playing the same game, touching Katie under the agitated water where there was no chance of being detected by the camera. His hand slipped behind her and cupped her half-covered ass. He squeezed it, and pulled her even closer. Her breasts pressed firmly against his chest, her nipples tightening, yearning to be touched by his strong hands or tantalized by his soft, warm tongue.

He kissed her harder, welcoming her warm response. Katie's passion equaled Eric's as they kissed. Katie wished circumstances were different. She wished she was the only girl on Eric's agenda and this date was real – not a group date on national television. She admitted if it weren't for the show, Eric was not someone she would have considered going out with. But now that she was with him, she wanted to see where things would lead. She wanted to jump him right there in the spa's Jacuzzi. It had been too long since she'd been with a man.

Her better judgment kicked in and she pulled back. Eric opened his eyes and his look questioned why Katie had stopped. Katie smiled and timidly lowered her eyes. Their legs were still touching under the bubbly water, and Eric's hand moved back onto Katie's leg.

Katie raised her eyes again to meet Eric's gaze. His eyes were greener than she had ever seen them. She smiled teasingly and adjusted her position on her seat. Their legs were touching more now, as she was lined up next to him rather than facing him. Her movement had forced his hand from her thigh, but his other arm was still around her back.

"I'd say that was worth the wait," Katie said, referring to the kiss, but also alluding to what was yet to come. "I'm not usually a patient person, but I guess under the circumstances, I have no choice."

"They say patience is a virtue. I have to admit I don't have much of it myself."

"Then this will be a good learning experience for both of us." Katie smirked.

Eric looked frustrated, but returned Katie's smile. He looked up at the ceiling, raised his arms and groaned to let off steam. Then he put his arm back around Katie's shoulder and gave her a quick squeeze.

"Tell me, Katie. Where exactly is Glens Falls?"

"Glens Falls is north of Albany, about an hour," she told him, impressed that he'd remembered the name of her hometown.

"How far is that from New York City?"

"It's about three hours, depending how you're traveling. It's a nice place to live, quaint, historic. It was a good place to grow up, not too big, but not too small either, busier in the summer months when vacationers come up to Lake George, but not far from skiing country in the winter."

"Do you come from a big family?"

"No, actually, I'm an only child. How about you?" Katie asked, before she was forced to go into the story of her father.

"I have two sisters and two brothers."

"Wow. That's a big family. Are your siblings older or younger?"

"My sisters are older, and my brothers are younger. I'm the middle child."

"Ah. I've heard about middle children. They are trouble makers, right?"

"No more so than only children," he laughed.

"Only children are independent and self-sufficient," Katie informed him.

"So are middle children. At least I am. I had to be, once my brothers came along. My mother was busy with them, and my sisters weren't interested in helping me with my homework, or playing with me. My father had to work mega hours to support all of us, so I didn't see a whole lot of him. I think I've done well for myself. But my family is a great supporting force. They're always there for me. We all live in the area, so we stay in touch. My youngest brother is the farthest away at college, about two hours away. We still get together over the holidays, and usually have big family dinners. I love having siblings, especially now that we're adults. I don't know how you got along being an only child."

"I had to take responsibility for every broken vase in the house, I'll tell you that."

Eric laughed.

"It wasn't that bad, really. I always wanted a sister, but I kind of liked being the only one, too." She figured she might as well get into the father issue. "Plus, it was just me and my mother. My father took off when I was a kid, and my mother never remarried."

"Oh, I'm sorry."

"It's OK," Katie said and touched his arm reassuringly. "I never felt like I missed out on anything. I have a great relationship with my mom, and I had a lot of girlfriends."

"And boyfriends?"

"Some," Katie smiled.

"What was the most serious relationship you've had? Ever been engaged or anything like that?"

"You're getting right into the tough questions," Katie commented.

"I have to."

"I understand. I have nothing to hide. I haven't had any relationships as serious as engagement, or even living together. I date about once a month now, I'd say. I haven't met anyone that I've wanted a serious relationship with."

"Do you think you're afraid of relationships because of your father taking off?" Eric read her like a book.

"I don't think so," Katie began, considering the question. "It's not like I haven't wanted a relationship. I just haven't met the right person. What about you? How have your past relationships been?"

"I've had a couple of long relationships, but never to the point of engagement, or even considering it."

"How long is long?"

"Well, I went out with the same girl for three years of high school. And I went out with a girl in college for about a year-and-a-half."

"And the topic of marriage never came up?"

"It came up, all right. It was never me bringing it up, though!"

Katie laughed with Eric.

"And now you feel you're ready for a commitment?" Katie asked.

"I am at that point in my life, yes. If I met the right person, I would be ready to commit."

"That's how I feel, too," Katie agreed. "I don't go through life meeting guys and hoping they're 'the one.' I believe things will happen for me when the time is right. I'm ready to settle down and think about marriage, and having a family, but I'm not desperately seeking it out. I don't feel my biological clock is ticking, or anything like that. I'm open to the idea, with the right person. Do you know what I mean?"

"I do," Eric assured her. "I know exactly what you mean."

"Good," Katie smiled.

"We should probably get back to Lois and Madison."

"If we must ..." Katie agreed wistfully.

Eric leaned in and kissed her. "I'm glad we got a few minutes alone," he said.

"Me, too," Katie said, and kissed Eric again. His lips were every bit as soft as she had imagined.

"I don't want to go," he said.

Katie smiled and stared into his green eyes. He wanted more. Good. Her strategy was working perfectly. She had to leave him wanting more. If that meant leaving herself wanting more also, it was a price she had to pay.

Eric kissed her again, and they both moved to get up. The Jacuzzi continued bubbling tauntingly, as they climbed out and grabbed towels. The last thing Katie wanted to do was meet up with Lois and Madison. She probably looked flushed and flustered. She could handle slowing things down with Eric for the moment, but she didn't feel like jumping back into the multiple-woman date.

Fortunately, Lois and Madison had gone for manicures and pedicures, and they weren't done yet. Eric and Katie sat at the refreshment bar to wait. The delay made it easier to make the transition back to group date. They had time to cool off.

Katie loved her time with Eric, but had to admit to feeling a little jealous she wasn't getting a manicure and pedicure. Her nails were beginning to look shabby, between the chipped polish and obvious need for a fill. Shabby nails aside, Katie felt she had capitalized on her time alone with Eric.

Katie and Eric chatted and sipped refreshing mimosas. Lois and Madison came along shortly. Lois looked relieved to be back with the group. Madison was probably starting to get on her nerves.

Katie pretended to be surprised and happy to see them, as though this were a chance meeting. Lois pulled up a chair. Madison ignored her and made a straight shot to Eric. She shoved her hands in his face and wiggled her fingers.

"Aren't they beautiful?" she forced Eric to take note. She hadn't been in the room ten seconds and already reclaimed her position as the center of attention.

"Nice," he said and smiled politely.

"And my toes match!"

From Eric's expression, he clearly did not share her enthusiasm. He leaned back slightly from the table as a precaution in case she stuck her feet in his face.

Madison did extend her leg toward Eric to show him her toenails, but stopped short from shoving her foot in his face. Her toenails were bright red to match her fingernails, and could have been seen from across the room.

Eric gave Madison the compliment she was fishing for.

"Let's see yours, Lois," Katie said, even though she couldn't care less about Lois's manicure and pedicure. She merely wanted to put Madison back in her place. Lois showed the other her fingernails. They were a tacky iridescent purplish-pink.

"That's a pretty color," Katie gushed.

"Thank you," said Lois. Madison ignored them. In fact, Madison ignored them for the remainder of the date. Katie was relieved she'd gotten some time alone with Eric in the hot tub. Poor Lois had barely gotten a glance all day.

They went for facials next, and called it a day at the spa. Eric decided he was hungry on the way home, and they stopped for pizza. It seemed spontaneous, but he had to have cleared it with the crew first. The cameras weren't disheveled at all and were evidently expecting the stop.

By that point, Katie wanted the date to be over. Madison was looping her arm around Eric's and dominating the conversation. Katie tried to keep her and Lois involved, but Madison continued cutting them out. Eric seemed a little embarrassed, but did nothing to put Madison in her place. He indulged in all the attention Madison was giving him.

Much to their surprise, the date wasn't over after the pizza. Eric took them to a Dodgers game. Since the women had proven their athletic abilities, it was only fitting to spend some time together at an athletic event. Katie and Lois were able to regain control of the date. They sat on either side of Eric and showed him how true fans behave. They drank large draft beers, hooted and hollered, ate whole salted peanuts, spitting and dropping the shells all over the ground around them.

Madison sat and sulked. After the sixth inning, Madison came back from the bathroom and claimed she had a stomachache, putting an end to the date. They walked back to the limo. Katie got in first, purposely positioning herself away from the door. Lois was next, followed by Madison and Eric. That meant Madison was next to Eric, but also closest to the door, which meant she would have to be the first one out, and Katie would be the last, giving her a few seconds alone with Eric. When they got back to the mansion, Eric gave them each a hug and thanked them for a great day. Katie made sure to hold eye contact for several long seconds. She smiled mischievously at him.

"I'm looking forward to next time," she said and winked.

Eric grinned back, his eyes turning greener. He leaned over and kissed her, which was more than the other girls got. The other girls were waiting outside the limo for her, so she didn't delay too long. She backed out of the limo and kept her eyes on Eric the whole time.

"Goodbye, Eric."

"Goodbye, Katie," he responded, his eyes longing for her not to leave.

She turned her back to him. She definitely left him wanting more …

Chapter Eleven

Katie, Lois and Madison were immediately grilled for details by the other girls. There wasn't much to tell, as far as Lois and Madison were concerned. Katie played down her experience in the hot tub. The other girls couldn't believe how boring it sounded. They assured the others it was a boring date, but Eric had been a perfect gentleman. It was a daytime date, which was much more casual and friendly than a night-time date. Besides, Madison had cut the date short with her upset stomach; who knows what else may have been in store for them.

The other girls left them alone and returned to what they were doing. Their curiosity wasn't exactly satisfied, but apparently no further details were forthcoming. Katie divulged all the intimate details to Tina in private, later in their room.

The next morning, the other group date commenced. Ann Marie, Brittany, Kristin, Tina and Valerie were picked up by the *Soulmates* limo at eleven. The destination had not been revealed to them, which left the other five women at the mansion to speculate.

Katie and Lois were not interested in spending another day with Madison and were prepared to ditch her at the first possible moment. The chance materialized after lunch. Madison announced she was going to swim and find a shady spot by the pool. She wasn't risking getting another sunburn, but didn't want to be cooped up inside either.

Lois excused herself to go upstairs and change. Katie bowed out, feigning a headache; she voiced her intentions of going upstairs to take a nap. Jenny and Samantha didn't question her. They went upstairs and changed into swimsuits and met Madison by the pool. Lois didn't frankly care if they questioned why she wasn't showing up right away.

Katie stayed in her room half an hour to be sure no videographer was lurking outside her door. She could see from her window that one videographer was definitely at the pool. She was almost certain the other was, too.

One of them was definitely assigned to Jenny for the day, since her single date was to take place that evening, while the other was evidently assigned to the rest of them. However, he seemed to have taken a liking to Madison. Katie would bet he was following around his favorite little diva.

She slipped into the hall and looked around. All was silent. She went upstairs to Lois suite and tapped on the door. Lois opened it promptly and let her in.

"What's going on?" Lois greeted her.

"Not much. My head feels better now. I think I just needed a few minutes of peace and quiet."

"Tell me about it. My ears were ringing all night."

"I don't think I can stand another day with Madison."

"I know I can't," Lois grunted. "Unfortunately, Eric seems to like her."

"Do you think so? I got the impression he was just being polite."

"No, he likes her. I don't know what it is, but guys seem to be attracted to girls that other girls hate. Madison made sure she was the center of attention all day, and Eric ate it up. I felt like we weren't even there most of the time. But at least you got some time alone with him."

"I know. I was glad of that. Otherwise I would feel exactly like you do right now. I don't know what he would see in Madison. Zeb's the only man around here who doesn't seem totally intoxicated by her, but he's probably gay."

"Definitely," Lois snorted. "Zeb. What kind of name is that anyway?"

"Nickname. Short for Zebonowicz. I have no idea what his first name is."

"I'm probably being eliminated," Lois said, ignoring Katie's explanation of Zeb's name. "Eric didn't seem to have any interest in me whatsoever."

"You can't be too sure with Eric," Katie said, but was thinking how predictable he was most of the time.

"I'm pretty sure," Lois said. "I say fuck it. I'm partying it up for two days. You want a cigarette?"

"No, thanks."

Lois lit up. Katie noticed she was using a water glass for an ashtray. From the looks of it, she'd been smoking in her room right along. Katie hoped if Lois did get eliminated, the room didn't reek of smoke after she departed. Katie had grown up with smoke-filled rooms and closets of clothes reeking of smoke due to her mother's nasty habit. All the remaining girls would have a chance at moving into the suite, if Lois was kicked off the show. Katie for one, didn't particularly want to move into a smoky suite.

"I'll tell you something," Lois was saying. "I love this suite, but I'll be damned if I'm going to hide up here all day. Madison can bite me."

"We should just go outside," Katie reasoned. "Madison's undoubtedly sitting under an umbrella. We can sit in the sun, as far away from her as possible. Maybe she fell asleep again."

"I guess ..." Lois said noncommittally.

"Come on. We'll fix some drinks first."

"That sounds good," Lois said, but sat still and sucked on her cigarette.

"You're the one who said you wanted to party."

"That's true. Plus, if I have a good buzz by dinner I might tell little Miss Madison to go fuck herself!"

"That's the spirit! Let's go."

Katie was grateful Lois put out the cigarette. They headed down to the bar and had two drinks before heading outside, bringing a third drink along with them. They walked along the far edge of the pool, opposite where Madison was lounging under an umbrella. She appeared to be reading a paperback novel, one of those seedy romances judging by the half-dressed woman on the cover wrapping herself around the bare, muscular leg of her want-to-be lover. Madison wasn't turning any pages, so she may just have been asleep. Her eyes were hidden behind sunglasses, so it was hard to tell. She made no notice of Katie and Lois, at any rate.

Jenny had already gone inside to get ready for her date.

"Hi, ladies," Samantha greeted them, as she walked by. "I was just going to take a walk. Would you like to join me?"

"I think we're going to get some sun," Lois answered for the both of them.

"Thanks anyway," Katie added with a wave.

Katie wasn't exactly thrilled to spend the afternoon with Lois – especially when she lit cigarette after cigarette – but she really didn't foresee Samantha being any better company than Lois. Samantha was nice, but rather boring. Lois was anything but boring. She might qualify as tactless, loud and bluntly outspoken, but she certainly was not boring. Katie found her quite entertaining, actually. Katie liked the fact that Lois didn't pretend to be something she wasn't. Lois was Lois, take her or leave her, and Lois didn't seem to care which.

Katie didn't particularly care what the other girls thought of her either, but she did want to be the same Katie whether in Eric's presence or just in the girls' presence. She didn't want to be perceived as fake, or having multiple personalities. In that respect, she and Lois were alike. It was probably the single similarity they shared, other than their distaste for Madison.

After a couple of hours of soaking up the sun and conversing with Lois, Katie was ready for a break. The cigarette smoke, although not as stifling as it had been inside, was killing her. She opted to go for a dip, which was the most diplomatic way of getting away from Lois. She swam for about ten minutes before Lois called out to her to ask if she wanted another drink.

"Sure, if you're going."

"I'm going. I'm ready."

Lois headed off to the mansion, while Katie swam a few laps and enjoyed having the pool to herself. When Lois returned, she was accompanied by Ann Marie, Brittany and Tina, who had returned from their date. Katie climbed out of the pool and met them, accepting her drink from Lois.

"Thanks, Lois."

"No problem. I'm glad I went in. These guys were inside getting grilled by Jenny and Samantha for details."

"Do tell," Katie insisted.

"Yes, do tell," agreed Madison, who had suddenly joined them from behind. Lois spun around and gave Madison a dirty look.

"Share and share alike, Madison," Tina compromised diplomatically. "You didn't give up many details of your date yesterday."

"What do you want to know?"

"I don't want to know anything, now. Katie already filled me in."

"Hey, Madison," Lois interjected. "Eric should be here any time to pick up Jenny. If you hurry, you might catch him."

"Why aren't you running in there, then?" Madison demanded.

"Eric already saw me in a bikini yesterday," Katie answered nonchalantly.

Madison's face said it all. She realized Eric had not yet seen her in a bathing suit, and he was due at the mansion any minute. She wasn't giving up an opportunity to draw attention to herself.

"Yeah, you didn't give up any details to me, Katie. I want to hear everything when I get back," said Madison.

"You were there!" cried Katie.

"You know what I mean," Madison called over her shoulder, as she scurried inside.

"Yeah, Katie," said Ann Marie playfully, but with a hint of bitterness. "How did Eric happen to see you in a bathing suit, but not Madison?"

"He and I went in the Jacuzzi at the spa," Katie answered casually. The other girls were listening attentively, but had not picked up on Ann Marie's change in tone. In fact, Ann Marie was still smiling at her. She wouldn't have picked up on it either had she not known Ann Marie so well.

"Eric asked Katie to go in the Jacuzzi alone with him, because he already had a single date with me and

133

Madison," Lois explained on Katie's behalf. "He wanted to be fair."

"That's fair," Brittany agreed. "So, how was he?"

"Nothing happened," Katie insisted. "We just kissed, and you already know what that is like."

"You passed up an ideal opportunity," Brittany said.

"Not exactly ideal. The cameras were in there," Katie pointed out.

"So, what?" Brittany retorted. "As Barbara has said many times, *Soulmates* is not rated X. They would have edited it out."

"You are sick," Tina spoke up.

"I'm not sick. I go after what I want. If you don't that's your loss."

"I don't think this is an appropriate setting for sex," Tina argued, and Katie and Lois nodded in agreement.

Brittany shrugged.

"I could see if you were the only one he was interested in," Ann Marie reasoned. "I mean, I would sleep with him if I was sure he was the one for me."

"And what if seven girls think he's the one?" Lois demanded. "Do you really think he would commit to one if he could sleep with seven?"

"Exactly," said Tina. "I wouldn't sleep with him even if I were in the final two. And I don't respect any woman who would."

"Be prepared to lose respect for a few women …" Brittany commented.

"You try on shoes before you buy them," Ann Marie added.

"So, sleep with him after the show is over," Tina offered, "if you're the one he wants. By all means, sleep with him before you marry him. I'm just saying this is not the appropriate time. I didn't come here expecting a free-for-all sleeping with the *Soulmate*, so he can choose who is the best in bed. And Brittany, I have nothing personal against you, but I don't want to sleep with any man you've been with."

"None of us want seconds," Katie agreed, "to anyone here."

"Then be first," Brittany argued.

"That's not the point!" Tina stated firmly. "No one should be sleeping with him. That's not why we're here."

"Sex might not be the driving factor, but it happens," Ann Marie said. "Eric is a guy. He'll take it all if he can get it."

"And there are plenty of women here who would give it to him," Brittany said. "If you want to uphold your morals, be my guest. But don't expect to be around much longer."

"Do you really believe you have to be promiscuous to avoid elimination?" asked Tina, a look of disbelief on her face.

"I believe you have to be competitive," Brittany replied. "You have to be willing to do what it takes. Obviously sleeping with him doesn't guarantee you won't be eliminated."

"It guarantees humiliation when you are eliminated," Tina rebuffed.

"I'll drink to that!" Lois laughed loudly. She and Katie knocked their glasses together. Their drinks spilled over the edges, but they didn't care, if they even noticed.

"How long have you two been drinking, anyway?" asked Tina, with a look of amusement.

"I don't know, two o'clock or so," Katie answered.

"That's five hours ago."

"It was closer to three o'clock," Lois spoke up, waving her hand as a dismissal.

"Maybe we should go in to dinner," Tina suggested.

The girls filed back to the mansion's dining room. The buffet was already set up, and Valerie and Samantha were filling their plates. As they greeted each other, Kristin came in.

"What happened?" Valerie asked as she took a seat at the table, noticing the disturbed look on Kristin's face. Samantha took the seat next to her, and Kristin plopped herself down in a chair across the table from them.

"She is such a conniving little bitch," Kristin spat.

All the girls at the buffet stopped spooning food on their plates and turned to listen.

"We realize that," Valerie prompted. "Where is she now?"

"She went up to her room for something," Kristin answered.

"Probably to watch Eric drive away from her window," Lois said with a snort.

"She can't. She faces the back, remember? She had a fit over it on Sunday."

"I must have missed that one," Lois said.

"That's one disadvantage of having your own private, heavenly suite," Brittany said sarcastically. "You miss out on all the bedtime conversations."

"So, what happened?" Valerie prodded. "Did you see Eric?"

"Of course. Madison and Jenny practically knocked each other over trying to get to the front door. Jenny wanted to answer the door because – hello – it was her date. Madison just can't stand to have the attention on someone else."

"Don't we know it," Katie said to Lois.

"No shit," Lois was saying at the same time.

"The only reason I lagged behind," Kristin continued, "was because I knew Madison was going to try to screw up Jenny's date. I think she actually expected Eric to invite her along."

"Pathetic," Brittany said, and turned back to the buffet. Katie was beginning to think Brittany said half of what she did for the simple pleasure of getting a rise out of the others. No one took the bait this time.

"She butted herself right between Eric and Jenny," Kristin went on. "She latched herself onto his arm and led him into the sitting room. Then she saw I was in there, and she spun him around to the opposite end of the room. Well, I looked at Jenny, and she looked at me, and we followed her to the other end of the room and sat right down with them."

"Good for you," Valerie commended her.

"She was practically sitting on his lap. She kept touching his knee and rolling her hair like she does." Kristin demonstrated the hair roll. "And poor Jenny wanted to leave. She didn't want to sit there and watch the bride of Frankenstein mooch all over her date."

"Was she upset?" Samantha asked with concern.

"I'm sure she was, but you know Jenny. She doesn't have a mean bone in her body. She just sat there politely and waited. Well, I wasn't so polite. After a few minutes of that bullshit, I stood up and started wishing them a good time on their date. Jenny took the hint and stood up, and Eric went right along with her. And Madison was running behind them all the way to the door. I swear, she was about to invite herself on the date."

"What does he see in her?" Valerie asked. "She is nothing like the rest of us. She acts about ten years younger than anyone here."

"I don't get it either," Kristin agreed. "He only sees what he wants to see. And let me tell you, the second he left, she turned on me."

"She did?" Valerie was surprised.

"Oh, she lit into me. She wanted to know what I was doing there, and ranted and raved about how I was trying to sabotage her."

"Sabotage her?" Valerie repeated in disbelief. "What were you doing to sabotage her?"

"I'll tell you what she's doing," replied Madison angrily from the doorway. "She's trying to turn the rest of you against me. She's so jealous that Eric and I might have a future, she'll do anything to make me look bad."

"You do that fine on your own," Kristin retorted.

"You go out of your way to be mean to me, and you know it. You feel so threatened by me, you do everything you can to put me down."

"Oh, and I suppose the sunburn was all my fault, too," Kristin demanded.

"You could have woken me up!" Madison cried. "And now you're sitting here having a conversation behind my back."

"You were trying to have a conversation with Eric behind everyone else's back. Did you think he was going to tell Jenny forget it and go out with you instead?"

"No, I didn't. I didn't expect him to. That's not why I was there."

"Why were you there?" Kristin asked pointedly.

"Why were you there?" Madison shot back.

"I don't have to answer to you. I can go anywhere in this house I please."

"Whatever, Kristin. You know as well as I do, you were there to come between me and Eric. Like I said, you're trying to sabotage me."

"And you were trying to come between Jenny and Eric. So, you're right. I was there to stop your effort to ruin Jenny's date."

"You're trying to ruin my night, and it's not going to work. I'm not hiding in my room from you. I'm going to eat my dinner now, and I suggest you stay away from me."

Kristin burst out laughing.

"Go ahead and eat, if you can find anything you're not allergic to. I'm not leaving. Like I said, I can go anywhere in this house I please."

"Whatever," Madison said again and headed for the buffet. Her hands were shaking as she picked up a plate. The other girls at the buffet quickly turned away and resumed filling their plates.

Dinner was awkward, to say the least. The table was broken into groups of separate conversations. Katie sat with Tina and Lois. Katie and Lois ate heartily, but also downed a few more drinks with dinner. Brittany sat next to Kristin and joined in a less-heated discussion with Samantha and Valerie. Madison tried to make small talk with Ann Marie. Madison took her time eating, purposely staying at the table longer than Kristin. Kristin, who opted not to eat, went outside to "make a phone call."

"I apologize for having that conversation in front of you," Madison said for everyone to hear. "I just felt as though I had to expose Kristin for what she really is."

Brittany opened her mouth to speak, but changed her mind. No one said anything.

"I'm sorry if I ruined anyone's dinner," Madison paused as though waiting for someone to insist she hadn't.

"The only thing upsetting my dinner is that my drink keeps running out!" Lois said loudly, beginning to show signs of intoxication.

"I'll fill you up," Ann Marie offered, probably more so to get away from Madison than to be nice to Lois. She picked up Lois's glass. "Come help me, Katie."

Katie didn't want to miss anything, but she followed Ann Marie to the bar.

"We need to talk," Ann Marie said under her breath.

"Bathroom," said Katie, then hiccupped loudly. "Don't tell me Kristin's rubbing off on me! She gave me the hiccups!"

"The booze gave you the hiccups."

"So, I had a few drinks today. You're a fine one to talk."

"Shhh," Ann Marie hissed and grabbed Katie's arm, pulling her quickly to the ladies' room.

"What is wrong with you?" Katie asked when they were safely inside.

"Shhh. I don't want any cameramen lurking outside the door listening."

"All right, but I really do have to pee," Katie giggled and entered a stall.

"That's fine," Ann Marie said with a touch of sarcasm that was completely wasted on Katie in her inebriated state.

Katie used the bathroom and came out to wash her hands. "OK. What's up?"

"I really wish you weren't drunk right now. This is serious."

"I'm not drunk!"

"Shhh!"

"All right, all right," Katie lowered her voice. "What is so important?"

"I need to talk to you about Eric."

"What about him" Katie asked flippantly as she fingered her hair into a neater state.

"I need to know how you feel about him."

"I feel good. We made out in the Jacuzzi yesterday, and he was hot for me. If things were different, I would have jumped him."

"Hormones aside, how do you feel about him, emotionally?"

"I like him. I'm hoping to stick around, and see what develops."

"Well, I'm asking you not to."

"What?" Katie stopped fussing with her hair and stared at Ann Marie.

"I had a really great time with him today, and I think we might have something. Remember when we started all this, we discussed what we would do if one of us really liked him? I'm telling you, I am truly beginning to have feelings for Eric, and I'm asking you to back off."

"I'm not backing off. He likes me, too. Maybe I have a chance with him."

"You can't possibly like him. He's not even your type, remember? You've said so since day one. But he is my type, and we really hit it off today. I'm asking you, as we agreed, to back off."

"You can't ask me to back off, and not the others. If you are so sure about him, why aren't you asking Madison and Jenny and Samantha to back off? He likes them too, you know."

"I'm asking you, as my friend – my best friend – to back off."

"Ann Marie, this is not some singles' club where you and I both want to hook up with the same guy. This is a contest to win this guy's heart. You're the one that talked me into doing this, and I'm doing it. I'm not giving up now."

"Yes, I talked you into doing this, and I'm glad you're here with me. But we agreed if one of us started to have feelings for the guy, the other one would back off."

"And what if we both have feelings for him?"

"But you don't, Katie! You don't have feelings for him. If you had met Eric on the street, you would have kept walking."

"Maybe, maybe not. But now that I've gotten to know him, I don't feel that way."

"You can't feel the way I do."

"You don't know how I feel," Katie spat.

"No," Ann Marie conceded, "but I know how I feel. And I know you are not right for Eric. Deep down, I think you know it, too. Please don't let your pride get in the way. I know you have a competitive spirit when it comes to me. You want to beat me at this for your own ego. I understand that about you. You're still my friend, though. If you keep up this charade of 'trying to win Eric's heart' you are just going to get hurt."

"That's my decision."

"I know it's your decision, and I hope you can take a step back and look at the whole picture. Eric is not the one for you. You know that. But he might be the one for me. In your effort to beat me at this game you're playing, you could be robbing me of my one chance at happiness in this lifetime."

"Are you serious? You could be robbing me of the same thing," Katie pointed out. "That's why I'm saying let Eric decide."

"I shouldn't have bothered trying to talk to you when you're drunk."

"I am not drunk!"

"This isn't a game, Katie. This is our lives. I'm begging you, if you are my friend, you will step aside."

"I'm not stepping aside. You won't see any of the others stepping aside."

"But what if I am the one who is supposed to be with Eric?"

"If you and Eric are meant to be together, then Eric will choose you. I'm not stepping aside. You made me quit my job and come here. Now I'm here and I'm sticking it out."

"I didn't make you quit your job. Besides, you got your bonus. You already got what you came for. You can go home and face your mother, and you can get another job. You know damn well you don't want Eric. You just don't want me to have him."

"That's crap."

"No, it isn't. You are so jealous that I might end up happy, while you'll still be alone. When will you stop letting your jealousy come between us? We're supposed to be friends."

"Jealous?" Katie's voice escalated. "Why the hell would I be jealous of you?"

"You shouldn't be. That's my point. But you are. You've always been jealous of me. You can't stand the fact that I have a real family. I have a father who loves me; I have brothers and sisters. I'm pursuing the career you gave up, because you couldn't handle the pressure. And now, I have a chance at a future with a great guy, and you are so insanely jealous, you can't stand the fact that I could have a husband and a family of my own, while you have nothing."

"Did you dream up that ego overnight? I'm not jealous of you now, and I never have been! And I wouldn't say I have nothing. If you really think that's who I am, I don't know why we were friends in the first place. If you think you and Eric have a future, go for it! But don't ask me to back off," Katie said and headed for the door. As she pulled in open a videographer zoomed in. She had no idea how much the camera had picked up through the door, or how long it had even been out there. She turned back to Ann Marie, and spoke with exaggerated annunciation.

"Game on," she said.

"It's not a game!" Ann Marie yelled and slammed the door.

Katie strode past the videographer, who followed her closely. She pretended not to notice and went about her business, fixing drinks for herself and Lois before rejoining the other girls in the dining room.

"What took you so long?" Lois slurred, accepting her drink from Katie.

"I got side-tracked. Did I miss anything?" she asked, noting Madison's absence.

"She got sick of being ignored and took off."

"You didn't say anything to her?"

"I didn't have to. I think she knows no one likes her."

"Where's Ann Marie?" Tina asked.

"She's in the can," answered Katie.

"She's been gone a long time," Tina commented.

"Maybe she's taking a crap. I don't know. Hey, I lost my hiccups! I'm also losing my buss. Come on, Lois. Let's do shots."

"Now you're talking!" Lois cried and stood up, rather unsteadily. "I told you I wanted to party!"

"Yes, you did!" Katie confirmed and followed Lois to the bar.

Chapter Twelve

Katie slept until noon the next day. She was the only one who wasn't downstairs when Eric came to pick up Samantha for their date. Even Lois had gotten up. Katie didn't care; she didn't need to fawn all over Eric like the others, and she certainly didn't need Eric to see her hungover. She looked as bad as she felt. She had to get herself together by elimination time.

She spent the day nursing her hangover and avoiding Ann Marie. Every time she thought about their argument, her head pounded harder. She couldn't stop thinking about it, no matter how hard she tried. She kept thinking of things she should have said, and remembering things Ann Marie said that bothered her. How could Ann Marie, after all these years, accuse Katie of being jealous?

She was relieved when Tina came up to get ready for the elimination. She needed to talk this out with a neutral party. She didn't think she had been in the wrong, but she wanted someone else's opinion.

"How are you feeling?" Tina asked.

"I'm better, thanks. I think I'll be presentable for the elimination."

"I should hope so. You've been up here all day."

"I didn't feel like socializing. And I didn't feel like dealing with Ann Marie. I'm sure you heard, we had a big fight last night."

"I heard. What was that all about?"

"Eric, actually."

"I'm not surprised. I know you had a good time with him the other day, and Ann Marie is obviously smitten with him. It's not unusual for a man to come between friends."

"I know. We talked about this before we even came on the show. I was concerned what would happen if we both ended up liking the guy, but it didn't seem very likely. We've always had different taste in guys, so we've never ended up liking the same guy before."

"You've never been put in this situation before," Tina pointed out. "There's only one guy."

"True. And I'll be honest with you, Eric is not the type of guy I would typically date. But I do like him, so far. And I want to get to know him better just to see what happens. The whole point of this show is to find true love. I'm not sure if Eric is my true love or not, but I'm not giving up now. Ann Marie asked me to back off last night."

"What does she want you to do? Quit?"

"She didn't say, exactly. She just said she was beginning to have feelings for him, and as her friend, I should back off."

"So, she wants you purposely to get eliminated?"

"I guess so. We didn't get that far, because I said no way. I think it should be Eric's decision if and when I am eliminated."

"I completely agree. There are enough people around here trying to manipulate Eric's decisions, and that is plain wrong."

"I'm glad you think so. I felt like she was personally attacking me, which is totally unfair. I told her how I felt. I told her straight out that she was out of line asking me to back off and not asking the others."

"I still don't understand what she expects you to do. Does she want you to go to Barbara and tell her you want out? Does she want you to act like a jerk in front of Eric, so he kicks you off? I don't get it."

"Maybe act cold towards him, or something. I don't know. She seems to think they have something special. I told her if that's the case, Eric will choose her. Maybe I'm being selfish, but I can't make myself give up. What if he and I have something special, and I throw it all away?"

"You're not being selfish, Katie. You are here to discover if Eric is your true love, and you owe it to yourself – and to Eric – to stick it out. And you're right. If he likes her, he'll pick her, and if he wants you, he will pick you. And if he wants someone else, he will pick someone else. You and Ann Marie will have to live with Eric's decision, no matter who ends up with him. It's too bad your friendship is suffering because of this."

"That's why I'm doubting myself. I keep thinking a guy isn't worth ruining our friendship over, but Ann Marie obviously doesn't agree. She said some pretty hurtful things last night. Now I'm wondering how we stayed friends all these years. She thinks I'm jealous of her, and the only reason I won't back off is my own ego. She said I don't want Eric, I just don't want her to have him. I'm not jealous of her, or anyone else here. I've told you many times, if you end up with Eric, I'll be happy for you."

"I'm not going to end up with Eric, girl. We both know that."

"You don't know that."

"Yes, I do. And I'm OK with that. There is no spark between us. He's a great guy, but I don't see it happening."

"But if you did, theoretically, I would be happy for you, Tina. I'd wish you and Eric the best of luck and move on. I wouldn't be mad and I wouldn't hate you because of it."

"What if Ann Marie ends up with him? Would you be mad or hate her?"

"I would now, after the fight we had! I told her last night 'game on' and I meant it. I'm pulling out all the stops. I will never let Ann Marie have Eric."

"Just be careful, whatever you do. I agree with you that Ann Marie was out of line asking you to back off. It's unusual that you two were friends before the show, and that you've both come this far. She never could have gotten away with approaching any of the rest of us and asking one of us to back off. But now that you aren't allies any more, you need to watch your back. Be careful what you say to the others, on camera and off."

"I won't be talking to the others. You're the only one I've talked to about anything personal."

"I'm not going to be here any more …"

"Tina, don't say that."

"I'm being realistic, girl. I'm not going to be able to watch your back any more."

"You don't know that for sure."

"I'm pretty sure."

"But I need you!"

"I know, and I'm sorry! I would love to stay and be here to support you. But the truth of the matter is Eric and I have no future. There are enough women here trying to manipulate his feelings. I can't come on to him just to get a bid into the next round. Now, give me a hug and let's get ready to go downstairs."

Katie embraced her friend.

"I'm going to miss you, if you do go," Katie said.

"I'll miss you, too," Tina said and patted Katie's back. "You've got my numbers, and my email address. You keep in touch."

"I will."

"OK." Tina nodded. "Now go doll yourself up, girlfriend. You want to look hot for the cameras."

Katie did as she was told. She hoped Tina was wrong about being eliminated, but she had a sinking feeling she was losing her roommate.

She took care getting ready. She felt like wearing black, but decided to go with a pink dress for something different. It was soft and clingy, subtle yet sexy. She didn't want to dress too revealing, but she did want to remind Eric of their time in the hot tub and show him what was to come if he kept her.

She was semi-confident in her own chances of advancing to the next round. She had moments of uncertainty, but tried to maintain her confidence. She hated having feelings of insecurity, even if they were fleeting. She knew Eric had enjoyed her company the other day; she simply couldn't gauge how he felt about the other women. She wasn't privy to the intimate details of the others' dates. All the participants held back detail, the same as she had about her experience in the hot tub – except maybe Brittany, who seemed to enhance her details.

Katie could only hope, and wait. She fixed her makeup to perfection, adequately covering any signs of heavy alcohol consumption the previous day. She had trouble with her hair and was not completely satisfied with its turnout. Her hair always seemed unusually limp the day after a drinking bout. She had been sure to double-shampoo and skip the conditioner, but the results were disappointing.

Tina assured her no one would notice at all; it looked fine. Katie would be the only one who thought it looked limp, simply because it wasn't as full of body as she preferred. Katie told Tina she was probably right, and thought again how much she was going to miss her. Tina had been her rock through the majority of this affair. She had come here for Ann Marie, planning to have the time of their lives. Things hadn't turned out as planned. Sure, she was having a good time, but she and Ann Marie hadn't spent much time together at all, and now they were feuding.

She couldn't help secretly hoping Ann Marie would be eliminated tonight. She knew if they both stayed, things were only going to get worse. And if Tina left, she would have no confidant. She had nothing to look forward to, except the possibility of spending a few more days with Eric.

Katie went into the elimination filled with anxiety. She and Tina made small talk on the way downstairs. Kristin and Valerie were right behind them on the stairs, so they made no reference to their previous conversation. It was a somber descent to the front sitting room. They filed in along with the others and waited for instructions. It felt like a receiving room at funeral services. No one spoke, and the air was thick with the sickly-sweet smell of flowers and a mix of perfumes.

Shane came along shortly. Katie was thankful his cologne overpowered the other smells in the room. He looked as hungover as she felt. He smiled and hid it as best he could, welcoming them and explaining they would each have a brief interview before the elimination began. They would also get a few minutes alone with Eric, as usual, to plead their cases before he made his final decisions.

They were taken to Eric one at a time in no particular order, and took turns giving interviews in the library in the meantime. Eric was set up on the back terrace on wicker furniture among urns of flowers and twinkle lights. Any chance of having a truly private word with Eric was obliterated by the cameras.

Katie approached Eric with a smile when her turn came.

"How are you, Katie?" Eric asked as he rose to greet her. He gave her a quick kiss and hug.

"I'm great," she lied. "How have you been?"

"Great!"

"I've missed you."

"I've missed you, too," he said. "It seems like we haven't seen each other in ages."

"It does. It's like time has been slowed down, or something. I feel like we've known each other for years, and haven't seen each other for weeks."

"It does seem like we've known each other forever. I feel so comfortable with you. But time is flying by in my eyes. I can't believe I have to make another decision already."

"How are you doing with that?"

"I feel sick about it. I have to send four people home today. It's not easy breaking people's hearts. Some of the girls feel pretty strongly about me, which is scary. I mean, some of them claim to have these feelings when we barely know each other."

"Some women are looking at you as their future," Katie surmised. "They might think they're in love with you, but they're just projecting their dreams onto you. They know they want a man in their future, and they are desperately trying to mold you into that man."

"You're right. I've noticed an insincerity in certain people. But I am still having a lot of trouble sorting out which emotions are real and which are fabricated."

Katie took his hands in hers and held them in her lap.

"I can help you with one thing. I can't speak for the others, and I won't offer any opinions on them. I will tell you, sincerely, that I am interested in you. I honestly don't know at this point if we are quote-unquote *Soulmates*. I don't think we know each other well enough to determine that yet. But I am, definitely, interested in finding out. I had a great time with you the other day at the spa, at the baseball game, and especially in the Jacuzzi …" She paused and smiled sheepishly. "I would love to stay and see where things lead. I think you're a great guy and we'd have a lot of fun together."

Eric smiled at her.

"Thank you, Katie, for your honesty. I can't tell you how many lines of bull I've heard during these private talks. I will take everything you've said under consideration, I promise."

"That's all I ask," Katie said, dropping his hands and standing up. She smiled warmly at him.

Eric stood and gave Katie a nice, long hug. He squeezed as though he never wanted to let go. Then he kissed her gently. Katie prayed it wasn't the last time their lips would touch.

She returned to the group reluctantly. A few ladies had yet to see Eric, and a few had interviews to give. The others sat and chatted with a polite nervousness. Shortly, they were called to gather on the porch for the dreaded elimination.

Barbara was there, shouting orders and looking more frazzled than usual. She had an arrangement prepared for the ceremony, but ended up changing it twice before shooting began. She finally decided to stagger the ten women over all three steps, with two on the ground, one on the first step, four on the second and three on top.

Ann Marie and Brittany got the front row, and Jenny was centered between them on the first step. The three of them formed a little triangle. Katie, Kristin, Lois and Madison were spread across the next step so that all were visible between the women in the front two rows. Samantha, Tina and Valerie were centered on top, almost perfectly aligned with the bottom three.

Katie was beginning to feel weak by the time they started filming, between the remains of her hangover and the heat of the lights boring down on them. She realized for the first time that she hadn't eaten all day. She was determined to stay focused and not to pass out. That would be too embarrassing.

Amazingly, Shane nailed his speech on the first attempt and didn't ask for any retakes. He looked as though he wanted to get through the filming as quickly as possible. He went through his usual spiel, and then called for Eric.

Katie took a deep breath. She had to concentrate on breathing in order to prevent herself from passing out under the lights. Madison dropped first.

It could be no coincidence that Madison began to wither the moment Eric stepped on the set. Valerie caught her from behind and helped to lower her to a seated position on the steps. Madison had not lost consciousness. She sank down and put her head between her knees.

The set burst into activity. Barbara yelled "Cut!" and ran forward with several others to tend to Madison. Katie's knees grew weaker, and she sat down to gain her composure. Tina stepped over to Katie quickly and kneeled down beside her.

"Are you OK?"

"Yeah, it's just so hot ..." Katie's voice sounded vague in her own ears.

"Just relax. I'll get you some water."

One of the crew members had already fetched water for Madison, and Tina flagged him down.

"We need some water over here, too," Tina called authoritatively.

Barbara looked up to see who dared snap orders on her set. She gave Tina a surprisingly approving look and turned to Zeb. She barked some instructions at him, and he ran off to comply.

Madison and Katie were coming around within a few minutes. The crew was gathered around Madison, and had pushed Valerie out of their way. Valerie had joined the majority of the girls, who had gathered around Katie. Ann Marie and Brittany were the only ones who had walked away, stepping back from the stairs and the hot lights. Eric wanted to check on the girls, but Shane held him back.

"You don't want to show any partiality," Shane said.

"I was going to check on both of them," Eric retorted. "The cameras aren't even rolling."

Shane held his arm.

"Just stay back, Eric. The staff will take good care of them. We don't need you passing out, too."

Eric wiped the sweat from his brow and fidgeted uncomfortably in his tuxedo.

Zeb was back soon enough with several industrial fans. The crew went to work setting them up per Barbara's instructions. A beverage cart arrived as well, and all the ladies were encouraged to drink some juice or water.

"I don't know why they can't move us inside," Kristin complained. "Someone is going to end up with heat stroke."

Tina brought Katie some more water and helped her to stand up. Madison was struggling to her feet also.

Katie didn't believe for a minute that Madison's collapse was for real. It was clearly a cry for attention. In spite of disbelieving the validity of Madison's collapse, Katie was actually grateful to her for drawing all the attention. Katie would have been mortified if she had been the only one having the close call.

Barbara personally checked on Madison and Katie before proceeding. Once the fans were in place – creating the illusion of tropical winds – the ten ladies in contention were settled perfectly back into their places, and Barbara called for action.

"Eric will say a few words, and then we will begin eliminations," said Shane as he stepped aside to leave Eric standing alone in front of the women.

"Good evening, ladies," Eric began. "I want to thank you all for bearing with me for a moment in this heat. I just need to tell you all what a wonderful time I've had and how much I hate elimination days. I've had a chance to get to know everyone better over the last few days. Even though I know what I want in a future wife, I feel like I'm struggling letting any of you go, because each of you has admirable qualities. And I don't feel like I've seen all the qualities you possess yet. I feel bad letting four of you go without getting to know you completely. But, I have to. I just want you to know that you are all great ladies. If the circumstances were different ..." he trailed off without finishing the sentence.

"So, thank you, all of you, for taking part in this experience with me. I feel like I'm losing four great friends today, but I also know I have to say goodbye to some in order to bring me closer to my destiny.

Eric took a deep breath. He reached for the first gift from the infamous gold box. Six beautiful strands of pearls lay in waiting in the velvet-lined box. They represented a future with Eric, and they sat tauntingly in front of the ten women.

Eric withdrew the first necklace from the box and held it in his hands. He hesitated dramatically, although perhaps not intentionally.

"Samantha," he said.

Samantha smiled graciously. She didn't look surprised in the least as she moved swiftly down the porch steps and hugged Eric. He gently looped the necklace around her neck and clasped it. Samantha's hand instinctively went to her throat, fingering her new set of pearls, as she turned back to Eric.

"Thank you," she said.

"You're welcome," he answered and smiled. There was an obvious attraction between them. Their date must have gone well today.

Samantha was positively glowing as she returned to her place on the steps. The other girls eyed the pearls enviously. There were five more strands and nine empty necks.

"Jenny," Eric said.

Jenny squealed and moved her arms in a running motion as she sailed forward to receive her pearls.

"Thank you! Thank you!" she said.

"You're welcome! You're welcome!" Eric said back.

Jenny giggled and covered her mouth. She was so giddy that she appeared to be drunk. Katie hadn't seen Jenny drinking before the shoot, but she hadn't been around the others all day. Just because they didn't have a social hour before eliminations didn't mean Jenny hadn't indulged earlier. Although Katie didn't know why Jenny would have felt the need to get drunk. Jenny was on everyone's sure-pick list. She didn't have any reason to worry about being eliminated. Maybe the pressure was getting to her.

Jenny returned to her spot, and Katie made a mental note: two necklaces down; four to go.

Eric slowly picked up the third necklace. He stared at it in his hands for what seemed like an eternity before raising his head to face the women once again.

"Katie."

Katie stood perfectly still for a few seconds while reality sunk in. Eric had called her name! She was safe!

She smiled and carefully stepped down, passing Ann Marie without a sideways glance. She could feel her former best friend's eyes burning into her back as she collected her pearls.

"Thank you, Eric," she said with a brilliant smile.

"You're welcome, Katie," he smiled back.

Katie accepted a quick hug from Eric, then turned to face the other women. Ann Marie's face showed no signs of jealousy or hatred, but then again it wouldn't. Ann Marie's acting skills were impeccable.

Katie knew she was smiling when she passed Ann Marie, and she didn't care. She smiled up at Tina, who was grinning back at her. Tina's smile was probably the only genuine one in the crowd.

Katie was safely back in place when Eric picked up the next necklace. She reminded herself there were only three more. She hoped one of them belonged to Tina, and not Ann Marie.

"Valerie," Eric said.

Valerie's mouth turned into a huge smile, but for once she kept it shut. She hurried forward and hugged Eric before receiving her necklace. Eric didn't seem to mind. He returned the affection, and then clasped the necklace around Valerie's neck.

"Thank you!" she said excitedly and hugged him again, also giving him a quick peck on the cheek.

"You're welcome."

Valerie turned gracefully and strode back to her place in the upper corner. She was undeniably gloating as she passed Madison. Her triumph was short-lived, because Eric called Madison's name next.

Madison went forward. She showed no signs of nearly passing out less than thirty minutes earlier, but had a radiant glow. In fact, she looked like she'd had a makeover since the last elimination. Katie hadn't noticed before, but Madison's golden hair was streaked with white-blonde highlights. Her skin was suspiciously tan, as though she'd had it sprayed; her burn couldn't possibly have tanned down so smoothly, the way it had been peeling. Her skin had transformed from splotchy and dry to perfectly bronzed. Her nails at been done at the spa the other day, so that was no mystery. The rest of the changes must have come about on Mother's Day, when Madison had left the premises. If that was the case, Katie was getting permission to leave the mansion before her next date. She needed her nails filled and repainted in the worst way, even if the spray-tan was unnecessary.

Madison got her pearls, thanked Eric profusely, and sneered at Kristin on her way back up the stairs. Kristin looked disgusted, as did Lois. Katie snuck a sideways glance at Tina behind her, who rolled her eyes.

One more string of pearls rest atop the red velvet. It signified advancement for either Ann Marie, Brittany, Kristin, Lois or Tina. Katie kept her fingers crossed for Tina but she doubted it would do any good. Tina had been certain she was going home tonight, and she had actually seemed relieved. Katie hated hoping for Brittany, Kristin or Lois over her oldest friend, but she couldn't help it. She didn't want Ann Marie there anymore. She wanted Ann Marie to skulk back home to "nothing." She was so relieved Eric had already called her name.

Eric picked up the final necklace. He turned it over in his hands and rubbed the pearls as though he were still contemplating his choice. The tension in the air was less bearable than the heat.

Finally, Eric looked up. Katie couldn't tell If he was looking at Kristin next to her, or Ann Marie in front of her. Then he broke the silence.

"Ann Marie," he said.

Katie couldn't see Ann Marie's reaction, but they all heard her exhale loudly. Then she made a whooping noise.

Katie didn't watch Ann Marie receive her necklace, but looked back at Tina. She made a little pout at her, but Tina simply smiled. She didn't appear to be upset at all, but of course, she'd been expecting this.

After Ann Marie settled back into place, Shane came forward and gave his usual pep talk to those eliminated.

"Thank you, ladies. If you did not receive a necklace tonight, I'm sorry, your journey ends here. You must say goodbye to Eric. We want to wish you the best on your own personal quest to find your *Soulmate*."

Shane proceeded to call them forward one at a time to say goodbye to Eric. Brittany was first. She didn't look disappointed in the least, but strode forward and held out her hands to Eric. She leaned forward and kissed him, then squeezed his hands.

"Goodbye, Eric. Good luck to you."

"Thank you, Brittany. The same to you."

Brittany took her leave with her pride intact. Evidently, the opportunity to have sex with Eric hadn't arisen, or if it had, she wasn't worth keeping.

Kristin approached Eric with open arms. She gave him a big hug.

"Bye, Eric. I had a great time, and I wish you nothing but the best."

"Thank you, Kristin. I appreciate it."

"Well, you're a great guy and you deserve the best," she said, and lowered her voice somewhat. "You have some great ladies here to choose from, but beware.

One of them is putting on an act for you. She is not who she pretends to be while she's around you, and if you keep your eyes open, you'll see for yourself."

"OK..." Eric said unsteadily, with a look of confusion and surprise.

"Good luck," she said, and teetered away with a smug grin.

Eric still looked dazed when Lois came forward. Lois smiled in spite of the plain disappointment on her face. At the same time, she appeared to have been expecting elimination. She gave Eric a big hug.

"Kristin already said it all," Lois said without further elaboration. "You deserve the best."

"Thank you, Lois."

Lois walked away, still looking disappointed but satisfied that she'd reinforced Kristin's comments without being derogatory herself.

Katie fought back a glimmer of guilt that the two of them could have been referring to her. She knew they meant Madison, but the way Kristin had said "putting on an act" hit too close to home. She couldn't stop thinking about it, while Tina said her goodbye to Eric.

When Tina was done wishing Eric well, she turned and waved to the girls.

"Take care! I'll miss you," she called to the group collectively.

The girls called that they'd miss her too, but no one would miss her more than Katie.

Chapter Thirteen

The Soulmates mansion was unusually quiet the next day. The six residents remaining assembled in the front sitting room to hear the agenda for the next round. The room was already set up for the shoot, and the women sat on the couches, while Shane spoke from his usual spot in front of the fireplace. He looked as though he had recovered from whatever had been ailing him yesterday.

"Good morning, Ladies, and congratulations. We have a lot to do today, so we're getting started early. I will tell you, first of all, the next elimination will take place Monday and two women will be eliminated. Eric will be seeing more of you between now and then. He will date three of you on a one-on-one basis, and the other three will have a shared date. Date number one will take place later today, but first we need to address the issue of the empty suite on the third floor."

The ladies smiled as they listened.

"As you know, Lois is no longer with us, which means the luxury suite is available. It would be a waste to leave it vacant, so we are presenting each of you with the opportunity to claim it. We will be taking a vote, and the winner will move in immediately following our meeting. To make it fair – and to make sure we're not here voting all day – you cannot vote for yourself."

The girls nodded and laughed a little.

"Go ahead and take a sheet of paper from the coffee table, and write the name of the person who you think deserves the suite most."

Kate took a slip of paper and thought for a moment. Ann Marie and Samantha were the only ones left sharing a room, so it made sense that the others would be voting for one of them. She would be damned before she'd vote for Ann Marie. She scribbled Samantha's name on the paper and looked around for somewhere to deposit it. Shane motioned her to hang on to it.

The others finished voting after giving it some thought. Shane turned toward Jenny, who was seated in the first position on the couch nearest him.

"Jenny, please show us your vote," Shane instructed. The girls looked at each other with a sudden realization that everyone was going to know for whom they'd voted.

Jenny turned her sheet over to face the camera.

"Katie," she read.

Katie's look of surprise was sincere. Madison went next. Her vote was for Ann Marie. Katie was next. She flipped her sheet over for the camera.

"Samantha," she said.

"OK," Shane recapped. "We have one vote for Katie, one vote for Ann Marie and one vote for Samantha, so far."

Valerie voted next.

"Samantha."

"Samantha has two votes," Shane updated, as though they couldn't figure it out.

Samantha held up her sheet.

"Ann Marie," she said.

"That's two for Ann Marie, two for Samantha, one for Katie, and one vote left to count. Will Ann Marie's vote create a tie, or break one?"

Shane paused, while Barbara reorganized the cameras. Undoubtedly a commercial break would air at this strategic moment. Katie was relieved to know that Ann Marie couldn't possibly win, since she couldn't vote for herself. Of course, Katie couldn't win either, but she didn't want the suite after Lois smoked in it. Barbara called for action again.

"Ann Marie," Shane said with a smug grin. "Please reveal your vote."

Ann Marie slowly turned her paper over.

"Samantha," she said.

"Oh, thank you!" Samantha was thrilled, but added quickly, "I don't want to lose you as a roommate, of course, but thank you!"

"You deserve it," Ann Marie told her.

"Samantha," Shane was saying. "Congratulations. You may begin moving when we are finished. But I must advise you to make it quick. Eric has selected you for his first single date, which will take place later today. I can't give you any details at this point; that would ruin the surprise. I can tell you formal attire is in order."

Samantha's face lit up. How could one person be so lucky? She had already gone on a single date with Eric, and he chose her again! On top of that, she got the private, luxury suite. Katie was jealous, and she didn't care if her face revealed her true feelings. The other girls wore disappointed expressions as well.

"Samantha has had a wave of good luck today," Shane continued, "but there is good news for two more of you. A total of three women will be going on single dates with Eric – one tomorrow night and one Saturday. The remaining three will have a shared date tomorrow afternoon. Eric wanted all of you to know that he is looking forward to spending time with each of you. He selected three women he felt he needed to get to know better. Are you ready to hear who Eric has selected?"

"Yes!" they answered.

"Of course," was Valerie's response.

"You seem awfully anxious. Are you sure you don't want to wait until tomorrow?" Shane teased.

"No!" they cried.

"All right, all right. I'll tell you today. Tomorrow night's date will be … Madison."

"Yeah!" Madison squealed delightedly.

"Saturday will be … Katie."

Katie smiled excitedly but refrained from screaming out like Madison.

"That leaves Jenny, Valerie and Ann Marie, who will share a date with Eric tomorrow. You three should be ready at 10:00AM. Madison's date will begin tomorrow at 7:00PM and Katie's will be 7:00PM Saturday."

"Is my suggested attire formal also?" Madison asked. The others stared at her in disbelief. She was so concerned about herself, she couldn't even wait for Shane to finish his speech.

"Details of your date will be forthcoming," Shane assured her without missing a beat, and continued. "You will all, in fact, receive personal invitations with as much detail as possible. We won't give out too much information before hand, of course. What would a *Soulmates* date be without the element of surprise?"

"So true," Valerie agreed.

The others said nothing, but smiled politely for the sake of the cameras.

Katie felt lost when she returned to her room. Tina was gone, so she had no one to talk to. Any of the other girls she had socialized with in Tina's absence were either gone or not speaking to her.

Her options for making friends was extremely limited. Samantha was busy moving into the luxury suite with the help of Ann Marie. Madison was absolutely out of the question; she couldn't handle being in the same room with Madison, let alone befriending her. No, Katie would rather die of loneliness than stoop to striking up a conversation with Madison.

That left Valerie and Jenny. Valerie was rather annoying, with her know-it-all attitude. She was personable enough but could never fill Tina's shoes. Valerie was over-confident, pretentious and self-absorbed. Katie frankly didn't trust her. She would undoubtedly use any information she could obtain against the other women. Katie had no proof of Valerie's intentions, but sensed she would do and say anything to win. Valerie seemed to be all about winning in every aspect of her life; whether she truly cared for Eric remained to be seen. Katie didn't want to get burned by Valerie. She knew she would be better off staying away from her. Let Valerie victimize one of the others.

That left Jenny as the only logical choice. Jenny had been careful to keep on neutral territory. Her roommate Riann had left early on and she hadn't made any especially close bonds with any of the others. She was friendly and polite to all of them. She wasn't catty or jealous-acting. She was probably the only one who was genuine in her actions. When Jenny gave you a compliment, she meant it. When she didn't like something, she kept her mouth shut.

Katie decided she would try to hang out with Jenny, if anyone. Her first priority was to arrange a manicure and pedicure. She figured tomorrow would be a good time to go, because Ann Marie, Jenny and Valerie would be gone on their date, leaving her alone in the house with Madison and Samantha. She couldn't bear to spend another day with Madison. She had nothing tangible against Samantha. She simply had a bad feeling about her. Anyone who acted that nice had to be acting, period. Samantha seemed too perfect. She had to have a flaw somewhere, and Katie resolved to find it. In the meantime, she wasn't allowing herself to be vulnerable to Samantha's niceties. She didn't want to be sucked in like Ann Marie obviously was. There was something about Samantha that Katie didn't like; she just couldn't put her finger on it yet.

As it turned out, Katie didn't have the opportunity to befriend anyone. She spent the day alone, arranged for her manicure and pedicure for tomorrow, brought her lunch up to her room, and took a much-needed afternoon nap. All the activity was beginning to catch up with her.

She ate dinner with the group and joined them afterwards to watch movies. She and Ann Marie were cordial towards each other in front of the others. They didn't go out of their way to speak to each other, but didn't totally ignore one another either.

When Samantha returned from her date after midnight, she was blushing and dreamy-eyed. She wasn't forthright with the details, but left no doubt that her date with Eric was fabulous. Madison said nothing, but glared enviously at Samantha. Ann Marie, for being so taken with Eric, didn't appear jealous in the least. Maybe Ann Marie wasn't in love with him after all. Maybe she wanted Katie to back off for Samantha's sake. Something was suspicious between the two former roommates, unless Ann Marie was an even better actor than Katie gave her credit for. Even Katie couldn't help donning a look of disappointment that Samantha's date had gone so well.

Valerie and Jenny had the same look on their faces. They were trying to be nice, but couldn't help feeling as though their "boyfriend" was cheating on them.

    This endeavor was a lot tougher than Katie had imagined it would be. She was glad when Samantha excused herself to go upstairs. None of them could concentrate on the rest of the movie after Samantha's interruption anyway. They stared at the screen, but had something else on their minds.

    The next day came and went quickly. Katie took a cab to a nail salon. She didn't tell the others where she was going, because she didn't want company. Madison and Samantha were the only ones in the house as it was, since the other three had already left for their date. They hadn't returned by the time the dinner buffet was set up, so Katie and Samantha were the only two at the dining table. Madison was upstairs getting ready for her 7:00PM date. Katie allowed herself to make small talk with Samantha. She told her where she had gone earlier, and they chatted about their hometowns.

    Samantha lived just outside Sarasota and worked as a customer service representative for a credit card company. Katie had never been to Florida and asked a lot of questions. She preferred hearing about Florida over talking about herself.

    After dinner, they went their separate ways. Samantha said she wanted to call her family to check in, and retired to her third-floor suite. Katie didn't blame her. Samantha could relax in privacy, make her phone calls, take a bubble bath, fix a nice drink, whatever she felt like.

    Katie decided to sit outside. She heard the others coming in from their date, but didn't wait to see them. She headed out to the pool to catch whatever rays of sunlight were left. There weren't many, so she only stayed out a short time. When she headed back inside, she found the others having drinks. Ann Marie, Jenny and Valerie were riled up from their shared date and wanted to keep the momentum going. Samantha was there too, and was giving a few more details about her date the previous night. Katie was reluctant to join them, but Valerie was insistent.

"Come on, Katie," Valerie said. "We're all friends here. Ann Marie, pour her a drink."

Ann Marie did as she was told and didn't let on she was still mad a Katie. Katie was expecting her drink to be either very strong or very weak, but Ann Marie mixed it perfectly.

"So, what happened after that?" Samantha asked, prodding the others to continue their account of the day's events.

"Eric said he wanted to spend time alone with each of us," Valerie continued smugly, "so I volunteered to go first. I'm sorry, ladies, but I felt like I really needed that time alone with Eric. I was afraid if I waited, I would lose my chance."

"We all got our chance," Jenny said sweetly, as an assurance there were no hard feelings.

"The first thing Eric hit me with was who Kristin was talking about at the last elimination."

"He asked us the same thing," Jenny added for Katie's benefit, as they had already told Samantha about Eric's mutual inquiry.

"I'll be prepared for that question tomorrow, then," Katie surmised. "What did you guys tell him?"

"I said, in my opinion, Kristin was talking about Madison, because it was no secret the two of them didn't get along," Valerie answered.

"I told him it was definitely Madison," said Ann Marie, "because she is a completely different person when she's around Eric, and I truly believe he needed to know that."

Katie wondered what details Ann Marie truly believed Eric needed to know about *her*. Ann Marie could have spilled her guts about all of Katie's past, if she'd wanted to.

"I told him I couldn't answer that," Jenny was saying. "I didn't feel it was my place to discuss any of you with Eric, and he respected that. Besides, for all I know Kristin was talking about me."

"She wasn't talking about you," Valerie laughed. "She liked you."

"Well, I'm using myself as an example. All I mean is that she could just have easily been talking about me."

"We all know who she was talking about," Valerie insisted. "But getting back to my date – I mean our date. I was a little surprised that Eric's first question to me was about someone else. I told him so, too."

"You did?" Katie interrupted.

"Of course, I did. And he apologized. He agreed we would only talk about each other for the rest of our time together."

"And did you do a lot of talking?" Jenny asked sarcastically, but with a laugh.

"No… we didn't," Valerie admitted.

"I'm telling you, Eric is playing all of us," Jenny said. "He made out with all three of us today. He must think we don't talk to each other."

"Or he doesn't care," Valerie said.

Jenny gestured at Samantha and continued, "The two of you were hot and heavy last night, and he's probably enjoying himself with Madison right now. I'm not saying I didn't enjoy my time alone with him, but I'd be naïve to think I'm the only one he wants to be more than friends with, if you know what I mean."

"I feel like my boyfriend is cheating on me," Samantha agreed.

"It feels even worse when the 'other women' are on the date with you," Ann Marie added.

"It's a major reality check," Jenny replied. "It really makes you stop and think about this whole situation. There are six of us and only one of Eric. I know how I feel when I'm with him, and he's good at making you feel like you're the only woman when you're alone with him…"

"Yes, he is," Valerie interjected.

"…but when your time with him is over, you have to remember your odds aren't that great," Jenny finished.

Katie thought about the Jacuzzi incident and wondered how it compared with the other girls' experiences. Maybe her time with him hadn't been as intimate as the others' time with him.

"Our odds keep getting better," Samantha offered optimistically.

"I don't know what to think," Valerie remarked. "I thought I had a pretty good idea of who Eric liked and who he didn't. Then he turns around and chooses Madison for one of the singe dates – again. He seems to like all six of us. I have no idea who will be going home next elimination."

"I don't want to go home yet, and I don't want to see any of you go, either," Jenny said, "but I also don't like the feeling that I'm part of a harem."

"This is definitely a lot harder than I thought it would be," Katie added.

"Let's talk about something else," Ann Marie suggested. "We all know what we're up against, as far as Eric is concerned, without rehashing the painful details of our individual time with him. Let's just enjoy our time together as five beautiful, eligible women."

"Hear, hear," Valerie raised her glass.

The girls clinked their glasses together and agreed not to talk about Eric for the rest of the evening. They did fairly well sticking to their plan. Eric's name only came up about once an hour when one of them questioned when he and Madison would return.

They had been out a long time. It was after midnight. The five women had been in and out of the hot tub and were reassembled at the bar area. They were enjoying themselves. Ann Marie was the life of the party, as usual, even though she said nothing directly to Katie all night. The other girls didn't sense any tension between the two of them; it was as though they didn't know each other. They didn't totally ignore each other, but they didn't act buddy-buddy either.

Midnight turned to one, and still no Madison. The girls were getting drunker and rowdier by the minute. It was after two-thirty when Madison finally arrived.

Eric actually walked her inside, and the girls were surprised to hear Eric's voice. They charged to the front foyer to interrupt good-bye kisses.

Madison had her arm over Eric's shoulder. He was holding her up.

"What happened to you?" Valerie asked, stepping forward to help Madison to a chair. Her foot was bandaged and she was carrying her shoes.

"I had a little accident," sighed Madison.

"We can see that. What happened?" Valerie redirected her question to Eric. His story was more likely to resemble the truth.

"We had a lovely date at the emergency room," he said. "I'll let Madison tell you all about it. It's late. I'm going to turn in."

"You don't have to leave," Ann Marie told him.

"The party was just getting started," Jenny said with a slur.

"So, I see," Eric said patronizingly. "No, really, ladies. It's been a long night. I'm beat. Madison, I hope your foot feels better."

"Thank you, Eric!" Madison gushed. "You were a doll tonight."

Eric bent and kissed Madison on the cheek.

"Good night, ladies," he said and made a fast exit.

"Good night," they cried wistfully.

The second the door shut behind him, they turned back to Madison.

"What the hell happened?" demanded Ann Marie.

"I am so clumsy!" Madison swooned, her eyes welling up with tears. "Our date had barely started. We were supposed to go out on a yacht for dinner. I took my shoes off to walk through the sand, and I didn't put them back on when we got to the dock, because I didn't want to break a heel. Don't you know, I stepped on a nail. We couldn't tell in the dark how rusty it was, and I hadn't had a tetanus shot in years, so Eric insisted on taking me to the emergency room."

"Oh, no!" Samantha cried empathetically.

"No way," was Ann Marie's response.

"I couldn't believe it!" Madison smiled through tears. "We were in the emergency room all night. We missed our dinner entirely. Eric was so sweet, though, the whole time. The hospital cafeteria was closed, so he got me all kinds of snacks out of the vending machine. Neither of us dreamed we would be there so long! We were starving when we finally got out of there. I swear, all night for a bandage and a tetanus shot. I thought I was going to need an amputation by the time they got around to looking at it."

"Let's not get carried away…" Valerie interposed.

"Of course, I'm exaggerating," Madison said, "but it was completely unacceptable servicing time. I know my injury wasn't fatal or anything, but you would think they would zip the easy cases through to make room for all the gunshot wounds."

The others started at Madison. No one knew how to react to her. She had no sense of political correctness whatsoever.

"Hey, this is LA," Madison shrugged and continued her narrative. "Eric was so wonderful through it all."

She was misty-eyed again.

"He really kept my spirits up. He was an absolute doll from start to finish. He took me through the Burger King drive-thru in the limo when we left the hospital, we were so hungry! I didn't want to hobble into a restaurant at one o'clock in the morning. Can you imagine? The kid that waited on us had this priceless look on his face, to wait on a limo at the drive-thru! I'll never forget that kid's face. Oh!" she sighed dramatically. "Our date wasn't entirely ruined, but if Eric does keep me around next elimination, it will be completely out of pity."

"A little pity can go a long way," Valerie laughed.

"I'm going up to bed now. No, no, don't get up. I don't want any help. I have to learn how to do things for myself. I might as well start now."

"There's no need to play the martyr," Ann Marie said in a sicky-sweet tone, the sarcasm completely lost on

Madison. "I'd be happy to help you up the stairs – just this once."

"OK, just this once. By tomorrow, I'm sure I'll be able to get around well enough on my own."

Ann Marie helped Madison to the stairs, looking back at the others on her way up. She made a face at them and tried not to laugh.

Valerie waited until they were out of earshot to speak.

"Move over, Miss Scarlet," she said in the best southern accent a woman from Boston can manage. "Miss Madison has arrived!"

Chapter Fourteen

Katie slept in the next day. Eric wasn't due to pick her up until seven, so she relaxed all day and pampered herself. Details of the date were forthcoming, as Shane had promised, on a formal invitation slipped under her door. The time and date was printed on the invitation, and Eric had hand-written a note underneath. It said, "please wear the black dress you had on the night we met. I'm looking forward to seeing you – Eric."

Katie had no knowledge of what the other girls' invitations were like. She was pleased hers had a hand-written note, and that Eric remembered the dress she was wearing the night they met. Seven o'clock could not come fast enough!

Katie took her time getting ready and made her way downstairs from her room at 7:03PM. Eric was already there, standing in the doorway of the sitting room and visiting with the other five women whom he'd already dated this round. He heard Katie coming and turned to watch her descent down the grand staircase. She wore the black strapless dress, as requested, with sleek black sandals. She had gotten matching French manicure and pedicure, taking a page from Brittany's book, which had turned out spectacular. She wore the strand of pearls Eric had given her the other night. Her hair was pulled up in the back, and strategically placed curls danced along the back of her neck and in front of her ears.

She felt like a princess, as she went carefully, step-by-step down the stairs to greet her prince. Eric waited in awe with a speechless smile. Several of the women peeked out of the sitting room to catch a glimpse of their competition.

"How are you, Eric?" she asked as she came off the bottom step.

"You look incredible," he said, stepping forward to take her hand. "Shall we go?"

"Positively," she said with a smile and a glance over his shoulder to the door of the sitting room. The women were gathered at the door now, struggling to see Katie and Eric's departure. "Good night, ladies!"

Katie wanted to say, "Don't wait up," but held her tongue. She didn't want to arouse any more jealousy than she already had. This was no time to create enemies. Time with Eric was critical, and some women would soon be stooping to bad-mouthing the others to sway Eric's choices in their favor.

Katie soon found out her suspicions were correct. She had to do some damage control. Eric hit her with the tough questions as soon as the limo pulled off the access road.

"I don't want you to feel like I'm bombarding you with questions," he started apologetically. "I just need some answers, and I trust you to be honest with me. And I want to get the tough part of our date over with, so we can enjoy the rest of the night."

"That's fine. I'll help you any way I can. Hit me."

Eric smiled, relieved that Katie was willing to open up to him.

"I feel like some of the girls are trying to manipulate me into choosing them, and I've heard a lot of stories this week, to say the least. I'm not the kind of person who buys into gossip. I do think you can learn a lot about people by listening to what they have to say about their adversaries. So, what I'd like to talk about, first of all, is the last elimination. Kristin was trying to tell me something about one of you six women. Do you know who she was talking about?"

"You seem very uncomfortable today, Eric," Katie said, instead of addressing his question.

"I do feel a little out of my element," Eric admitted, glancing at the camera. "If you're uncomfortable talking about this, we don't have to."

"I'm not uncomfortable talking to you about anything. In regards to your question about the elimination, I think Kristin was talking about Madison. The two of them had a few disagreements publicly, and both were vocal about their feelings toward one another. They started as roommates, and I think they got off on the wrong foot. I don't know whether there's any validity to what Kristin said, but that's how she felt about Madison."

"That's pretty much what the others thought, also. I already asked everyone that question, but I wanted to hear your opinion. I always feel like you're straightforward with me, Katie."

"I try to be. I think you would be wise to ask Madison's opinion on the matter. She deserves a chance to give her side of the story."

"I did speak with Madison yesterday. She admitted Kristin was talking about her. She told me Kristin didn't like her from the start, and that she thought all along Kristin was trying to sabotage her. I don't know what goes on in the house between you girls, but I hope things haven't come to sabotaging each other."

Katie laughed. "I think Madison tends to exaggerate. No one has tried to sabotage anyone."

"I wouldn't be too sure about that," Eric said. "Maybe sabotage isn't the right word, but there is a lot of back-stabbing going on. Some of the others have even made derogatory comments about you."

"Really? I didn't think I'd pissed anyone off," Katie answered casually, knowing full well Ann Marie was the only one she'd pissed off, as well as the only one who had any damaging information against her.

"I don't know if you pissed anyone off, but I've been forewarned you aren't completely honest."

"What have I not been honest about? Ask me anything you want to know."

"I hear you're an actress," Eric said cautiously.

"I did some acting," Katie admitted. "Remember I told you I used to live in New York City? I did a couple commercials to pay the bills. I also worked for an accounting firm. I tried bartending for a couple months, but I was too scared of the customers. Actually, I worked a lot of odd jobs back then. There's probably a lot you don't know about me yet, but I wouldn't say I've been dishonest about anything."

"No, and I didn't mean to imply I thought you were dishonest. I personally feel like you are one of the few I can trust. I just wanted to clear up some of these things the other girls brought up. When I want to know something, I go to the source."

"Good. What else do you want to know?"

"There's just one more thing, and it's kind of related to the other subject. It was mentioned to me, because you are an actress, that you don't really have any feelings toward me, you are acting …"

"Do you think it's an act?"

"No, I don't. I think it's a case of jealousy. But I want to hear it from you."

"I think you already know the truth, but if it will make you feel better, I'll tell you. I do care about you. I think you're great. I think we're great together. I'm not acting – I'm obviously not that good," Katie laughed nervously. "But you don't have to take my word for it."

She leaned over and kissed him. She started gently, brushing her lips against his. She kissed him softly several times, pulled back slightly, then leaned in for more. Their lips met more forcefully now, both of them succumbing to their desire. They moved their bodies closer and embraced. They kissed harder, tongues mingling, their mouths warm.

Katie smoothly pulled back and raised an eyebrow.

"I'm convinced," Eric said, sounding short of breath.

"Good," Katie said, and decided to put a little pressure on Eric, "because I've heard some stories about you, too."

"You have," Eric replied with obvious apprehension.

"I have," Katie repeated. She remained smiling to try to make the conversation seem lighter. She wanted to be careful about sounding jealous, but she wanted Eric to know she cared at the same time.

"Hit me," Eric said, copying Katie's phrase from earlier.

"I've heard that you have been enjoying kissing all six of us, and I was wondering if you have set limitations."

"Wow," was all Eric said. Clearly, he had not been expecting that question.

"Let me rephrase that," Katie offered to let him off the hook slightly. "I realize you have to test your physical attraction to all the remaining women. I just want you to know that I, for one, don't intend to sleep with you for the sole purpose of staving off competition. Some of the others would do just that. I don't think it would be appropriate for you to have sex with one of us unless it truly meant something to you."

"I understand," Eric said quickly, "and I do have limitations. I don't plan on sleeping around with the six of you. I'm not like that. In fact, I don't intend to sleep with any of you, but by the same token, I'm not saying it couldn't happen, either. If I find my true soulmate, the woman I'm going to marry, I don't see anything wrong with letting passion run its course."

Katie was speechless, and an awkward silence loomed heavily on the moment. She finally gained her composure and found her voice.

"That answer was more honest than I expected," she said and smiled again. "I understand."

"Good," Eric said. "Now if there are no more tough questions, would you like some champagne?"

"Champagne would be lovely," Katie smiled into Eric's eyes. "That was an easy question."

"That's all I have left is easy questions." Eric opened his arms, then reached for the bottle of champagne. It was already uncorked and chilling. He lifted the bottle out of the ice bucket and raised it to show Katie.

"They didn't want me to put out a window," he explained.

"I don't blame them," Katie laughed.

Eric grinned and poured the champagne. He handed Katie a glass and raised his to touch hers.

"To a spectacular evening alone together," he said as they clinked the glasses.

Katie kept her eyes on Eric as she sipped the champagne. She could get used to living like this, dressing up in gowns, driving around in a limo, sipping bubbly with an extremely hot guy.

"How does your typical date in Pittsburgh stack up to this?" Katie asked playfully.

"It doesn't," Eric said. "This entire experience has been incredible, sometimes too incredible. I think some of the people get so caught up in the experience, it doesn't even matter who the *Soulmate* is. I'm sure I'll go back to my boring life and be happy with simple dates again. Some of the girls have grown to expect the royal treatment, I suspect."

"No doubt," Katie said. "Not to mention living in the mansion, having all your meals catered, not having to work all day ... reality is going to hit hard for all of us soon."

"It is, and reality is going to change. I know I'm not going home the same person I was when I came here, and I hope I'm not going home alone ..."

"Would you say your goal is to meet someone and have them move to Pittsburgh?"

"That would be ideal, but I'm not against moving, either. I already own a house, which I'd have to sell, but I can do my job from anywhere."

"You would rather stay where you are, though?"

"I'd rather stay, definitely. I grew up in Pittsburgh and my family is close by. It would be a big adjustment for me to relocate, especially out-of-state."

"It would be an adjustment," Katie agreed, "but change can be good. I don't have any qualms about leaving Glens Falls, or New York State for that matter."

"So, you'd rather move?"

"I think so. I don't have anything keeping me there. I live in an apartment. I don't have a career there. The only family I have is my mother. I'd miss her, but we would visit each other. We don't usually hang out together anyway. We talk on the phone a few times a week, and we can do that from anywhere."

"I bet she'd miss you."

"She would. She's an extremely independent person, though. She's used to being on her own. It's not like we live together. I haven't been under her roof since I was eighteen, and trust me, I could never go back there."

"Why not?"

"My mother is a great person, don't get me wrong. I just don't want to live with her again."

"Aw, come on," Eric laughed. "Why not?"

"For one thing, she smokes like a chimney. For another, she's a bit of a control freak."

Eric laughed louder.

"Honestly, my mother and I are great friends. We've only had each other to depend on. Sometimes we're more like sisters."

"Do you have any other family nearby – grandparents, aunts, uncles, cousins?"

"Not really, no. My mother has one brother, who lives in Maine. We used to go visit on summer vacations, but I haven't been in years. He has two kids, which makes my grand total of cousins two. My grandparents died before I was born, on my mother's side. I don't know anything about my father's side."

"Have you ever been curious about him and his side of the family?"

"Sometimes, but not in years. I think I fantasized when I was a kid that I was a long-lost granddaughter of some rich, old lady who lived in a castle and owned a lot of horses. I mostly only thought things like that after having a fight with my mother. I don't think I've been curious since reaching adulthood."

"That's sad to me," Eric replied. "I come from a big family, and I couldn't imagine life without them. I'll tell you all about them over dinner. In fact, my family is so big, it'll probably take that long."

Eric kept his promise and told Katie about his entire family on both sides, encompassing four generations. Katie enjoyed hearing about them, but knew she couldn't possibly keep them all straight. She paid special attention to immediate family's names, ages and marital status, but let the information on aunts, uncles, great aunts and great uncles go in one ear and out the other. She would worry about remembering their names when she met them, should that occasion ever arise.

As Katie and Eric got to know each other, they found they were very different from each other, yet compatible. Katie was a small-town girl with a big-city heart. Eric was a city-person from birth. Katie wanted a career in the arts, but settled for working with numbers. Eric was a computer programmer, but enjoyed the theater. They both had an attention for details. The main difference was Katie was a bit of a loner, while Eric was a big family person. Katie had never known what a big family was like and wasn't accustomed to having a lot of people in her personal space. She preferred the anonymity of the city, yet she had admittedly been enjoying living in the mansion and having a roommate. Granted, she had been lucky enough to get Tina for a roommate; had she gotten someone like Madison, she'd have pulled her hair out by now.

Katie found she was curious about Eric's big family and liked listening to Eric talk about them. She was open to the possibility of being a part of that family, even if it felt strange at first. She was a little scared, though. She couldn't help being somewhat guarded around Eric, in light of what she'd been through with her father. Her mother had impressed upon her that men were not to be trusted – all men. Even though Katie didn't totally believe that, she had always kept her guard up on dates.

It was hard for her to open up to Eric, but she knew it was necessary if anything were to become of this experience. She tried to keep the conversation light and flirtatious, but she answered the serious questions with honesty.

She was relieved when dinner was over. She felt tired from the pressure of answering Eric's questions correctly. She hadn't exactly been saying what she thought Eric wanted to hear, but she was extremely careful how she phrased herself. She worried about her answers to the point of obsession that Eric was making decisions based on what she said.

She felt much more comfortable when the date turned from psychological to physical. Katie could relate physically where she felt she failed emotionally.

They took the limo back to the *Soulmates* cottage where Eric was staying. The night had turned chilly, so Eric lit a fire for them to snuggle in front of the fireplace. He poured them each a glass of wine.

"This is so relaxing," he said, putting his arm around her shoulder and pulling her closer.

"It is. I could fall asleep."

"Are you tired? I can take you home."

"No, that's OK. I'm just so comfortable," Katie turned to Eric and smiled.

"You look beautiful. Thank you for wearing the dress."

"You're welcome. I'm glad you like it."

"I do. I liked it the day I met you. I was literally blown away when you walked into the room."

"Thank you. I was just relieved you met me before Kristin," Katie laughed.

"Kristin had nothing on you."

"Well, she had one thing, or should I say two," Katie joked, referring to Kristin's huge boobs.

"I think your body is perfect," Eric whispered into Katie's ear. Katie smiled into Eric's deepening green eyes, and for the first time all night felt awkwardly aware of the cameras.

"They don't stay all night," Eric whispered, sensing Katie was uncomfortable. He leaned in and kissed her reassuringly.

Warmness flooded over her body as Eric's soft lips pressed against hers. She melted into his arms, immobilized by his touch. She had never been in love before, but she knew this feeling had to be more than pure lust. There was definitely something between her and Eric. Katie wanted to believe he was the one for her, but she still felt like something was missing. She was highly attracted to him, and she wanted to be the last woman standing in the worst way, but was it true love, or was it simply her competitive spirit?

Katie ignored her doubts and concentrated on kissing Eric. Whatever became of her and Eric, her priority should be savoring each second of this experience, indulging every one of her senses in the grandeur.

Eric was right about the cameras not staying all night – which actually made Katie even more uncomfortable, as she pondered about how Eric had spent the time completely alone with the other girls. The last bit of filming was Eric leading Katie by the hand to the bedroom. I was a staged scene, just part of the show. Katie didn't mind filming it, because it got rid of the cameras for the rest of the night, but on the other hand, she did have concerns about looking like a slut on national television.

After the cameramen packed up and left, Katie and Eric resumed their positions in front of the fire.

"I'm sorry about that," Eric apologized. "They want the show to be racier than I'm making it, so they've been spicing it up a little. And just so you know, our conversation earlier in the limo was fabricated as well. I don't really care who Kristin was talking about at the last elimination."

"I thought you were acting weird," Katie admitted.

"I told Barbara I didn't want to do that, but she insisted. She said it was controversy that made the show so successful, and I could check my contract if I had any objections."

Katie suddenly felt anger rising up inside her. If Eric had staged that conversation, what else had been staged? She felt like a fool.

"What else did Barbara make you do?" Katie demanded, wondering if Eric even liked her at all. She got to her feet quickly.

"Nothing, I swear," Eric jumped up after her.

"And your choices? Have you made all your own decisions at eliminations, or did Barbara coach you on that, too?"

Katie turned to leave, but Eric grabbed her by the arm.

"No. You've got to believe me, Katie. I've made all my own decisions. Everything I've said to you up until today has been true."

"How can I believe you, Eric? This is a TV show, even though we ignore that fact much of the time. Barbara wants ratings, and I can appreciate that. I have no objection to helping her get good ratings. If that's what the director wants, that's what the director gets. What I need to know is what you want. What motivates you? Why are you even here?"

"I'm here for the same reason as you, Katie. I don't blame you for being mad. I didn't want to manipulate you into that conversation. I'm sorry."

Eric held Katie's arms so that she was forced to face him.

"I'm sorry," he repeated emphatically, looking her straight in the eye.

Katie could see he was being truthful. She let out a sigh.

"I'm the one who should be sorry. I over-reacted," she said.

"No, I don't blame you. I felt like I was betraying you, and I don't like that feeling. I promise it won't happen again.

Katie nodded and let her eyes drop toward the floor. She felt like an idiot. She had probably blown her chances on getting to the next round, because she had let her emotions get in the way. All along, she had been playing this game skillfully in her opinion, and now she set herself up to lose.

"Forgive me?" Eric asked sweetly.

"Of course," Katie said, then added. "Can I ask you something?"

"Anything."

"If we had met under different circumstances, would I be someone you'd be interested in?"

"Absolutely. No question," Eric answered without hesitation. "Do you want me to take you home?"

Not knowing if she could answer her question the same way, Katie decided Eric was forgiven. He had been honest with her right along, and she had not been totally honest with him. She had no right holding this against him. He had a contract, just like she did. If his contract entailed having a conversation about something he cared nothing about, who was she to judge?

Katie smiled, taking Eric's hands in hers and giving them a squeeze.

"No, I'd like to stay. Let's enjoy the rest of our night together – alone."

Eric grinned, his green eyes dancing.

Chapter Fifteen

Katie took her own advice and enjoyed the rest of the evening with Eric. He walked her back to the mansion in the wee hours of morning. She entered through the back entrance from the terrace and scurried upstairs undetected.

She felt horrible in spite of the fact the remainder of the date had been pleasant. In fact, the evening had been incredibly romantic; Katie simply couldn't shake the bad feeling that had overtaken her. She couldn't explain precisely what was wrong; it was just a feeling of impending doom.

The next elimination was coming up, and frankly Katie didn't know her own fate. She hated uncertainty and the gnawing possibility of saying goodbye to Eric forever. She wasn't even sure if it was the prospect of losing Eric that bothered her, or the mere act of losing. She wasn't totally sure how she felt about Eric. She was utterly confused as to how she felt and what she wanted for her future.

She cried herself to sleep that night, alone in the room she had shared with Tina. She felt so lonely without her there, and without the friendship of Ann Marie that had always been unwavering, unquestionable. The worst part of not knowing what was going to happen with Eric was not being able to talk to anyone about it.

She woke the next morning with the bad feeling still in the pit of her stomach. She had no desire to see the other girls, no inclination to discuss the details of her date with them. She certainly didn't feel like being on camera. She was beginning to regret allowing Ann Marie to talk her into this fiasco in the first place. She had no job. She had lost her best friend. She had gotten no closer to a career in acting and she probably wasn't going to end up with the guy.

She wasn't even positive she wanted to end up with Eric. He was a great catch and would make an excellent husband and father. There was no doubting his merits. He was intelligent, successful and sexy; he had a great laugh and a super sense of humor. He could take her away from it all – her knight in shining armor. But was it love? She had no idea if she was falling in love with Eric, or if she was falling in love with the future he represented. He was her ticket out of the pathetic series of events she called her life.

She had a lot of thinking to do, and she wanted to hibernate in her bedroom all day and do just that. Hunger set in, changing her plans. She knew she had to face the others eventually, so she showered and went downstairs for lunch.

They were all there, and they were anxious for details of Katie's night. The last thing Katie wanted to do was relive her dreadfully emotional date, but she couldn't leave the others with nothing. They had all shared their experiences to varying degrees; she had to tell them something.

She told them about dinner, and how she and Eric had talked all evening. She mentioned the fact that he'd asked her about Kristin's comments at the last elimination.

"Why did he ask you?" Madison wanted to know. "He already talked to me about it."

"That's what I told him – talk to Madison. He said he already did."

"What else did he say about me?" asked Madison, predictably falling into Katie's plan to take the focus off her date. The conversation turned to Madison's rivalry with Kristin, and all the mean and terrible things Kristin had done to her. Katie actively participated in the discussion rather than taking her usual route of ignoring Madison, and her feigned interest encouraged Madison to dominate the rest of the lunch-hour conversation.

After lunch, Katie retreated to her room. She didn't feel like being sociable, but she didn't feel like being alone either. It was depressing to sit in her room all alone, now that Tina was gone. She changed her mind and went outside to sit by the pool. She could bring a book down with her to keep the others away. She could either read to pass the time, or pretend to be reading it and daydream about Eric. Plus, she would get some last-minute sun before the taping tomorrow – the dreaded elimination.

She felt sick to her stomach as she changed into her bathing suit. She knew very well it was nerves, although she tried to pass if off as cramps. Her period was due any time. With her luck, it would come while she was sunbathing. She tucked a tampon in a tote bag, along with a towel, tanning lotion, sunglasses and a paperback book, all compliments of various *Soulmates* sponsors. She stopped by the kitchen and grabbed a bottle of water before heading outside.

Valerie was the only one out there, but the others would probably be along shortly. Katie smiled and waved, but sat on the opposite side of the pool. She turned her chair slightly to make it look like she was trying to get the perfect angle of sun. When the other girls came outside, they would come across Valerie first, which would hopefully prompt them to sit with her. Katie hoped she would get the privacy she desired.

She didn't exactly get her wish, but she did avoid socializing with the others most of the day. Barbara ordered a meeting after dinner. Katie spent the afternoon sunbathing, and then went upstairs to shower. A meeting after dinner meant cameras, and she didn't want to sit around sweaty and smelling of coconut tanning lotion.

Katie went downstairs for the meeting refreshed and in perfect filming condition. As she passed by the front sitting room, she noticed it wasn't set up for a formal shoot, but had one unmanned camera off to the side of the room. Katie went on to the dining room and helped herself to the dinner buffet. She made small talk with the others. Dinner was a somber event, as none of them had much to say while worrying about the upcoming meeting.

The six ladies gathered in the sitting room after dinner. Barbara arrived shortly thereafter, seemingly in a rush as usual. She talked at her top speed.

"I'll try not to keep you long, ladies, but I do need to go over a good deal of information. As you know, tomorrow is the next elimination. The field will be dropping from six to four. In light of Memorial Weekend coming up, we want to get this shoot off as quickly as possible; we want to try to squeeze in two single dates this week before we break for the holiday. We will shoot the other two dates after Memorial Weekend. Our plan is to shoot the elimination first thing in the morning, so we can still use tomorrow as a travel day. I'll talk about the shoot first and then the travel arrangements."

Madison began to ask a question, but Barbara held up a hand to stop her.

"Save your questions, Madison. I have a lot to go over, and I will undoubtedly answer everything while doing so."

Barbara gave Madison a stern look and wasted no time in resuming her speech, to be sure Madison didn't get the opportunity to argue.

"Even though we are shooting in the morning tomorrow, we still need to recreate the atmosphere of an evening elimination. We will still wear evening gowns. We will still have a social hour. The only difference will be the location. We are going to shoot the elimination indoors. We don't have time to waste, so our best bet is to shoot indoors, where we can control the environment and manipulate the setting to appear as though it is evening. No one will be the wiser."

Barbara paused for a breath, briefly peering over her glasses at the six women and scanning for initial reactions.

"We'd like to use the front foyer and the staircase. We'll step out there momentarily to block some positions. If we can't get the shot I want, we'll try a few other places, but I'm hoping the staircase will suffice. It truly is the best option in the house. The elimination will be otherwise the same as usual, as far as format. I already mentioned two of you will be eliminated at this point. However, because of the upcoming holiday and single dates next round, all of you will be receiving travel itineraries for tomorrow. Don't get excited when you see it; it does not mean you've been eliminated. You are all traveling home tomorrow after the elimination."

Madison was about to burst from keeping her questions to herself, but Barbara ignored her and continued.

"The two of you that are eliminated, unfortunately will be staying home. The four remaining will go on individual dates with Eric, spread out between this week and next week. Separate travel arrangements will be forthcoming to those four individuals, and will be provided after the elimination ceremony. With that in mind, tonight is the last night in the *Soulmates* Mansion for all of you. Therefore, you will need to pack all your belongings and take them with you tomorrow when you depart."

"What if we forget something?" Madison asked before Barbara could stop her.

"We'll get it to you. I'm not concerned about that," Barbara brushed her off. "Let me recap, so we're clear on everything so far. The elimination is being shot tomorrow at 8:00AM. Be downstairs dressed and beautiful no later than 7:00AM if you want to participate in the social hour."

"Wait a minute," Madison interrupted. Barbara crossed her arms and tapped her fingers on them in frustration.

"If we are not down here at seven o'clock in the morning, we don't get any time with Eric before the elimination? That's not fair."

"There's nothing unfair about it, sweetheart," Barbara responded curtly. "If you feel it's important to participate, you'll be there. Set your alarm."

"Can I get a 4:00AM wake-up call?" Ann Marie laughed.

Barbara lips moved into half a smirk, but she made no comment. Instead, she continued, "You should get your packing done as much as you can tonight, because some of your flights are early afternoon. You will receive your itineraries in your rooms today. You will not be returning to the *Soulmates* Mansion after you leave tomorrow. All future events will take place elsewhere, so be sure to take all your belongings with you. Two of you will be eliminated tomorrow. We will shoot four individual dates next round – two this week and two next week after the holiday. If you advance to the next round, you will receive further travel instructions. The next elimination after that will take place next Friday in Pittsburgh, where three of you will remain for the next round. Details will be forthcoming as necessary to those of you advancing. For now, let's concentrate on tomorrow's shoot. I want you to line up on the staircase. We'll mark of some spots and see if we can't get the lighting right. If we can't, we'll try a few more options."

Barbara gave Madison a little push towards the door.

"Come on, Madison," she said. "Let's move quickly on this. If you have more questions, you can see me after we've finished. We need to get started now, in case we can't get the shot we want in the foyer."

Madison nodded and said nothing. She looked like she was on the verge of tears. She moped, defeated, into the foyer, where they spent the next ninety minutes standing on the staircase in various positions. The only break they got was when Barbara ordered them upstairs to change into the shoes they'd be wearing for the shoot. Actually, the break was lengthier than Barbara intended, because Madison claimed she hadn't decided what she was wearing yet.

Barbara was visibly perturbed, but refrained from chastising Madison. She resumed arranging and rearranging the women on the staircase until she was satisfied. Zeb marked spots with masking tape. Finally, they were excused. Madison, of course, stayed behind to bombard Barbara with her hundred-and-one questions.

Katie hurried upstairs to pack. She put all her things into her suitcases except what she needed for the shoot tomorrow, and a change of clothes for traveling. The dress and shoes she could easily slip into the garment bag after the elimination.

She tried not to think about the elimination itself, but it was impossible. She had to believe Eric would choose her, when compared to the other girls remaining.

If she had to choose, Madison and Ann Marie would be going home for good. Unfortunately, the choice wasn't hers; it was Eric's, and for some reason he liked Madison. Katie had no idea how Eric felt about Ann Marie, but if he felt the same way Ann Marie claimed to feel, he would probably be keeping her, too. If those two made it into the next round, Katie's chances decreased drastically. Both Jenny and Samantha were loved by all. If Eric was smitten with those two as well, she and Valerie were fated to leave.

Katie was not ready to leave! She liked Eric. She couldn't imagine flying home tomorrow and never seeing him again. The end was coming too soon, and there was nothing she could do at this point to stop it. An hour with Eric tomorrow morning surely wasn't going to affect the outcome. His decisions were surely solidified already.

On that note, Katie went to bed. She barely slept all night, on account of her constant fear of oversleeping. The last time she checked her alarm, she still had thirty-five minutes before it was due to go off. She shut it down and got up. She was surprisingly wide awake in spite of the sleepless night, but she knew it was going to catch up with her later.

It did, on her afternoon flight home. As she sat on the plane, her body was exhausted, but her mind was racing with the day's events.

The shoot had been surreal. They drank champagne and nibbled hors d'oeuvres at seven o'clock in the morning. It felt weird, but Katie accepted the experience as practice for her acting career. She nursed the same glass of champagne for the entire hour. Ann Marie and Madison didn't, and both were showing the effects by the end of the social hour. Katie watched them and hoped they would drink themselves out of the game.

She thought her wish might come true, when Barbara sent them upstairs after social hour. Barbara wanted the ladies to make an entrance down the staircase for the elimination. They had to stand in line waiting at the top of the stairs in their heels for over thirty minutes, while Eric was supposedly contemplating his choices. Katie was in the front of the line, behind Valerie, while

Madison and Ann Marie brought up the rear. With any luck, one or both of them would fall down the stairs and break a leg. For Madison, such a fall might be fatal, considering the anguish she'd suffered over stepping on a possibly-rusted nail. The only problem was, they would probably take others out with them on the way down.

At last, they got word that Eric had finalized his decisions. He waited at the bottom of the stairs with Shane, the ceremonial gold box positioned between them. Zeb motioned Valerie to start her descent. She did so in her formal, Miss America style, gliding down the center of the staircase to the bottom step, and then stepping sideways toward the bannister to take her place on her X'd spot.

Katie was next. She strode downwards carefully, her eyes on the camera. She came to her place opposite Valerie, but one step up. The other four women came down in the same fashion, one at a time, staggered one step apart on either side of the staircase. Valerie, Samantha and Madison completed the left side by the bannister, while Katie, Jenny and Ann Marie lined the right, by the wall.

When they were settled in and Barbara was satisfied with the shot, Shane stepped forward. He opened the ceremonial gold box and removed one of four small jewelry boxes, which he held in his hands as he spoke.

"Good evening, Ladies. As you know, two of you will be eliminated tonight. The four chosen to advance will receive from Eric this exquisite pair of sapphire pendant earrings." Shane opened the box to reveal, indeed, the most exquisite earrings Katie had ever seen.

"Never fear," Shane continued in a lighter tone. "We aren't going to make Eric put the earrings on you."

The girls smiled. Madison giggled.

"The two women not chosen will be removed from the *Soulmates* mansion tonight, and removed from Eric's future. The remaining four women will also be moving out of the *Soulmates* Mansion – but moving on with Eric to the next round. Individual dates will take place on more comfortable turf – your own. This will be your chance to show Eric your world. At this point, you've invested a good deal of time and emotions into your relationship with Eric. If you know in your heart that Eric is not your *Soulmate*, you may step down at this time and eliminate yourself from the competition ..."

Shane paused, but no one stepped down. No one ever had in any of the previous seasons. Women who weren't crazy about the *Soulmate* were generally eliminated in earlier rounds. What man would keep a woman around who wasn't crazy about him? The six women left in this case would fight to the death for Eric.

Shane, getting no takers, snapped the jewelry box closed, handed it to Eric and bowed out of the picture. Eric stepped forward.

"Good evening, Ladies," he said with a slight smirk, emphasizing the word "evening." He quickly sobered. "I never dreamed what a difficult decision this would be. I thought things would be more clear-cut by now. I know I'm lucky to have gotten the opportunity to date six beautiful, genuine ladies, but now I'm cursed with the task of saying good-bye to two of you. Quite frankly, I don't want to. You are all special in your own way, and I want you to know how much I've enjoyed my time with each of you. Now I need to do what is necessary to bring me one step closer to my ultimate goal. I have to choose the four ladies I feel are most compatible with me, the ones that best share my visions for the future."

Eric looked down at the jewelry box in his hands and collected his thoughts. The girls stared, anxiously awaiting his decisions. It seemed eons before he looked up, and it was difficult to tell exactly whom he was looking at.

"Katie," he said.

Katie's heart began to race. She had been certain he was going to call Jenny behind her. She was momentarily frozen in her spot, but quickly recovered and came forward to receive her gift.

She gave Eric a hug first, squeezing him tighter than she intended in her excitement. Then she stepped back and accepted the jewelry box. She beamed up at him, his green eyes making her melt inside.

"Thank you, Eric."

"You're welcome, Katie," he returned her smile.

Katie returned to her place on the stairs feeling closer to Eric than ever, after their brief exchange. Her heart was pounding in her chest. Was she falling in love with him? She wasn't convinced but she had to force air into her lungs, before she passed out on the stairs.

Eric was taking the second small box from the velvet-lined container. Katie took deep breaths through her nose and listened up to find out who else Eric had chosen.

"Samantha," he said.

Samantha smiled and let out a small noise as she stepped between Katie and Valerie. She looked thrilled but confident, not at all surprised that Eric had chosen her. She glided forward and gave Eric a peck – on the lips – followed by a warm embrace.

"Thank you so much," she said and accepted the small box.

"You're welcome," he said back, smiling at her with those dazzling eyes.

Katie felt a pang of jealousy. Clearly the two of them had chemistry. Katie suddenly felt threatened. If she was falling in love with Eric, she needed to step up her game. She couldn't depend on her sex appeal and casual flirtations if she was going to win Eric's heart. She needed to start making a deeper connection.

Samantha swiftly resumed her position on the stairs behind Valerie. Madison appeared to be glaring at the back of Samantha's head. Katie apparently wasn't the only one feeling threatened.

Eric, in the meantime, picked up the next box and held it in his hands. He looked as though contemplating his next call. He was halfway done. He had two names left to call, and four women sweating out his decision.

"Valerie," he said.

Valerie let out a tension-breaking squeal.

"Thank you, thank you," she cried as she stepped forward.

She kissed Eric on the cheek and threw her arms around his neck.

"Thank you!" she said again.

"You're welcome. You're welcome," Eric laughed.

Valerie was absolutely beaming as she turned from Eric. Katie smiled at her. Katie couldn't help smiling at Valerie's enthusiasm, and Valerie didn't pose as much of a threat to Katie. Valerie struck her as the type of woman that men admired and appreciated as a friend, but not the type of woman to fall in love with. Valerie was strong, outspoken, business-like and possibly too independent for a man's liking. Men unfortunately preferred women like Madison, who were vulnerable and needed rescuing.

Madison was one of the remaining unchosen women, along with Ann Marie and Jenny. Katie couldn't foresee Eric selecting anyone other than Jenny. Jenny was so sweet and personable, while Madison was fake, and Ann Marie was overbearing. Eric obviously went for the sweet type, because he'd kept Samantha. Perhaps he couldn't see through Madison's façade.

He called Madison.

She swooned and swept down the stairs past the other girls without a sideways glance. Katie watched Valerie's face, as she turned to watch Madison alighting. She was smiling out of politeness, but her eyes told a different story. If Katie was reading Valerie's expression correctly, it said, "Here comes Scarlet O'Hara."

Madison grabbed the jewelry box out of Eric's hands and threw her arms around his neck. She nearly knocked him off his feet. She drew back and kissed him, then resumed her strangle hold.

"Thank you!" she cried. "Oh! I'm so excited."

"You're welcome," Eric grinned.

Madison took her time getting back up the stairs. Katie watched her climb back to her position and took advantage of the opportunity to snuck a glance at Ann Marie. She was mounted at the top step of the frame. She was clearly upset, but trying not to show it. Her emotions had overcome her acting skills, after all. She had been adamant about her feelings for Eric, but he apparently didn't feel the same way.

Katie was bubbling inside, she was so happy to have been chosen. Madison was moving forward, but Ann Marie was not. That took a lot of pressure off Katie. She didn't have to worry about all the gory details of her past surfacing unsolicited. She didn't have the stress of competing with her best friend – probably ex-best friend at that point. She did still have formidable opponents, which she recognized, but she could handle that. She was just so relieved that she was still in the game, while Ann Marie wasn't.

Katie was brought back to reality by the flight attendant coming by with the drink cart. Katie accepted a soda and leaned back again to relax and analyze the day's events. Somewhere behind her, eight or ten rows, sat Ann Marie, undoubtedly in sorrow. Katie was glad she couldn't see her. She didn't want to deal with Ann Marie. Eventually, she would have to face her and try to work things out – they had been friends too long to stay mad over a guy. What if Katie ended up marrying Eric? She had always imagined Ann Marie as her maid of honor. She couldn't imagine a future *without* Ann Marie. That bothered her more than the prospect of a future without Eric.

But she had made a commitment to *Soulmates* and she was going to fulfill her duties on the show. She would pursue a relationship with Eric at all costs. In the end, she would make up with Ann Marie – with or without Eric at her side.

Katie's head hurt from the stress and exhaustion. She reclined her seat and let herself doze off.

Chapter Sixteen

Katie felt strange being home again. She was so used to living out of a suitcase, she didn't bother to unpack for three days. She slept most of the time, or lounged in her pajamas and watched TV from her couch. She didn't go see her mother until Saturday.

She simply didn't know what to do with herself. She had to save what little money she had left of her bonus to pay her bills indefinitely, since she had no job. She needn't bother looking for a job at this point, since she had no idea what her future held. Maybe she should be searching for a job in the Pittsburgh area; she didn't want to jinx herself, but the thought occurred to her to check out the Pittsburgh job market.

She debated with herself all day about what she should be doing, but at the end of each day, she had virtually done nothing. Daydreaming about Eric all day passed the time sufficiently. Plus, Barbara called every other hour to check in with her.

Barbara wanted Katie's input on the upcoming date on Wednesday. More specifically, Barbara was pushing Katie to introduce Eric to her friends and family. Barbara understood easily enough that Ann Marie had been Katie's best friend, and it wouldn't be productive to bring her along on a date with Eric. Convincing Barbara to leave Katie's mother out of it was another issue altogether. Sharon Cohen adamantly refused to be filmed, and Katie didn't attempt to convince her otherwise. Katie respected her mother's wishes, and quite frankly agreed with her. If she and Eric truly reached the point in their relationship that necessitated the meeting of parents, she firmly believed the introductions should be private.

Barbara tried to show Katie the other point of view – Eric's. How would he feel that Katie wouldn't let him into her life? She made Katie think about being the *Soulmate* herself, and how she would feel if put in Eric's position. Would she continue a relationship with someone who wouldn't introduce her to his family? This was, after all, the point in the relationship where friends and family were introduced. It was part of the schematic progression of the show.

Katie agreed with Barbara's points, but wouldn't budge on the issue. She would explain to Eric why her mother wasn't willing to participate and she would level with him regarding her past friendship with Ann Marie. Eric may be offended or hurt, but he might react with compassion. Katie had already confessed her vulnerability as far as family was concerned. Eric knew what happened with her father; he might completely understand Katie's reluctance to force her mother into such an uncomfortable situation. He may even feel relieved that Katie had spared him of the ordeal.

Barbara wasn't happy about it, but she resigned herself to work with what she had. She insisted that Katie explain the absences to Eric on camera. Katie was fine with having a heart-to-heart with Eric on TV. She felt Barbara was making a bigger deal out of this than need be, but Barbara was used to calling the shots. The fact that she lost control of a decision probably bothered her more than the fact that Katie had no friends or family to participate on their date. Whichever the case, she got over it and planned a superb date for the two of them.

Eric met Katie at a pub near her apartment a little after noon on Wednesday. Katie was so excited to see him that she gave him a huge hug. She had missed him more than she thought possible. He looked great, dressed casually in jeans and a golf shirt. She felt so comfortable and relieved to be in his arms, she didn't want to let go. Eric returned her affection, and kissed her on the lips.

"I missed you," she said, smiling into his green eyes.

"I missed you, too, Katie. I feel like I haven't seen you in so long."

"You haven't, considering we're used to seeing each other every day."

"What have you been doing with yourself?" Eric asked, letting her go and sitting down across from her in a quiet booth in the corner.

"Not much. I've been trying to catch up on some sleep from all the traveling and activity. The time zone has me thrown off a little too. You must be exhausted. Did you fly into Albany this morning?"

"Yeah."

"How was your flight?"

"Not bad at all. No problems."

"Did the *Soulmates* limo pick you up at the airport?"

"It sure did," Eric said with a smile. It was a joke around the house that there wasn't actually a *Soulmates* limo. There were many rented limos donning temporary magnetic *Soulmates* logos on their side doors. "As a matter of fact, it's waiting out front for us."

"Good. We'll be needing it."

"Where are we going?"

"I have a few things planned," Katie said vaguely, enjoying teasing Eric since he wasn't privy to the date-planning for once. "Would you like a drink first? We aren't in a hurry, and I'd like to have a talk over lunch."

"Sure," Eric agreed and ordered them a couple of beers and sandwiches.

"Who are we hanging out with today?" Eric asked when the waiter had gone.

"Actually, that's what I wanted to talk to you about."

"Oh?" Eric looked surprised.

"I don't want you to take this the wrong way, because it has absolutely nothing to do with you personally." Katie paused and took a deep breath. "My mother refused to come on the show. It's not because she doesn't want to meet you. She's a very private person. She didn't feel comfortable being on television. She didn't even like the idea of me going on the show to begin with. She thinks I'm being exploited."

Katie paused, as the waiter delivered their drinks. She poured her beer into the iced glass he'd brought and took a swig before continuing.

"I respect my mother's opinion. I would never force her into an awkward situation against her will. I just hope you don't hold it against her when you do eventually meet her. And I hope you won't hold it against me when you decide who to eliminate next."

"I won't hold it against either of you," Eric assured her. "I completely understand. My parents weren't exactly thrilled about the idea at first either, especially when they found out they'd be on TV, too. They came around, though. My parents have always been very supportive."

"My mother is more of the silent supportive type. She gives her opinion, good or bad, and then keeps her mouth shut and lets me make my own decisions. Whatever I decide, she accepts, but there's no persuading her to change her opinion about it. I've always been OK with that system. She's never forbidden me to do anything. She sometimes guilts me into going along with her, but most of the time she's been fair. And I think I've done pretty well so far. I haven't made any decisions that totally screwed up my life – yet."

Eric laughed and took a swig of beer.

"Your mother sounds cool. I'm disappointed I won't get to meet her today. I admit I'm a little intimidated, but I think I'd like her."

"I think you would, too. She is cool. She's more of a sister to me than a parent most of the time. And since her opinion does mean a lot to me, she has agreed to call me on my cell phone when she gets home from work. The two of you can have a private chat."

"That's great. Maybe I'd better take it easy on the drinks until later," Eric laughed and raised his glass.

Katie lifted hers as well and tapped it against his spontaneously.

"Enjoy yourself," she said. "You don't have to be on guard for my mother. Just be yourself. She'll love you."

"I'm taking your advice," Eric said and downed half the glass. "So, do we have some of your friends joining us?"

"Actually, no," Katie answered quietly. She was dreading telling Eric about Ann Marie more than she had feared telling him that her mother refused to meet him. "My best friend and I had a falling out recently. I didn't feel it would be appropriate to invite her."

"That's too bad. What was your fight about?"

"A guy."

"Really?"

"Yes, but it was more than that. We have always had a competitive relationship. I let her talk me into a project of a competitive nature, and we clashed. We had a huge argument. She accused me of being jealous of her and implied that I've always carried this jealousy my entire life. So, the argument started over a guy, but it unveiled this ugly resentment she's had for years. I feel foolish for not seeing it before now. I'm kind of glad it's out in the open, and I'm sure we will work it out eventually. We have been friends for so long, I can't imagine not being friends with her. She's like my left hand."

Katie paused, as the waiter dropped off their sandwiches.

"I'm sure you'll work things out," Eric said. "And when you do, I'd like to meet her."

"Funny thing about that," Katie began, diverting her eyes. "You have met her."

"I have?" Eric was trying to piece things together.

Katie had a horrible feeling in the pit of her stomach. She was trying to keep the conversation light in spite of the subject matter. She was afraid Eric would feel like she'd been lying to him.

"Yes, you've meet her," Katie admitted, making herself look at Eric. "Up until last week, my closest friend for the majority of my adult life was Ann Marie Monaghan."

Katie searched Eric's face for a reaction. His expression was one of surprise, but he didn't appear angry. He was still connecting the dots in his head. Finally, Eric spoke.

"This 'project' Ann Marie talked you into doing was *Soulmates*, and the guy you were fighting over was me?"

"Yes."

Eric nodded and took a drink, trying to digest this new information.

"We didn't say anything about our friendship to anyone in the house or on the set. We didn't want you to feel you had to choose between us, and we didn't want you to worry about possibly coming between friends. We felt it would be best for everyone involved if our friendship wasn't common knowledge. The only one who knew was Tina, who was my roommate, while she was at the mansion."

Eric nodded but said nothing.

"I don't want you to feel like we've been dishonest with you. It seemed unfair to the other girls for us to have a friend in the house. And we know so much about each other, we didn't think it would be fair to you if we talked about each other – good or bad. We decided it would be best for everyone if we simply stayed away from each other. We never imagined we would both end up liking you so much. We have very different taste in men, so it seemed unlikely that we would end up fighting over … a man … you …"

Eric stared intently at Katie. He didn't look mad. He looked thoughtful, but not upset. His green eyes were dark and cloudy, deep in thought on how to react to this strange turn their conversation had taken.

"Turned out we both had strong feelings for you," Katie continued. "We got into an argument. I told Ann Marie I didn't want to do or say anything that would sway your opinion of her – or me. I wanted you to look at the two of us, and the other women for that matter, for who we are as individuals and make your own decisions. And I think you've done that. I know there's been a lot of backstabbing going on, but I have not been part of it. I have shown you who I am and let you decide from there if I'm someone you could be interested in. I can't answer for the others. I don't know what they've told you about me or anyone else. At the very least, I can leave this experience with a clear conscience, that I didn't do or say anything to turn you against Ann Marie. You made your mind up all on your own, as far as I'm concerned."

Katie paused and waited for Eric to say something. She felt ashamed and embarrassed. It was one thing confessing the truth to Eric; it was entirely another doing it on national TV. She felt like an idiot. No matter what Eric said in response to her confession, Katie knew their relationship was probably over. Eric undoubtedly thought she was a liar and a fake, and she didn't blame him. She was, wasn't she?

She had to tell him the truth, though. If they had any chance at a relationship, he had to know the truth about her past, and her relationship with Ann Marie wasn't the worst bombshell she could have dropped. Katie knew she had done the right thing. Now the ball was in Eric's court. He could forgive her, or not. Katie hoped the issue was smaller than she was making it in her mind.

"Under the circumstances," Eric said finally. "I don't blame you for not being totally honest. I'm sure there are worse skeletons in the closet, so to speak. I can't say I'm not surprised, and I can't say I'm not disappointed."

Katie nodded and took her turn keeping silent. She looked down at her hands in her lap and picked at the corner of a nail tip that was coming loose.

"Katie," Eric said, and pulled at her arm to get her hand in his. He squeezed her hand. "I'm disappointed because you've been my rock through this whole experience. You've been my friend. I feel like you let me down, like you didn't trust me enough to tell me the truth. I understand why you did it, but that doesn't make it right."

"I know. I'm sorry. I understand if you don't want to finish the date with me."

Eric was taken aback.

"Of course, I want to finish our date," he said. "I'm glad you told me the truth. And I appreciate the fact that you haven't been gossiping about the other girls. Obviously, you and Ann Marie know a lot about each other. You didn't use any of that information to your advantage. I respect that. I especially respect you, because Ann Marie didn't play by the same rules."

Katie raised her eyebrows. In actuality, she wasn't surprised. She had known Ann Marie was responsible for planting the doubts in Eric's mind about her sincerity previously. The whole "acting" conversation could only have come from one place, and Katie had figured that out long ago. It was working to her advantage that she'd kept her mouth shut. She could have told Eric a thing or two about most of the other girls, but she felt it was best to let them sink their own boats. Eric would discover the truth on his own. He had seen through Ann Marie. He would eventually see through Madison.

"Ann Marie had plenty to say about you, but don't feel singled out. She had a lot to say about the others, too."

"I won't take offense, then," Katie laughed. She decided it would be wise to end that conversation and move on with their date. She didn't want to ask Eric what Ann Marie had said about her. She was still here, while Ann Marie wasn't. Whatever information Ann Marie had divulged, it hadn't swayed Eric's opinion and couldn't cause any further damage. She would merely look petty if she dwelled on it. Madison, she was not! She lifted her beer glass for a toast.

"Are we cool, then?" She asked.

Eric smiled and tapped his glass against hers.

"We're cool," he said and proceeded to finish off the rest of the glass.

Katie took a few gulps out of relief, but refrained from finishing the whole beer. It was early, and she wanted to make the most of her day with Eric.

They ate a leisurely lunch before taking a driving tour of Glens Falls in the *Soulmates* limo. Katie showed Eric the building she lived in, the house she grew up in, and her high school. She showed him a few points of interest along the way. The limo merged onto the Northway at the end of town. Eric wanted to know where they were headed, but Katie didn't give up any details. Their journey wasn't very far, as they exited the highway at Saratoga and pulled into the harness track.

"Is this part of the tour, or are we really stopping here?" Eric asked excitedly.

"This is the place," Katie answered.

"I've never been to the races," Eric admitted.

"Never?"

"Nope."

"You're in for a treat."

The limo let them out by the front. The videographer followed them to the gate, then went back to the limo.

"That's the best part," Katie told him. "They aren't allowed to film inside during the races. They'll be in our private box during dinner, but we could actually get to spend a lot of time unchaperoned if we're creative – and gamble."

"You mean, the more bets we place, the more privacy we'll get?"

"Precisely."

"I don't even know how to bet, but I'm a fast learner."

"I'll teach you. It's easy."

Katie explained the basics of horse track betting to Eric over dinner. She showed him the program listing the races and the horses' statistics, and explained the order to place a bet.

"So, you're an old pro at this," Eric surmised. "How much money have you won?"

"I don't bet enough to win much. Five bucks here and there."

"You can bet five bucks?" Eric was astounded.

"You can bet two bucks if you want."

Eric laughed. "All right. You're not a hard-core gambler. I thought I was seeing another side of Katie."

"No," she said. "I do it for fun. I don't have that much money to lose."

"Let's have some fun, then. Lead the way."

Katie took Eric to the betting windows. He was like a little kid, he was so excited to try something new. Katie was excited to have given him this experience. Being away from the scrutiny of the cameras allowed her to let down her guard and let more of her true personality shine through. She still couldn't believe Barbara had suggested coming here. Barbara had been very accommodating indeed. She had called ahead and made all the arrangements. They had been allowed to film earlier in the day, so she was able to get some footage of the facility before Katie and Eric arrived. She reassured Katie that *Soulmates* was only an hour show, and they had four days' worth of dates to condense and an elimination to squeeze into that hour. She only wanted to shoot the highlights of each date, and she agreed that the couples needed time off the camera to be themselves. Katie was surprised to hear that from Barbara. She had been under the impression the cameras ran nonstop, whether the participants were aware or not.

  Katie took full advantage of her time alone with Eric, regardless of whether they were near a camera. They held hands and flirted. It felt more natural than any date they'd had so far.

  Her mother called on the cell phone, as promised. Eric spoke to her enthusiastically. It sounded like they had a great conversation, and he definitely scored points.

  After the races, the cameras were back on, but the couple didn't let that deter them from kissing in the limo on the way back to Eric's hotel. The videographer followed them all the way upstairs to the door of Eric's room, which they shut in her face.

  "I'm sure I'll be portrayed as a woman without morals for coming back to your room," Katie laughed.

  "It's good for ratings," Eric said nonchalantly, managing his best impression of Barbara.

  Katie couldn't stop giggling. Eric opened a bottle of champagne and sent the cork flying across the room, which made Katie laugh even harder.

  "I warned you I was dangerous with corks," he laughed.

  "I guess you weren't kidding," Katie replied and accepted a glass of bubbly. She began to take a sip, but the bubbles fizzed straight up her nose, and she sneezed.

Another fit of giggling onset. Eric grinned at her in amusement.

"I can't believe we didn't clean up at the track," he said. "I thought I might be able to quit my job and retire in the Bahamas."

"I can't believe you've never been to the races before, the big sports fan that you are."

"Is horseracing a sport? I'm more of the football-baseball kind of guy."

"I like baseball …" Katie offered.

"Who's your team?"

"The Yankees, of course."

"Pirates. More importantly, football?"

"I don't really watch it."

"You're going to. Your team is the Steelers."

"All right …"

"Hockey?"

"I don't follow it."

"Penguins."

"Penguins. What kind of name is that?"

"Names don't matter. One of the greatest players of all time was a Penguin."

Katie had a blank look on her face.

"Don't tell me you've never heard of Mario Lemieux?"

"I don't follow hockey," she repeated defensively. "I don't think I've ever seen a hockey game in my life."

"We'll have to remedy that."

"I'm willing to try new things. I like baseball. I'll gladly watch that with you."

"Yeah, you were a good sport at the baseball game."

"See? There's a sports fan in me. It may be deep inside me, but it's in there."

"We'll draw it out one way or another," Eric said and leaned in for a kiss.

Katie's giggling fit was gone, and she returned Eric's affection. His lips were warmer and softer than any she'd ever kissed. She wanted to badly to climb into bed with him and forget about everything for one night. She didn't want to marry him tomorrow, she just wanted to live her life today without worrying about the consequences for once.

Of course, she wouldn't allow her desire to take over completely. There was too much at stake. She was playing a game, and she needed to control her every move. Strategically speaking, *not* sleeping with Eric was far more advantageous at this critical point in the game.

Katie did allow Eric to kiss her all he liked. They kissed and talked until three in the morning. She had never experienced a date like this in her life. She wanted to believe a future with Eric would be filled with experiences like this one. She wanted to advance to the next round and further. Hopefully, her concealed relationship with Ann Marie wouldn't hurt her chances. She didn't think the fact that her mother refused to come on the show would be a factor. She had no control over others' actions, and her mother had called as promised. Eric couldn't very fairly hold that against her.

Katie didn't want the date to end. The reality that this date could be their last loomed heavily. She wanted the night to end on a positive note, but she couldn't stop thinking about the possible finality of the situation.

The *Soulmates* limo drove her home, and Eric rode along. They were quiet during the ride, with Katie nestled against Eric's chest. She felt very comfortable in his arms, as though that was where she belonged. The camera, unusually noninvasive, seemed to blend into the background.

The limo stopped on the street outside Katie's building, and Eric walked her to the door. The camera stayed on them, but from the limo, rather than hovering on top of them.

Eric kissed her goodbye. It was a long, lingering kiss Katie didn't want to end.

"Thank you for a memorable day," he said.
"Thank you. I really enjoyed it."
"Me too," he said. "See you in Pittsburgh."
"I can't wait," Katie smiled and kissed him again.

Eric reluctantly drew away and made his way back to the limo. Katie stood motionless, watching him go. She waved as the limo pulled away, even though she couldn't see inside it. She watched it roll down the street until it was out of sight. She took a deep breath and let it out with a whistle. She was exhausted, but exhilarated at the same time. She put her arms out and spun around, tipping her head up to the stars. If it was, in fact, her last date with Eric, it had been an awesome one.

Chapter Seventeen

Katie went straight to bed. She didn't even notice she had messages on her cell phone until after she got out of the shower the next morning. The first message was from her mother. She had called after hanging up with Eric last night.

"Hi, Katie. Good, you turned your phone off. I'm glad your attention will be on the rest of your date. I just wanted to say Eric sounds like a perfect gentleman. I feel slightly better about this fiasco after having spoken to him. Enjoy your night. I'll give you a call tomorrow."

Katie smiled and hit delete. It meant a lot to her that her mother had made the effort. It was her mother's way of silently supporting her, as she had tried to explain to Eric yesterday.

The second message was from last night, too.

"Hey, there. It's me," spoke Ann Marie's voice. "I know you probably don't want to talk to me, but I have a few things to say, one of them being I'm sorry."

She paused, seemingly contemplating what to say next.

"You can call me back if you want. I really wish you would because I think we need to talk. I know you're going to be flying to Pittsburgh by the end of the week, and it's really important that we talk before you go. OK? OK, then. I'll catch you later."

Katie hit delete emphatically. She had no desire to talk to Ann Marie. Eventually she knew she would resolve things with her, but she wasn't ready yet. She wasn't ready an hour later, when her phone rang again. Her first instinct after checking the caller ID was to let the voice mail pick up, but she couldn't avoid Ann Marie forever. She hated to do it, but she answered the phone.

"Hello."

"Oh, hi," Ann Marie seemed surprised. "I was expecting your voice mail again."

"I'm here. I was just getting out of the shower," she exaggerated.

"Well, I'm glad I caught you."

There was an awkward silence.

"Yeah, I just listened to the voice mail you left me. You wanted to talk?"

"I think we need to, don't you?"

Katie didn't respond.

"Well, I need to talk, so I'm just going to say what I have to say. You can take it or leave it. We've been friends too long to leave things in limbo."

"OK," Katie said for lack of anything better to say. She was curious to hear Ann Marie's apology.

"I'm sorry I freaked out on you in LA, first of all. I didn't mean half of what I said. I think I was just so freaked out by how intense the whole experience was, and how quickly things were going. I know I talked you into doing it in the first place. It seemed like it would be fun – and it was fun at first – but it turned into this cut-throat competition. And it wasn't even about Eric, totally. I mean, I did like Eric. He's a great guy. But I knew on some level, he wasn't going to be my husband someday. I wanted to win, and I wanted to pursue a relationship with him, but I realize now that I wasn't in love with him. I don't know what I was thinking. I just got caught up in the whole romance of it. I think I wanted to have a relationship so badly that I tried to make Eric into 'the one' even though I knew subconsciously we wasn't. I became obsessed, like he was my last chance or something. I had to win, and some little part of me believed I could ask you to step aside, and that would leave the road clear for me. I don't know why I even thought that. It's not like it was between you and me. There were all those other girls, too, obviously some of which Eric was very attracted to. But you were my friend. I could count on you to step aside, so I made you my target. In my crazed state, I thought I could simply ask you to step aside, because I can always count on you to do things for me."

"You mean you can always manipulate me into doing what you want."

"I don't manipulate you! I've talked you into a few things, sure, but that's how things have always been with us. I'm adventurous, and your more reserved. That's part of our relationship. You have to admit that."

"Yes, I agree. You're the risk-taker. You're the free spirit; I'm the grounded one. I try to talk you out of things, and you try to talk me into them. I get that about us. I also admit I'm sometimes glad you talk me into doing stuff. I'm glad I did *Soulmates*. It's been good for me. We had some fun. We met a cute guy. We made a little money. You were right. I get that. What I don't get is why you personally attacked me. You said yourself it wasn't all about Eric. I could understand if it was an argument over a guy. But it wasn't just about Eric. It was about some deep-seeded jealousy I didn't realize existed. You said some pretty hurtful things, and I don't think you can play it off as getting caught up in the excitement and romance and competition. You made me question the entire basis of our friendship."

"Katie, your friendship is very important to me. I never would have asked you to do this if I thought it would put our friendship in jeopardy."

"What about all the things you said?"

"You have to take what I said in context. We were in a situation where we were acting. We agreed not to let on that we were friends in front of the camera."

"That secret's out," Katie mumbled.

"What?"

"Never mind. Continue what you were saying."

"I was just explaining that you're taking what I said out of context. I was angry; you were drunk. We had a conversation that got out of hand. It never should have happened."

"You're right about that. It shouldn't have happened, but it did. Why can't you simply take accountability for the things you said? You accused me of being jealous of you – not just jealous of your relationship with Eric, jealous of your entire life. Is that truly how you feel? I need to know, because it came as a shock to me. If you really think I'm so jealous of you, why have you stayed friends with e all these years? I need an explanation."

"I said it in anger."

"So, it doesn't count, because you were mad when you said it?" Katie demanded. "It must have some truth to it, or at least crossed your mind."

"I was trying to be hurtful, because I was mad at you."

"Oh, that's bullshit, Ann Marie. If you wanted to be hurtful, you'd have said I was too ugly or stupid for Eric, or something off the top of your head. You said I was jealous of you – jealous of your family and your career, and everything you apparently have that I don't. You didn't just spew that out in the heat of the moment. You've obviously put some thought into the subject. Now that it's out, I want to know the truth. Lay it on me. I can take it. Let's hash it out now and get it over with. I don't think we can remain friends if I have a doubt in the back of my mind that you think I'm jealous of you."

"I don't think you're jealous of me, exactly. I think there have been times in your life that you wish you had some of the things that I had, but that's normal in a friendship. The grass is always greener sort-of-thing. I elaborated on that point because I wanted Eric, and I didn't want you to have him. I was afraid you would try to compete with me for the sake of competing, because that's how we are. I was afraid that you didn't like Eric, but you still wanted him just to keep me from having him. I shouldn't have brought up the whole jealousy subject. It wasn't about jealousy so much as competition."

"It seemed to me that you were the jealous one."

"I was! I admit it! I liked Eric, and it tore me up that he liked you more than me. I did not want to go home when I did. And it pissed me off that it was my idea in the first place, and you were doing better than I was."

"How do you know that? We weren't on the same date with him. How do you know my date didn't bomb?"

"You and Eric have chemistry. I'm not the only one that could see that. It killed me, knowing that you were going to move on with him, while I was losing his interest."

"So, you threw that jealousy crap in my face to shake my confidence? That was a low blow."

"I know, I know. I'm sorry. I don't carry around a deep-seeded jealousy of you, and I don't think you do either. You're my best friend. I'd give you everything I have if it would make you happy. I never should have let a guy come between us. I shouldn't have made you audition, and quit your job and all that. I'm sorry."

"You didn't make me quit my job. You can stop feeling guilty over that one. As far as auditioning, I'm glad I did. It's been a good experience. The bonus money will hold me over until I get another job. I don't think I'll gain a husband out of this, but I'm not about to lose my best friend over it, either."

"Are we still best friends, then? I promise I won't talk you into doing anything ever again."

"You've been talking me into doing things for years. I would never take any risks if it weren't for you. Sometimes taking a risk can be a good thing."

"Forgive me?"

"I forgive you."

"I'm relieved. I'm really, really sorry I hurt you. I hope you and Eric get together, if it was meant to be."

"I don't know, Ann Marie. I feel so close to him when we're together. It's hard knowing I'm not the only one he's dating. Every time I feel confident about our relationship, I remember the other girls. I don't know how things would turn out if I was the only one. I just don't know."

"Hey, I understand. You've got some stiff competition. He's obviously attracted to you, but he's obviously attracted to some of the other girls, too – one of which I'll never understand why …"

"Madison, yeah. I don't get that either. She and I are totally opposites. How can he possibly like both of us?"

"I don't know. Maybe he feels sorry for her."

"He felt sorry for Julia, too, but he didn't choose her."

"I don't know. Like I said, I'll never understand why he's interested in her. I hope he sees through her pretty soon. I'd hate to see him make the mistake of choosing her in the end."

"I think he'll come to his senses sooner or later. The more time they spend together, the more her true personality will come out. I don't particularly feel threatened by Madison. I can't picture Eric spending the rest of his life with her."

"No, I can't either. I would feel more threatened by Samantha and Valerie, if I were you."

"Definitely."

"Did you already go on your date with him?"

"Yeah, yesterday."

"How did that go?"

"It went great, as far as dates go. I feel good about our relationship. I just don't know how I stack up against the others."

"It's hard to say, sweetie. We have no way of knowing how the other dates went. What does your mom think of him?"

"That's another issue. My mother flat-out refused to be filmed. You know how she is. She did talk to Eric on the phone last night, and they seemed to get along fine. I didn't ask either of them for any details of their conversation, but Eric was upbeat when he got off the phone. And my mom called me back and left me a voice mail that she approved. That made me feel better. I just hope Eric doesn't hold it against me when he makes his decision. It's not that she didn't want to meet him, personally; she didn't want to meet him on TV."

"Did he seem offended?"

"No, not at all. He said he totally understood."

"Then I wouldn't worry about it. I'm sure he wouldn't hold it against you."

"Maybe not, but I also told him the truth about us."

"You told him we're friends?" Ann Marie sounded deflated rather than surprised, as though she realized Eric learned she'd been playing games with him.

"I told him we were friends."

"How did he react?" Ann Marie asked, her interest not completely unselfish.

"He took it well enough. I couldn't help feeling guilty for keeping it from him. I'm afraid I may have screwed things up."

"Why? What did he say?"

"He didn't say anything derogatory. I just feel like I let him down, in a way. He's been telling me all along how he trusts me, and how easy it is to talk to me. I'm afraid he's not going to trust me now."

"Did you tell him about acting, too?"

"He already knew that," Katie answered lightly. She wasn't going to give Ann Marie the satisfaction of thinking she had contributed to Katie's demise. Eric knew all he needed to know about her acting career. After all, she wasn't an actress for a living; she was an Accounts Payable Clerk.

"That's good," Ann Marie said without much enthusiasm. "So, when do you fly out?"

"Tomorrow morning. Barbara plans to shoot the elimination tomorrow night."

"What do you think your chances are?"

"I don't know ..." Katie began. "I'd like to think they're good, but you never know."

"I know. It's gut-wrenching to wait it out."

"It is. And it's totally unnatural. It's ten times worse than waiting for a guy to call you after a date."

"Oh, absolutely. Fifty times worse," Ann Marie laughed.

Ann Marie was right about that. Katie had never felt so nervous in all her life, as she arrived at her hotel room in Pittsburgh the following day. She had hours to kill before the elimination. She wanted nothing more than to take a nap, but she couldn't sleep. She changed into her bathing suit and a wrap and headed down to the hotel spa. She wished she could splurge for a massage, but opted to sit in the sauna, which was free. It had the added benefit of rejuvenating her skin, so she was satisfied with her choice. When she was done in the sauna, she took a few laps in the pool to cool off. Then she went back upstairs to her room to shower and start getting dressed.

Fortunately, she hadn't run into any of the other women. She wondered if their rooms were near hers, or if they were dispersed throughout the hotel. She didn't care to see any of them before the elimination. Frankly, she didn't care to see any of them again in her life, but she had to be careful what she wished for. She would have to see two of them again, as long as she remained in the competition.

Katie tried not to think about the others as she got ready. She had to trust in her relationship with Eric in order for it to work. She couldn't expect to have a future with him if she didn't think positively. On the other hand, she didn't want to get her hopes up simply to be crushed. She let out a sigh. She wanted to be optimistic, but she didn't want to be disappointed, either. She was a nervous wreck. Maybe she would be better off getting eliminated tonight. It would spare her this horrible pit-in-her-stomach feeling next round. Again, she had to be careful what she wished for. She wasn't about to vote herself off the show.

By the time Katie went downstairs, her palms were sweaty and her cheeks were flushed. She kicked herself for staying in the sauna for so long. It was easier to blame her hot flash on the sauna than attribute it to stress, which was more likely the cause. Whatever the case, her face was as red as her dress, and no amount of powder in the world was going to fix it.

Katie arrived at the Riverview Ballroom, which was the designated location for the shoot. Barbara was bustling around, attending to last-minute details. She directed Katie to a screened-off section of the room, where she would be interviewed. Samantha was in there now, and Katie would go next. Valerie was seated off to the side, apparently having already gone. Madison was just entering the room.

Katie didn't have to wait long for her turn, and it was just as quickly over. She was so nervous that she couldn't remember how she'd answered the questions.

She was angry with herself for losing control of her emotions, but she couldn't help herself. Her acting skills were overridden by her personal feelings for Eric. She had wanted this to remain an acting experience, but it had become a love affair. She couldn't do anything now to stop her feelings; she was too deeply invested in the relationship to hold back.

After each of the four women gave their interviews, Barbara lined them up in alphabetical order in a straight row. Katie was on the left, followed by Madison and Samantha. Valerie stood on the right. Katie had been expecting a social hour, but was relieved to learn it would be omitted. Each woman would instead have a private word with Eric before he finalized his decision. Each girl was filmed walking from her spot in line to the screened-off area, where the individual talks would take place. Then Barbara allowed them to sit while each one had the actual talks with Eric. At least they weren't expected to stand the entire duration of the four talks.

Katie was first. She stepped behind the screen to find a completely different set-up from their individual interviews. A white lattice arbor covered with silk ivy and twinkle lights had been set up. A lavender, plush seat was centered under the arbor. Eric stood in front of the loveseat with his hands clasped and waited anxiously.

Katie felt a rush of emotion upon seeing Eric. Tears of relief welled up in her eyes, but she held them back and smiled brilliantly. She extended her arms and grabbed Eric's hands, unclasping them from each other and squeezing them tightly in her own. She gave him a kiss, dropped his hands and threw her arms around his neck. They embraced tightly.

Her heart had been beating out of her chest, but she felt a wave of calmness flow over her. She was in Eric's arms, where she belonged, even if only for a moment. She embraced him tighter and rocked from one side to the other. She stepped back to look into those stunning green eyes she was growing to love.

"I'm so glad to see you," she said. "I can't believe how much I missed you."

"That's good to hear," Eric admitted. "I thought it was just me."

Katie laughed lightly and let Eric guide her to the loveseat. They sat down, and Eric took Katie's hand in his.

"Thank you for coming to Glens Falls and seeing my hometown – what little there is to see."

"I loved it. I had a great time. And now you're in Pittsburgh."

"I'm here! I'm ready to cheer for the Pirates, and the Steelers, and even the Penguins."

"You're in luck. The Penguins are still in the playoffs."

"Oh, yeah?" Katie laughed. "Can you get us tickets?"

"You never know …" Eric said and smiled at Katie. He was the same playful, outgoing Eric she was falling in love with, and didn't seem at all nervous. Of course, he wasn't the one on the verge of rejection. All he had to do tonight was break someone's heart; his own ego would be intact.

"You never know," Katie repeated. "I would love to see my first hockey game with you."

"I owe you one. You took me to my first horse race."

"Did you really like it?"

"I loved it," Eric assured her. "It was one of the best dates I've ever had."

"I'm glad," Katie said, but she was wondering if he would say that to the other girls as well. She hated doubting Eric, but she wasn't naïve either. If she was falling in love with him, then so were the others. He could easily be stringing them all along. She decided to fish for more information. "I hope you weren't too disappointed you didn't get to meet my mother."

"Not at all. I mean, I would have liked to have met her. I hope I do meet her someday, but I got to talk to her on the phone. She sounds like a great lady. I can see where you got a lot of your traits."

"You can?" asked Katie, uncertain if that was good or bad.

"You're a lot like you're mom, yeah. You're independent, strong, intelligent, confident ... you say what's on your mind. I admire that. I feel like I know you – the real you. That's saying a lot under the circumstances. We haven't known each other very long, but I feel like we've been friends forever. That's due to your openness and honesty. I really appreciate that."

Katie smiled and felt slightly less apprehensive. She wanted to believe Eric was going to choose her, but considered the possibility his compliments were a way of letting her down easy.

She felt a sudden urge to plead her case. She didn't want to appear desperate, but she had to give Eric a reason to keep her. Of course, his mind may already be made up. Not knowing where she stood made it highly difficult to plan her strategy. Cool confidence, while certainly within the realm of her acting skills, wasn't in her nature. Playing the helpless waif seemed to work well for Madison, but that wasn't the answer, either. She had to be strong yet show her vulnerability at the same time. She looked him straight in the eye and smiled sincerely.

"Thank you for being my friend through this whole experience. It hasn't been easy, but it's been worth it – you are worth it. And just so there's no doubt in your mind about my feelings for you, I am crazy about you, Eric. I have enjoyed every moment we've spent together, and I know our future is only going to get better."

She looked down at their hands, still joined. Eric squeezed her fingers.

"I've enjoyed every minute with you, too, Katie. And trust me, you are worth it."

He reached over and hugged her. She smiled and let out her breath in relief, but she felt like crying. Their interaction was too similar to a goodbye for her to have any hope of a future with Eric.

She hid her insecurity and left the interview with a forced smile. If Eric was letting her go, she wished he would come out and admit it. It was torturous to wait and be told in front of the others. How humiliating! And then to have to spend the night in the same hotel with him and the others. Katie hated the idea of being under the same roof after such a devastating rejection. She wouldn't want to wait for a morning flight; she would almost rather wait in the airport all night.

She sat by herself, while the other girls met with Eric one at a time, and tried to prepare herself for the inevitable. She wanted to look gracious on camera, not shocked or bitter. She wanted to be a good sport. She didn't want to burn any bridges, so to speak. She tried to play over the scenario in her mind, searching for the right words to say an authentic goodbye to Eric. She wouldn't be getting a dress rehearsal; she had to depend on her improvisational skills.

She worried herself sick, as one girl after another came and went to Eric's lair. Katie tried frantically to put together some acceptable goodbye, thanks-for-having-me speech in her mind, but she couldn't concentrate. Her hands kept sweating. She wiped them on a napkin to prevent any unsightly water spots on her dress. She was thankful the dress was sleeveless, which should conceal how sweaty her underarms were. The dress was partially backless, with the material flowing from her top vertebrae around her neck, over her breasts and around the back to rest just above her tailbone. It was red and risky, but at that moment it was keeping her cool. She knew she looked fabulous in it, despite her flushed face and sticky pits.

Valerie was finally going in. Katie fanned herself with the napkin. She stood up, realizing her crotch was also getting sweaty. The last thing she needed was a sweat spot on the back of her dress, which wasn't unlikely considering she was wearing a thong. Now that the worry was planted on her mind, she would make sure her backside was never facing the camera, regardless if her fear was unfounded.

The only thing making her feel any better was the sight of Madison's pout from across the room. Madison looked twice as bad as Katie felt. Maybe Eric was letting

Madison go, or maybe Madison was vying for attention again. Whatever the case, Katie didn't like her. She couldn't figure out what Eric saw in her. It made no sense.

Madison's attention was suddenly drawn to the curtained-off area, where Valerie was emerging. Shane went in to talk to Eric, and Barbara told the women to take ten. Katie didn't want another ten minutes to contemplate her fate. She wanted to get it over with.

She got herself a glass of water. Her throat felt dry and constricted, as though her voice wouldn't come out if she tried to talk. She sipped the water and tried a relaxation technique from an acting class. She had calmed down some by the time Barbara realigned them for the shoot. Shane stepped forward to address them.

Katie continued breathing deeply and completely disregarded Shane's speech. He couldn't possibly be saying anything she hadn't heard before. She tried not to appear disinterested and she took notice when Shane held up a sapphire heart necklace that three of them would be receiving. Then she zoned out again.

When Eric stepped forward, she tuned back in. She hung on his every word, searching for a clue in his words that might foreshadow her destiny.

"Good evening," Eric began.

The ladies smiled and greeted him politely.

"I appreciate you letting me into your lives this past week. I've gained a lot of insight into your personal character, and I feel I've gotten to know all of you better. I'm probably starting to sound like a broken record, but I have to say how difficult this decision was for me, and how great you all are. You are four unique, outstanding women, and any man would be lucky to have a future with any one of you. But I have to let one of you go. I have given this a lot of thought, so please don't think it's been easy for me."

Eric's eyes scanned each of their faces as he spoke. They were resting on Valerie when he completed his speech, as she was positioned on the end. He didn't linger, but turned for the first of only three necklaces in the ceremonial gold box.

I seemed eons before he spoke again.

"Samantha," he said, and Katie's heart sank. She had been hoping he would call her first again, but no such luck. Katie had a bad feeling he wasn't going to call her name at all. Waiting was agonizing.

She didn't want to watch Samantha and Eric together. Samantha was sickeningly sweet, with her soft voice and southern twang. Her white blond hair was too perfect to be natural. It was long and flowing, and probably received one-hundred strokes-a-day. She pulled it aside to make room for Eric to fasten the necklace around her neck. She was already wearing the sapphire earrings he had given her, and the set perfectly coordinated with her deep blue even gown, not to mention her sapphire-blue eyes. She had worn no necklace to the elimination, even though the low-cut neckline called for accentuation, almost as though she had prior knowledge of the gift.

Katie shifted her weight on her aching feet. Her own dress would look stupid with a necklace. Maybe she wasn't getting one anyway.

Samantha was hugging Eric and gushing with her usual thank you's. She had all the cool confidence Katie lacked. She was like a seasoned contestant in a beauty pageant. She flipped her hair over her shoulder as she spun around to return to her spot. She touched her new necklace affectionately, straightening its position on her chest.

Katie watched Samantha and caught a look at Madison, as well, who stood between them. Every emotion Katie felt was displayed plainly on Madison's face. Madison had a half-pout, half-scowl and shifted her feet nervously. Her eyes shot invisible daggers at Samantha. Madison turned her attention quickly back to Eric, as she anxiously awaited the next name. She looked at him pleadingly, but expectantly, silently willing him to choose her and do it next.

Katie drew her own attention back to Eric, who was carefully lifting the second necklace from the chest. It dangled from his fingers teasingly. He looked up, and his eyes were unquestionably on …

"Madison."

She gasped and trotted forward. She wore a cream-colored gown that probably cost more than Katie's entire closet, but eerily resembled the Bride of Frankenstein. She had worn her pearls with it and asked Eric if she should take them off.

"Wear them both," Eric suggested and clasped her new possession around her neck. As was typical, Madison's first concern was securing the monetary prize.

Katie felt anger rising up inside her. How could Eric have feelings for that spoiled little brat? If she got sent home now when Madison got to stay, she would question if she ever knew Eric at all. Her chances were down to fifty-fifty. It was her or Valerie. Either way, Eric had made a mistake in Katie's eyes. Madison was not the woman for Eric. Madison was an immature, self-centered, calculating bitch. If he ended up with Madison, he was not the man she thought he was.

Madison was busy fawning all over Eric and wasn't aware of the looks of sheer contempt on the other girls' faces – Katie and Valerie because they realized Madison had beaten one of them out. Samantha, although safely on to the next round, clearly didn't appreciate sharing her man with Madison.

Katie leaned around Samantha to exchange glances with Valerie. One of them was eliminated, and Katie had a hunch her luck had run out. In spite of Eric's assurance he wasn't angry with her, he had been disillusioned with her, possibly enough to let her go.

As Madison returned to her position, Katie took a deep breath and prepared herself for the bad news. She had screwed up and now she was going home.

Eric took the last of the three necklaces from the velvet-lined box. His hands were shaking slightly as he settled it between his fingers. He stared intently at the necklace, swinging back and forth like a pendulum and twinkling in the light of the cameras. As he finally raised his head, he closed his eyes and took a deep breath. He opened his eyes and turned his head to one side.

"Katie," he said.

Katie was momentarily paralyzed, while the realization sunk in. Eric had granted her another chance! She felt exhilarated. She smiled and stepped forward. She had been given new life, while Valerie was the one rejected.

"Thank you, Eric," she said and pulled him into her arms. She held him tightly and lowered her voice. "I won't mess up again, I promise."

Eric patted her back soothingly.

"You're welcome, Katie," he said audibly. He drew back and placed the necklace around her neck. She no longer cared that it didn't match her dress. It was hers, and it was from Eric. It was a symbol of hope for their future together.

Chapter Eighteen

Shane directed his farewell speech to Valerie, and Eric walked her out. The cameras followed to film their "private" goodbye. Katie was glad to know they had reached the point of one-on-one goodbyes for those eliminated, even if it was on film.

The other girls were seated for dinner, and Eric joined them shortly. They weren't thrilled at the prospect of dinner for four, but it beat ordering room service for one. It was a difficult mix of emotions for all of them – relief, joy, jealousy and frustration. Each of the women wanted to be alone with Eric, but each was grateful to be with him at all. Even Madison was more pleasant and less pouty than usual.

They were also aware they needed to get along during the next round, because they would all be spending time together and meeting Eric's family. None of them could risk appearing spiteful or ornery in front of Eric's family and friends. They had to be on their best behavior.

Katie didn't foresee any outbreaks. Madison's rivals were gone, Samantha hadn't made any enemies, and she could rely on her acting skills.

They had dinner and drinks at a leisurely pace, although it was still relatively early when they called it a night. Eric assured them they would have a busy day tomorrow.

The girls rode the elevator together to their rooms. They were all on separate floors. Samantha got off first on the fourteenth floor, while Madison was still riding upwards when Katie existed on floor nineteen. Madison had pressed twenty-one, but quickly checked her room key. She pushed at the buttons again, covering both twenty-two and twenty-three. Katie believed Madison's every move was calculated. Her apparently random tapping at the buttons was her was of making sure the other girls didn't learn which floor she was on. Katie couldn't imagine why she or Samantha would care where Madison's room was, and they could have found out easily enough had they wanted to. Katie surmised Madison was paranoid and weird.

    Katie said goodnight to Madison as she got off the elevator. Katie had half a notion to run upstairs three flights just to see Madison's face when the door opened. The notion passed as quickly as it had come. Madison wasn't worth the energy, and her feet hurt. Besides, she needed to concentrate on herself and her relationship with Eric. She needed to pretend other girls weren't involved. Hopefully her relationship with Eric was genuine, in which case the other girls would bear no significance.

    Katie went straight to bed. She left the TV on and pretended to watch it for a few minutes, but exhaustion set in. It had been a long, stressful day, and she needed plenty of rest for the weekend ahead.

    The next morning, she got up early enough to subject herself to the sauna again. She spent only seven minutes in the sauna this time, and then jumped in the pool for a few minutes to cool off. Adequately refreshed, she headed back to her room to shower and prepare for the day.

    She had no idea what to expect. She knew she'd be meeting Eric's family over the next few days, or at least his parents. She expected to meet a few of his friends as well. The prospect of meeting the friends scared her more than meeting the parents. Parents were easier to impress, because you were expected to be on your best behavior. As long as you used good manners, parents were generally satisfied. Friends were harder to handle because they expected you to be yourself. They could easily be Eric's complete opposite, and they could easily take a disliking to any of the three women. More importantly, friends would have far more influence over Eric's decision than his parents would. Parental approval was appreciated, but not essential. In fact, some of the men Katie had dated had completely given up trying to find someone who would please their mothers.

    Katie went downstairs to tape her interview as instructed. The interviews had been consistently her strong point. She exuded confidence, but kept a sweetness in her tone. She was careful not to say anything negative about the other girls, even if asked a direct question about an incident. Katie understood the interviews were extremely important in developing rapport with the viewers. She knew if anything were to become of her acting career through this experience, it depended on the public's opinion of her. The audience had to love her and empathize with her; they had to want to see more of her almost as much as Eric wanted to see more of her. Katie put her best effort into making her interviews special. It meant more air time, at the very least.

After interviews, a family luncheon was planned. The girls were called into the room one-at-a-time, and stood together in the front of the room. Then Eric introduced them all to his family.

"Katie, Madison, Samantha, I'd like you to meet my family, the Werner's. These are my parents, Doug and Maureen. This is my eldest sister, Laura, and her husband Geoff. This is my other sister Emily, and her husband, Bob. And these are my little brothers, James and Justin."

Katie found it funny that Eric still referred to his brothers as little. They were twenty-six and twenty-two years old respectively, and both were taller than Eric. In fact, both were attractive men by Katie's standards, although Justin was too young for her.

The family stepped forward and greeted the girls, shaking hands with each of them much like a reception line at a wedding. They were quickly seated at a large round table for lunch. Eric was centered between his parents at twelve o'clock. Around the table to Eric's left sat Mr. Werner, followed by Katie, Laura, Geoff, Bob and Emily. Madison was next, followed by James, Justin, Samantha and Mrs. Werner. Katie was relieved to be seated close to Eric, and was also pleased to have Mr. Werner next to her as opposed to his wife. Eric's father seemed much more personable and easier to impress. Eric's sister Laura and her husband, Geoff, were both outgoing. Katie recalled all the information about them she could from her previous conversations with Eric. The family members were impressed with what she knew.

Samantha seemed to be holding her own on the opposite side of the table. She and Mrs. Werner were getting along fabulously. Justin was positively gaga over her. Madison didn't seem to be faring as well. She and Emily barely spoke throughout the entire meal, one of them obviously having rubbed the other the wrong way. James was socializing politely, but not giving Madison half the attention Justin was giving Samantha.

By the end of the luncheon, Katie was satisfied that she had made a good first impression with the family. Each girl would spend an hour with Eric that afternoon, as well as an hour each with two family members. Katie had her hour with Eric first. Katie noted Samantha had been assigned to Emily, and Madison to Mrs. Werner.

Katie had been hoping to get her hour with Eric last, but made the best of her schedule. She and Eric went to the hotel bar and found a quiet spot in the corner. Katie wasn't sure if it was a good idea to order drinks before her one-on-one with Eric's mother. Eric reminded Katie of the advice she'd given him before his conversation with her mother. Katie smiled sheepishly and took her own advice.

"What was I thinking?" she said to Eric with a laugh, and ordered a glass of wine.

Eric returned Katie's laughter and took her hand from across the table. He assured her, "You'll do fine. I think I did with your mom."

"You did," Katie told him, but she wasn't so sure about her own fate. She took it easy on the wine as a precaution, nursing one glass through the entire hour. The time couldn't have gone faster. She wished she could order another glass of wine and spend the rest of the afternoon with Eric, maybe make a trip to the hot tub together. How nice it would be if things were different! The afternoon would turn into evening. They could go to dinner and retire to Eric's room early – better yet, they could order room service and spend a romantic evening alone together.

Unfortunately, those options weren't available. Katie embraced Eric and kissed him goodbye.

She met Mrs. Werner outside on the terrace, the designated meeting place. Knowing her interview followed Madison's, Katie felt slightly less apprehensive about impressing Eric's mother. She knew she was better for Eric than Madison, and Mrs. Werner's scrutiny would work to Katie's advantage.

Mrs. Werner stood when she noticed Katie approaching. Katie gave her a quick, friendly hug. She thought Mrs. Werner looked a little frazzled after spending an hour with Madison, but maybe she was misreading the expression. It could have been Mrs. Werner's natural disposition.

"How are you, Katie?" she asked congenially.

"I'm well, thank you. How are you holding up through all of this?"

"It's different, but I'm hanging in there."

"It is different," Katie agreed, nodding toward the cameras.

Mrs. Werner sat down and motioned Katie to take a seat next to her. She wasted no more time on niceties.

"Tell me about yourself, Katie. Where are you from?"

"I'm from Glens Falls, a little town in upstate New York."

"I'm familiar with it. What do you do there?"

"I've been working as an Accounts Payable Clerk for a mid-sized company. I've always had a knack for working with numbers. I've been contemplating going back to college for my masters," Katie said, trying to depict herself as motivated and having direction in her future. She immediately realized her casual comment was a big mistake.

"That's wonderful. You have a business degree, then?"

"I have a BA from SUNY New Paltz," Katie answered and tried to change the subject. "I moved to New York City after I graduated and spent three years there. I never really found my niche, though. I moved back to Glens Falls last year to try and save some money.

"You family still lives there?"

"Yes," Katie said, averting the bullet. She went on to tell Mrs. Werner all about her mother and family – or lack thereof. Mrs. Werner never returned to the subject of Katie's schooling and career aspirations, which kept her acting background a secret for the time being. Katie opened up about her father, and kept Mrs. Werner on that subject for most of the hour.

The time passed quickly, and Katie gave her potential future mother-in-law a quick hug goodbye. She left the interview feeling positive. She was confident she had scored some points by expressing her vulnerability, although she may have exaggerated a bit. She also felt somewhat guilty, pretending to be something she wasn't. If she and Eric were to have a future, he and his family would have to come to terms with the fact that she was a trained actress. She simply didn't want to be burdened with trying to prove her feelings for Eric were genuine at this point, and not a charade. Gaining Eric's trust and admiration was hard enough as it was. Besides, as Eric had previously pointed out, she could have far worse skeletons in her closet; she hoped the other two women did. The path would be cleared for her and Eric if it turned out Samantha had been previously married and Madison had recently been discharged from a mental institution.

Katie went to meet with James with her head held high. She knew the toughest part of her day was over.

James was waiting for her in the lounge outside the lobby. James bent down to give her a hug, and they had instant chemistry. He smelled terrific! He sat on a small couch and motioned for her to join him. There was plenty of room for Katie next to James on the small couch, but she opted to sit in the chair next to him. She probably screwed up the shot, but the cameras would have to adjust. She couldn't sit that close to James for an hour. It was going to take a conscious effort not to flirt with him. The further away she sat, the better. Even from across the luncheon table earlier, Katie had noticed an immediate attraction to James. She caught him looking at her several times, and she felt lit up inside when he was looking at her.

She wanted to make a good impression, but she wanted James to see her as a match for Eric, not for himself.

The hour with James went the quickest of all. They talked about everything, yet about nothing. Katie could have sat there all afternoon. She was lucky that wasn't an option. She and James were getting along so well, they were likely to skip the group dinner that was planned.

Katie went back to her room and evaluated her performances that day. She knew she'd scored points with Mr. Werner, Laura and James. She had barely spoken to Emily and Justin, but didn't suspect either of them would have much influence on Eric's opinions. Certainly, making no impression at all was better than making a bad impression. Mrs. Werner seemed amicable enough, but hadn't exuded the warmness of her husband.

Katie had no idea if the other contestants had impressed the family, but she suspected Samantha had done well, from what she had witnessed. She could only hope that Eric's family saw the same Madison she and the other girls at the mansion had gotten to know. Katie didn't waste much time thinking about Madison. Everyone she knew who had met Madison agreed that she was not the woman for Eric. Eric's family must be telling him the same thing. Katie didn't perceive any possibility of her own elimination this round.

Katie took an hour nap while she had the opportunity, and was actually able to get some sleep. She needed to rest and had no inkling what was in store for her the rest of the night. She doubted it would be an early night, whatever was planned.

All she knew was to be dressed for a formal dinner in the Riverview Ballroom at eight. She had planned to wear Eric's favorite black dress, but had been pleasantly surprised to find Barbara had sent a dress up to her room. It too, was black, but had spaghetti straps and silver scrolling throughout that was only visible when the lights hit it. Katie immediately fell in love with the dress's elegant simplicity. She knew she would never be able to afford to buy anything like it for herself.

Katie reveled in every moment she spent in her princess-like dress. She strode into dinner proudly, well aware of the others' admiring eyes. Even though Madison and Samantha had snazzy new dresses also, they were not nearly as spectacular as Katie deemed her own. Madison's was red, which was not her color. Samantha's was white, which was pretty, but too reminiscent of a bridal gown. Katie thought it made her look desperate to plant a seed of marriage in Eric's head.

Katie soon learned that she was dressed up for nothing. Shane dropped the bomb that only one of them was dining with Eric and his parents. The other two would have a separate agenda for the evening. Katie was angry at having been deceived, especially when Shane announced Samantha would be Eric's sole date that evening, but she tried to be a good sport. Madison, on the other hand, was furious. Her face turned as red as her dress. She said nothing, but crossed her arms tightly over her chest and glared at the others.

Shane led Katie and Madison across the hall to another formal, yet smaller, dining room. Katie assumed she and her rival would be dining with the rest of Eric's family, but she was wrong again. They were to dine alone with Eric's best friend, Mike Holden.

Shane explained that the theory behind splitting the girls up was to give Eric's family the opportunity to see him interact individually with the women. Tomorrow night, Katie or Madison would have a turn to join Eric and his parents for dinner – of course, which one of them was yet to be announced. The third lady would have a lunch date on Monday. Shane also pointed out that although a lunch date wasn't as glamorous as a dinner engagement, it would be the last date before elimination, which had its own advantages.

Katie didn't care which date she got. She needed the time with Eric's family. Katie had a gut feeling she would get the dinner date, and Madison would get lunch. She felt like Madison was struggling this round, and the true competition was down to her and Samantha. She didn't want to jinx herself, because she'd been wrong about Madison before ...

Her best strategy was to concentrate on making the most of her time with Mike. She needed to act just as excited to spend the evening with him as she would have with Eric. While Madison pouted and sulked, she would win Mike's affection.

Her plan worked well. Mike was friendly and easy to talk to. He seemed to be enjoying himself more so than sizing them up. Of course, Katie didn't let her guard down too much, knowing his hidden agenda to report back to Eric.

Katie liked Mike. He was fun, like a brother. At least, spending time with Mike was how Katie imagined spending time with a brother would be. He was not her type, which made things easier, since there was no obvious physical attraction as there had been with James. She felt like she could relate to him platonically, without appearing to come onto him. He wasn't ugly or anything, although slightly overweight. His hair was thinning a bit. He had hazel eyes behind his glasses and adorable dimples.

Katie had no problem scoring points with Mike. She dominated the conversation without trying, while Madison clammed up. She made several efforts to include Madison in the conversation. Katie could have ignored her, killing and burying her chances, but charitably tried to include her, which surely scored even more points with Mike. Katie had no doubt by the end of the evening that she had come out on top over Madison. Winning the best friend's approval was big.

Katie's confidence level skyrocketed. As predicted, she was chosen to have dinner with Eric and his parents the following evening. Realistically, she understood Samantha was a much more formidable opponent than Madison; she wasn't anticipating blowing away tonight's audience as she had Mike. Nevertheless, they seemed to like her well enough, which was important, and she got to spend time alone with Eric after dinner, which was even more important.

Katie made it through dinner, then accepted Eric's offer to show her around Pittsburgh. He took her on a driving tour in the *Soulmates* limo, similar to the one she had given him in her own home town, but quite more exciting. They ended the tour at Eric's house. Eric grabbed a bottle of champagne from the limo and escorted Katie to the door.

They paused. Instead of finding his keys, Eric pulled Katie into his arms and kissed her. It was a long, passionate kiss, and he held her tight. Finally, he pulled back, slowly, reluctantly.

"I've been waiting to do that all night," he said, grinning. His green eyes sparkled in the light on the porch.

"It was worth the wait," Katie smiled back.

Eric stared at Katie with adoration, then found his keys and let them in.

Katie had no idea what the house looked like from the outside, in the dark, but the inside was lovely. Eric hadn't done much in the way of furnishings or decorating, but the house had great potential. The front door opened to a ceramic-tiled foyer overlooking a sunken living room. A brick fireplace dominated the opposite wall. Beyond the living room was the dining room, where a modest-sized table stood under a brass chandelier. French doors leading to an outdoor patio were on the far wall behind the table.

"It's not much," Eric was saying, following Katie's gaze as she took in the surroundings, "but it's mine."

"I love it," Katie said, feeling at home immediately.

"I haven't had time to do much decorating yet, and I'm not very good at that sort of thing, but it's coming along."

"It's beautiful," Katie assured him. "It's got to be hard to furnish a house all at once."

"It's home," Eric said and raised his arms wide. He took Katie's hand and let her inside. They went through the living room and dining room to the kitchen, where he grabbed two champagne flutes from a cabinet.

Katie found herself wondering what kind of guy actually owned champagne flutes.

Eric began to remove the foil wrapping from the champagne bottle, but Katie stopped him.

"Maybe you'd better step outside to do that," she suggested.

Eric laughed, but took Katie's advice. He stepped back through the dining room and out the French doors onto the patio. Katie watched, as he popped the cork. Champagne sprayed out violently, some dripping down the bottle and onto Eric's pants. The cork was nowhere to be found, but the lack of the sound of shattering glass told them nothing had been damaged.

Katie laughed at the sight of Eric's pants.

"You really need to get some practice popping those corks," she told him, as he entered the dining room from outside.

"You'd think I would have gotten it down pat by now," Eric said. He poured them each a glass and toasted to their evening together. Then he reversed roles by excusing himself to change into something "more comfortable."

Katie made herself at home on the couch, while Eric was absent. She looked around and tried to take in as many details as she could. She was eager for clues about Eric's life outside of *Soulmates*. There wasn't much to take in, as Eric had few possessions visible. Katie wasn't exactly sure how long Eric had lived here, but he really needed to do something – unpack or go shopping.

Eric returned and accurately read the expression on Katie's face.

"I told you, I haven't done much with the place."

"I see that," Katie laughed. "You need some help in that area."

"I do."

"At least some paint."

"I know. I'm just not very good at that sort of thing. I don't know where to start."

"I'm not sure," Katie admitted, never having owned her own home. "The good thing about paint is that you can paint over it if you don't like it."

"That's true," Eric sighed and looked around. "What would you suggest?"

"I would say something warm, like a creamy yellow or sand color, maybe even red."

"Red?" Eric questioned. "Wouldn't that be too bright?"

"I don't think so. Besides, it doesn't have to be sports-car red. You could go more of a brick or crimson. That would be nice."

"Do you think so?" Eric asked, stepping closer to Katie and sitting down next to her on the couch. Clearly, he had little interest in paint colors. He was humoring her and biding his time to move in for a kiss. Sensing Eric's impatience, Katie playfully continued the discussion.

"You need to be adventurous. I admit, you can't go wrong with butter yellow, but wouldn't red be more exciting?"

"It's excitement you seek?" Eric asked, leaning closer.

Katie grinned in reply and let Eric kiss her. She had been waiting for this moment all evening – to be alone with Eric in a real environment. It felt wonderful to be in his arms, in his house, in his living room, with no cameras or other women invading their privacy. If circumstances were different, she would have loved to have been in his bedroom. Maybe it was better this way, to be forced to wait. She didn't like feeling restricted, but she didn't want to be made a fool of, either. Here she was in Eric's arms, but the two other girls could be there tomorrow, or yesterday. Katie wouldn't allow herself to lose sight of the fact that other people were involved, and there were consequences to her actions.

She made out with Eric on the couch, and enjoyed every minute of it. Eric mentioned moving into the bedroom once, but Katie brushed off the suggestion. She certainly wanted to go, but she knew it was inappropriate. She hoped Eric wouldn't hold it against her. She couldn't imagine ending up with him and finding out later he'd slept with Samantha – or worse, Madison. It wasn't fair to herself or to the other women, to let things go too far. She even felt a little irritated with Eric for suggesting it, in spite of her gratefulness that he'd reassured her he did want her.

She felt torn. Eric accompanied her back to the hotel in the limo. He kissed her goodbye in the hotel lobby, and she went back to her room alone. She had mixed feelings about the evening, but altogether, she felt her chances were still good.

Chapter Nineteen

Katie was relieved to find she had a light itinerary the following day. She was expecting to be subjected to another session of sucking up to Eric's family, while Madison had her private luncheon with Eric. Her day was just the opposite, virtually free other than a promotional photo shoot and her interview.

Katie's confidence grew as the day progressed. The photo shoot went well, and she couldn't help but assume the fact that she was doing a photo shoot at all meant she was in the top two. She brought up that very point to Samantha over lunch.

"Madison did have a photo shoot last night, while you were at dinner," Samantha told her. "She made quite a big deal about it, as they whisked her off. I was just glad not to have to spend the evening with her. I don't want to say anything mean about anyone, but I really can't see Eric with Madison. It's nothing personal. I'm sure she's a very nice woman."

"I'm not so sure," Katie retorted, throwing away any concern of appearing catty on camera. If Eric couldn't see through Madison's façade, hopefully the viewers would. "I feel like Madison has been manipulating Eric from early on. I don't see where she has feelings for anyone except herself."

"You may be right," Samantha shrugged, without any true commitment. "I don't know how she is feeling, honestly. I don't particularly want to know, but I do know I would hate to see Eric end up with her."

"Are you worried that might happen?" Katie asked, trying to sound casual, forking some lettuce but not bringing the bite to her lips as she anxiously awaited Samantha's reply.

Samantha paused as she slowly chewed her bite of salad.

"My heart tells me no."

Katie nodded and took the bite she'd been holding.

"But that doesn't mean much," Samantha added quickly. "According to my heart, Madison was going a long time ago."

Katie nodded again, a little more emphatically.

"So, it's not just me," Samantha surmised.

"Not at all," Katie assured her. "I think we all saw a very different side of Madison than Eric has, having lived with her. I truly thought he would have seen through her by now."

"I think he's beginning to – not that I've talked to him about her or anything. I haven't talked to Eric about any of the women. I don't think that would be ethical. I'm basing my opinion completely on my observations this weekend."

"I've had similar observations," Katie told her. "I don't want to get my hopes up too high, but I have been getting vibes from the others that maybe Madison isn't the favorite."

"Yes," Samantha agreed. "I couldn't have put it better myself."

"I hope your heart and my intuition are right."

"We'll find out soon enough," Samantha said with a hopeful smile.

"Yes, we will."

Katie finished as much of her salad as she could stomach, with the tingling of nerves eating away at her insides. She wished Samantha luck, and actually meant it. She would rather see Samantha in the final two than Madison, in spite of the fact she felt she had a better chance against Madison. But that remained to be seen.

Katie pondered over it on her way back to her room. Either way, she didn't have an optimistic outlook on her ultimate future with Eric. If Madison had made it this far, who was to say Eric wouldn't choose her in the end? Obviously, Eric saw something in Madison the others didn't. Katie had a sinking feeling if Madison did make it through tonight, Eric would be choosing Madison overall. She didn't want to believe that would happen. The last thing she wanted was to lose to Madison. But she had to ask herself if would it be any easier losing to Samantha?

Samantha was definitely a formidable opponent. She had it all – looks, personality. She was beautiful, charming and compassionate. She hadn't taken part in any of the bantering that had occurred at the mansion. Her feelings for Eric seemed authentic. Katie wanted to believe Samantha was putting on an act, because she was almost too nice, too polite. Her job as a customer service representative for a credit card company seemed to have seeped into her personality. She spoke to others as she would speak to a customer. She was respectful and attentive, practically to the point of being patronizing. Katie didn't completely buy it. No one could be that perfect all the time.

There was no mystery what Eric saw in Samantha. She had no visible faults. Her perfection was enviable. Katie had to figure out a way to beat her, and it wasn't going to be easy.

Katie didn't want to get too far ahead of herself, but she wanted to be certain she was prepared for any outcome. She would be shocked and heartbroken to be eliminated at this point, but it would almost be better than eventually losing Eric to Madison. That outcome would be the most devastating of any. Of course, she didn't believe there was much of a possibility of that happening. She was ninety percent sure Madison would be going home tonight. That ten percent shadow of doubt, however, forced her to draft a farewell speech as a precaution. She had no choice but to accept the possibility that today may be the last day she would ever see Eric.

She prepared herself mentally as she primped herself for the big event. Barbara had sent up another dress. This one was even lovelier than the last. It was a dark indigo color, almost black, with tiny beads covering the bodice and a long, silk skirt. Katie couldn't fathom what it must cost retail. She was almost afraid to wear it – almost.

The only pressing decision left was whether to accessorize. She felt naked without any jewelry, and hated to appear presumptuous by not donning any. She definitely had to wear something. She shuffled through her new collection of divine pieces. The necklace with the Soulmates logo looked tacky next to the other items. She would probably never wear it again in her life. Still, she had been thrilled to receive it.

The gold bracelet was nice, but she had nothing to go with it. The pearl necklace didn't quite coordinate with the beaded dress. Then her eyes came to rest on the sapphire pendant earrings and matching heart necklace. She had overlooked them at first, assuming they wouldn't go with an indigo dress. On second examination, she realized they were perfect. The beading on the dress was dappled with blue specks. Most of the beads were black, but some were iridescent in dark shades of purple and blue.

Katie had to hand it to Barbara. She had a knack for crafting perfection, from the wardrobe, to the set, to the gifts they were presented, and even the food they ate. Every detail was not merely planned, but scrutinized. The show's success was clearly attributable to Barbara's diligence. Katie took on a new respect for what she had previously viewed as Barbara's nit picking.

Katie was grateful Barbara took such care in selecting the wardrobe. She didn't get to keep the beautiful dresses, but she did get to keep the jewelry. Whatever became of this experience, she would always have a few exquisite pieces of jewelry to bring her fond memories.

Katie put on the sapphire earrings and necklace, and went to the full-length mirror for a final self-appraisal. She was stunning. Not a hair was out of place.

She got a quick drink of water, and then touched up her lipstick. She added a bit of powder to her nose, so her skin wouldn't shine too much under the lights. Satisfied with the results, Katie headed downstairs to confront her fate.

She gave her interview first. This interview was far more intense than the others had been. She found her confidence waning under the pressure from questions such as, "How do you cope with the reality that you may never see Eric again," and "How would your family react to news of an engagement?"

For the first time, Katie envisioned a serious marriage proposal. She had considered the possibility of marriage, but she had never actually imagined Eric down on one knee, offering her a ring. The image was terrifying and was immediately followed by the image of her getting up and turning off the TV in disgust.

Katie didn't mention her apprehension in her interview, but gushed that her family would be thrilled for her, of course, after the initial shock wore off. It was somewhat of an abrupt occurrence, after all. The entire relationship had been fast-forwarded. Nevertheless, Eric was a special person, one that any potential mother-in-law would welcome to the family.

Katie had her doubts that Sharon Cohen would be thrilled to learn her daughter was engaged to a man she'd known barely a month, a man Sharon herself had never even met – not that she hadn't been given the opportunity. No, Katie was certain her mother would not be thrilled with news of a marriage proposal.

Katie felt her throat tighten at the thought. Her voice was audibly higher for the rest of the interview. She kept reminding herself it was acceptable to appear nervous. She wanted to appear self-confident, but not cocky; she definitely didn't want to appear immature and terrified at the prospect of marriage. If Eric didn't believe she was serious about marriage, he would never even consider keeping her for the next round. Madison and Samantha had undoubtedly made their aspirations of marriage perfectly clear long ago.

Katie left the interview with what felt like a rock in the pit of her stomach. She couldn't identify exactly which thought was scarier – getting chosen or getting eliminated. She wanted more time with Eric! She shunned the thought of never seeing him again, but she shuddered to think of changing every aspect of her life to run off and marry this man she technically barely knew.

She needed air. Katie took the elevator downstairs to the lobby level and stepped outside onto the terrace. She wasn't worried about being missed, knowing Barbara would find her if she were gone too long.

The sun was beginning its late afternoon decent, causing the majority of the terrace to be shaded. Katie welcomed the coolness of the shade, as she had been warm inside and would soon be stifling under the lights. She wanted to sit, but couldn't risk wrinkling her dress. Instead, she strolled slowly around the brick courtyard. She paused by the bench she had shared with Eric's mother. The thought of Mrs. Werner someday being her mother-in-law was bizarre. She moved along promptly. She concentrated on her breathing techniques and tried not to think about the fate that awaited her inside.

She stayed outside no more than ten or fifteen minutes. She was feeling considerably calmer and didn't want to irritate Barbara by holding up the shoot. She was ready to get the shoot over with, truth be told. She returned upstairs to find she hadn't been missed at all. In fact, they didn't appear to be any closer to shooting than when she'd left.

She stood near the interview area and tried to catch part of Madison's interview. She stayed back far enough to appear casual, as though she wasn't eavesdropping. She couldn't hear much, but she could see Madison smiling and wiping back tears at the same time. Maybe she knew she was at the end of her run with glory.

Madison's tears dried up immediately upon concluding the interview. She strode away and went to speak with Barbara about something. Madison pointed to the back of her shoulder, where her dress was seamed. Katie saw no wardrobe malfunction from her position, but presumed the shoot would not begin until Madison's concern was rectified. Barbara flagged down Zeb to care for Madison's issue.

Over an hour elapsed before Shane made a physical entrance. The women had been arranged and rearranged until Katie's feet were sore. She couldn't wait to get this ordeal over with.

Shane addressed the ladies in his usual manner. Katie was growing weary of Shane's act. His attitude on camera was full of compassion and interest in the girls' lives and well-being, while off camera, he wanted nothing to do with any of them. Shane was a Hollywood snoot, as Katie and Ann Marie liked to call actors who thought too much of themselves. One would never have guessed from Shane's rehearsed speeches that he wasn't best friends with the women. He smiled at each of them, making direct eye contact and addressing them by name.

"Katie ... Madison ... Samantha," he recited, his arms outstretched as though physically embracing them. "We are down to three. This is our last elimination, so to speak. One of you will be leaving us forever. Two of you will be chosen as finalists. The two finalists will not be brought together in this way again. Instead, each of you will be whisked off on private, romantic excursions with Eric. Then Eric will have to face his ultimate decision, which he will communicate to you individually in private.

"As we approach that long-awaited day, we must say goodbye to one of you. Tonight's event is a bittersweet one. I won't delay long in turning things over to Eric. I know he has a lot to say. I would, however, like to show you the exquisite trinkets which await two of you in our ceremonial gold box."

He opened the box. Inside, the velvet lining was inclined to display two brilliant diamond and sapphire tennis bracelets. They were, indeed exquisite, as they sparkled under the hot lights. They coordinated perfectly with the necklace and earrings Katie had coincidentally had the foresight to wear. Of course, Madison and Samantha had intuitively done the same. Unfortunately, one of the three women was not to receive a matching tennis bracelet.

Katie tried not to gawk at the gold box, which Shane purposely left open on the velvet pedestal. Katie whole-heartedly wanted to continue her relationship with Eric, but she coveted one of the tennis bracelets as well. They were spectacular. Losing Eric would be emotionally difficult to bear, but losing a diamond and sapphire tennis bracelet would be insurmountable. She could no doubt find another "Eric" in the world somewhere, but she could never, ever afford a piece of jewelry like the ones sitting before her.

Finally, Shane introduced the man of the hour. Eric entered looking as handsome as ever. He was excited and nervous at the same time, apparent from his smile and constant wringing of his hands.

"Good evening, ladies," he said, smiling at each of the three remaining contenders, but careful not to gaze too long at any one of them.

The women smiled back but didn't speak. Katie didn't think her voice would have come out had she tried to speak.

"You all look beautiful," Eric continued. "I'm amazed at how truly beautiful each of you are, inside and out. I have been so lucky to have gotten this far, and to have three incredible women to choose from. I can't believe it. And I can't believe how fast our time together went. I ... um ..." he faltered. "Um ... I'm sorry. Do I need to start over?"

"Keep going, Eric. We'll edit it," Barbara instructed.

"I'm sorry," Eric nodded, them bowed his head to gain his composure. He paused only a few seconds, but the slip-up made his speech seem very rehearsed. Katie was surprised and disappointed, but let the feelings pass. Had she been in his position, she certainly would have rehearsed what she was going to say.

"I honestly can't believe how fast this has all gone," Eric continued. "I came into this experience with fairly high expectations. I'll admit, I had my doubts about finding a potential wife here, but I did believe I would make a real connection with one special woman. I never dreamed I would be presented with three potential wives. It's just not like me to be so taken with three completely different types of women. You are each unique and special in your own way. I don't want to let any of you go."

Eric paused and looked down at his feet. He took deep, deliberate breaths. He was obviously overwhelmed with emotions – perhaps so overwhelmed he'd forgotten his speech.

"I have to," he said finally. "I don't want to hurt any of you. I want you to believe that in your hearts. I had no idea coming into this, the magnitude of emotions involved. I just want you to know that it is not my intention to hurt any of you. It is an unfortunate byproduct of this process. If I had the choice to do this all again, I honestly don't know if I could, knowing what I know now."

He paused again, and the tension in the room thickened. Eric was genuinely distraught over this elimination – whether by the decision itself or merely the vocalizing of his decision, Katie wasn't sure.

"But I know that letting one of you go brings me closer to my ultimate destiny. That is why we are all here, after all."

Eric stopped, as though he had planned to say more, but opted against it. His hand quivering slightly, he reached for the first tennis bracelet. He turned it in his hand, feeling for the clasp. He looped it over his left hand and watched as it settled into place. The room was silent, as everyone waited, staring at Eric and the tennis bracelet sparkling in his hands.

"Samantha," he said finally, looking up to see her reaction.

She was beaming, her cheeks flushed, as she stepped forward. She hugged Eric and said something softly in his ear.

Katie's heart was pounding out of her chest. It was down to this – her and Madison. She felt like she couldn't breathe. She stole a glance at Madison. Madison's face looked pale against her dark hair; Katie's own face felt pale as well. It seemed to take Eric forever to fasten the bracelet on Samantha's wrist, and then it seemed another eternity before he lifted the final bracelet from the gold box.

This was the end for one of them, Katie thought. She had to be chosen. She couldn't imagine not being chosen. But it was Eric's decision, and Eric for some reason liked Madison.

Then he spoke.

"Katie."

Katie exhaled. She felt the blood rush back to her extremities. Eric had chosen her! She grinned uncontrollably and stepped forward, throwing her arms around him.

"Thank you," Katie felt as though she had waited so long to hear Eric call her name, and then everything happened very quickly. Before the news had fully registered, she had already received her bracelet and returned to her place, while Eric and Madison had departed for their farewells.

Barbara immediately whisked Katie and Samantha away for another interview. They were never reunited with Eric. As Barbara soon explained, they were not to be reunited with Eric until their private excursions.
After the interview, Katie returned disappointedly to her room. Something wonderful had happened and she had no one to share it with. Her advancement was not filled with the elation it should have been, but she felt celebratory nonetheless. She flopped down on the bed and started laughing out loud. Madison was gone! Her instincts had not failed her. She stood up and spun around in circles in her beautiful gown. She spun until she became dizzy, and then flopped back down on the bed.

Maybe dreams do come true.

Chapter Twenty

Katie was plagued by the feeling something was amiss the next morning, but she had little time to ponder over it as she rushed to make her flight. However, she had plenty of time on the plane to contemplate the entire weekend's events. She had not been informed where she was headed until she received her ticket at the airport. Her final destination was St. Thomas, US Virgin Islands. Her apprehension changed gradually to excitement, in spite of the fact that the view from the plane was a vast expanse of ocean. Katie opted to shade her window in lieu of staring at the plain, blue, never-ending scene below. As the pilot announced they would begin their descent, Katie opened the shade to catch a glimpse of Caribbean green waters. It had clouded up, and she couldn't see much until they were very low. She still didn't see any landing strip, and they were flying extremely low over the beautiful, jewel-colored water. The plane touched down, and much to Katie's relief they were on land, not sea.

They rolled slowly to a stop next to a tiny airport. Katie immediately noticed the cameras waiting for her. Then she saw Eric. A rush of adrenaline swept over her. Her fears dissolved, magically transformed into hope and exhilaration. Katie felt like her feet never touched the ground from the plane into Eric's arms. She kissed him on the lips and embraced him again. Her feet were still airborne as Eric lifted her and spun her around, gripping her tightly. Katie found herself giggling like a school girl. She kissed Eric again, as he lowered her back down to stable ground.

They were interrupted by a sudden downpour of rain. Katie had barely noticed they were still outside. She had never exited a plane outside a terminal, but she also had never seen a terminal as small as this one, either. Eric tucked Katie under his arm and whisked her into the tiny building, safe from the warm, tropical shower. Directly inside they passed a tiki bar dappled with rum drinks, and they grabbed some as they shot through the miniscule airport. On the other side of the building, their official

Soulmates transportation awaited, this time a black van with tinted windows, the *Soulmates* logos affixed to the doors.

They climbed in and dug into a bottle of rum. Katie laughed and winked at Eric, nodding at the bottle of champagne he had opted not to open.

"Too many windows," he explained.

"That's probably a wise decision," Katie agreed. "Besides, this rum is totally hitting the spot."

"Isn't it?" Eric grinned, snuggling closer to his date. He leaned in for a quick kiss.

Their kiss was interrupted by an abrupt curve which threw them apart. Katie turned to the window to see they were on an extremely curvy, mountainous route with spectacular views. Katie found herself thrown back into Eric's lap several times, which neither of them minded other than the sporadic spilling of their drinks. She giggled and licked rum from her fingers the entire way to the hotel. They arrived soon enough, even though they seemed to have twisted and turned all the way to the opposite side of the island.

The tropical shower stopped as quickly as it had started, and the radiant sun efficiently disposed of any evidence of rain. They exited the van to a gorgeous day. Eric took Katie's hand and led her through the meticulously landscaped grounds to their suite, which was the most luxurious lodgings she had ever seen.

The high, beamed ceiling housed several large fans. There were flowers everywhere – exotic, brilliant blooms in huge cobalt blue vases. There was a separate seating area and kitchenette. The furniture was rich mahogany, the four-poster king-sized bed centered on a raised platform, from which one could perfectly view the ocean waves outside the wall of glass opposite. The sliding door nestled inside the glass wall led to a large private balcony with a marvelous view. The hotel was built into the side of a cliff, so while their accommodations seemed to be on the ground floor, their balcony was a marble platform hovered over a rocky bluff. The bathroom, complete with a double Jacuzzi tub, was marble as well.

Katie laughed, as Eric kicked off his sandals.

"This is incredible," Katie gasped, scanning the room again to take in every last detail.

"Isn't it?" Eric said again, grinning like a child in a candy shop.

Katie couldn't help grinning herself. She was ecstatic to be here, in such an exotic, tropical setting, with Eric no less. She didn't even care that the cameras accompanied them everywhere they went.

They sat on the balcony, enjoying their rum drinks and snacking on a platter of fresh fruits and cheeses that was waiting for them in their room. Neither had ever been to St. Thomas, or any place in the Caribbean. Eric confessed he hadn't taken any vacation in years. Between working long hours and becoming a homeowner, he hadn't devoted much time to anything else in his life. Katie made him promise to take a decent vacation after his duties on the show were fulfilled. Eric whole-heartedly agreed, although admitted much of his commitment on *Soulmates* had been rather like a vacation.

Katie had to agree. *Soulmates* had been the best vacation in her life – the accommodations, the food the drink, the entertainment and the companionship were unsurpassable. This abbreviated trip to St. Thomas was the icing on the cake.

The couple didn't stay on the balcony very long. The heat was becoming uncomfortable, and the sound of the ocean waves taunted them. They changed into bathing suits and took a walk down a wooden-planked path with hundreds of steps leading to the ocean. They took a short stroll along the water. Although romantic, the beach was even hotter than the balcony, and the water line was ridden with shells. Katie didn't want to walk very far without her sandals on, but she didn't want to wear them, either. They ended up settling on a private corner next to one of the resort's meandering swimming pools. They were at the end by a small waterfall, which trickled gently in the background. Their own dedicated pool boy kept the rum drinks coming.

The heat was almost unbearable. They didn't sit long before they had to jump into the pool. They relaxed the rest of the afternoon in the sun, alternating between chaise lounges and the pool. They talked and joked, growing serious just long enough for short intervals of kissing.

Katie felt more comfortable around Eric than she had ever felt with a man in her life. They had a strong connection from the beginning. Admittedly, he was not the man she had imagined herself spending the rest of her life with, but he was a great catch. He was mature and ready for a relationship; he had a stable job, a nice house and a normal family. He was handsome, had a nice body and a super sense of humor. What more could a girl ask for?

Still, Katie didn't know if this was love. She had never been in love, so she had no comparison. She hadn't felt any so-called "sparks" when Eric kissed her, but she did feel horny. They definitely had a physical attraction. She knew Eric felt that attraction as well. He hadn't been unable to take his eyes off her all day long. And they got along superbly. They laughed non-stop.

But, was it love? The question weighed heavily on Katie, even more so because she knew Eric had prior relationships to compare. She didn't want to assume it was love. Maybe Eric clearly knew it wasn't ... Yet she had to maintain the intensity to stand a chance with him. Was she setting herself up to live a lie, or was she taking all the steps necessary to secure her future happiness?

She kept up with the charade the rest of the day into dinner. It was the most spectacular date she had ever experienced – or even imagined. She felt like she had landed a stint on a daytime drama and was acting out the dream. Real dates didn't go this well, and were far less glamorous.

Dinner was a private affair on their balcony. There was an array of foods: mahi-mahi, shrimp, marinated pork and chicken, grilled vegetables, and delectable salads of artichoke hearts, garbanzo beans and julienned carrots. Katie felt like she was eating hand-over-fist, tasting a little of everything, then tasting it all again. Dessert was a chocolate fountain for two, and was served just after Katie declared she couldn't eat another bite. Somehow, she found room, as Eric fed her chocolate-covered strawberries and chunks of fresh pineapple.

"This is the best fruit I've ever had," Katie swooned after each bite.

"Anything tastes good after, what, fifteen rum drinks?" Eric laughed.

"That's probably true, but we're nowhere near fifteen drinks, unless you're combining our consumption."

"I don't know … we've been drinking all day."

"Yes, we have. And I'll admit my taste buds may be altered from all the rum, but my emotions are intact. I have to tell you, Eric, this is the best date I have ever had."

"I'm glad you're enjoying yourself."

Katie shot him a glance. "Don't patronize me."

"I'm not!" Eric grinned. "I'm having a great time. You know what? This is the best date I've ever had, too." He slapped his hands on his thighs and lifted his head to meet Katie's glance. His demeanor was still teasing, yet sobering.

"Your best date so far," Katie blurted out before she could stop herself. She immediately regretted what she'd said, and rephrased her comment to camouflage her jealousy of Samantha. "I mean, the night is young."

"So, it is," Eric agreed, his green eyes lighting up. Much to Katie's relief, Eric had not detected her insecurity.

"What should we do next?" Katie asked, raising her eyebrows tauntingly.

Eric took her hand and led her inside. After a long and extremely arousing kiss, they decided it would be best to get some air. They could seize the opportunity to indulge in their surroundings while enjoying each other's company. Neither party was anxious to leave the suite, but neither was prepared to deal with what might happen if they stayed.

Both admittedly wanted more than what their current situation would allow, but they were acutely aware of the inappropriateness. They discussed this predicament as they strolled hand-in-hand around the resort gardens.

The sun had almost completed its descent – a far less awe-inspiring sight than those sunsets they had witnessed in California, but nevertheless romantic. They enjoyed the warmth of the breeze and the smell of tropical flora. They found as they walked, they distanced themselves from the cameras.

"I'm glad they backed off and gave us some privacy," Eric confided, "but I'm also a little uneasy to be left alone with you. I don't know if I can trust myself to be a gentleman."

"I know," Katie concurred, turning her gaze from her toes to Eric's profile. "I hope you don't doubt my feelings for you, because I really would love to take this relationship to the next step, but I don't think that would be fair to the third person involved in all this. And I hope she would extend me the same courtesy."

"Of course," Eric said. "I totally understand."

"You don't think I'm not attracted to you, or prude or anything?"

"I think I know you pretty well," Eric assured her. He stopped walking and turned to face her. He grabbed her around the waist and pulled her close. When their lips met, all tentativeness disappeared. They didn't hold back, but indulged in the moment, allowing waves of passion to sweep over them much as the sound of the ocean waves sweeping over the beach nearby.

They kissed, as the last gleam of sunlight faded into the soft, velvety night. The warm, tropical breeze steadily confronted the beads of sweat on their bodies, causing goose bumps to erupt down Katie's arms and legs. She shivered involuntarily in spite of the upper-seventies temperature of the night.

"Shall we head back?" suggested Eric.

"Sure," Katie said, ready to get more comfortable with her date, yet reluctant for this moment to end. She had never before felt so consumed by a man.

They walked back to the suite hand-in-hand. Neither said a word, but every few minutes they would look at each other and smile. The silence was comforting, rather than awkward. The cameras followed at a distance, but left them in privacy at the door to their suite.

Once safely inside, Eric decided to interrupt the serenity. He picked up the bottle of champagne that was waiting on ice and raised his eyebrows at Katie.

"Shall we?"

"I think we should," Katie agreed. "It's a special occasion, and you haven't put out a window in a long time."

"I've never actually put out a window," Eric reminded her, as he removed the gold wrapping from the top of the bottle. "Hopefully, I won't start tonight."

"Let's hope not," Katie giggled, standing clear and readying her hands near her head to protect from any stray, flying objects. "They would probably kick us out."

"You really have no faith in me," Eric surmised, his grin teasing, green eyes dancing.

"I didn't say anything!"

"You didn't have to," Eric laughed, as he pointed the bottle away from his date.

The explosion was impressive, but the cork caused no damage.

"I think I'm getting better at this!"

"You should be," Katie joked. "You've had enough practice."

"All right. I've had just about enough out of you," Eric said threateningly, throwing his arms around her and dragging her down to the couch on top of him.

Katie let out a small squeak when she landed on Eric. She started to giggle but quickly regained her composure. She had been yearning to be in this position all day and she wasn't about to waste a second. She made no attempt to get up, but rather leaned even harder against Eric and kissed him. All the passion she had been holding back for weeks was released at last, and she kissed him without concern for anything but each other. Her worries, inhibitions and feelings of guilt evaporated.

Eric returned her enthusiasm. He pressed his mouth harder against hers, their tongues intermingling intensely. Kate relished in the moment, but pulled back after a short time.

"I've been waiting all day for that," Eric whispered, his eyes still half-closed.

"Mmm … I have too," Katie replied, letting her body slip to the side of Eric's so that she was half on him instead of full frontal. She stroked her finger along his strong jawbone, where the five-o'clock shadow was beginning to emerge. Eric fully opened his eyes and met Katie's gaze. He reached up and grabbed a lock of hair that had cascaded over her shoulder, and smoothed it over her back.

"I can't believe how fast this whole thing has gone. We're already at the end, and there's so much more I want to know about you."

"We have all night," Katie reminded him optimistically. "Ask away."

"I just want to look at you," Eric responded, his eyes tracing her face, consuming every detail.

Katie couldn't help wondering if Eric believed this would be their last date. His expression was dreamy – hopefully more wistful than regretful. Perhaps he was imagining their future together. Katie couldn't tell if Eric was contemplating how he would ask her to marry him, or how he would let her down easy. She hoped he was indulging in the moment they had just shared, and contemplating how he was going to let Samantha down easy.

Katie smiled and kissed him again.

"You have your whole life to look at me, if you want," she said soothingly, rubbing his cheek.

The dreamy expression left Eric's face, and his playful grin returned. His greed eyes lit up, with that delightful charm Katie was growing to love.

"I don't want to waste a minute," he told her and pulled her close. She was in his arms again, and he was kissing her and stroking her hair. He sat up a bit, propping himself on his arm so he could reach her better. He rubbed her back and pulled her body tightly against his. All of the playfulness was quickly replaced by passion.

Katie at last felt a surge of confidence that Eric was going to pick her in the end. His soft lips couldn't possibly kiss anyone else the way he kissed her, with such intensity. She was going to be his; there was no turning back.

Her fears dismissed, she returned his passion. She had never been one to wear her heart on her sleeve, but she let her inhibitions go for the time being and kissed her "boyfriend." She let him caress her, knowing she should hold back, but desperate for more.

As it was, Eric held back in the end. He went so far as to cup her breast through her shirt, slowly pushing the shirt open and kissing her bare breast gently. She would have torn her clothes off at that point, but Eric withdrew, returning to eye level and taking her in his arms once again. He embraced her, sitting so still Katie thought he may have fallen asleep.

"There is no doubt that I want you," he whispered. It was nothing Katie didn't already know. His body was pressed so firmly against hers, she could feel every muscle.

"There is no harm in waiting," Katie smiled, knowing that when the time finally came, it would be the best night of her life. She knew it was right to wait, but her heart was still racing, and her breast still tingling from the touch of his warm mouth.

She was glad the cameras weren't in the room. Barbara had assured them there were no hidden cameras and explained her intention was to leave much to the imagination of the viewers. If they didn't know what happened behind closed doors, it made the finale more exciting. Essentially that meant the entire viewing public would assume Katie and Eric had slept together, but Katie supposed there were worse things in life.

All things considered, Katie was relieved to spend some time alone with Eric. Even though they had gotten to know each other fairly well during the short period of time they had known each other, she felt as though there were many unanswered questions. She certainly didn't know enough about Eric to consider a marriage proposal.

She wondered what type of commitment he would be asking for, because marriage seemed far too sudden.

Finally, Eric drew back and faced Katie. His eyes were greener than ever, his skin flushed. He bore a serious expression, but quickly relaxed. He smiled, and a sheepish grin emerged across his lips.

"I'm sorry," he confessed. "I got carried away."

"You're fine," Katie told him, thinking he actually had enormous restraint.

"I really like being with you, and I tend to forget we're in this ... situation, for a lack of a better word."

"You don't need to explain, Eric. I understand completely. I'm in the same ... situation." She smiled and rubbed his shoulder.

"I wish things were different, but then we would never have met. I have to be grateful for that, even though it's difficult."

"I know."

"So ... to get super serious on you, what do you want the outcome of all this to be?"

Katie was paralyzed by the point-blank question. She had played the future out in her mind many times, but she truly didn't know what she wanted the outcome to be. Her competitive side wanted to win more than anything in the world. Her practical side said, "then what?" What on earth was she getting herself into? Winning Eric presented a whole separate set of issues – marriage, relocation, eventual motherhood – all of which were terrifying. Yet how could she tell Eric she was terrified of the prospect of spending her life with him?

Katie didn't know how to respond to Eric's question. Tell him the truth, and she would ruin her chance of being chosen. Tell Eric what he wanted to hear, and she could force herself into a future she wasn't sure she wanted. She had to say something. She couldn't squash her chances with Eric after she'd come so far. He was awaiting her answer.

"I don't know, exactly," she began cautiously. "I don't want to sit here and tell you I want to have two kids named Bobby and Sally, because I don't think we know each other that well yet. But I do love being with you. I know I want more. I want an opportunity to date you in the real world, and have a normal relationship. I want things to progress naturally."

"We kind of skipped all that," Eric confessed.

"Well, we're on an accelerated schedule. We've dated, I've met your parents, and we're on this glamorous, romantic getaway together. We've gone through the natural progression of a relationship at a completely unnatural pace. I'm ready to take the next step with you, that's for sure. I'm just not certain what the next step should be."

Eric nodded but was silent.

Katie felt the need to elaborate.

"I'm not saying I don't want to consider marrying you," she began carefully, trying not to seem presumptuous. "I'm just saying we don't have to run down the aisle tomorrow."

"Oh, no," Eric agreed. "Not at all. I came into this to find a potential wife, but I want to do all the things couples do before they get married. I want to go on real dates. I want to go to the movies, or to the mall, or join a golf league together. I want to spend time together, get to know each other's families, maybe live together. Like you said, I don't plan on eloping after the final taping of the show."

"No?" Katie asked, needing reassurance.

"Not at all. I still want to have all the things you have in a relationship."

"Then, do you think you could give – one of us – an engagement ring?" Katie asked timidly.

"I do," Eric said after only a second of thought. "I don't see why two people can't enjoy all the aspects of dating and engagement at the same time."

Katie smiled and rested her head on Eric's shoulder. If Eric thought they could do it, then that was good enough for her. This heart-to-heart talk eased her concerns. She breathed a sigh of relief and relaxed into Eric's arms. This was exactly where she belonged at this moment in time. Whatever happened tomorrow happened; she needn't worry herself about the future when the present was so precious.

Chapter Twenty-One

Katie was home again before she knew it. She felt like the entire trip to St. Thomas had been a dream. One minute she was in Eric's arms, and the next she was back in her tiny, lonely apartment. Twenty-four hours had somehow elapsed, and she lay awake in her own bed and yearned for the warmth of Eric's body next to hers.

Last night, she and Eric had shared the most incredible, romantic night. Even though they didn't make love, they bonded in a way Katie couldn't imagine him bonding with Samantha. She wanted to revel in the vivid recollection of every detail of yesterday. She could still smell Eric's cologne; she could see his piercing green eyes. She could feel his breath on her bare shoulder, his lips on her breast. She shivered suddenly, her nipples tightening as the wave of emotions passed through her body as forcefully as they had last night.

If she closed her eyes, she could almost trick herself into believing she was still there. She and Eric had moved from the couch to the bed after a while. She had changed into a short, creamy-colored silk negligee, and Eric wore only a pair of boxers. They had actually discussed lying naked next to each other, but agreed the temptation would be too great.

Katie wanted nothing more than to strip down naked in front of him and to forget about everything else. Her more reasonable side knew that resistance was still the key. She had to leave Eric wanting more. So, she donned the sexy, little number that left just enough to the imagination, and slipped into the bed slowly enough to give him a glimpse of her body. Now he had seen her in a bikini and a sheer negligee. He had seen enough to know if he wanted more, and Katie was certain that he did, in fact, want to see more.

They fell asleep in each other's arms, after talking much of the night. It felt so natural to Katie, lying there with Eric, that she forgot to be afraid. She let her guard down and let him into her life. She felt the warmth radiating off Eric's body as they slept, and it warmed her heart. She felt loved and secure in Eric's bed, in Eric's arms, like he was her savior and protector. He was the one who had been able to eradicate her deeply-imbedded fear of men. She had almost completely forgotten the feelings of loneliness, guilt and unworthiness instilled by the abandonment of her father. She felt healed. She felt as though she were finally where she belonged.

She slept well that night in Eric's arms, which was probably equally attributable to the amount of alcohol she'd consumed as to her newly-discovered comfort level with a man. Between that and the pure exhaustion of the schedule they'd been keeping, she slept better than she had slept in a long time.

She probably wouldn't sleep again until this ordeal was over. She wouldn't see Eric again for three days, and that may be the last time she would ever see him. She couldn't think that way. She had to keep a positive attitude. Her romantic getaway with Eric had been a fantasy-come-true. These few days without him would soon be a distant memory. She and Eric could look back and laugh at the entire experience. They would say all the little things they couldn't say during the taping. They would share their thoughts on the other women: Katie would confide in him all the code names she'd made up for the other girls, and Eric would laugh and say, "That is so true!"

Katie couldn't wait to share everything with him. She wanted him to know how he made her feel. And she wanted to know when he first realized that she was "the one." Most of all, she wanted to be in his arms again, and she longed to hear those three little words she had never allowed any man close enough to feel, let alone vocalize.

She thought about what she would say when Eric chose her, and how she would respond. She tried not to think about receiving a marriage proposal, because the very thought still made her stomach ache. She decided it would be best if the proposal came as a surprise. She didn't want to appear too prepared; the finale would be much more exciting if spontaneous.

Katie tossed and turned much of the night, because she was simply too excited to sleep. The question in her mind was no longer if Eric would choose her, but rather how he would do so, and what would come next.

Katie had no qualms whatsoever of moving to Pittsburgh. She had felt lost ever since she left New York City, and quite frankly felt lost during most of her time spent there as well. Her future seemed to have no purpose. Her life was one audition after another, with no end in sight. She was constantly practicing for a role she had yet to land. She was beginning to think it would never happen, either in her so-called acting career or in her real life. She was going nowhere. If she couldn't get a job playing a wife on TV, she didn't know how she expected herself to be a wife in real life. This question weighed heavily on her. She didn't know if she was ready to be someone's wife, but she definitely wanted to move forward in life. She was stuck in a rut and needed to get a fresh start, in a fresh city. She needed to try something new. Eric was exactly what she needed.

She awoke the next morning feeling as though she hadn't slept in days. It was after ten o'clock, and she didn't feel guilty about lounging a while before starting her day. She literally had no reason to get out of bed at all, if she didn't want to. She had no job, no commitments. Her bills were paid for the time being. She should probably call her mother to let her know she was still alive. She could stand to make a trip to the laundromat as well.

Katie put off calling her mother until after she showered. She needed to be fully charged before engaging in that particular conversation. She didn't really want to talk to her at all. She knew her mother would have tons of questions, not the least of which regarding marriage. She knew she would have to approach the subject eventually, but given their history, she saw no justification for opening that can of worms any sooner than necessary. In the event that Eric miraculously didn't choose her, she wasn't about to have wasted the time and energy an argument with her mother required. Besides, the last thing she needed was an "I told you so." She wasn't ready to convince her mother that she might get engaged, just to be dumped two days later. She seriously doubted that would be the case, but with Sharon Cohen, one did not passionately argue one's case until one was absolutely certain.

Katie opted to leave her mother a voice mail on her cell phone, rather than call her at work. She would prepare for battle another day. She did, however, make another dreaded phone call – this one to Ann Marie. She should have called yesterday, and was surprised Ann Marie hadn't tried calling her yet. Ann Marie was not generally a patient person, and must have known Katie was back in town.

"What's up?" Katie asked when her best friend answered.

"What's up?" Ann Marie repeated indignantly. "You tell me. What's going on? When did you get back? What happened with Eric?"

"I got back yesterday."

"Yesterday?" Ann Marie barked. "Why didn't you call me?"

"I did call you," Katie pointed you.

"You know what I mean. Why didn't you call me yesterday? You know I'm dying to hear all the details! Where did you go? How far did you go with Eric? Are you still in the running?"

"Calm down and I'll tell you everything."

Ann Marie quieted and listened, as Katie narrated every possible detail about her dream date with Eric. Ann Marie was very attentive, and barely interrupted except for an excited interjection from time to time.

"It was awesome, Ann Marie," Katie concluded. "I had the best time. I can't believe I'm back home already. I still feel giddy."

"Are you in love?" Ann Marie prodded teasingly.

"I'm not sure, exactly ..." Katie admitted. "I mean, I've never been in love before. I have no prior experience on this type of thing. I know what I'm feeling. I had an incredible time with Eric and I definitely want to win this thing, but I can't honestly say I'm in love. Does that mean I'm not?" she asked insecurely, clearly disappointed with herself.

"Not necessarily. Everyone feels love in their own way. Some of those girls were gaga in love with Eric the second they met him. That doesn't mean it's real love. And it doesn't mean what you're feeling isn't."

"That's a relief. I'd feel guilty stealing him away from Samantha if I'm not even really in love."

"No, you wouldn't."

"You're right, I wouldn't," Katie laughed.

"Wait a minute!" Ann Marie realized. "Does that mean Madison is gone?"

"She sure is."

Ann Marie squealed. "Finally!"

"You can't tell anyone. I'm not supposed to talk about it."

"Of course not. I know that. Besides, who would I tell?"

"I know, I'm just so nervous. I really want this to be the start of something. I don't want to lose Eric after coming this far. What if he's the one?"

"What if he is?"

"If he is, I'm scared to death, but my point is, shouldn't I know that by now? I realize, given my past, I'm not going to hear wedding bells as quickly as other girls do, because I've got a lot of issues with marriage in general. But I will hear them eventually, won't I? I don't want to get too excited yet, but I truly feel something for Eric, and he obviously feels something for me."

"Do you think he's going to pick you?" Ann Marie asked excitedly.

"I think he is."

Ann Marie squealed in delight. Katie was grinning from ear to ear, and her face felt flushed.

"I am so excited!" Ann Marie cried.

"Are you sure? No hard feelings?"

"Of course not! I told you that! I am thrilled for you. What are you going to say if he asks you to marry him? I'll die of excitement."

"Don't get ahead of things. I haven't prepared an acceptance speech."

"But you would accept."

"I guess so. I haven't really thought that far ahead."

"You are so full of shit, Katie," Ann Marie called her best friend's bluff. "You don't do anything without thinking it through, analyzing the situation from every angle and reanalyzing it just to be sure. I know you. You most certainly have thought about it."

"I've thought about the possibility of it happening, sure, but I don't know how I would respond."

"You better get on that, if you think he's going to ask you."

"I know. And you're right. It's not like me not to be prepared for every possibility. On the other hand, I don't want to be presumptuous. I don't know. I get scared every time I start to think about it. I want a relationship with Eric. I want to move forward with him, but marriage is a whole different ball game. I'll be psyched if he picks me, but I don't necessarily need a marriage proposal. I certainly don't want to bank on getting one just to be disappointed."

"I understand your need to be cautious, but Katie, you've got to be prepared also. This is going to happen quickly. And you still have your career to consider. You need to make this season's finale red hot! Don't lose sight of the whole reason you did the show to begin with."

The words suddenly sounded harsh to Katie. They had discussed this very topic many times. Katie had done the show for her career, admittedly, but now her future was at stake, and another person's future was at stake. Eric was not just the leading man playing opposite her; he was a decent person with genuine feelings. Katie had invested a good deal of time and effort in convincing Eric she was in this for more than just her career. She thought she had gotten past that.

Nevertheless, she supposed Ann Marie had a point. Whether or not things worked out with Eric, she had landed a part on a TV show; she had done her best to bring excitement to the show, to follow direction well from Barbara. She had made contacts in the industry. The exposure was a good thing, no matter what happened with Eric.

"I'll be prepared when the time comes, for either outcome," Katie tried to assure her friend, as well as herself.

"But you think you got it?" Ann Marie repeated, knowing that the vocalization of the words would boost Katie's confidence.

"I think so, but you never know. Weirder things have happened."

"No, no. You're smart not to discount Samantha. The woman literally has no faults, as far as I could tell. And Eric seemed pretty smitten with her."

"I know. It was sickening. She seems almost too perfect."

"I know, I roomed with her. I tried to find a dark side, believe me, but there wasn't one. She doesn't even have any annoying habits."

"Her perpetual politeness is annoying."

"Annoying, but not a fault."

"Politeness can be annoying to a fault. It was overkill, admit it."

"It was constant, but I don't think Eric was annoyed by it. I think he actually liked it."

"He did, but hopefully he liked my raw honesty better. I think Samantha's true colors will come out eventually."

"I don't know … "Ann Marie hesitated to agree. "She seemed pretty sincere."

"Whose side are you on?" Katie demanded jokingly.

"I want whatever is best for you, my friend."

"Thank you for your support," Katie commented, in her best political-campaigning tone.

"Don't be sarcastic. I know I wasn't exactly supportive before, with the whole jealousy factor going on, but I'm over all that. I'm not hung up on Eric. I realize he wasn't the right guy for me. If you think he's the right guy for you, I'm behind you one-hundred percent."

"I'm glad to have you on my side, honestly. I hated fighting with you. You're my best friend. And besides, you always win. But seriously, I need your support now more than ever. I'm a little scared how this is going to end. I think Eric is going to pick me, and that scares the crap out of me. I'm going to need your help getting through this."

"You know all you have to do is ask."

"I'm asking. If Eric does propose to me, I'm going to need your help convincing my mother that he's an OK guy. She is going to freak out."

"She is going to freak out," Ann Marie concurred. "And she's not going to listen to me any more than she'll listen to you. I'm the bad influence that prompted you into a dead-end career, remember?"

"That's never intimidated you before."

"I'm not intimidated now. If you want me to give your mother my opinion, I will. I'm never short of giving my opinion. I'm just saying, your mother has never put much faith in my opinions in the past."

"No, but at least I won't have to face her alone."

"Wimp."

"I'm not usually a wimp! You know how she feels on the subjects of men and marriage. I'm dreading telling her. That's just wrong. What girl in her right mind would be petrified of telling her mother she's engaged? That should be one of the happiest moments in a girl's life – sharing with her mother the incredibly exciting news that she's found the man of her dreams, and he's fulfilled her deepest desire by asking her to marry him. That would be a normal thing for a mother and daughter to celebrate together. Most mothers can hardly wait to start planning every detail of the special day and go shopping for dresses. But in my screwed-up life, it's a nightmare. Men are evil, marriage is the seal of death, and Sharon Cohen is always right, no matter what."

"I don't envy you in that respect," Ann Marie replied. "That's one conversation I wouldn't be looking forward to either. But, you can cross that bridge when you come to it. I will be there for you to help however I can. For now, concentrate on what you're going to say when your man proposes to you on national TV."

The girls squealed together at the prospect.

"I can't wait! This is killing me. I just want to get it over with and move on with my life, and start planning my future. Which reminds me, I have one more favor to ask you."

"You already owe me big time for talking to Sharon."

"Not yet, I don't. I will owe you. But seriously, I could never get married without you by me side. Will you be my maid of honor?"

"Of course, I will! I'd be honored. I couldn't imagine you getting married without me by your side. I'll be jealous as hell that you're going first, but I'll get over it."

Katie laughed. Ann Marie had a good point. Anyone who knew the two of them would have bet money that Ann Marie would be hooked up long before Katie – if Katie ever got married at all. But that remained to be seen. Marriage could be a long way off. Katie's engagement might be so prolonged that Ann Marie may end up getting married first.

The girls laughed and talked of the future for almost two hours. It felt great to have her best friend back! Katie's confidence was soaring, between that and her recent trip to St. Thomas. She was ninety percent sure Eric was going to pick her. They had a chemistry she couldn't imagine existed between him and any other woman.

Katie was confident, yet still bothered by the fact that Eric was on an equally romantic date with Samantha at that very moment. The sick feeling in her stomach returned every time she thought about it. It was a mixture of jealousy and betrayal.

Such a strong attachment to a man was new for Katie. She had always preferred to keep it casual. If she was seeing a man who was also seeing other people, it put less pressure on her to commit. Neither party got overly attached. Katie got a free dinner once in a while and could move along any time she felt the urge. She never had to broach the subject of the seriousness of a relationship and where it was going. She certainly never had the fear of an ensuing conversation on marriage, neither with the man nor with her mother. Katie's aloofness had probably benefitted her in getting this far with Eric. She hadn't minded sharing him with the other girls – until now.

Katie was confused by these new feelings of jealousy but knew they must be completely natural. The man she just spent the night with was off on a romantic rendezvous with another woman. This particular other woman was extraordinarily beautiful, charming and captivating. Fortunately, Samantha was also reserved and proper. She didn't seem to be a total prude, but probably wouldn't allow Eric to do anything other than kiss her. This supposition brought Katie great relief. The thought of Samantha succumbing to any type of sexual contact with Eric was absurd; it simply was not in her nature to get carried away to that point.

So, while Katie did not entirely discount Samantha as a fierce competitor, she did feel she held the advantage in physical attraction. If Eric had made his decision yesterday, Katie knew she would have won easily. She wished her date had been second rather than first. Hopefully, his feelings toward her would remain as strong and as fresh in his memory as hers had toward him. He couldn't very well concentrate on Samantha if he was still dreaming about her, after all.

Katie could still smell his cologne if she closed her eyes. She didn't know how she could stand to wait until Saturday to see him again. They were flying her to Pittsburgh for the taping of the finale. She was relieved to see the end nearing, but that also brought reality closer. She would have to transition her life. She was ready for the show's conclusion, but she was saddened that her television debut was coming to an end as well.

Looking back, she could hardly believe she'd resisted Ann Marie's idea of auditioning in the first place.

Soulmates had turned out to be the best gig she'd ever had. She had been living like a star for weeks. A limousine took her everywhere she wanted to go, every meal she ate was catered, and every dress she wore was several hundred dollars beyond her budget. She had a lovely collection of jewelry, was tanner than she had ever been, and experienced the most incredible dates imaginable. She had no complaints about her time spent on *Soulmates*, other than the fact it was coming to an end, and she would need to find a real job, which brought her full circle to where she began.

She was no closer to knowing what she wanted to do with her life. She knew she didn't want to waste any more time as a part-time Accounts Payable Clerk in Glens Falls. There was no future for her here. She had known that for a long time, but had been too scared to do anything about it. Eric made her realize there was more in live, if you were willing to take a chance.

She was finally ready for that chance. Whether it meant pursuing her acting career or settling down to have a family, it was time for her to start living. If Eric would have her, she would say yes. The thought of marriage intimidated her still, but not nearly as much as the thought of spending the rest of her life alone. She didn't want to turn into her mother – so cynical and guarded. But even her mother had someone. She had a daughter who loved her. Katie would have no one if she kept living her life as she had been.

The fear of being alone the rest of her life had been subconsciously eating away at her for years. Suddenly, it was clear to her. She didn't fear having a relationship or a family with a man. She feared not having one. She feared growing old in solitude.

With this revelation and fresh outlook on her future, Katie was able to prepare herself for the finale shooting. She rehearsed both scenarios in front of her bathroom mirror until she was satisfied she wouldn't look like an idiot. She prepared for the worst, but had new hope for the best.

She and Eric had shared a wonderful experience in St. Thomas. They definitely had chemistry. They conversed easily, laughed at each other's jokes and fit perfectly in each other's arms. It had to be love! She had to be the one Eric was choosing. She was close to becoming his fiancé and that thought no longer frightened her, but thrilled her. She didn't think she could wait another minute to reunite with *her Eric* and confess their love for one another.

Chapter Twenty-Two

Barbara called Friday morning to confirm travel arrangements. They had decided to shoot the finale in Pittsburgh rather than their traditional location of LA, since all three remaining parties lived in the Eastern Time zone. Katie downloaded her travel itinerary to her cell phone, and a driver picked her up the following morning before the sun was up to take her to the Albany airport.

She had only a carry-on bag, as she was spending one single night and flying back tomorrow. She needn't have brought anything at all – Barbara had everything she needed waiting for her in the hotel room.

Katie fantasized, as she perused the hotel room, what it would be like if she were to make it big as an actress. The concessions were endless. The room was filled with complimentary items from various sponsors, from make-up to clothes to jewelry. She had seventeen gowns to choose from for the shoot that evening. She had no idea if she got to keep any of this stuff, but she knew the make-up and undergarments were coming home with her. No one would expect those things back!

Katie flipped through the rack of dresses and wondered how she would ever decide which to wear. She noticed all the dresses were different in some ways, yet had similar features. All had either a plunging neckline or a peek-a-boo cut in front. All were neutral colors, but dark shades, ranging from merlot to emerald, and at least half were black. Some had sparkles and some were flat, but all were very dark.

Having hours to spare before the shoot, Katie decided to try on all seventeen dresses. Some she immediately filed under "no" and some she kept under "maybe." After trying them all on, she still had ten on the "maybe" side. She compared them and easily eliminated half, keeping four black and one emerald green.

All five contenders were equally exquisite. There was no way to decide, even after trying them on for a second time with all accessories in place, including shoes and panty hose. She eliminated three more black dresses, keeping her favorite of the blacks and laying it out next to the emerald green one. She just couldn't decide between the two.

Fortunately, Barbara sent up a hairstylist and a make-up artist, who helped her choose. They agreed that the black dress was stunning. The pearl necklace coordinated nicely without overwhelming the look.

Decision made, the hairstylist took over. She left most of the front down and formed it into tight ringlets with a narrow curling iron. She created a French twist in the back and embellished it with strategically-placed pearl-tipped pins.

"Your color looks perfect. I'm glad we didn't need to touch it up."

"Thank you," said Katie politely, her mind racing with the amount of money she had spent on her hair before coming on the show. It was money she didn't have at the time. A free touch-up would have been welcomed, not knowing how long it would be before she could afford to go get one.

The make-up artist was next. He worked around the strands of hair that framed Katie's face. He worked along quickly. Katie would have required hours to apply that amount of make-up on herself. And, unfortunately, her face would look as though she had caked on a ton of make-up. The professional's application, although heavy, was tasteful and perfect.

The cameras had arrived in the middle of the make-up session. They captured the footage and stayed focused on Katie, as she paced the floor and waited. Eventually, Zeb showed up to interview her. Katie had felt confident taping every other interview all season, but now she was a nervous wreck. Her intuition that Eric was choosing her had evaporated into skepticism. She wanted to believe he was, but the fear of being hurt had overcome her previous optimism.

Zeb's questions were going in one ear and out the other, as her ability to focus waned. Zeb encouraged her to free-flow her feelings to ease the pressure of coming up with answers to specific questions. Katie took a deep breath and let her feelings flow.

"I'm a little overwhelmed right now, because I'm afraid this may be the last time I'll ever see Eric. I want to believe it won't be, but there are no guarantees. Eric is special to me. I've never felt this way about anyone before, and I don't want to lose him. Our date in St. Thomas was a dream come true to me! It made me realize what a great thing Eric and I have, and how much I have cherished my time with him. I am so ready for the next step. I want the waiting to be over! I just want Eric to tell me his decision, so I can move forward with my life. I feel very strongly that Eric should be a part of my future, and I'm tired of waiting to get started."

Katie paused and sipped some water. Her eyes were welling up with tears in spite of her efforts to control her emotions.

"That's good, Katie," Zeb encouraged her. "Good stuff. Let's talk a little bit about what you expect your future to hold."

Katie nodded, set the water glass down, and resolved herself to continue.

"I have no idea what my future holds," she said. "I'm going through the motions right now and hoping for the best. I really want a future with Eric. I would pack my bags and move to Pittsburgh in a heartbeat. I literally have nothing holding me back …" except the terrifying prospect of her mother, she thought. "I'm just ready to embrace my future, whatever is in store for me. I think Eric would make a great husband and father, and I would love to explore that option with him."

Katie smiled and shrugged, as though it were that simple.

Zeb asked a few more question and instructed the cameramen to wrap it up. He told Katie to sit tight and someone would be up to get her shortly.

Katie nodded and resumed pacing the floor of the small hotel room. Her feet were becoming sore from the new shoes. She knew she should sit, but she didn't want to mar her dress. A wrinkled posterior would not do for such a special occasion. She walked over to the window and leaned against the wall. She lifted one foot at a time and slipped off the shoes temporarily.

She stared out the window in contemplation. The wait was increasing her nervousness. Was she waiting while Eric dumped Samantha, or was she waiting to be dumped? She considered calling the front desk to ring Samantha's room, just to see if she answered, but it was too risky. Plus, she didn't want to hear the news from Samantha. If Eric was planning to propose to her, she would simply have to wait for the surprise.

It seemed to be taking forever. Hopefully, the delay was a good sign. Maybe Eric had finished breaking up with Samantha and needed some time to recompose before meeting with her. Katie hated to speculate and get her hopes up, but the longer she waited, the better she believed her chances were becoming.

The rap at the door startled her.

"One moment," she called, slipping her shoes back on and hurrying across the room.

It was a small girl with dark, curly hair that Katie recognized from the set.

"Ready?" She asked.

Katie nodded and tried to answer, but her voice was stuck deep in her throat.

The girl led her down the corridor and around the corner to the elevators. She stepped back when the doors opened and allowed Katie to enter first. Then she stepped in, entered a key into the panel and turned it. She pressed the button for the twenty-second floor and twisted the key loose.

"Good luck," she said and stepped back out of the elevator.

Katie gave a weak smile and nodded again. She took a deep breath as she was pushed upward to the top story of the hotel. The elevator doors opened to a large foyer, where Shane was waiting. The cameras were there as well, capturing every second of Katie's arrival. Shane smiled at Katie reassuringly and held out his hand to help her over the threshold. Katie reminded herself to breathe as she accepted Shane's hand and smiled back nervously. He tucked her hand into the crook of his arm and patted it gently, as he escorted her slowly from the elevator to the door of the penthouse.

Katie was grateful for Shane's guidance as she stepped carefully along the tiled floor, pain stinging her feet with each step. She was overcome by the pounding of her heart. She could actually hear it beating, and glanced sideways at Shane to see if he had noticed as well.

If Shane had noticed, he showed no sign of it. He continued leading Katie on her way to conform her fate – good or bad. He pressed his hand over hers as though he were a tower of support. Only Katie knew the truth, that Shane didn't have any personal dealings with the participants whatsoever. He appeared to be everyone's best friend on TV, but in reality, touching Katie's hand was not the soothing act it appeared to be.

Shane escorted Katie to the opposite end of the foyer to the door of the penthouse suite. Shane paused and turned to Katie with a smile and a nod, as an indication that his job was done, and she was on her own from there.

"Whenever you're ready," he said reassuringly and patted her hand again.

Katie nodded and faced the door. This was it. Eric was in there waiting for her. She was finally getting the news, good or bad. She inhaled deeply and opened the door. Whether she was ready to hear Eric's decision had no bearing at this point. The film was rolling, and she was anxious to meet her fate.

"The show must go on," she thought, as she stepped into the room. She couldn't see Eric from the doorway, just the cameras and what seemed like one-hundred people manning them. The reality of what she was about to do slapped her across the face. These people working on the set were about to bear witness to an intense and private conversation, one that would not be privy to the general public for months. Yet it was an immensely personal and critical event in Katie's life.

Katie was so overwhelmed by the revelation that this moment had finally arrived, she was too distracted to take in the details of her surroundings. She was vaguely aware that the room was fabulously decked out with all the romantic indulgences imaginable – flowers everywhere, red velvet underfoot, candles and twinkle lights offset by the hot glare of the camera lights. It was beautiful and enchanting, yet corrupted by the presence of the multitude of cameras, lights and personnel.

Katie rounded the corner into the main room of the suite, and there stood Eric, waiting for her. Everything else disappeared from her view, as she focused on the love of her life. None of the bells and whistles around her mattered, as long as Eric confessed his love for her.

He smiled when he saw her. She let out her breath, which she had inadvertently been holding, and smiled back. She breathed normally now, set her eyes on Eric and stepped forward intently. The mixed scents of many varieties of flowers and scented candles pierced her nostrils, as she passed across the room, making her momentarily dizzy. She pushed forward without faltering. Nothing mattered now except Eric. As she reached him and they clasped hands, everything else faded into the background. The pain drained from her feet, and the dizziness subsided, as she regained her equilibrium. It was nothing more than her and Eric, finally reaching the defining moment they had anticipated as well as dreaded.

Eric held Katie's hands and stared at her in awe, taking in every marvelous detail.

"You look incredible," he said finally, breathlessly.

"Thank you," she answered quietly, her voice sounding unusually high in her ears.

He gave her a hug, then resumed holding both of her hands and staring into her eyes. Katie smiled at him. She was so happy to be with him again that she temporarily forgot why they were here. She had missed him terribly the last few days. It felt wonderful to be here with him again, regardless of the circumstances.

She stared into his green eyes. They looked different from the last time she saw them – still loving, but darker, more serious and lacking their usual playfulness. Eric had something important on his mind, and Katie couldn't wait to hear all about it.

"Katie," he began abashedly.

Katie smiled in anticipation. She nodded to let him know it was OK. He could tell her anything. She was his best friend, his confidant, and hopefully soon to be his fiancé.

"Katie," he said again, squeezing her hands. "I knew you were special from the moment I met you. The first time I saw you, and you told me not to forget your name, I was blown away. You were such a knockout, you didn't need the nametag; I couldn't have forgotten your name even if I tried. You looked phenomenal in that black dress – and you look phenomenal now. I'm still blown away every time I set eyes on you.

"I remember thinking when I first saw you, that you were way out of my league. I didn't know what a guy like me could possibly have in common with a girl like you. What would we ever have to talk about? I kept you around, because I was intrigued. And I was so glad that I did, because once I got to know you a little, I realized that even though we don't have a lot in common, we do have a lot to talk about. We are true *Soulmates*, in a way, because we have similar souls. We have a connection, a rapport that you don't have with just anyone. The more time I spent with you, the more apparent that became to me.

"When we had our first date alone together, I was thrilled that the special chemistry we had was stronger than ever. I felt so comfortable with you. I've told you before, I feel like we've been friends forever. We have that kind of relationship where I feel like I can tell you anything. I appreciate that more than you'll ever know, because this process has been difficult for me. You have helped me to get through this, even though I couldn't confide in you or talk to you about all of my struggles."

Katie kept smiling and nodding. She wanted to speak, to respond, but her voice was trapped deep in her throat. Her thoughts were rushing around in her head, and she didn't know what to say, so she remained silent.

Eric was beginning to ramble. The words were flying by in Katie's mind so quickly that she was only absorbing about a third of what he was saying. She wasn't sure where Eric was going with his speech, but she was acutely aware that he had used the word *Soulmates*. That word stuck in her head; that had to be a good sign.

"You must know that this decision has been the biggest struggle of all. I can't say that I experienced love at first sight, or put my finger on the exact moment when I knew who I was going to choose. There was a lot of internal debate, and it has come right down to the wire. All I can do at this point is move forward with my decision and pray for the best. I'm ready to start my future. I feel sad to see this whole experience coming to an end, because I have had the thrill of my life on *Soulmates*. But, I'm anxious to move forward also. I want to get married, to settle down and think about starting a family."

Katie's perpetual smile widened and she blushed in anticipation of Eric's next question. The lights bore down on them, and beads of sweat appeared on Eric's brow. Katie shifted her feet anxiously in anticipation, waiting for him to drop to one knee.

"But … I'm sorry to say that my future is not going to include you, Katie."

Katie's smile faded as the message sunk in, but her face remained flushed. She opened her mouth to respond, and a small sound came out of her throat, but no words. Eric continued before she could try to find her voice.

"It kills me to tell you this. I never meant to hurt you. I know we have strong feelings for each other, and that we probably would have been happy together if we'd tried. But it boils down to the fact that I love someone else."

Eric struggled for the right words. Katie felt as though she'd been stabbed.

"I know I owe you an explanation and honestly speaking, I don't have a decent explanation. I wish I did, for your sake and for mine. There is nothing wrong with you, Katie. There is nothing you did or didn't do that steered me in one direction or another."

'Okay …" Katie answered unsteadily, surprised her voice came out at all. She didn't say the word meaning she was accepting what he was saying, but more of an OK, I'm listening; go on with your explanation, and it had better be good.

"I do wish you would have let me into your personal life a little more. I mean, the fact that I've never met your family tells me that you don't completely trust me, or at least trust me enough to make me part of your life."

Katie's heart began to race. She knew that whole fiasco with her mother would come back to haunt her! Damn Sharon Cohen. Damn her to hell. She was ruining Katie's life with her hatred and paranoia. She was a selfish bitch!

"I didn't think you would hold my mother's actions against me," Katie said defensively, yet meekly.

"I don't, Katie. Believe me, that isn't the reason. It's just part of an entire trust issue with you. I don't feel like you trust me enough to let me see the real Katie. I think there's a lot about you that's still a mystery, and although I would gladly give a lifetime to discover it all, I've already reached that level of trust with someone else."

Katie nodded and averted her eyes.

"I never wanted to hurt anyone, especially not you. You are a beautiful, special person, and you have a lot to offer. My feelings for you were very strong, so please don't doubt my intentions. Every second we spent together was special to me. But I know in my heart that there is a better match for me."

Katie wanted to run, but she mustered up the courage to find her voice.

"All I ever wanted was for you to be happy." She swallowed and smiled wanly, biting back tears and resisting the urge to tear his limbs off. "Of course, I feel horrible that I'm not the person who's going to fulfill your every desire, but I'm truly happy for you, that you found what you set out to find."

"Katie," Eric shook his head and embraced her, rocking from side to side. "You are amazing. You're going to make some guy very happy, trust me."

Katie smiled and brushed back a tear.

Eric walked her to the elevator in silence and pushed a button. The wait was excruciating. Katie felt the temporary numbness she'd been feeling dissipate. The pain swept over her body. Her feet ached again. Her skull throbbed from the sickly-sweet mix of fragrances and the strain of holding back tears. Her body felt extremely hot. Her face felt beet red, from the heat of the lights as well as from the embarrassment.

Where the hell could the elevator be? There were only twenty-two damn floors to this hotel. Katie stood in silence and continued to avert her eyes from Eric.

Finally, a soft ding signaled the arrival of the elevator, and the door opened. Katie wanted to climb into the elevator and disappear, but Barbara was barking instructions behind her. She wanted to film Katie entering the elevator, but would hold the doors open to shoot from outside looking in. She wanted to film Katie's reaction as though the elevator were moving. When they were done, she would film the doors closing and edit it in.

Fortunately, Barbara sent Eric back to the suite, so he wouldn't witness Katie's reaction. Barbara wanted fresh, raw emotions. She didn't want Eric there, inhibiting Katie from divulging her true feelings.

Katie, naturally, was trying to regain her composure, while the cameras were setting up. Barbara was running around frantically, trying to get the cameras ready before Katie was able to do so. She didn't want Katie calm and composed, taking it like a man. She wanted "frivolous, pre-menstrual emotional" and she wanted it now.

The cameras in place, she addressed Katie directly.

"What the hell happened in there? I thought you were a sure win," she baited her.

"I don't know what happened," Katie said, taking Barbara's direction without skipping a beat. "I'm still in shock, I think. I was so sure Eric and I were right for one another."

A curly lock of hair was stuck to her cheek by a salty tear that had escaped. She brushed it out of her face and crossed her arms in front of her chest dejectedly.

"I feel like I just got plummeted by a Mack truck. I mean, I don't want to sound like I was over-confident, because I knew there was another person involved and there was a possibility Eric was choosing her. I just didn't believe that would happen. I can't believe it did happen. I'm in shock!"

"Do you know why Eric didn't choose you?" Barbara asked from outside the elevator.

"I don't really understand why Eric didn't choose me. He said we were *Soulmates*, and isn't that the whole point of the show – to find your *Soulmate*? I don't understand how he could call me that and then turn around and pick someone else. That makes no sense."

Katie paused and wiped away a tear. Much to her surprise, the tear was genuine and not manufactured. The fact that Eric didn't choose her was starting to hit home now. She had been going through the motions and trying to be gracious, but she truly didn't believe this was happening. She hadn't thoroughly prepared herself for this outcome, even though she had promised Ann Marie she would. She honestly didn't think she would be in this position. She was the loser, number two, the runner-up. I had happened so fast.

"This is bullshit," she said, anger beginning to replace the shock. "It's just wrong. I honestly don't know what I did wrong. I feel so stupid." She swallowed to hold back an uncontrollable flow of tears.

"Why do you feel stupid?" Barbara prodded.

"I feel like an idiot, like I should have seen this coming. I know how I feel about Eric, and I thought he felt the same way."

"Do you think Eric knows how you feel, for sure?"

"I thought I made my feelings for Eric clear, but maybe I didn't. I don't know. It's too late now, but I hope I did everything I could to show him how I felt. I don't think I held back my feelings. We were pretty honest with each other from the beginning. I'm sure I'll think of things I could have done differently, things I should have said, but there's no point beating myself up over it. I've lost him. It's over."

"Do you think your decision to keep your family out of it affected Eric's decision?"

"I'm afraid my mother's insistence not to meet Eric had a big impact on Eric's decision, even though he assured me it wouldn't. He told me it was OK at the time, but I feel like he held that against me in the end. I hope that wasn't the deciding factor, but it seems like it played a big part."

"What are you going to do now?"

"I don't know what I'm going to do now. I have no job, no boyfriend, no future to look forward to. I'm in shock right now. I had plans for a future with Eric. I was thinking about moving to Pittsburgh, getting married, and possibly starting a family. It's pretty devastating when your entire future gets torn out from under you."

Katie swallowed hard to keep from sobbing. Tears were streaming down her cheeks in spite of her efforts to hold them back. She had never been a dramatic crier, but more of a silent sufferer. She refused to lose her composure completely on national TV. She was going to be a sophisticated mourner, the beautiful victim, horribly betrayed by the man she loved. In spite of the pain she was feeling, she was very conscious of how she wanted to be portrayed. She didn't want to be a babbling, pathetic idiot; she wanted to evoke empathy from the viewers. She wanted them to feel bad that Eric hadn't chosen her; she wanted the audience rooting for her and suspecting Samantha as she had.

None of that should have mattered, but to Katie, *Soulmates* was once again just an acting gig. She had come on the show as an actor with the intention of jumpstarting her acting career. A bruised ego wasn't going to transform her into an emotional drama queen like Madison. She would keep her head high, shed the obligatory tear or two, and wait to have her true breakdown in privacy.

    Barbara sent her on her way, but also sent a camera along to film her return to her room. She wanted to shoot Katie packing a suitcase and grabbing a taxi in front of the hotel – no more *Soulmates* transportation for the loser. Barbara mentioned filming it later, after Katie had a chance to revive herself, but Katie insisted she'd rather get it done. She wanted to meet her obligations and be left the hell alone. She couldn't get out of there for real until tomorrow, and she desperately needed to be alone to sort out all that had happened. It didn't seem possible that Eric had let her go, but it was starting to sink in.

Chapter Twenty-Three

Katie had trouble coming to terms with the fact that Eric had essentially broken up with her, even after she was finally left alone in her hotel room. It still didn't seem real. And if it was real, was there a camera hidden somewhere in the room to capture her response? She felt like she was on candid camera and Eric would walk in any moment with a grin on his face, and tell her it was all a joke – Barbara's idea, of course.

Katie looked around at the concessions she'd been given and wondered if they were her "parting gifts" or if Samantha had been given the same products. Samantha! It was the first time she thought about her since she left Eric's suite. So, it was true. Eric was in love with Samantha and was gone forever. The two of them were undoubtedly together right now, celebrating their newly-proclaimed love.

Katie despised her. She was a fake. She was nothing but a beautiful, empty shell. She had a sweet demeanor, but it was only skin deep. She had no depth, no truly endearing qualities. She was like a Barbie doll, pretty and compliant but lacking any thoughts of her own.

What a joke! Katie couldn't believe Eric hadn't seen through Samantha's façade. Granted she was attractive and personable, she had a decent job and probably a nice, normal family. But she had no inner beauty, no gusto. She kept her opinions to herself, didn't ruffle any feathers, and went through life doing what she perceived everyone expected her to do. She didn't break any rules, hurt any feelings, owe any debts. She was like an exquisitely decorated Easter egg that had been hollowed of insides for posterity. She would undoubtedly make the perfect wife, as she would take to heart her vows to love and obey. She would give Eric all the children he wanted, and they would be spoiled rotten by their hollow, non-confrontational mother.

The thought of Samantha becoming a mother reminded Katie of her own mother. Thinking about her mother was the last thing she wanted to do, but she couldn't help it. Sharon Cohen had most definitely played an integral part in Katie's demise.

Katie was furious with her mother for refusing to meet Eric. Sharon Cohen was going to have to get off her high horse and stop forcing Katie to live her life without male companionship. Katie was fed up with feeling guilty every time she had a boyfriend. Every time things started to have a glimmer of promise for a future, good-old Mother stepped in and squashed all her chances of having a normal relationship with a man.

Things were going to change between Katie and her mother. Her mother was going to have to accept the fact that Katie wanted a husband and a family of her own. Her negativity was depriving Katie of developing a healthy, happy relationship whether inadvertently or intentionally. Knowing that Sharon Cohen never did anything without calculation, Katie tended to believe it was a knowing attempt at sabotage. Her mother was going to have to stop trying to run her life; she had to let go and allow Katie to make her own mistakes.

Katie swallowed her pride and packed up her things. She crammed her small carry-on bag full of every item she could fit, and regretted packing lightly for this trip. She decided to take advantage of the situation – she had to get something out of this whole ordeal. She went downstairs to the hotel gift shop and bought a large, expandable duffle bag, toted it back to her room and filled it with every concession imaginable – all the make-up, accessories and food items. The dresses and shoes had been removed from the room while she was out filming, but the rest of the goodies were hers for the taking. She wasn't leaving anything free behind.

She checked one bag and carried on the other, and everything made it back to Albany. She carted her bags through the airport, loaded them into a cab and lugged them upstairs to her apartment. She had almost completely unpacked by the time she realized these small concessions were no substitute for Eric. She missed him already. She sunk down in the middle of the kitchen floor and buried her face in her hands.

She needed a good cry. She had been holding back her emotions, trying to be a big person, a gracious loser. Now that she was in the privacy of her own home, she could let it out. She cried, allowing the painful emotions to overcome her. She quit trying to put on a front and realized it was OK to feel sorry for herself. It was OK to be mad – mad at Eric, mad at Samantha, mad at her mother, and most of all mad at herself. She was mad at herself for falling for Eric in the first place and doubly mad for letting him go. There had to have been more she could have done to hold onto him. She had fallen short; she had let herself down.

Katie allowed herself a good cry and time to mourn, before she resumed any productive activity. She knew she couldn't completely move on yet. They still had one more show to film. She knew she had to get through the final show before she could put everything behind her. Eric would be there with Samantha, making their first appearance as an official couple. She would have to face them together, along with all the other girls, too. Katie knew she'd need her friends beside her. She pulled out Tina's cell number and dialed her first. She would call Ann Marie next, but right now she just wanted some sympathy. Tina would listen and console, whereas Ann Marie would more likely say, "I told you so," or "I always knew you guys weren't compatible" or some other painfully true statement. Ann Marie didn't intend to be mean, but she was brutally honest, and Katie wanted first to hear some soothing, albeit patronizing words.

Katie talked to Tina for almost an hour, and then to Ann Marie for almost two. The conversation with Tina went exactly as expected, and after speaking with her, Katie had the strength to call Ann Marie. The conversation with Ann Marie went surprisingly well. Ann Marie had the common sense to keep most of her comments to herself, but did point out that Samantha was too perfect to dump. Katie, nor any of the other girls, had a fighting chance against Samantha.

Katie tried not to feel slighted by Ann Marie's insights. Ann Marie meant well, but often lacked tact. At any rate, the two of them were booked on the same flight to Los Angeles to fulfill their obligation to *Soulmates*. Season Seven would be wrapped in in the usual fashion. All the cast was reunited in LA to view the completed premier episode. The women who had been eliminated would learn who Eric had chosen, and they would all be presented with the opportunity to confront Eric, or the other girls as the case may be, and gain closure to the entire experience to varying degrees.

Katie definitely planned on confronting Eric. She didn't want to portray "the woman scorned" exactly. She would be gracious and accepting, but she would demand some answers. She deserved an explanation. Unless she was completely naïve, Eric had led her to believe that she was "the one" and she needed him to know that he had indeed hurt her.

Katie prepared for the event as she would for any other acting gig. She practiced her "lines." She anticipated Eric's reaction and prepared counter-attacks. She played over the season's events to make sure she didn't have any grudges held against her by the other girls. She didn't think she had encountered any personal conflicts, other than the one with Ann Marie. That interaction wasn't going to come back to haunt her, so she doubted any other mysterious vendettas would surface.

Katie and Ann Marie had separate itineraries, but met up by the boarding gate in Chicago O'Hare during the layover for their connecting flight to LAX. They were both tired from traveling and not overly enthusiastic about the long day ahead of them. Added into the length of the day was the three-hour time difference from New York to California. The actual shoot wasn't until that evening in Los Angeles, and the girls didn't want to look bedraggled. They were both equally intent on looking their finest to rub in Eric's face what he had missed. Surely, they weren't alone in their intent. The rest of the girls undoubtedly felt slighted by Eric as well and would all want to look their best. It wasn't going to be easy given the fact they'd been traveling all day.

Katie was surprised how the adrenaline kicked in once they arrived. She was excited to see some of the girls again, especially her ex-roomie Tina. She honestly didn't remember some of the faces, let alone the names to go with them. She didn't know why Barbara had bothered to bring in all twenty-five women; the first ten to be eliminated were a waste of airtime. Eric wouldn't even remember them, probably.

But Katie supposed, since they were gathered to view the premier, everyone involved would be anxious to see the results, even those that had only been in that first episode. They all deserved their five minutes of fame, whether they lost in the first round or the last. None had suffered the loss as deeply as Katie had, but she wouldn't begrudge the others their opportunity for closure. This regrouping of the case was, after all, to bring closure to the season and the experience as a whole.

Barbara had the girls grouped by the episode in which they were eliminated. The ten to leave first were to be introduced alphabetically by first name, with Amanda at the head of the line. Shane did the announcing, and the women listened and awaited their turns nervously.

"Amanda Rawles... Andrea Romero... Chelsea Simon... Desirae Sanzone... Faith Ennis... Iris Chapman... Karen Taylor... Maeve O'Brien... Patty Pritt... Simone Rose."

The live audience applauded. Katie had been surprised to learn they were filming in front of a live audience. She shouldn't have been, having seen previous episodes of the show, but it must have slipped her mind. The audience itself wasn't all that intimidating. It was composed of friends and family of the producers, as well as Eric's and Samantha's. Most of these people had been on the set before, at one point or another.

Shane's voice continued calling the names of the next set of ladies who'd been eliminated. The anticipation was almost as bad as The Price is Right except that you knew your name was coming eventually.

"Danine Giacomo... Heather Hines ... Julia Chrisman ... Olivia Parker ... Riann Hathaway."

He was already up to the top ten.

"Brittany Latrelle ... Kristin Moore ... Lois Denato ... Tina Bailor."

Ann Marie turned back to Katie and winked.

"Ann Marie Monaghan ... Jenny Greison ... Valerie Beck."

There was a long pause while Shane talked to the girls. Apparently, they weren't calling Madison and Katie out right away, which rather annoyed Katie that she was stuck waiting backstage with Madison. The last thing she felt like was small talking with little-miss Drama Queen. Fortunately, Madison was preoccupied listening for her name to be called so she could begin her grand entrance.

"I can't hear what Shane is saying," she complained more to herself than to Katie.

Katie didn't bother to respond. She was irritated as well that she couldn't see or hear what was going on in there. They were missing something good, from the hooting and hollering that erupted. Katie, unable to stand still, began pacing. Madison ignored her. Eventually, a guy with a headset motioned for Madison to go.

"Wish me luck!" she called over her shoulder to Katie, who rolled her eyes. Shane's voice was once again audible.

"Let's give a warm welcome to the woman you loved to hate ... Madison Jaynes."

Madison donned her semi-permanent beauty-queen smile. She seemed thrilled by Shane's introduction, as though she only heard the word "loved" and nothing after that. She pranced away to the sound of applause and waved to the audience. Katie thought she heard a "boo" through the crowd also, but chalked it up to wishful thinking – although it did sound suspiciously like Ann Marie for a second.

Katie was glad to be alone. They weren't letting her in straight away, either, so she let her mind wander, knowing the guy with the headset was getting paid to pay attention for her cue. She couldn't help thinking about Eric. She would be reunited with him soon; at least, they'd be in the same room.

Katie practiced her speech and damned Barbara that she couldn't see what they were doing in there. She'd have to wait and watch it on TV, at the same time half of America viewed it. That didn't allow for any damage control, not that she had any influence over what footage *Soulmates* aired anyway. She was at their mercy. She felt grateful that Barbara seemed to like her, or she may be getting a slam for an introduction much as Madison had. Shane's sarcasm wouldn't be wasted on her.

The guy with the headset held his finger up to indicate she'd be called in a minute. Katie was relieved and proud to hear her introduction.

"She's here in our studio, America's sweetheart, our own 'girl next door,' Katie Cohen!"

Katie was pleased to hear the applause as she entered the set. The noise level was much higher than when Shane had announced Madison's name. Surely, she wasn't imagining that.

Katie smiled graciously. She truly felt like Miss America parading across stage. She wasn't wearing the gown or the tiara, and she hadn't won the contest, but she felt equally special. After all, she reminded herself jokingly, the runner-up got to step in if anything happened to the winner. Too bad things didn't work that way. She knew she would never have Eric, no matter what happened between him and Samantha. She threw out a little wave to her fans and stopped in front of Shane, who was offering his hand. He shook her hand warmly, smiling as though they were the best of friends. Katie took it all in stride.

Shane motioned Katie to take a seat in the low-armed chair that was set up opposite him. A small table between them held a pitcher of water and two empty glasses. The rest of the girls were seated in an arc around them. Ann Marie was positioned perfectly so they could make eye contact without shifting or leaning. Katie couldn't help wondering if Barbara had planned that on purpose. Of course, she had – everything Barbara did was purposeful.

Katie continued smiling, as the applause filled the studio. She was thrilled to have received such a positive response, unless they were merely cheering on Barbara's instruction. Although that possibility was very real, Katie scanned the crown and smiled appreciatively.

"Welcome, Katie," Shane began.

"Thank you."

"How are you feeling? Have you been able to come to terms with everything that's transpired?"

"I'm doing pretty well, under the circumstances."

"As well as can be expected," Shane inferred.

"Exactly. I'm hanging in there. The initial shock has worn off. I still feel badly about it, but I'm moving forward."

"That's exactly to be expected," Shane said compassionately, as though he'd been through it a thousand times. He had, in fact, been through it seven times as the host of *Soulmates*, but he had never been emotionally invested in any of the participants. In his personal life, Katie doubted he felt a thing. He probably drifted from prospect to prospect, taking what he wanted and leaving before any emotions came into play at all. Katie had no evidence of this, other than the absence of a wedding band on his finger. However, judging from Shane's mannerisms on the *Soulmates* set and his deliberate separation from the cast, one would naturally assume he was a shallow, conceited snob.

"It is to be expected," Katie agreed. "And I can accept the fact that it's going to take some time to heal. It's just hard to know what to do with myself. I had all these plans, and now that's not going to happen."

"Are you still searching for answers as far as what happened? I mean, you are going to have an opportunity to speak with Eric. What do you plan to say to him?"

"I really just want to know why. I feel like we had a great relationship starting, and I thought he felt the same way. You know, it hasn't been easy for me to open up to someone as much as I opened up to Eric, after all I've been through in my life. I think my own inhibitions were my downfall, which totally sucks, but that's part of who I am. I don't think he should hold it against me that I'm slower at opening up than other girls."

"You'll get your chance to ask him. Let's take a break, and when we come back, we'll have Eric Warner and his new fiancé, Samantha Kearney, here live!"

Katie felt her stomach turn. She kept smiling for the cameras, but inside her blood pressure boiled. Her temples flooded with pain, her eyes burned from the dryness of shedding so many tears the last few days. It was the first time she had heard that they were engaged. He had proposed to Samantha only moments after breaking her heart. She was nauseated by the thought.

Katie's head was spinning, as the crew around her bustled to rearrange the stage. Katie's single chair was being moved next to Shane, and was replaced by a matching love seat. Katie would have liked to leave now, but there was no going back. She tried to stay calm and push forward. She told herself it was perfectly acceptable to show her vulnerability; it was expected. She'd recently been dumped by this guy and was about to be confronted by him and his fiancé. Any normal woman would feel intimidated right now.

Katie was relieved she was no longer in perfect alignment with Ann Marie. She feared if she looked at her, she would burst into tears. She did glance over at Tina, who set her jaw and nodded, silently telling Katie to stay tough. Katie nodded back and took her seat next to Shane. Barbara made a few adjustments to some of the other girls and repositioned two cameras before they continued.

Katie was only vaguely aware that they were filming again. Shane was talking, and Barbara was spouting directions, but Katie's mind was back in St. Thomas. It didn't seem possible that she'd spent the night in Eric's arms, feeling so safe and secure, and now she was sitting in this studio, about to be humiliated again. What was she thinking, getting herself into this position?

She should have resisted Eric's charm. She should have gotten past the first round, collected her bonus and turned a cold cheek. She probably could have found a new job by now. She'd be back on her feet already, but no, she had to fight to the finish. What a huge waste of time!

Her thoughts were interrupted by an eruption of applause in the studio. Eric was entering from one side, and Samantha from the other. The happy couple was being brought together again by *Soulmates*. They flew across the stage and into each other's arms, to the raving applause. Katie felt sick.

Samantha and Eric engaged in the most nauseating of embraces, Shane standing at their side, applauding and beaming like a proud parent. Katie clapped along mechanically, her hands moving apart and then together, but producing no detectable sound.

Katie was appalled to watch, but like a witness to a bad accident, she couldn't look away. Her heart was broken. She actually felt a stabbing pain in her heart. Was she having a heart attack? She couldn't be; things like that only happened to Madison.

Katie snuck a peek at her old nemesis. Madison was not feigning politeness by clapping, but sulking like a child, her teeth clenched, her eyes round and misty. Looking at Madison made Katie feel better, and the heart pains subsided. Her anxiety attack passed, and she was able to don her good-sport smile and greet Eric and Samantha in turn.

They both hugged her warmly – Samantha maybe more so than Eric. That made Katie hate her even more. Samantha seemed genuinely sorry for her. What a bitch! Didn't she have any faults?

They all took their seats, and Shane turned to Eric and Samantha first.

"How does it feel – finally to be able to proclaim your feelings in public?"

"It feels great," they each agreed in their own words.

"How long ago did you know, Eric, that Samantha was the one for you?"

"I'd like to think I knew, on some level, the first time I met her. I definitely knew there was something special about her. But this isn't a typical situation where you meet someone and it's bam love at first sight. You're meeting twenty-five lovely women at the same time, all of which have the potential to be that special someone. So, I wouldn't say I could pinpoint an exact moment that I knew I wanted to be with Samantha. It was a gradual process."

"And you had it narrowed down to two beautiful women, both of whom you had strong feelings for. And I'm sure Katie wants to know, too – what exactly was it about Samantha that won your heart?" Shane asked.

"Samantha is," Eric began, searching for the right words, "everything I wanted in a woman. She is not only beautiful on the outside, but on the inside as well. And this is nothing against Katie, because she's obviously got special qualities of her own, but Samantha makes me feel special when I'm around her. She makes me a better person. She completes me, so to speak. She was the woman I described as the perfect woman for me when I started this show, only I hadn't met her yet."

Blah, blah, blah. Katie wanted to punch him. He had the nerve to sit there and recite one cliché after another, as if she weren't even in the room.

Eric turned to Samantha at that point and kissed her, as though he was so overwhelmed by emotions he couldn't keep his lips off her. The whole display made Katie want to puke – smelly and green and all over the two of them. They disgusted her.

The audience, in the meantime, was applauding. Katie attributed their idiocy to the fact that most of them were friends or relatives of Eric and Samantha. Those that weren't were merely following suit. If one idiot started clapping, they all did. Some of the idiotic women behind her were clapping along enthusiastically. It wasn't a wedding, for God's sake. They didn't have to clap every time the happy couple kissed.

"That's wonderful," Shane was saying. "We love to be responsible for romance here on *Soulmates*."

When the applause had once again subsided, Shane pulled Katie into the conversation.

"I'm happy for you two, I truly am. But let's let poor Katie off the spot. I know it's uncomfortable for all of you, and I want to thank you all for agreeing to appear together today. We don't want the lovely Katie leaving *Soulmates* with any bad feelings. Katie, you've got some things you'd like to get off your chest, don't you?"

"I do, Shane. Thank you. And let me be the first to say I'm not here to make this uncomfortable for anyone. I'm happy for you guys, too. Insanely jealous," she added lightly, "but happy for you."

The audience chuckled politely, which was the reaction Katie had been hoping for. They seemed to be empathetic and supportive. Even Shane seemed somewhat on her side.

"I really just want to know why. I mean, unless I was totally feeling something that wasn't there, I thought everything was going great. I was shocked, to say the least, when you let me go. You've always said how comfortable you feel talking to me, and how you feel like we've known each other our whole lives. We have a chemistry between us that is real; I'm sure I didn't imagine that. I don't understand how you can go from the way we were in St. Thomas, to breaking up with me. I just don't get it."

Katie wanted to say more, but stopped. She had prepared rebuttals for every possible answer Eric came out with, but what would it matter? He wasn't going to change his mind. Pointing out that she thought he'd made a huge mistake wasn't going to get her any further ahead.

"I don't really know how to respond, Katie, and I'm sorry," Eric began. "Let me say this. Everything we experienced was real. I wasn't faking anything, or making anything up. The chemistry you felt was truly there. We are, no doubt, compatible. And there isn't anything that you said or did that made me question our ability to have a relationship or a future together. I don't have anything against you, and there was no defining moment when I realized Samantha was the right choice for me. I didn't string you along intentionally, or anything like that. What it came down to was the simple fact that Samantha is a better match for me. That's not to say anything derogatory about you, because I never meant to hurt you. I had strong feelings for you. I just had stronger feelings for Samantha."

Katie was speechless. She had consumed hours preparing responses, but at the moment she was blank. Her pain and anger had dissolved into numbness. She was defeated. She saw no purpose in arguing or belittling Eric at this point. She needed to swallow her pride and be a good sport. She took a deep breath and exhaled slowly to conjure up enough confidence to do what needed to be done.

"Eric," Katie said softly and smiled. "Don't beat yourself up over it. I understand you made your decision. I'm not going to pretend I'm not disappointed, but I need to bring closure to this experience as much as you do. I'm glad you found someone. I hope things work out the way you want."

"Thank you, Katie. You'll be fine," Eric said and stood.

"I know I will."

He leaned in to her. She stood and welcomed his embrace. It still felt good to be in his arms – natural, as though they fit together perfectly. He was still the same Eric, and she still cared about him. She squeezed him and patted his back.

That was the end of her courtship with Eric. He let her go, and she left the hot seat and took her place with the other girls – next to Madison.

As she settled in to watch the official preview of the first episode of *Soulmates* Season Seven, she pondered if maybe Eric was right. Maybe they weren't made for each other at all. They made a great couple, but she had said since day one he wasn't exactly her type. Maybe she had been banking on something that she should have known all along wasn't going to happen.

Chapter Twenty-Four

The preview was fantastic. Katie watched intently and was impressed with how good she looked on screen. She came across exactly as she had hoped – confident but not presumptuous. No wonder Barbara liked her. Her profile and interview was immaculate; the camera loved her.

Katie became more convinced as the show progressed that she was destined to be an actress. She needed to get off her hump and get her name back into circulation. After this premier aired, she might just be a hot commodity.

As Katie watched, she felt as though a weight had been lifted. She had gotten through the worst of it. She could relax now. The rest of today's shoot would be a breeze. The tenseness in her muscles gradually relaxed, and she could actually smile again. She found herself laughing out loud at the part when Kristin got the hiccups.

She was very pleased with the finished product. Barbara's editing team was top notch. The episode ended with a shot of the fifteen girls who had advanced, and a quick sampling of the following episode. They showed a snippet of the girls moving into the mansion, as well as the group dates. The preview mainly focused on Eric's single dates with Madison and Lois, and ended with a shot of all fifteen women aligned on the front porch of the mansion in anticipation of Eric's selections.

Katie couldn't wait to watch episode two! She had been present for the taping of episode one in its entirety and experienced it all first hand, but the next show would reveal all the details of the other dates she hadn't been present for. She would get to see exactly what had happened behind closed doors, all the details that the other girls had omitted from their narratives.

She was especially interested to see Madison's one-on-one interactions with Eric. She was curious for clues as to what Eric ever saw in that spoiled brat! Katie was fairly certain Madison was an entirely different person when she was alone with Eric; she didn't know to what extent Madison acted differently, and couldn't wait to find out. She couldn't believe she'd have to wait and watch it on TV with the rest of America.

The studio filled with applause, as the *Soulmates* logo appeared on the screen. It faded to black slowly.

Shane took over once again. He asked Eric a few questions about the beginning of the season, and if his first impressions of the women had held true, and if there were any surprises along the way.

Eric maintained that his first impressions were pretty accurate, but he was pleasantly surprised at what a great group of women he had to choose from. He reiterated what a grand time he'd had on the show, and that his *Soulmates* experience was all that he'd expected and more.

Shane moved on to address some of the frictions that had existed in the mansion throughout the season, which quickly evolved into Madison vs. the rest of the world. Katie got to experience all of Madison's huffing and puffing first-hand, as she was seated right next to her.

"I truly felt ostracized in the mansion," Madison was saying. "I felt like everyone was jealous of me, because Eric liked me right from the start, and they held that against me. I couldn't walk into a room without feeling like they had just been talking about me. And the sad part is, I didn't even have to live at the mansion. I live close enough where I could have gone home. But then I might have missed something, which really isn't fair to me."

"Plus, it's against the rules," Shane added, pointing out that Madison commuting wasn't a valid option.

"But why should I have to go anyways?" Madison continued as though Shane hadn't spoken. "I had as much a right to be at the mansion as everyone else. If people don't like me, that's their problem. I shouldn't have to inconvenience myself and possibly miss out on something when I wasn't even the one with the problem."

"But, Madison," Kristin interjected. "Doesn't it seem odd that everyone in the house had a problem with you? And it's not like we had problems with anyone else, just you. Doesn't that kind of turn on a light bulb that maybe the problem was you all along?"

"I don't have a problem with any one of you!" Madison cried, missing the point. Her cheeks began to flush. "Even though you guys were mean to me, and talked about me behind my back, I haven't said or done anything to any of you. I just ignored it and kept reminding myself of the real reason I was there – for Eric. You guys were just jealous that Eric liked me better."

"Then wouldn't we be jealous of Samantha?" Brittany pointed out. "And Katie?"

"Not if you thought I was the biggest threat," Madison retorted, and in her twisted little mind, actually believed it.

"The only one who thought you were a threat was you," Lois cackled.

That comment ended the Madison issue. Shane changed his line of questioning, asking Valerie how she felt to have Eric meet her family, only to eliminate her. Madison sat and sulked the rest of the time.

After hearing from several of the rejected women, and allowing them to have any last words to Eric, Shane turned the focus back on the happy couple.

"So, what is next for Eric and Samantha? Have you discussed wedding plans?"

They exchanged glances before answering, not sure how much information the other party wanted to divulge.

"We have," Eric nodded, his permanent grin intact. "We haven't picked the date yet, but we're thinking of next fall."

"Beautiful!" Shane responded automatically.

"It takes a long time to plan a wedding," Samantha took over, "and we want to make sure we have plenty of private time for ourselves, too."

"Yeah," Eric added. "We don't want to add the stress of planning a wedding to our new relationship. We'd like to spend some time together first."

"That's a wise decision," Shane agreed. "There's no rush, after all."

"The whole *Soulmates* experience is such a rush, we want to slow the pace down," Eric explained. "You know, you pack so much into such a short time, when you're on the show. We want to take a step back and enjoy our time together. I don't want to be on a date and thinking, 'OK, who am I seeing next and who do I like better?' I just want to enjoy Samantha and give her my undivided attention."

They smiled at each other.

"I feel like we need time to be alone together," Samantha added. "I know Eric had a lot on his mind during our time together, and I did, too. My mind was racing with fears and anxieties and insecurities. I'm looking forward to spending time alone with Eric now that we have both cleared our heads. It'll be nice to express our feelings freely. I feel like I've been holding back just a little bit." She held her finger and thumb close together to articulate her point.

"What would be your next step, then?" Shane inquired.

"We'll have to deal with the long-distance relationship for a while," Eric offered, after glancing at Samantha as though to gain her approval. "Samantha is going to get her resume together and start scoping out the Pittsburgh employment opportunities."

"That's great. Any apprehensions on your part, Samantha?"

"None, whatsoever."

"But I bet you'll miss that warm Florida climate," Shane prodded.

"Oh, yes. The weather will take some getting used to. But as far as I'm concerned, we've overcome much larger obstacles than the weather. I'll deal with it. Besides, we had such a great time on our ski getaway, I may end up a winter lover!"

"That's right. You two hit the slopes together."

"We sure did," Samantha continued. "I wasn't half bad, either! I surprised myself."

"You did great for your first time," Eric assured her and wrapped his arm over her shoulder. "You'll be a genuine ski bunny before you know it. And we'll vacation to Florida and visit your family. You'll have the best of both worlds."

"No doubt I will," Samantha agreed, her cheeks flushing with the excitement of being in love.

"Keep us updated on the wedding plans," Shane insisted, and the happy couple agreed they would. Shane turned his attention to the camera. "There you have it! Another *Soulmates* success story!"

"Cut!" Barbara yelled, zooming to Shane and barking orders around the room. "Everyone stay put. We have a couple retakes."

Barbara hustled around the room and shouted directions. She got the retakes she wanted, and gave Shane a few more questions for Eric. They wrapped up in less than an hour.

Katie could hardly believe it was over. All the anticipation, the inner struggles, the mystery, the romance was gone. She had been in a whirlwind of emotions for months, and now had nothing to feel but emptiness. She sat, unmoving, as Barbara gave her "thank you" and disclosures speech – refer to your contract, etc. She had a stage assistant passing out paperwork, which included a web address for a questionnaire she needed filled out by everyone at their earliest convenience. She ended by inviting them all to a farewell buffet that was set up across the hall.

Katie met up with Ann Marie to go grab a bite to eat. Some of the other girls were headed across the hall as well, while others opted to boycott. The friends heard snippets of conversations as they made their way across the crowded room.

"I'm going back to the hotel and ordering room service," Lois was saying. "*Soulmates* is footing the bill."

"You guys think I had it easy," Madison was telling Jenny. "I'm not being put up in a hotel room tonight. I get to drive home by myself. You think it's an advantage to live close by, but for me it's been a handicap."

Katie and Ann Marie exchanged glances, rolled their eyes, and kept moving before they got dragged into the conversation.

"He wouldn't have the balls to set foot in there," they overheard from Heather, who was evidently referring to Eric making an appearance at the buffet.

"Excuse me, Katie," Barbara was suddenly next to them. "Can I have a word with you, please?"

"Sure," she answered, then to Ann Marie, "I'll meet you in there."

"No problem."

Katie followed Barbara back through the crowd and waited, as she made several stops along the way. She finished doling out instructions and motioned Katie to follow her. They exited the studio through a side door and went across the hall to a small office. Several people were busy at work, glanced up at Barbara as though poised and ready for orders, but quickly turned their attention back to the task at hand after ascertaining Barbara wasn't here for them – this time.

Katie followed Barbara through the office to another door, which opened into a small conference room. Two men and a woman were present already, and they stood to greet Barbara and Katie.

"Verne Bauer," the more distinguished-looking of the two men introduced himself and shook Katie's hand. Katie felt her heart rise up in her throat. Verne Bauer, the executive producer, was shaking her hand! She quickly found her voice.

"Katie Cohen," she said.

"Pleasure to meet you," Verne said, somewhat automatically, and took his seat, as his colleagues introduced themselves. Katie turned to meet the woman, but could still feel Verne's gaze upon her. Her attention was still on him as well. She couldn't help reminding herself if Ann Marie's agent hadn't slept with him, she never would have gotten this gig.

"Michaelina Hughes," the woman said. "Senior Casting Director. We met in New York."

"Yes, nice to see you again," Katie said and smiled.

"Jose Munoz," said the other man, taking his turn and shaking Katie's hand. His greeting felt warmer than the others. "Marketing Director."

"Nice to meet you," Katie said politely.

"I've been working with your face all season. I feel like I already know you," Jose told her. "And I must say, you've been a pleasure to work with."

"Thank you," Katie beamed, still unsure why she was brought to meet them.

"You've done a great job on the show, Katie," Barbara began, sounding more factual than complimentary, and motioned Katie to take a seat. "*Soulmates* has been a success story from the first season. It takes a specific personality type to make this show a success. I believe you have that personality type."

"Thank you," Katie said, wondering why Barbara was feeding her ego in front of the executive producer.

"Season Seven will be no less successful, no doubt," Verne input. "But to keep a show successful, to give a show like this longevity, you've got to keep your audience engaged. You've got to change it up just enough to keep them guessing, raise the controversy level, but maintain the pieces that the viewers love. My continued support in the production of *Soulmates* is based on its ability not only to keep viewers, but also to attract new viewers. It's a must in this industry. One bad season can kill a show like this."

"Yes," Katie agreed, trying to follow along intelligently.

"Which brings us to you," Verne went on. "We are hoping, with your experience on *Soulmates* and your ability to take direction well, that you might be able to help us keep that momentum going."

Katie's heart was racing faster than it had all season. What was Verne getting at? Was a job offer coming out of all this? Did they want her to join the

Soulmates staff? It wasn't exactly the outcome she had hoped for, but a job on the set of *Soulmates* might be a great starting point.

"We are predicting *Soulmates* Season Seven is going to be the most successful yet," Jose picked up. "From a marketing standpoint, you are an extremely likeable person, one that the public can really relate to. People like to watch people like you have their dreams come true."

"We'd like to offer you a part on the next season," Barbara took over. "We're looking for a cornerstone to drive Season Eight off the charts, and we think you have the potential to be our next *Soulmate*. We've brought Michaelina in to complete the screening process."

"If that's a prospect you'd be interested in," Michaelina added, as Barbara obviously assumed Katie would be agreeable.

'I'm flattered," Katie stammered. She didn't know what to say. Of course, she was interested! It was a job, wasn't it? Hopefully it was a paying job. That was the big question. "Yes, I'd be interested in learning more," she answered tentatively.

"It's a big commitment, I know," Barbara continued. "There are a lot of details. I can get a contract delivered to your room for your perusal."

"That would be good."

"I'll have that sent up right away. I'll leave you with Michaelina, then," Barbara said and shook Katie's hand.

Katie stood to shake hands with the men, and they followed Barbara from the room. Katie took her seat once again across from Michaelina.

"Katie, as the Senior Casting Director for *Soulmates*, I interview many candidates for this position. I wade through pages and pages of applications, reference letters, background checks, you name it. We have, essentially, already done that for you last season. You've done all the pre-screening interviews and questionnaires, and you've already proven your ability to relate to an audience. That makes my job easy. It is a rare occasion that Verne and his crew come to me with a candidate.

Clearly, Verne sees dollar signs when he looks at you, and I have to agree with Jose, you are very marketable. The *Soulmates* team feels strongly about you. Tell me, Katie, how did you feel about your experience on *Soulmates*?"

"My experience was great, obviously in spite of the fact that I got my ego crushed and my heart broken."

"Is it something you would consider doing again?"

"I would definitely be interested in looking over the contract. I've honestly never considered the possibility of being 'The Soulmate.'"

"It's a different perspective. I can certainly understand if you have apprehensions, because you so recently went through this devastating breakup on national TV. It's not easy. It takes a strong person to go through what you did and still have your dignity intact. The fact that you got hurt, however, is a huge part of your appeal. The audience can relate to you, and they'll be rooting for you to make a comeback, so to speak. Typically, we wouldn't make such a huge casting decision so abruptly. In fact, we'd have to bump a few potential *Soulmates* to put you in for next season, but Verne thinks it's worth it to keep the momentum going."

Katie nodded.

"With that said, we want to start filming right away, since we are piggybacking the two seasons. Clearly you have the attributes we look for in a candidate, and Verne sees you as our next prospect, so we don't want to waste any time getting rolling on this. I don't want to push you. I know you want to review the contract, but I would ask that you do not delay a decision. Your appeal to the audience will be immediate. It's Season Eight or nothing – two or three seasons down the road the audience will have lost much of the emotional investment they've put in you."

"I understand," Katie insisted. "I'll look over the contract tonight."

"Good. We'll have a lot of work to do, and I like to get my part started as early as possible. As you can imagine, the screening process can be very involved. I want to make sure I get the right mix of candidates for your liking, which is much harder with men, I might add. I admit, I have more to choose from when filling a cast of women. As you probably already know, we've only had two female *Soulmates* in seven seasons, and one of those seasons was our lowest-rated to date.

"That's not to say anything negative about the girl," Michaelina added quickly. "She was a lovely girl. It's just that men don't create the dynamics that women do. I'm happy to be working with you as our next *Soulmate*, of course. We need to cast people who will relate to our audience and move them."

Katie listened and nodded politely, as Michaelina droned on. By the end of the conversation, if one could call it such, Michaelina had done most of the talking, and Katie was convinced she was a fast-talking, opinionated casting director who seemed to think she was a lot more important than she really was. She had most likely insisted on "interviewing" Katie to put her seal of approval on the deal, to appease her own ego. Katie, nevertheless, thanked Michaelina warmly, and meet up with Ann Marie at the buffet.

Ann Marie had finished eating, but was having a glass of wine with Tina.

"Where have you been?" she asked.

"It's a long story," Katie said briefly, glancing around to see who else was in earshot. She wanted to confide in her friends, but knew this wasn't the place to do so. She filled a plate, grabbed a glass of wine and joined the girls. They caught up and reminisced, but Katie didn't give the reunion her full attention. Her mind was too busy replaying the events of the last hour.

She was going to be the next *Soulmate*. She was going to meet twenty-five eligible bachelors and date them! She couldn't believe how her prospects had changed in the last hour. She was heartbroken and lost, but now her life had a new direction.

She couldn't wait to get a look at the contract. She wondered how much it paid. It had to pay pretty well, considering the bonus she'd gotten last season. The money was the least of her concerns. She would have all her expenses paid. She would get to live in the guest house behind the *Soulmates* mansion, eat gourmet, catered meals and drink champagne, and travel on exotic dates. What was there to think about?

Katie's mind raced, imagining herself throughout the season – the men fighting for her affection, her hand in marriage.

Her mind stopped short, as she realized the whole point of the show was to find your *Soulmate*, the person you wanted to spend the rest of your life with. Was she truly ready for that?

Ready or not, Katie made up her mind to go for it. She had nothing to lose, and everything to gain. It would help her career; it would mend her broken ego, and who knows? Maybe it would lay the groundwork for her future. Maybe she truly would find her *Soulmate*.

The End

Made in the USA
Middletown, DE
24 March 2020